SAPPHIRE SUNSET

Also from Christopher Rice

Thrillers
A DENSITY OF SOULS
THE SNOW GARDEN
LIGHT BEFORE DAY
BLIND FALL
THE MOONLIT EARTH

Supernatural Thrillers
THE HEAVENS RISE
THE VINES
BONE MUSIC: A Burning Grill Thriller
BLOOD ECHO: A Burning Girl Thriller
BLOOD VICTORY: A Burning Girl Thriller

Paranormal Romance
THE FLAME: A Desire Exchange Novella
THE SURRENDER GATE: A Desire Exchange Novel
KISS THE FLAME: A Desire Exchange Novella

Contemporary Romance
DANCE OF DESIRE
DESIRE & ICE: A MacKenzie Family Novella

With Anne Rice
RAMSES THE DAMNED: THE PASSION OF CLEOPATRA
RAMSES THE DAMNED: THE REIGN OF OSIRIS

SAPPHIRE SUNSET

Sapphire Cove

Christopher Rice
Writing As
C. Travis Rice

BLUE
BOX
PRESS

Sapphire Sunset
By Christopher Rice writing as C. Travis Rice

Copyright 2022 Christopher Rice
ISBN: 978-1-952457-87-6

Published by Blue Box Press, an imprint of Evil Eye Concepts, Incorporated

This is a work of fiction. Names, places, characters and incidents are the product of the author's imagination and are fictitious. Any resemblance to actual persons, living or dead, events or establishments is solely coincidental.

Acknowledgments from the Author

Sapphire Cove would never have opened for guests without invaluable reads from some wonderful writers I'm proud to call my friends—J.R. Ward, Jill Shalvis, Tere Michaels, Lauren Billings, and the incomparable Eric Shaw Quinn, my producing partner at Dinner Partners and my podcast co-host on "TDPS Presents CHRISTOPHER & ERIC."

For invaluable insight into the operations of a large hotel, I'm indebted to Troy Pade. For insight into Marine Corps operations, major thanks to Lt. Col. M. Matthew Phelps, US Marine Corps. The last time Matt helped me on a book about a Marine, Don't Ask Don't Tell was still in force, and I couldn't use his actual name on the acknowledgments page. Any errors or embellishments in these areas are the work of the author, and not these experts in their fields.

It's a dream to be back working with the amazing ladies at Blue Box Press. There are not enough thanks in the world to Liz Berry, MJ Rose, and Jillian Stein for seeing the type of romance I wanted this to be and committing to it wholeheartedly. They're not only great publishers, they're amazing friends. Major gratitude as well goes to Kim Guidroz, for her sharp editorial eye, and to Kasi Alexander for additional proofreading.

As always, I'm grateful to Christine Cuddy for her sterling legal guidance and Cathy Dipierro and the team at The Unreal Agency for their fantastic web management.

Prologue

When Logan Murdoch was sixteen, his dad caught him watching porn, and their lives changed forever.

It felt like an eternity, but all told, it probably only took Chip Murdoch five seconds to realize the guys in football uniforms on Logan's laptop were working themselves into a frenzy without any assistance from a nubile female cheerleader. Maybe because the sound was off and there'd been no all-male moans to clue him in. The next thing Logan knew, his six-foot-four kickboxer of a dad was shuffling off down the hallway like he'd been kneed in the stomach by the Jolly Green Giant.

A few breathless minutes later, dressed in the first clothes he could pull from his dresser with trembling hands, Logan found his dad sitting on the foot of the lounger in the backyard where he usually smoked, staring up at the scrubby hillside behind their house that coughed a rattlesnake or two onto their patio every spring. But he wasn't smoking. Shaking one loose from the rumpled pack on the table next to him would have required concentration he didn't seem to have.

Up until then, Logan had never known fear like that in his life.

Years later, he'd discover a more sudden and visceral version of it after he joined the Marines. But the fear of getting blown apart was distinct from the fear of losing everything you care about because of who you are. Nothing came close to the total, bone-deep vulnerability he felt from head to toe in that moment. There's dying, and then there's eking out an existence without love or family. At sixteen, both prospects seemed equally dire.

For a while, his dad just stared and stared. Like he thought a meteor was coming to wipe out the planet, and he didn't have time to run.

That, or he was trying to permanently unsee his son's junk.

Whatever the case, Logan was pretty sure his old man hadn't been this shell shocked since Logan's mother died suddenly when he was three.

Chip Murdoch was a hard guy who'd had a hard life, born to a mom who'd loved heroin more than her kid and a father who'd grieved his wife's overdose with a belt. In other words, Logan's dad hit the streets at sixteen and never looked back. There was a year or two of running with bad crowds, even sleeping under a few bridges, before he made a life for himself in construction that ensured he'd never have to enter the snake pit of his family again—a family who'd never sent Logan so much as an email or a Christmas card, which was all he needed to know about them. For most of those difficult years, Chip Murdoch's height and brawn, which he'd passed on to Logan, had been the key to his survival. Protecting him on the streets, aiding him in a job devoted to manual labor, making him a hit with the ladies, the most important of which had been Logan's mom.

Guys like that didn't put up with a homo for a son.

And so as Logan stood there, waiting for his dad to rouse from his shock, he was braced for a fist to the face, even though the guy had never raised a hand to him in his life.

Instead, his old man swallowed. "Well, looks like I won't be passing on my shitty history with women."

Then he ordered Logan into his truck.

In silence, he drove them south to Fallbrook, that hilly little town just east of Camp Pendleton's rugged stretch to the sea. The Marine base would later play a huge role in Logan's life, but in those days it was shrouded with grown-up mystery and video-game fueled fantasies of war games. When they crested the winding gravel road that brought them to his aunt's lonely ranch house atop a boulder-strewn hill, that's when he learned that yes, his mom's sister Fran was a lesbian, and her housemate Pam wasn't just her good friend. And as his dad wandered their property in a daze, Logan sat at a butcher block table in a kitchen hung with so many knickknacks it looked like a TGI Fridays, across from the women who would become his gay moms. The three of them drank chamomile tea out of big glazed ceramic mugs painted bright primary colors as Fran asked him important questions his dad couldn't. Was he experimenting?

Using condoms? Doing things online with strangers he shouldn't?

He gave honest answers. His dad's relaxed attitude toward Internet parental controls had helped Logan create a rich and vivid fantasy on his hard drive. Women played no role in it. But it was all dirty movies, like the one he'd been caught watching that day. No stranger danger involved. As for real-world experiences, just a few fumbling misfires with other boys at school, none of them repeats. That was all.

After gathering the essential intelligence, Fran went for a walk with Logan's dad. Later, Logan realized whatever shitty things his dad probably had to say in that moment he'd said to his sister-in-law so he'd never have to say them to his son.

But that night, when his dad told him it was time to head home, Logan started blinking back tears the minute he heard the man's casual tone. "I thought you were going to leave me here," Logan blurted out. Then a big, wet humiliating sob burst from him like a breath he'd been holding in for hours, and his dad reached up and planted a hand on his shoulder.

"You're my boy." Chip Murdoch's grip became a brief hug. Kinda awkward, but a hug, nonetheless. "You got that? You'll always be my boy."

They drove home under a clear, star-flecked Southern California sky, the wind pouring in through the truck's open windows as they listened to Lynyrd Skynyrd, his dad's favorite. Logan had never been much of a Skynyrd fan, but that night, the melancholy chords of *Simple Man* wound their way through his soul, turning into an anthem that meant freedom. It was a song about a mother's advice to her son, and he was pretty sure his dad played it every time he wished the love of his life was there to help him raise their boy. Maybe she had been in spirit, and that's why the greatest secret Logan had ever kept didn't destroy his family after all.

Also, nobody had told him he had to delete all that porn, and that was a relief too.

Years later, when his dad's life hit the skids, when he wrecked his back and a career in construction as a result, all because he'd refused the doctor's orders to stay out of the kickboxing ring while recovering from a minor sprain, when it became clear to everyone who knew him that Chip Murdoch's idea of saving for a rainy day had been to hold two palms over his head, Logan's friends asked him how he could justify putting his whole life on hold just to manage the fallout of his stubborn old man's lousy life choices. Was he really ditching his dream of becoming a Navy

SEAL just so he could grab the first job that allowed him to support his dad?

The answer was simple.

Yes.

Because men like Chip Murdoch, hard guys from hard backgrounds, usually kicked their gay sons to the curb. But his dad had done the opposite.

Had he been perfect? No. Would he have been so accepting of Logan's sexuality if Logan had turned out to be the kind of gay guy who loved things his dad found girly or soft? Maybe not. But what it came down to with his dad was simple. Chip Murdoch gave better than he got, especially when it came to his son, and he deserved to be loved through one of his lowest moments.

And that's how Logan Murdoch, a former staff sergeant in the Marine Corps who'd once been blasted out of a Humvee only to dust himself off and help the guys who were more injured, ended up landing a job at one of the poshest resorts in Southern California.

1

The jacket was a perfect fit. A sign of good things to come, Logan thought.

After he'd aced his final interview and background check, management at Sapphire Cove provided him with three matching blazers and three pairs of khaki pants to go with them, all tailored to measurements they'd taken in their back offices.

Now, standing before the only mirror in the trailer he'd shared with his dad for months, Logan smoothed the lapel bearing the hotel's bright gold logo with both hands. Then he smoothed it again. The gentle motions quieted nerves that had been vibrating for days.

It wasn't just a blazer. It was a promise the hotel had kept, as evidenced by the way it flattered his broad chest and bulky shoulders. And kept promises were exactly what he needed.

Truth be told, he'd gone back and forth between dreading his fancy new gig and nursing excited daydreams about it. Fantasies of escorting some Harry Styles type to his private villa, only to have the gorgeous little Hollywood twink slide his phone number into his palm. And as an added bonus, maybe his new movie star husband would be the type who didn't drag every Marine he met for wars said Marine didn't start or vote for. That would be a refreshing change of pace.

Before he could savor this swell of contentment over his new uniform, there was a deafening crash from the kitchen.

He found his dad ass flat in front of the refrigerator, one hand holding to the handle above his head. Logan figured the old man had gone over sideways when he tried to open the door. When he saw his dad's new silver crutches leaning unused next to the sofa in the main room, his jaw ached, which told him he was grinding his teeth in frustration. Again.

"Old man, I swear to God with you."

"I just wanted a sandwich," Chip groaned.

"Then ask me to make it for you."

"You were getting ready."

Logan hoisted his dad to his feet, no small feat given they were about the same size.

"And you were doing that thing you do when you're nervous."

"What thing?" Logan let Chip's arm slide from around his upper back, lowering his dad carefully onto the worn sofa.

"That thing where you clear your throat over and over again and pace like an elephant. You know, like when you've got a date."

"It's not a date. It's a job. And elephants don't pace. Those are tigers, which is what I'm going to turn into if you don't start taking your recovery seriously."

"What if I get hungry while you're at work?" Teeth gritted against the pain, Chip rolled onto one side like a beached whale.

"Sally will be over in two minutes."

"Christ on his throne," Chip grumbled.

"Let's try for Chip Murdoch on his sofa, like the doctor ordered."

Chip's eyes rolled back into his head, and he groaned like he'd been stuck in the gut. And that was the idea. Sally was the only other resident in their trailer park, besides Logan, capable of frightening Chip Murdoch into silence. Her secret was that when Chip shouted at her, she shouted back louder and faster until Chip shut up and got tired. It was genius. But it was also a painful reminder. They were leaning on their neighbor because Logan's beloved gay moms were both gone now—Fran felled by a heart attack shortly after Logan joined the Marines, and Pam finally claimed by her years-long battle with cancer last winter. Just a whiff of chamomile tea would bring a lump to Logan's throat, transport him back to their kitchen in Fallbrook where they'd spent so many special hours. He and his dad could sure use some of their wisdom now.

Logan's dad waved his hands through the air as if he could make the prospect of Sally's imminent arrival disperse like cigarette smoke. Before Sally finished her harsh series of knocks, Logan opened the door, and in walked their neighbor, a proud tank of a woman who dressed solely for comfort and looked at everything in her path like she thought it might try to bite her and that was a good enough excuse to kick the living crap out of it before it tried. "Am I allowed to hit the sauce during this gig?"

"Wait until baby's asleep, at least." Logan gave the woman a half hug and a peck on the cheek.

She stood over the sofa and glared down at Chip like she was deciding which cuts from his body would make the best steaks.

Logan headed to the bathroom to brush his teeth, but the trailer was small enough that he could hear every word as if he were still standing next to the sofa.

"It's payback time, Chipster." Sally planted her hands on her hips.

"For what, Sassy Sally?" Chip kept his forearms crossed over his face like a vampire trying to avoid the sun.

"You think I didn't hear that thing you said to Lizzy Ramirez a few weeks ago? About how I look like I let my pit bull do my hair?"

"Son, you couldn't make other arrangements?"

"This one seemed like a fit," Logan called back, then spit.

"So did it work?" Sally asked his dad. "Did she sleep with you? 'Cause she told me she'd rather date my pit bull, so I'm just asking, is talking smack about my hair going to be a winning strategy for you around these parts or are you ready to give it up and learn some respect for women?"

"Son, are you paying this woman?"

Logan swirled his mouthwash and spit. "We worked something out, yeah."

He spritzed himself with more cologne. A special brand with a name he couldn't pronounce and a price tag that had made him swallow. But it smelled nice, and it seemed classy enough for a place like Sapphire Cove. When he returned to the living room, Sally hadn't budged from where she stood over her patient-slash-victim.

"I'm not going to have you sexually harassing my son in exchange for the chance to ruin my weekend, woman." Chip was staring up at Sally now, trying to look tough, even though the rest of his body wasn't along for the ride.

"He's fixing my dishwasher, you old perv," Sally said.

"Likely story."

"No one's getting sexually harassed," Logan said.

Sally sat down on one arm of the sofa. It looked like she was contemplating whether or not to knock him to the floor. "No, but I know someone who's gonna have to go put up with a bunch of rich bastards at the beach tonight just to take care of your old bones. You might want to thank him instead of giving him the ass."

"Right now, you are the only one giving anyone *the ass*, lady," Chip said.

Logan patted his dad on the chest. "I might be late, Pop. I'm going to take all the shifts they give me."

Suddenly Chip grabbed his wrist, holding it with unexpected strength. When Logan looked back, he saw something new in the man's eyes. Pain, guilt, a vulnerability he'd never shown when he was younger. A man who needed to be taken care of and feeling plenty of guilt over the reasons why.

"Thank you." In the silence that followed, even Sally seemed moved, as evidenced by the fact that she'd stopped harassing his dad.

Logan gave his dad a quick peck on the forehead and patted his chest, when what he really wanted to do was throw his arms around the old man and tell him it was all going to be okay. Because that was Logan's job. To make everything okay. And he had a ways to go. Because right now things were hovering at marginally shitty.

As he headed for the door, his father called out, "And don't let those fancy fuckers give you any shit. Half the folks staying there probably won the trip in a contest or something."

"Got it, Dad."

He was halfway to his truck by the time his dad started his usual speech about how no one who flew first class had actually paid for the ticket, how they either used miles or their companies footed the bill. Logan had heard it all before. And if it was how Chip made himself feel better about where they'd ended up, that was fine.

One thing was true.

Logan was about to drive out of a world where first class was something you made fun of and into a world where most people considered it a reward for a job well done. No more part-time bouncer gigs at that club in Anaheim that played nothing but Insane Clown Posse, where more than one female patron had become physically violent with him when he'd told her he wasn't into women. He was officially joining the security staff at a resort one travel website referred to as the jewel of the Orange County coast, independently owned by the same family since its founding in the 1960s and with a reputation for treating its employees almost as well as it treated its high-paying guests.

Working security at a place that nice would require a softer, classier touch.

Did he have it, or would he say the wrong thing to some billionaire guest and get his ass, and his dad's health care, kicked to the curb on day one?

Logan had never considered himself much of a design person, unless you were talking about Minecraft blocks. But a few hours into his first shift, the lobby at Sapphire Cove was melting his heart.

Maybe it was the giant crystal chandelier that sent shimmers across the white marble floor or the contended laughter of guests drifting in from Camilla's, the hotel's main restaurant. It could have been the gardenia-scented candles flickering inside the small, mirrored cubbyholes that flanked the entrance to the gift shop. Or maybe, after years of deployments to places where none of the locals had welcomed the arrival of his Marine Expeditionary Unit, Logan just enjoyed being somewhere people seemed happy to see him.

There was a hard tap on his shoulder, and a now familiar voice barked, "What's up, Jarhead?"

Buddy Haskins was exactly the type of guy Logan had expected to be working with when he'd landed the job. Thick as a brick wall, but standoffish in a way that said he didn't have any law enforcement or military experience and was threatened by Logan's. He spent most of their department meeting earlier sending dick pics to various women. Logan hoped the women had actually asked for them.

"Maybe a new nickname, Buddy," Logan said.

"How 'bout Bullet Sponge?"

Awesome, Logan thought. A deliberately insulting term more tech-reliant branches of the military used for Marines. Buddy knew this, he was sure. Not because he'd served. But because he was a prick.

"I'd prefer Jackass, to be frank," Logan said.

"Deal." Buddy slapped Logan on the back. "How's lobby duty, Jackass?"

"One nine-year-old kid who tried to smuggle out a bedside lamp in his backpack. Other than that, not a lot of bullets for me to sponge up."

"Look, I know it might not seem like as big a deal as the Marines, but if you don't think this job can get rough, wedding season'll prove you wrong, I guarantee it. One time this bridesmaid got drunk and two hours before the ceremony told the bride that she thought her dress looked like a car accident. Sheesh. That was war, my friend. An all-out *war.* I think there's still a dent from a champagne bottle in the wall over there. The groomsmen even got involved, and by the end there were helicopters, you understand me? *Hel-i-copters.*" To make his point, Buddy tugged at the collar of his dress shirt to reveal scars left by what looked like a single claw mark, a claw made of manicured nails. "Bridesmaid Battle, May 2015." He tapped the scar with one finger. "Never forget."

"Copy that."

"All right." Buddy clapped his hands then rubbed his palms together. "I got an assignment that might give you some more excitement. Javier called in sick, so you're going to help me guard the prince's graduation party. Follow me."

"The prince?" Logan asked.

A real prince? The hotel was nice, but it wasn't that nice. According to Logan's research, Sapphire Cove did its briskest celebrity business with fading reality starts hosting their second and third weddings.

"Oh, you haven't met him yet? Hoo, boy. You're in for a treat."

When they entered the wide corridor for the conference and event spaces, their feet swished over a thick spread of Pepto-Bismol and turquoise carpeting. The wedding off to their left had a loud and mostly off-key band, but at the end of the corridor on their right, the metal push bars on the ballroom doors rattled with fast-paced techno bass beats.

"Seriously, who's the prince?" Logan asked.

"Connor Harcourt, owner's grandson and the GM's nephew. He and most of the graduating class from UC Irvine are having a big blowout tonight in the Dolphin Ballroom. Our orders are to make sure it stays, and I'm quoting, *contained and private.* Translation—don't let any college grads puke up their guts on the lawn outside, and don't let any hotel guests in to steal the free booze."

Buddy stopped and turned so quickly Logan almost smashed into him.

"Oh, and I've got some barf bags back in the office in case you need 'em." He waggled his eyebrows like he and Logan were in on some secret together.

"For what?"

"Well, let's just say the Harcourt kid's got a fruity flavor, if you know what I mean."

Logan felt a wave of tension sweep his body from head to toe and saw Buddy flinch, which said the anger had written itself on Logan's face.

"Tangerine or pomegranate?" Logan asked before he could stop himself.

"All right, dude, don't get all PC on me. I'm just trying to warn you. You *will* see guys mackin' on each other in there, so steel yourself. And don't go hauling off on anybody if they check you out. A guy like you, all muscly and moisturized, you're gonna be just their type."

Their *type*? Logan thought. *Jesus.*

Sapphire Cove wasn't a tent revival church. But from what he'd seen of it, the resort's security team was a lot of hard guys looking for a softer route in life so they could either regroup or cash in. Logan didn't want to make assumptions, but he was pretty sure they weren't all gay friendly, and the ease with which Buddy had made his barf bag comment didn't exactly persuade him otherwise.

Logan felt a familiar, uncomfortable flutter in his chest, not as bad as the one he'd get helicoptering into hostile territory, but close. The flutter he'd get whenever someone who had the power to screw up his day asked him if there was a special girl in his life, and he just stood there, time stopping as he wondered whether he should tell an outright lie or just a lie of omission, weighing which one of the two would take a bigger bite out of his soul. *No, ma'am, no special girl* or *Just haven't met the right one yet.*

There was a price for going where you were outnumbered or unwelcome and trying to succeed, and it didn't always take the form of a door being shut in your face on the first day of the job. Surviving was one thing, but if you tried to get ahead, people were less tolerant of your mistakes, quick to paint your natural screw-ups as a result of your so-called identity. If it wasn't exactly like theirs. In other words, you had to be perfect all the time. That's what coming out now would really mean. Nobody would try to get him fired right off. They'd just start judging him by a harsher standard than anyone else, an effort designed to wear him down and eventually make him quit.

Well, if that turned out to be the case, they could suck it. He'd survived multiple deployments to Iraq and Afghanistan. He could survive some bigoted knuckleheads in the security department of a posh resort. Especially with his dad's medical bills at stake.

Logan stopped walking and stood his ground. "No barf bags for me, thanks. Since I pay pretty good money to watch college guys mack on each other online, I figure I'll just add it to my spank bank. Maybe save myself a buck or two."

He braced for a punch in the stomach. Which was insane because A, they were working, and B, Logan was about twice Buddy's size and could easily flatten him. But he didn't plan to take another step until Buddy addressed his insult in some way.

"Aw, shit. Sorry, man."

"About what?" Logan asked.

"That you gays can't get free porn the way we straights do."

Logan had to admit it was a pretty nice save, and Buddy delivered it with a winning smile. Still, the dude's assertion that two guys kissing was vomit-inducing was going in Logan's asshole bank. And it wasn't like Buddy had apologized for the comment.

As if to make nice, his grinning coworker held open the door to the lawn outside and gestured for Logan to step through.

Just to their right, the Dolphin Ballroom's terrace doors were open to the night, the flashing lights from the dance floor pulsing across the river of manicured lawn that sat between the terrace steps and an elegant balustrade that marked the approximate edge of a cliff that plunged to the resort's private crescent of beach far below.

There was no denying it—the thing that had allowed Sapphire Cove to stay independent was its prime real estate. It sat atop a promontory that gave it three different sets of stunning views—either up or down the coast or straight out to sea.

Personally, Logan preferred the vistas north and south. After dark, they featured twinkling coastal hills plunging toward the pitch-black ocean, whereas the view straight out to sea was just black. The resort didn't have any guest rooms on its eastern wall facing the motor court. Maybe not the best decision for the hotel's bottom line, but it meant there truly wasn't a bad view in the house, a fact trumpeted on all of Sapphire Cove's promotional materials.

The weather was beyond Southern California excellent. Warm, but also breezy enough to rustle the giant palm trees lining the resort's ocean-facing façade, making a sound like gentle rain.

By day, the hotel was four stories of pastel-pink confection that looked like a freshly baked cake seconds away from melting in the bright sun. At night, pinpoint lighting accentuated the many curves in its ocean-facing walls, turning it into a modern art sculpture nestled in a jungle of palms. At the base of the cliffs, the dark Pacific rolled toward Sapphire Cove's private beach beneath a vault of stars.

Buddy stepped onto the ballroom's empty terrace so he could take up a post next to the open doors. Logan did the same, scanning the crowd inside.

He was impressed by the party's setup. Maybe even a little dazzled. Lighting rigs had been brought in to give the ballroom a dim, blue hue with bright white accents, and the walls were covered with digital projections that shifted around each other like schools of lazy tropical fish slowly circling the room. But they weren't fish, they were detailed collages. Pictures of the graduates, it looked like, interspersed with the university's logo. The ballroom must have had five hundred guests in it, most of them on the dance floor. No way could they all have been included in these images, but the closer he looked, the more it seemed like that was exactly the case.

"Who put this shindig together?" Logan asked.

"The prince did. Family footed the bill, of course, but he's a little party planner." Buddy said *party planner* like it was the only gay slur he was allowed. "About to start in the events office here now that he's graduated."

Logan looked in the direction Buddy had just jerked his head, and his heart stopped.

Aw, God, no, please don't let that slice of heaven be the owner's grandson.

Talk about a dangerous temptation.

Bright blond hair in a perfect side part, big blue eyes, and an infectious, boyish smile offset by cherubic cheeks. Dance moves that said he knew how to turn himself into a fluid, pliable love machine in the bedroom. In the words of his best friend, Donnie, Logan liked guys he could fit into his back pocket but would kick their way out in five minutes because they were so full of energy and sass.

A high and tight little butt didn't hurt either, and Connor Harcourt was certainly sporting one of those. And in gray and white plaid pants tailored to show it off, no doubt.

He danced without fear. Smiled big and easy whenever he broke to take a selfie with his friends.

And he had dimples. The guy actually had dimples.

And he was a college graduate, which meant there was only about four years between them, even if right now Logan looked like twice the grown-up in his blazer and khaki pants and sporting an earpiece.

Stop doing the math. He's not for sale.

Suddenly Connor wasn't dancing anymore.

He was sprinting across the crowded ballroom. Protective instincts surging, Logan took a step forward until he saw Connor's destination—the spot where a server had hastily left a tray of champagne flutes right inside the swing radius of the catering kitchen's doors. The server had a good excuse. She'd been knocked backward by a colleague who'd come bursting through those very doors seconds earlier. Server one was now trying to hide the fact that her nose might have been broken as server two tried to help her without dropping his tray. Both looked up from their huddle in time to see Connor reach out and stop the door before it crashed into the flute-filled tray.

Frightened, they looked to their rescuer with dazed expressions, clearly terrified their jobs might be on the line.

Logan was too busy wondering how Connor had sensed the near collision from halfway across the room. Did the guy's Spidey senses work on things besides trays full of champagne?

Whatever Connor said to the servers had them laughing and relaxing their shoulders, even the lady with the possibly broken nose. Connor moved in closer, studying her face, then giving her a light pat on the back when he didn't see any blood. With Connor's blessing, the injured server hurried off into the kitchen to tend to herself. Hors d'oeuvres guy started circulating. Meanwhile, to Logan's total amazement, Connor picked up the champagne flutes and started carrying them through the ballroom. Some of the guests whooped and hollered, probably because they assumed the only reason the guest of honor would be carrying booze through his own graduation party was if he planned to chug it all himself. But Connor was intent to serve, and he didn't stop until the tray was empty.

Rich as all get-out and covering for one of his own staff. That's unexpected.

And it was pretty clear, given the collages and the way Connor served his guests, he didn't think of himself as the guest of honor. Not the only one, anyway.

Suddenly, Connor was distracted by a guest who danced right past him with a blinking glow-necklace around his throat. He pulled the guy close, pointed to his neck, and asked him some question over the music. That's when the guest pointed out the little dude who'd started handing out the new party favors. The gift giver was about Connor's size, with ink black hair and brown skin. Connor headed straight for him, his attention stolen right at the moment when Logan thought their eyes were about to meet.

When Connor caught up with his best friend, Naser Kazemi was weaving through the crowded dance floor, handing out fistfuls of blinking plastic necklaces that made Connor's skin crawl. Given how gratefully his gifts were being received, the Dolphin Ballroom would soon look more like a rave than a resort.

And that was not okay.

"Nas, a word please." Connor guided him to the edge of the dance floor with a hand against the small of his back. They were about the same compact size. *Pocket gays* is how they'd refer to themselves in polite conversation, *fun size* if they were setting up an Internet dating profile. Despite the fact that they were evenly matched at five foot, four inches, Connor had once been able to wrestle Naser off the sofa in their apartment during a fight about the outcome of *RuPaul's Drag Race*. Hopefully, such a use of force wouldn't be required in this moment. But he wasn't willing to rule it out.

Naser had to be stopped. Immediately.

Whenever he was required to do something other than stay home and calculate things for fun, Connor's best friend and roommate wore a similar outfit. A slim-fit Express dress shirt that was a neutral color—tonight it was beige—and black jeans completed by black dress shoes that could not be less suited for a night of drinking and dancing. It probably wasn't that big a deal. Naser danced like he was constantly afraid his mother was going to burst out of the crowd and drag him off the floor, demanding to know why he was making a fool of himself. It was a not very acrobatic routine that consisted of stepping side to side vaguely in time to the music, shooting humorless glances in either direction as he did so. Occasionally, Connor would grab his arms and raise them into the air, but Naser always retracted them quickly, as if his best friend had tried to tickle his pits.

"Why am I in trouble?" Naser whined. "I thought I was contributing. You said you wanted me to contribute."

That actually wasn't true, but he wasn't going to fault Naser for trying to loosen up a bit. He was also sloshed. In keeping with someone who was allergic to any gathering of over five people, Naser had spent the last hour thoroughly buzzed off one swallow of champagne.

"You hate the glow sticks? No!" Naser wailed. "You told me to bring something fun."

"Well, for starters, these *aren't* glow sticks."

"I guess not, but the party store was out, and these glow so..." Naser stared woefully down into the bag as if the revelation that sticks and necklaces were two entirely different things was one he'd be processing for a long time. Possibly in therapy. He was so disconnected from the idea of a party in general that in his eyes one annoying blinking thing was as good as any other.

"They are, but Naser, I actually suggested party hats. Not glow sticks."

"Did not!" Naser gave him a shocked stare. "You did not. You specifically told me to bring glow sticks."

Which these aren't, to his own gratitude, he managed not to say.

"Actually, I said if you wanted to help out, bring something like party hats or feather boas or some sort of costume element..." *that doesn't blink or glow or throw off the lighting design I spent hours calibrating.*

"Okay, well, the call must have dropped out then because all I heard was glow sticks and how you think I'm no fun."

"Those were different conversations. Naser, stop. Stop with the Bambi eyes."

But Naser's Bambi eyes were a potent weapon—big and dark and swimming and capable of filling with whatever emotion he wanted to fill them with. He'd used them to great effect over the years on his mother and sister and pretty much anyone else in his huge family of A-type personalities, on whom he'd sharpened his innate skills as a budding accountant and all-around human Day Planner. Throughout the years together at UC Irvine, their friends joked that Connor was destined to throw all of life's great parties, and Naser would make sure they didn't bankrupt anyone or catch fire.

Connor curved an arm around his best friend's back and pulled his face to his chest, a move that allowed him to deftly snatch the bag of hideous blinking necklaces out of Naser's hand.

"I never said you weren't any fun," Connor said, even though he knew it was kind of a lie.

"You said some people are the life of the party, but I'm the ICU of the party."

"A year ago." Connor started pulling Naser toward the nearest bar so he could secure his best friend some caffeine to go with his buzz. "When

I was drunk. And that's because you started reading a book at my birthday party."

"It was a good book."

"It was a pool party, Naser, and you were *in* the pool. Look, I commend your attempt to create a distribution event that raises the energy of the guests on the dance floor past the party's halfway point, thereby distracting them from the fact that their second wave buzz might be wearing off. Unfortunately, these necklaces just do not work with my lighting plan."

"I understand. Can I go home and read now?" Naser asked.

"No. There's still party left."

"But I'm doing the party wrong, and my feet hurt," Naser whined.

"You're not doing the party wrong. It's my fault for not giving you clearer instructions. And it's your party, too. However, due to a tragic misunderstanding, we'll need to eject this jewelry of the damned. These necklaces are not on the guest list."

"Are *they* on the guest list?"

Connor followed the direction of Naser's look.

At first, he guessed the three middle-aged men stumbling their way onto the dance floor might be family members of graduates. But only a few guests had brought relatives, and Connor had met them all. These guys were not among them. They looked like they'd come from the golf course by way of a Hooter's. Their polo shirts were bright primary colors, and one of them actually wore plaid golf pants. All three were sweaty and ruddy-faced and leering at Connor's friends Jose Villa and Ken Hong, who were bumping and grinding a few feet away. Jose and Ken had been a couple since junior year, so they moved against each other with the intensity of people who knew each other's bodies top to bottom.

Connor read the signs immediately: drunken douchebags, probably guests of the hotel, with enough liquid nerve to harass the one dancing gay couple they'd spotted as they'd walked past the open terrace doors outside.

The three men fanned out on all sides of Jose and Ken, parodying their moves with the grace of stoned penguins.

"Uh oh," Naser mumbled.

"Oh, I don't think so." Connor made a beeline for the invaders.

Drunky McGolfpants was doing his own version of a bump and grind against Jose's back. But it was more bump than grind, and God, if it didn't look like the guy was punching Jose with his crotch. Jose spun, finger raised. Connor had enjoyed enough wild nights in West Hollywood with Jose to know nothing good ever came of that raised finger. For the person standing in front of it, at least.

"Could you stop, dude?" Jose asked.

"Oh, wassa matter?" McGolfpants slurred. "You don wanna dance with me. I'm not *pretty* enough."

The music was still pumping, but the confrontation was drawing the attention of the other dancers.

Connor was calculating the best way to play both cool host and bouncer when a sudden, powerful force gripped his right shoulder. He spun, fearing another interloper had snuck up on him. Instead, he found himself staring up into a face that looked very sober, very focused, and so handsome Connor wondered if he'd accidentally been dropped into the pages of a men's fitness magazine he totally bought for the articles on nutrition, promise.

"I've got this, Mr. Harcourt." The security agent's voice was full of confidence and authority.

His nametag read *Logan*, and he was clearly new to the security department.

Because if Connor had laid eyes on him before now, it was entirely possible he would have thought of little else since.

He was tall. Not basketball player tall but climb-you-like-a-tree-and-hold-on-in-the-wind tall. Broad shoulders and a thick, muscled neck, and hands that looked like they were sculpted out of marble. Tan skin and fine dark hair. There was something adorable about the way he'd styled his hair into a side part, making it look like a boyish hat atop a guy who was all brawny man below. A small mouth and hard jawline gave a vaguely angry cast to his face, but it was offset by his expressive brown eyes underneath dark eyebrows that made him appear slightly devilish.

Maybe it's the eyebrows. They're making it look like he's undressing me with his eyes. But it's an illusion, that's all. The guy was probably straight, which meant that in addition to being as hot as lava, he'd be about as good for Connor's ass.

Connor, who usually talked a mile a minute, was speechless.

True to his word, Logan stepped past him. But it felt to Connor like he waited as long as possible before removing his hand from Connor's shoulder.

Jose and McGolfpants were now shouting in each other's faces, and his buddies, Drunky Dee and Drunky Dumm, were closing farther in, acting as if Jose's reaction to their friends' provocation was somehow worse than the provocation itself.

In his ear, Naser whispered, "Who is that security guy?"

"I don't know," Connor whispered back. "But I think my shoulder had an orgasm."

And, of course, at just that point, the music stopped, allowing the shouting between Jose, Ken, and their uninvited dancing partners to rip through the room. But it was quickly silenced by a commanding, decisive voice.

"Gentlemen, is there a problem?" Logan asked the crew.

"Yeah, yeah." Golfpants tried to stand up straighter and point a finger at Jose at the same time. The combined effort almost sent him over sideways. "This guy here's getting all worked up over a little joke—"

"I wasn't talking to you, sir." Logan turned to Jose. "Everything all right, guys?"

"No." Jose crossed his arms and stood his ground, looking sober as stone. "These guys are drunk and they're harassing us and they're saying all sorts of anti-gay crap."

The douches erupted in a slurred chorus of protests, most of it about Jose being too sensitive, and Ken chimed in with, *yes, pansy is actually a gay slur when you shout it at a gay man you don't know.*

"Are you guys guests of the party?" Logan asked.

"Musta thrown out the invite," Drunky Dee slurred.

"'Cause it was perfume scented," Drunky Dumm added.

"I'm going to take that as a no, which means it's time to come with me."

Golfpants leered. "You just want to get us alone so you can dance with us like nobody's watching."

Logan grinned. "Actually, if I dance with anyone tonight, it'll be Baby Blues over there. He's more my type."

Logan threw a look in Connor's direction when he said it.

Connor's face got hot. Logan's cheeks were flushed too. When their eyes met, there seemed to be a slender crack in the guy's stony composure. Maybe he was only joking and when he saw the hunger it brought to Connor's eyes, he regretted saying it. But another part of him thought, *Straight guys don't make jokes about other men being their type.*

"I think you're Baby Blues," Naser whispered into Connor's ear.

"Maybe it's you," Connor whispered back.

"My eyes are brown, queen."

"Chestnut. And they're gorgeous."

"Thanks, sweetie, but don't deny the obvious."

"He was kidding," Connor whispered.

"Nah uh. You're Baby Blues," Naser insisted.

"Is this real?" Connor whispered. "What's happening? Is he *real?* Did I hit my head?"

"All right, gents. I'll show you back to your rooms." With a closed fist, Logan gestured in the direction of the nearest exit doors.

The three drunks stood their ground, a portrait of wobbly entitlement.

"Nah, I think we'll hang out a bit," Golfpants asserted. "Maybe get ourselves a drink."

Logan walked up to Golfpants until they were nose to nose. "I think you won't."

"Is that what you get paid to do around here?" Golfpants asked. "Think?"

"You don't want to see what I get paid to do, *sir.*"

"All right, guys." Buddy Haskins, who'd been with the security department forever, suddenly emerged from the crowd like he'd seen enough. If that was the case, why had it taken him so long to react? He wasn't a guest. "Let's clear out."

Logan took a step back and gestured for the party crashers to file past him. Golfpants went first, then suddenly spun in Logan's direction. What happened next happened so fast Connor figured Logan was either waiting for it or a superhuman. Logan caught the man's flying fist and used it to wrench the guy's arm around his back. Golfpants yowled but was instantly immobilized. Now Logan was using the guy's arm like the handle of a lawnmower, driving him across the dance floor and toward the exit. Once they saw this quick and efficient display of force, Drunky Dee and Drunky Dumm walked ahead of Logan, heads bowed, eyes on the floor, as Logan drove his prisoner past Connor.

When they were inches apart, Logan winked at Connor. "Enjoy the party, Mr. Harcourt."

Connor couldn't remember the last time he'd been winked at like that.

And he certainly couldn't remember the last time a wink had sent shivers racing down his spine.

And as much as he wanted to stay right where he was in hopes of being hit by another wave of the guy's woodsy cologne, his guests had been harassed, and he needed to tend to them. But as soon as he threw his arms around Jose and Ken in turn, it was clear from their excited chatter they also couldn't think about anything except Logan.

Whenever a punch was thrown during a security incident, the aftermath could be time consuming for everyone involved. The sheriff's department might get called. Internal paperwork would have to be filed in case of a lawsuit.

So Connor waited an appropriate amount of time before embarking on the plan he'd thought up in the back of his mind while calling out numbers for the alumni association's raffle. After congratulating the winners, he stepped out into the hall, bound for the lobby.

It was totally normal and not weird, what he was about to do.

He was the party's organizer, the grandson of the owner, and soon he'd be working in the events office. Hell, it was his responsibility to check in on what had become of his homophobic party crashers. Even if it meant asking the incredibly gorgeous Logan incredibly detailed questions about everything that had transpired. And even if said questions were an excuse to gaze into the man's dark eyes.

These rationalizations were still circling in his head when he heard footsteps scraping the carpet in his direction and looked up to see a man who challenged his notion of what family meant.

Connor screwed on his best polite smile.

His uncle, clad in his self-styled general manager's uniform of black blazer, white dress shirt, and black dress pants, didn't return it.

According to family legend, there was a time in Uncle Rodney's life when he'd looked like Brad Pitt, but this was a time lived out only by Uncle Rodney, apparently, because in the old photos Connor could find, Rodney looked more like a slim Donald Trump with slightly better hair. And Connor was no expert at hotel management. Yet. But he'd been doing his homework ever since he was a young boy, and to his eyes, Rodney was more talk than skill. He could pour on the charm, for sure, wining and dining with the best of them—with the emphasis on the wine part. But he had to because the day to day of his job consisted of bringing in new conference clients to replace the old ones he'd alienated with broken promises. Unfortunately, Connor's grandfather was sold on his youngest son's bluster and confidence, which is why he'd placed Rodney in charge of the family's sole prize possession, Sapphire Cove.

"Heard we've got some dirty dancing going on in there?" Rodney asked in a tone that made it sound like Connor's graduation party was an unacceptable indulgence for the property.

"I'm sorry. Dirty?" Connor asked.

"Apparently we had an incident."

"Yeah, but not with dancing. With homophobic harassment is more like it."

"I see." But Rodney was looking everywhere Connor wasn't.

"You do? Because *dancing* is not what caused those guys to touch my friends inappropriately and call one of them a pansy."

"They're being dealt with, sport. Don't run to Twitter over it."

"I do Instagram. And you were coming to update me?" Connor asked.

"No. I have news. I need everyone out by ten."

"*Ten?*" Connor couldn't keep the anger from his voice. "That's two hours earlier than we agreed."

"We're getting complaints." Rodney studied the thumping doors to the ballroom as if he thought a giant, snarling dog might barrel through them at any moment.

"From who?"

"From the guests. Who do you think, sport?"

"It's nine thirty, and we've turned the music down twice already when you asked. And we ran sound checks today from points all over the hotel and everyone said we're well within—"

"We've got a banquet in here first thing in the morning, and we need to turn over the room."

"You didn't know this before now?" Connor asked.

And which is it? he thought. *Noise complaints or turnover time?*

"Plans change." Rodney's tone suggested Connor didn't need to be told why.

"It's my graduation party, Uncle Rodney. It's not like it's going to happen again next year. I'm probably never going to graduate from anything again."

"Yeah, well, your life is kind of one nonstop party now, isn't it, Connor?"

"Hopefully. I'm about to start working in the events office. Parties are literally my job."

Rodney gave a long sigh and rubbed the bridge of his nose as if logic, especially when it came from his only nephew, gave him a headache. "The

Laguna Hills Auxiliary Society is one of our biggest clients. I've got to move their annual breakfast out of the Seahorse Room because we've got a leaky pipe in the ceiling. If you really want my job someday, sport, these are the types of emergencies you're going to have to learn how to deal with."

"My graduation party has been on the books for four years. And it's not just my party. It's their party. Almost everyone I've ever talked to in my graduating class is here. And the last time I checked, this hotel's got three ballrooms. Why does the breakfast have to be in this one?"

"Ten thirty." Rodney glared at him, aggression replacing condescension. "Music off at ten fifteen."

"Music off at eleven."

"You're pushing it, Connor."

"Actually, Rodney, I'm planning it. The Berry-Stein wedding started before dusk, which means they're going to be winding down in another hour too. Which means if you clear everyone out of here at ten thirty, you're going to have a crush at the valet stand and an Uber and Lyft line that backs up all the way down the hill. That spells a ton of angry drunk people, most of whom will leave furious Yelp reviews on our profile first thing in the morning while they're marinating in the sour soup of their hangovers. To say nothing about the state of your inbox by tomorrow afternoon."

Connor was so proud of this little speech he was tempted to finish it off by tapping his uncle on the tip of his nose. But he figured that might earn him a swift kick in the ass.

He'd never gotten along well with Rodney, but recently something in the man's attitude toward him had shifted and gotten worse. Did he actually see Connor as a threat to his job? That was ridiculous. If Connor really was going to run Sapphire Cove someday, that day was so far off in the future there was no reason for Rodney to worry about it now.

"Music off at ten forty-five." Rodney's smile was so false it made Connor wince.

"Thank you, Uncle Rodney." Connor hated that he was having to show gratitude for holding his uncle to an agreement he'd made years before for a party Connor had been planning meticulously for months.

As Rodney headed off, there was a brief blast of music behind Connor, followed by the sound of the door clicking shut. Naser emerged, sober expression betraying he'd overheard everything.

"He's shutting us down early." Connor slumped against the wall next to where Naser stood just inside the hallway.

"Dick," Naser said.

"Don't pretend to be upset. I know you want to go."

"So? It doesn't mean you didn't do an amazing job. I just can't stand being around a lot of people unless we're all playing the same board game."

"Well, if we ever graduate from grad school, I'll arrange a five-hundred-person game of Scattergories."

Naser reached up and ruffled Connor's hair. "Don't be sad, Blondie. There'll be other parties, and you'll throw them all."

Connor smiled, but inside he was wondering if his uncle had planned to sabotage his graduation party from the moment they'd put it on the books. Rodney had treated Connor like an idiot for as long as Connor could remember, but this latest move was more aggressive than that. This was hostile. And it was coming just a week before Connor was scheduled to begin his employment with him.

"Thanks," Connor said. "Let's get the gift bags ready. Looks like we'll be handing them out earlier than we thought."

2

They'd warned Logan the hours around midnight could either be a nonstop crazy parade or peaceful as a tomb. Tonight, it was the latter.

After he'd finished dealing with the fallout from the party crashers, his supervisor had assigned him midnight rounds.

The shift consisted of walking the resort's perimeter while watching out for wayward kids or lovemakers too tipsy to make it all the way back to their beds. No doubt most of the senior guys were bored stiff by the routine, and so assigning it to him was probably a form of initiation for the new guy.

Or he was being punished for coming down too hard on the party crashers.

Either way, he didn't mind. The gorgeous views were worth it. While part of the shift meant being ready to respond to any call that came in through his earpiece, it sounded like Sapphire Cove was turning in for the night. On all sides of him, the laughter of pleasantly drunk guests danced on the ocean winds, and some of the sliding glass doors to the guest rooms overhead stood open even though the rooms were dark, suggesting the rooms' occupants had been lulled to sleep by the sound of the surf.

This was the perfect opportunity to take a deep breath and enjoy the peaceful and quiet night. Count his blessings he wasn't in some sand-blasted tent somewhere, trying to sleep through artillery fire from the surrounding desert hills.

But he was too damn busy cursing himself for what he'd said to

Connor Harcourt.

Baby blues?

What the hell had he been thinking, hitting on the guy so brazenly?

And yeah, it had just slipped out, and it had seemed like the best way to defuse the situation. And damn if the sight of the blush it had sent to his cheeks hadn't made Logan's heart race. But at best, the comment was unprofessional. At worst, he came off like a guy trying to get ahead in a new job by hitting on the owner's grandson.

The wink could be forgiven, even if Connor had let out a small gasp in response. Winks were private, personal, and they could mean a lot of things, most of them warm. Inviting Connor to dance with him? That could take him right over the cliff's edge.

When he reached the lawn outside the Dolphin Ballroom, he saw to his disappointment the terrace doors were already closed, the lighting rigs were being broken down, and maintenance was already rolling in a sea of ten-top tables for some brunch scheduled for the following morning. A brunch Logan was pretty sure had been slated for the Seahorse Room. He was also pretty sure Connor's party had been scheduled to go until midnight, but the guests were long gone.

Was Connor?

He was searching for a sign of the guy inside when a clear voice said, "Well, if it isn't my hero."

And there he was, the prince himself, walking toward Logan across the shadowed grass, blond hair blowing in the ocean wind and a little plastic bag bearing the UC Irvine logo dangling from one hand. When he entered the light streaming through the terrace doors, Logan was left breathless by the sight of the warm, open smile on his face.

Did the guy's confidence and energy ever wane? He'd been fully prepared to take on those drunks himself, and they were each about twice his size.

Logan tried to return the smile, but it felt like the only result was a spasm in his right cheek.

For most of his life, Logan had thought strength meant muscles and endurance and a battle scar here and there. But an entirely different kind of strength radiated from Connor Harcourt, and it came in a sparkly, strutting package. The strength that came from being out and proud and not needing to butch it up for a crowd.

And money, he thought darkly, in a voice that kinda sounded like his old man's after one too many Coronas. *Some of it probably comes from having tons and tons of money.*

"This"—Connor held up the plastic bag—"is for you, sir. It's the gift bag from the party. All the guests got one, and I figure you're entitled given the excellent work you did shutting down those jerks."

"Oh, I was just doing my job, Mr. Harcourt."

"Call me Connor, please. Like, really *please*. There are already three Mr. Harcourts, and spoiler alert"—Connor dropped his voice to a dramatic whisper—"they're all a lot older than me."

"Just doing my job, Connor. Truly. It's not necessary."

"I know, but I'd rather be nice than necessary." With a wink that set loose a hungry gnawing in Logan's gut, Connor set the gift bag on the nearby balustrade and started emptying it one item at a time.

So the prince wanted this to be an extended interaction. Logan's excitement and anxiety swelled in unison.

"How'd it end up with those guys, by the way?" Connor asked. "Did my uncle throw them out?"

"He didn't have to." Logan hoped his ramrod straight posture would distract Connor from the fact that he was taking little steps to bring them closer together. "They were so pissed they decided to check out early. Can't say they did the best packing job given how sloshed they were. After that, it was a matter of working with valet to make sure they didn't get behind the wheel. And, hey, if it makes any difference, by the end one of them was crying on me about his divorce."

"Excellent." Connor's smile made Logan's stomach wobble. "I think they all deserve a really good long cry. Maybe they can have one over at The Ritz in Laguna Niguel."

"Anyway. That's why I didn't make it back."

You're talking like you were a guest, jackass. Logan sucked in a deep breath through his nose.

"Well, I'm sorry about that." When Connor noticed Logan had closed most of the distance between them, he chewed his lower lip gently but didn't move an inch.

"Thank you. To be honest, I figured they might've put me on midnight rounds because they thought I came down too hard on those guys. Didn't realize the party shut down so early."

"Yeah, well, if there's one guarantee about the hotel business, it's that schedules are not always guaranteed. And you didn't come down too hard on those guys. Not in the slightest."

Connor avoided Logan's curious gaze as he took care to space out all the items in the gift bag.

Logan, meanwhile, felt like there was a beast inside of him choking on its short chain. If this were a crowded bar and Connor were a guy he'd just met, he'd already have said all the things necessary to get the guy wrapped around one of his legs while they headed for the nearest private flat surface. But this was his new workplace. And Connor wasn't some potential one-night stand. He was two generations away from being Logan's boss. And that's why Logan was awkwardly holding his hands behind his back. He was afraid he might pull Connor in for a long, wet one if he let his arms roams free.

"All right," Connor said brightly, "let's go through your loot."

"This should be interesting."

"Okay, well, there's a story here, so don't get your hopes up too much. I was a business administration major, and so most of the guests tonight were from the department, and I thought, wouldn't it be neat to find classmates who were already product testing and putting together startups and see if they wanted to donate something to the gift bag?"

"Cool."

"Well, sort of. The problem is most of them are edible, and they're not very good. Take for instance Bernie Killian's new vegetable chips. They're kind of tolerable, but only if you eat ten in a row and think about potato chips the whole time."

"So the tenth chip does the trick, huh?" Logan asked.

"Not really. It's more like thinking about nothing but potato chips for the time it takes to get down ten of these is what does the trick."

Logan couldn't control his laughter. "Awesome. What other goodies you got?"

"This"—Connor held up a small, bright pink tube—"is Marissa Atwell's new brand of organic, artisanal lip balm."

"What's *artisanal* lip balm?" Logan asked.

"I have no idea. And neither does Marissa. But it does answer the question, what would a dead frog taste like if I sucked it out of an exhaust pipe with my mouth?"

Logan laughed so loud they could hear him in the penthouse suite four stories up.

"Well, Connor, I gotta say, thanks for bringing me all of these terrible gifts."

"Yeah, well, you're on duty, so champagne didn't seem appropriate. And this was all I had. Seriously, though. Are you hungry? I could bring you some food."

"I'm good."

"What's your favorite snack food?" Connor asked.

"Anything that combines chocolate and peanut butter is basically a reason for living," Logan said.

"Let me go see what we have then."

"Actually, right now I think I'll be fine with your company."

You will be just fine if you shut the fuck up and stop letting your balls do the talking.

Connor was blushing again. And that was fine as far as Logan was concerned. If making Connor blush was as close as he could get to making Connor moan, he'd do it frequently and with pleasure.

"Thank you. I really am grateful for what you did in there. Seriously. The other security guys wouldn't have... There was just a lot going on in that moment they might not have understood."

"I get it," Logan said. "They weren't just drunks. They were bullies. They were trying to shame your friends out of dancing together."

"Exactly."

"And that was a pretty impressive party you put together in there. I wasn't going to let those jerks ruin it." Logan rested his elbows on the balustrade, pretending to stare out to sea when really he was hoping the conviction in his tone was sinking into Connor's pores.

"Thank you. You want to know what my favorite part of the whole thing is?" Connor emulated Logan's pose exactly. From a distance, they probably looked like two guys who'd come outside to study the stars instead of each other, when nothing, it seemed, could have been further from the truth.

"The dancing? You're pretty good at it."

"You know how to make a boy blush, Mr...."

"Murdoch. My last name's Murdoch."

"Like the guy from *Lethal Weapon.*"

"Yeah, his last name's actually Murtaugh, but you're not the first person to make that mistake," Logan said.

"Can I call you *Lethal Weapon* anyway? I mean, you've already come up with a nickname for me. It's only fair."

"Baby Blues, you mean?"

"Yeah. Baby Blues."

"You like it?" Logan asked.

"I brought you a shitty gift bag, didn't I?" Connor answered.

"Then *Lethal Weapon* it is."

"Look at us." Connor went to bump one shoulder against Logan's before realizing the height difference between them would make it almost impossible. He brushed up against Logan's bicep instead, then, eyes widening, he looked out to sea again. "We've already got nicknames. So anyway, have you met my grandfather?"

"They introduced me earlier," Logan answered.

"'Cause he was eating dinner at his special table at Camilla's, right next to the window?"

"Yep. Cool dude. Really nice."

"Yeah," Connor said, "and he doesn't just eat here every weekend because he loves that they make a fuss over him and he doesn't really have to do the work of running the place anymore. Although those are definitely perks."

"I'm sure."

"But what he loves is this," Connor said, "this moment right now. When the hotel's winding down for the night and you can hear people walking back to their rooms. And if you watch closely late at night on the weekends, you'll see him lingering out by the pool so he can take it all in. He says it's one thing to stand in the hustle and bustle of the lobby with people who might only be stopping off for lunch. But listening to the guests settling in, getting ready to spend the night under the roof you built. That's when he feels like the hotel's a true success. He calls it the magic moment.

"But see, me, I'm the opposite," Connor continued. "My favorite part of the whole party planning process is those last few minutes *before* the first guests walk in. You've got everything locked and loaded. Lights in place. Caterers in position. There's no time to really rearrange anything major, so you have to kinda sit with it even if you're not sure it works. You just have to be there. Surrender. Be with all the hard work and the expectations at once. There's something about that moment, the way it combines everything. Anticipation, excitement, fear of failure. I don't know, it's like… It's why I do this.

"Am I boring you?" Connor asked.

No, you're not, Prince of Sapphire Cove, Logan thought. *You are a new kind of beautiful I've never been this close to before, and the more I look into your baby blues, the more risk seems like reward.*

"I'm boring you," Connor said.

"No, you're not. And you don't talk like you just graduated college.

You talk like you've been throwing great parties your whole life."

"Planning them, maybe. With foam core and fabric swatches and printouts of possible place settings and pitch sessions to my mother in the living room, all of which abolished any doubts about my sexuality, I'm sure. But I don't want to bore you with the details."

"If it means I get to hear you talk about it some more with that twinkle in your eye, count me in."

"I think you're a little obsessed with my eyes, Lethal Weapon."

"The way you blush is a close second."

Something flashed in Connor's eyes, but it wasn't shock. It looked like a hunger, a sudden intensity that suggested he might grab Logan by the back of the neck and bring their mouths together. "Your turn. What about you?"

"My turn for what?" Logan asked.

"Your family. Do they know?"

"Oh, that I'm gay? Yeah, totally." Logan thought of laptops and fake football players with porno-perfect bodies and his dad wheezing like he'd been throttled.

Connor scooted in closer. "I sense the presence of a story."

"Well, it didn't involve foam core boards and fabric swatches."

"Makes sense. You seem like you were more of a *G.I. Joe* guy."

"*Assassin's Creed*, actually," Logan said. "But thanks, I guess?"

"I was close. Spill it. Tell me the story."

"My dad walked in on me jerking off to gay porn when I was sixteen," Logan said.

"Ouch. Did he tell your mom?"

"My mom wasn't around. She died when I was really young."

"Oh, I'm sorry."

"Yeah, no, I'm sorry. Don't mean to be a Debbie Downer." Logan turned from the balustrade, resting one elbow against it, looking directly at Connor now, which made the guy raise his head a little.

Connor looked like he was seconds away from emulating Logan's pose but needed to work up a little more nerve first. "You're not being a Debbie Downer. It's your life. And I asked."

"That you did. And I appreciate that. A lot."

"Okay," Connor said, "if you want me to change the subject, give me your pinky."

"My pinky?" Logan asked.

Connor extended his, and Logan took the hint, wrapping his around

Connor's. "I solemnly swear… Repeat after me. I'm serious."

"Okay. I solemnly swear," Logan repeated.

"I will never repeat to Connor's friends the shitty things he said about their gift bag items."

Logan tried saying it back word for word, but he was laughing too hard.

"Seriously," Connor said, "like, never. Ever."

"No worries. I don't really hang out with UCI kids anyway."

Connor straightened, hands on hips, tongue making a lump under his upper lip. "Oh, excuse me? We're not your style, huh? What kind of *kids* do you hang out with?"

"No offense. I just meant I didn't really do the college thing."

"What thing did you do?" Connor asked.

"The United States Marine Corps," Logan answered.

"Ooooo, impressive." Connor's eyebrows went up. "Thank you for your service."

"Hooh-yah," Logan said in a husky whisper.

"How long since your discharge?" Connor asked.

"A couple months."

"How's it been?" Connor asked.

The urge to pour out his dad's drama came on strong, but he stopped himself, worried it would come off like he was trying to manipulate the boss's family with his sob story. And in the end, would Connor Harcourt understand? If someone in the Harcourt family was forced into retirement by a medical issue, they probably took up watercolors on the veranda.

"Some family stuff to deal with," Logan said, "but otherwise, pretty great." He looked into Connor's eyes. "Especially now."

Connor took a small step forward, and suddenly they were inches apart, and it felt like all the little moves they'd made before now were just a silly prologue to this moment. This moment of sudden, unwavering eye contact and unspoken need. "So, um, do you dance as well as you catch punches in midair?"

"Are you asking me to dance, Mr. Harcourt?"

"I told you not to call me that."

"That's right. Apologies."

"And didn't you ask *me* to dance at the party?"

"In a passive-aggressive kind of way."

"I don't know, maybe it was your way of defusing the situation. And making the other gays feel more comfortable by outing yourself."

"Maybe," Logan said. "Partly."

"Or maybe you really want to dance with me," Connor whispered.

Logan swallowed, and suddenly the only sound was the huffing breaths he was taking through his nostrils.

From the way Connor's face fell, Logan realized the guy had misinterpreted his silence.

"I'm making you uncomfortable," Connor said. "Sorry."

"No," Logan managed, but it didn't sound convincing, and when he stood up straight and lowered his arm from the balustrade, Connor took it as a cue to step back. *Shit.*

"I am. That was kinda forward, I guess. Anyway…"

"Connor—"

Connor took several steps back. Each one tugged at the center of Logan's chest. The expression on his face blended regret and nervousness into a cocktail that made Logan's stomach go sour. "I really did just come out here to thank you. Truly. If you hadn't done what you did, I'm pretty sure those guys would have come back for round two, and it might have ruined the party. So thank you, Lethal Weapon. Sapphire Cove is lucky to have you."

The sight of Connor walking away was like watching a flight you'd raced to catch pull away from the gate, or your own car sliding backward down the driveway without you in it because you forgot to set the parking brake. Suddenly it felt like the potent connection they'd made would blow out to sea and be lost forever the minute the door closed behind Connor's perfect butt.

Logan had enough counseling under his belt to know that sometimes when something scared him, that meant it was good for him. Would Connor Harcourt qualify?

"Connor?"

Connor turned, but he was mostly in shadow now, so it was impossible to see his face.

"So there's sea caves here?" Logan said.

For what felt like an eternity, Connor didn't move, then he slowly approached until a sliver of light from the ballroom fell across one side of his face.

"There are," Connor said.

"Well, technically they're on my rounds, so if Sapphire Cove's really going to be lucky to have me, you should probably show me where they are."

They weren't on his rounds. The beach, maybe, but the guys told him they only checked it once or twice a night because it took them too far from the hotel's potential late-night hot spots—the event spaces and the bar inside Camilla's.

Maybe Connor knew this, maybe he didn't.

The intensity in Connor Harcourt's eyes made it look like he could hear the pulse roaring in Logan's ears. Logan almost wanted him to, wanted the guy to have some sense that it was wild hunger for Connor that had left him tongue-tied and reckless, and not a lack of interest.

Softly, the man they called the prince said, "I'd be happy to show you anything you like, Logan Murdoch. Follow me."

Then he slipped past Logan toward the gate in the balustrade, beyond which lay a set of wooden stairs that descended the cliff face to the beach below.

Defuse the mystery. Thank the guy for his heroic actions. Get Naser to stop nagging him about the whole thing so he could text him later with the sad news Luscious Logan—as Naser, Jose, and Ken had all swiftly nicknamed him—was straight and married and probably comfortable enough with his sexuality to make jokes about dancing with other guys.

Those had been Connor's intentions when he'd searched the property for the hero of his graduation party.

But Logan, it turned out, wasn't married to a woman or dating one. And he looked into Connor's eyes with a hunger that made Connor's breath catch inside a tiny space right below his throat.

Best of all, Logan didn't wince or draw back or go cold when he heard the sound of Connor's high-pitched voice. A *gay voice,* as more than one Tinder date had referred to it, and never as a compliment. The treacherous world of Internet dating was full of gay and bi guys who loudly proclaimed their exclusive interest in "straight-acting men," and he'd had more than one experience of having a prospect show lots of emoji-strewn enthusiasm for his profile photos, only to retreat into sullen silence once they met in person and realized Connor was just his mother's side of femme. They used code words, of course, little turns of phrase to make themselves sound less homophobic and sexist, but Connor had learned to recognize them all. Bubbly. Precocious. Lively. Spunky. Full of personality. A *talker*. So even after it became clear Logan was on the same team, Connor had waited for the inevitable recoil.

But the more he'd talked, the more he'd been himself, the more Logan Murdoch had leaned in. The wannabe dude-bro recoil never came. And wasn't that refreshing?

It was beyond refreshing.

It was intoxicating.

And now, as Connor descended the wooden staircase to the beach below, his hands felt tingly even though the air was distinctly cooler this close to the surf. He was headed to the sea caves, after dark, out of sight of everyone at the hotel, with one of the most attractive men he'd ever met. But calling Logan Murdoch attractive was like calling a redwood tree solid. Sure, it was technically true, but it didn't come close to describing the full extent of what you felt when you were standing before it.

"This way." Connor guided them along the base of the cliff, where the sand was hard packed and had less of a chance of getting in their shoes. He steered them through the shadows between the security lights studding the cliff face overhead, then toward the spot where a high, cast-iron gate taller than Logan blocked access to a narrow wooden boardwalk hugging the cliff's base where it jutted out into the sea.

"Not sure I have a key for that." Logan reached from behind Connor and gripped one of the gate's bars. Connor thought the guy might be about to press him up against the metal and take things to the next level right there. Instead, Logan gave the gate a small shake with his big hand that rattled it from top to bottom.

"You do. It's the same perimeter key that works on the pool areas."

"All right, then. Let's have at it."

Have at it. The words were deliciously direct and full of possibility, especially when accompanied by Logan's commanding tone.

The gate opened with a whine. Logan gestured for Connor to step through first. Gracing these furtive proceedings with such a gentlemanly gesture made Connor's heart flutter. Once on the boardwalk, wet spray misting his arms and neck, his heart started to thunder. When he heard Logan close the gate behind him, it felt as if he'd closed a bedroom door.

The ocean-facing stretch of the boardwalk was lined with informational placards about the sea life offshore and the history of the surrounding coast, and a few coin-operated telescopes. These had been Connor's mom's doing. A former high school teacher before she'd married a man she hadn't known was a multimillionaire until their fourth date, she was always trying to inject some higher purpose into the business of pampering vacationers. Sometimes it worked. Mostly it didn't. Thanks to Uncle Rodney.

After a few yards, the boardwalk made a sharp right turn. And then the cave swallowed them.

"Wow." Logan's voice echoed through the rocky chamber.

Here, the sounds of the ocean surf softened into something that was more like a gurgling brook. What whitecaps the cave's mouth captured were filtered down into something frothy and inviting amidst the labyrinth of low rocks within. The basic security lights at foot level threw a soft golden light across the metal struts that secured the rock ceiling overhead.

"I used to come here all the time as a kid with my friends," Connor said nervously. "There're all kinds of caverns back here we used to play and hide in before my mom found out and busted us. She still has no idea they don't go that deep. She still thinks you could get lost in here. But I've got an excellent sense of direction."

"Do you?"

"Yeah, I usually know where things are headed."

"Makes sense, I guess. Your life's kinda laid out for you, right? You'll probably run this place someday, right? Heir apparent and all that."

"Oh, God. Do they still call me the prince?" Connor turned, resting his butt against the guardrail so he could focus on Logan.

"Kinda."

"Is that a good thing? Should I be annoyed by that?"

"Better to be the prince than a peasant, I guess," Logan said.

"Are those really the only two choices?"

Logan laughed, but there was relief in it. As if Connor's snarky response had shined a light on possibilities he hadn't seen before now. "I guess not."

"Whatever. I'll let it go."

Silence then, save for the gurgling of the sea pushing its way past them and deeper into the cave.

Connor rested his elbows on the rail on either side of him, an attempt to look casual even though the sight of Logan leaning against the cave wall, hands in his pockets, studying Connor with a half smile made Connor feel welded in place. "All right, your turn."

"My turn for what?" Logan asked.

"I told you mine, and my grandpa's. What's your magic moment?"

"Okay." Logan straightened. "So if I remember correctly, it's like a moment when you're doing something you love and you feel the most satisfied by it. Is that right?"

"Exactly." Connor was thrilled that Logan had listened so closely.

"Well, my life is kind of starting over, so I'm kind of figuring out what it is I love to do. Kickboxing's up there, but that's more of a fast and furious kind of thing, and the high is mostly when I'm done. Not sure there's really a magic hour there. There was some stuff about the Marines that I loved, especially once I was a staff sergeant and I was in the zone for gunnery sergeant. But a lot of it was tough, and a lot to hold."

"I'm sure."

When Logan started toward him through the shadows, Connor's breath caught. His feet felt planted to the boards, and the sides of his face got tingly and hot.

"So if I had to pick," Logan said, "I'd pick this one."

"Walking rounds?"

"No. I'd pick the moment when I'm finally all alone with a guy who drives me wild, and I know we're about to kiss, but I'm not sure when. So there's this tension in the air, and I can feel it. Everywhere."

They were inches apart now, so close Connor had to look up at him to maintain eye contact.

"And we're both circling, waiting for the right moment. And I'm trying to take it kinda slow because I know one little touch"—Logan gently grazed Connor's cheek with the side of one finger—"and it might turn into a lot more than a kiss. But first, there's a promise to be kept."

"What promise is that?" Connor asked in a squeaky whisper.

"I believe you promised me a dance."

"Or you promised *me* one."

"Either way, seems like time."

Logan took Connor's hand, and suddenly they were in a pose Connor had never adopted with another man anywhere—sea cave, dance floor, or club—the starting position for a slow, romantic waltz. Sure, he'd done plenty of bumping and grinding, but never cheek to cheek with another man. He wilted into Logan's massive, powerful embrace, trying to take his time with it so he could savor every instant of new touch. Logan's body was as hard and unyielding as Connor had hoped it would be, but the grip of his hand in Connor's was powerful, and inside, Connor felt boneless.

His head came to rest against Logan's solid chest, and even though they weren't even looking at each other, even though their mouths hadn't met, he could already feel the same surge of overpowering desire that had roared through him the first time he'd ever truly lip-locked with another boy and realized *Yes, this is the way it should be. For me. Yes, this is who I am.*

The prospect of kissing Logan Murdoch felt like it would be just as revealing, just as full of potential. A moment that divided things into before and after.

"Obviously, I'm a slow dance kinda guy." Logan's deep, rumbling voice tickled Connor's ear.

"Works for me."

"I mean, there's not a lot of room in here to do a whole Lady Gaga thing."

"Doesn't seem like your style, anyway."

"Ever been line dancing?" Logan asked.

"Nope."

"I should take you sometime."

Something about the simplicity of this statement, the casualness of it, felt as powerful as their first touch.

Connor lifted his head from Logan's chest. "Are you asking me out on a date, Logan Murdoch?"

"I guess I just did, didn't I?"

Now he didn't simply graze Connor's cheek with one finger. He caressed the side of his face with one powerful hand, gently brushing Connor's bangs back from his forehead as he gazed into his eyes. There was something darker in his expression now, something determined but also thoughtful and kind of pained too. There were wounds there, Connor could tell. Maybe the wounds of war, but also from losing his mother so young. But so far, Logan seemed strong despite them.

"I could get in a lot of trouble for this, you know," Logan whispered.

"Not with me you won't."

And apparently that was what Logan needed to hear. With a low growl, Logan brought their mouths together, and the first feel of Logan's hot breath seemed to steal all the breath Connor was holding in his lungs, leaving him no choice but to part his lips and give himself to the man entirely.

So many ways to interpret that statement—*not with me you won't.* And a part of Logan's brain tried to file through all of them even as Connor's mouth rose to meet his.

Maybe Connor meant he'd never do or say anything to endanger Logan's job.

Or maybe Connor meant he only wanted to dance.

That one seemed as doubtful as either of them sprouting wings.

Or maybe Connor meant there were no consequences for him here at Sapphire Cove, and somehow that fact was supposed to protect Logan too.

And maybe Logan could no longer bring himself to give a fuck.

Logan knew it was the perfect kiss a second in. Perfect because he had no awkward awareness of Connor's lips or tongue or his own. No sense that their mouths had come together at the wrong angle and they needed to awkwardly adjust if they were going to keep going. Connor yielded to him perfectly, as if he sensed how hard the hunger inside of Logan had surged and was willing to let it carry him like the foam riding a wave. He smelled like a heady combination of citrus and sandalwood, accented with a hint of masculine musk from his time on the dance floor that said promising things about all the other delicious smells and tastes his body might offer.

Occasionally, Connor pulled back from their kiss, but he didn't break it. They were slight, these moves, and each time he brought his mouth back to Logan's, the kiss was just as passionate, just as potent. These breaks weren't moments of hesitation or doubt or breathlessness. He was recharging himself so he could give Logan more on each return.

He brought his tongue to the underside of Connor's earlobe and licked, waiting for a full-body response. With one arm curved around Logan's back and the other kneading the bulge of his cock, Connor held on for dear life, but the wave of bliss Logan was looking for hadn't come yet. Logan bit Connor's earlobe gently. Still it didn't come.

There's always a spot. Every neck has a spot, and so help me God, I'm going to find his.

Lower, down the nape of his neck. Long, wet, hungry licks until Connor let out a gasping cry, back arching, the pleasure so intense his grip on Logan's cock weakened as the grip on his back tightened so he wouldn't wobble off his feet.

Logan sucked. Hard. Savoring the sound of Connor Harcourt's stuttering moans laced with high, gasping breaths. Assaulting the tender, vulnerable nerve with focus. Backed them slowly up to the rail until Connor's back rested against it, allowing him to go even more limp in

Logan's embrace. If he didn't let up, Logan was going to blow right there in his uniform khakis. Then Connor lifted one leg and curled it around Logan's waist.

He drew back so he could look into Connor's eyes. They were lust glazed. And there it was, the sight he'd craved. Connor's moist lips as he gasped for breath, his pretty blond hair passion tousled.

"Hey, Jarhead, where you at? GM wants you in his office STAT."

Godmotherfuckingdammit.

There were few voices he would have wanted to hear in his ear less in that moment than Buddy's.

Connor, it seemed, had heard the crackle in Logan's earpiece too.

Now his groan was pained, disappointed, as he rested his forehead on Logan's shoulder as if to console them both.

"Shit," Logan whispered.

"Yeah, duty calls." Connor's words, however official in substance, sounded weak coming on a voice still thick with desire.

And for a minute, he thought about not answering the call.

For a minute, he even thought about chucking this job altogether so he'd have the freedom to fan the explosive little fire he and Connor Harcourt had started down here in the sea-spray misted dark.

But then he remembered the dad who was waiting for him at home, prone on the sofa before bad reality television, the crutches he refused to use resting on the wall beside him. The doctor's bills that were weeks overdue. The physical therapist's bills that would come due if his dad ever wanted to walk again without a limp. He remembered all sorts of things that made his skin go suddenly cold against Connor's delicious, inviting warmth.

"You need to go," Connor whispered into his ear. "I understand."

But I don't. I don't understand how I could have found someone so perfect in the worst of circumstances.

Slowly, he pulled himself free. Rested their noses together, saw Connor's eyes were as open as his. Good. He could see Logan's anger and agony and how much he didn't want to leave this cave. But maybe he could also see how this interruption had brought the awareness of all the consequences back in a flood.

"Go." Connor pecked him on the lips. "The next time I see you, I'll be sure to have some chocolate and peanut butter."

"Jarhead. Come in, Jarhead. The GM is our boss in case you don't know the lingo."

Logan hit the earpiece. "Copy that. I'm on my way."

"You better go, Lethal Weapon. My uncle's been on a tear tonight."

Logan nodded and started for the cave entrance, but as soon as he was within steps of the ocean air, he spun, drawn back to Connor as if by magnetic force. He kissed him wildly and without warning, half expecting the connection between them to have evaporated in the face of the interruption and all the unpleasant reminders it brought. But it was still there, yielding and hot and hungry.

"Phone," Logan said.

Connor reached into his pocket and pulled it free.

"Give it to me," Logan said.

Connor punched in his code and complied, and in another few seconds Logan had left a new entry in his address book. **Logan—your hero**. He passed the phone back to Connor. "Lethal Weapon's fine and all, but I put myself in there with the nickname I really want."

Connor smiled, chewed his bottom lip. Looked down at the phone Logan had handed back to him as if a delicious treasure was now concealed within. Logan allowed himself one more kiss, a long, powerful one as he gripped the back of Connor's neck. Then, checking to make sure there was enough hunger still in Connor's eyes for Logan to come back to, Logan turned and left.

3

"Talk about a trial by fire." Logan's boss flashed him a menacing smile and settled into his squeaking leather chair. The massive cherrywood desk between them was about two sizes too large for this windowless office.

Apparently Rodney had posed for a picture with every celebrity who'd walked through the entrance of Sapphire Cove, and then quickly hung the framed result somewhere on his walls. So far, Logan had spotted several Real Housewives of Orange County *and* Beverly Hills, along with some pop stars he didn't much care for and a few aging stars of old TV shows his dad streamed every night before bed. His celebrity search distracted him from the fact that he still smelled like Connor's citrusy cologne, even though he'd stopped in the employee bathroom to wash his hands and take some deep breaths until the tent in his khakis went down.

"Excuse me, sir?" Logan asked.

"Connor's party. Kind of a trial by fire."

"With all due respect, I've seen a lot worse."

Rodney grinned like he was modeling tooth whitener. Tooth whitener that burned his gums. He opened a deep desk drawer and pulled out a crystal decanter and two rock glasses. "You a scotch man?"

"Sure, but no drink for me sir. I'm still on the clock."

"Ah, you've barely got an hour left. Kick back and join me."

Rodney poured a glass and pushed it across his desk. "To new beginnings."

Logan accepted the drink and clinked it with Rodney's when the man raised his in a toast. But he only pretended to take a tiny sip. He hated scotch.

"So"—Rodney took a hearty slug—"tell me what happened at the party."

Logan did, relieved that it gave him the chance to lower the glass to his lap without taking a sip. He tried to sound neutral, professional, even as he was sure not to give the party crashers a free pass. Rodney listened, leaning back in his chair, shiny loafers crossed on the desk in front of him, but Logan felt like his boss was less interested in the content of his account and more interested in how Logan was delivering it.

"Is that it?" Rodney asked once Logan stopped talking.

"Yes, sir. I hope I handled the situation correctly. I know it's only my—"

Rodney waved a hand in the air. "No, no, no. You were fine. And you made the right call not to kick them out of the hotel entirely. I know that's probably what Connor wanted, but he can be pretty self-righteous, if you know what I mean. How was the party before that?"

"No incidents of any kind, but I wasn't there from the start. Sir, if there's some concern about how I handled the party crashers, I'd be—"

"My concern's more for you, to be frank."

"Me?" Logan was startled.

"Yeah, you're a cut above what we usually get here, Logan. Your military background, your fight training. I think you could be a real asset to our security department. So if my nephew ever makes you uncomfortable, I want you to come talk to me about it, okay?"

Well, that came out of nowhere. And for the first time, Logan sensed the presence of an agenda he hadn't quite anticipated, an agenda that was a few ticks off the one he'd feared. And reversed.

"Uncomfortable?" Logan asked.

"Unwanted attention, that sort of thing."

"What sort of unwanted attention?"

"Doesn't matter, as long as it's unwanted. If he's trying to tell you how to do your job. If he's hitting on you or… Look, I know you're gay. There's probably some workplace discrimination law against me saying that, but it's all fine since I don't have a problem with it. I can see past it. To the real you."

Ah, the real me, as opposed to the fake gay me?

"But," Rodney continued, "that doesn't change the fact that we need to make sure Connor's appropriate whenever he's in your presence. And honestly, you guys might be on the same team, but a big strong manly man like you, you're probably into other big strong manly men, right? You're not going to want a little f...flibbertigibbet like Connor getting handsy with you."

That *f* sound had been primed and ready to hook up with a far more demeaning word, Logan was sure.

He realized, suddenly, what he had walked into the middle of without meaning to. Realized it might have something to do with the real reason Connor's party was shut down before its scheduled end time. Logan wasn't about to be reprimanded for how he'd handled the drunks or his little trip down to the sea caves. There was bad blood between Connor and his uncle, and somehow Logan had ended up standing in a river of it.

His boss wasn't concerned for his personal boundaries. He was asking him to be a secret agent. Against his own nephew. The idea would have turned his stomach even if he and Connor hadn't just shared a mind-blowing kiss.

Given the pressure he was under, given how much he needed this job, a spirited defense of Connor in this moment could cost him everything.

But Logan couldn't bring himself to smile or chuckle or do anything to act like he was appreciative of his new boss calling him a big strong manly man, a gay man masculine enough not to trash when his back was turned. Unlike his own nephew.

"I think your nephew is amazing." Logan heard his words as if someone else was saying them. "That party he organized was off the charts, like something you'd see in a magazine. And he made everyone there feel like they were the guest of honor. I saw him treat the catering staff with a level of respect I honestly didn't expect out of him. And he was ready to handle the security incident himself before I intervened. I've never met someone as impressive as him."

Slowly, Rodney allowed all four legs of his desk chair to return to the floor before his feet joined them there. "Obviously he made a good first impression on you. But first impressions change. Let me know if this one does." Rodney's smile returned, but it was a vague suggestion of its former self. "I don't want to lose you, Logan. Every other weekend we've got a situation here go sideways that doesn't need to. A man with your experience might be able to keep things on the beam."

"That's exactly what I'd like to do for you, sir." Logan sat up as straight as he could, glass balanced on his knee, daring Rodney to make his repulsive request more specific.

Rodney nodded but didn't say anything further, a tactic no doubt intended to leave Logan hanging as punishment for not giving him what he wanted when it came to his nephew.

"Knock off early," he said. "You've earned it."

Not exactly a sendoff that implied he'd be fired tomorrow, but not a guarantee of the opposite either.

Logan rose, set the glass down on Rodney's desk, then he nodded at the man and left the office, eyes on the floor as he navigated the warren of windowless back offices that made up most of Sapphire Cove's administrative center. He dropped his earpiece in his locker, fetched his wallet and car keys from within, then it was out the side door and into the warm night air between the office door and the employee parking lot.

He was eager to get some distance between him and Sapphire Cove before he did anything else that put his father's medical future in jeopardy.

If he'd blown it, he'd at least walk away with his pride intact, but what good would his pride be when it was time to pay the doctors? If he wanted the paycheck and the benefits Sapphire Cove gave him from somewhere else, he'd need at least a few years of school under his belt. Who'd pay the bills in the meantime? Who'd pay for school?

He was almost to his truck when it occurred to him that maybe Connor might have waited around for him. Might even be expecting to pick up from where they left off. His phone buzzed, and he pulled it out. The text was from a number he didn't recognize.

Mtg seemed to go long so didn't want to cramp your style, Lethal Weapon. Or should I say...

The text was followed by a gif of a cartoon Superman standing atop a cartoon building, chest out, his cartoon cape blowing behind him in the wind.

So Connor had left the hotel. And probably because he knew lingering and waiting for Logan might seem suspicious and get Logan in trouble.

Logan raised his finger to type out a response. He wasn't sure what. Something sweet, something warm. But when his hand froze as if a million eyes were watching him, he stood there for a while.

Finally, he lowered his arm and pocketed the phone. All the romantic things he'd wanted to text Connor were knocking around inside of him like pool balls searching for pockets. He left Sapphire Cove feeling like nobody's hero.

When Connor got home, the condo was quiet, and Naser's bedroom was empty. There was no sign he'd returned home after Connor had poured him into an Uber with Jose and Ken. And that could only mean one thing. He'd ended up in another three-way with Jose and Ken.

And more power to him, even if he would return home eventually, completely freaked by the fact that he'd been their third yet again. As if the mere fact that two boyfriends had chosen to mutually have sex with Naser at the exact same time still meant someone had cheated on someone, and Naser would eventually figure out who had been wronged if he kept talking about it for hours on end while Connor grunted and ate ice cream.

Still, Connor could have used the distraction of Naser's misplaced guilt and kept hoping he'd hear the key in the front door.

No such luck so far.

Eventually, he nodded off, sitting up in bed.

When he woke up the next morning with sunlight peeking around the edges of his drapes, he'd keeled over to one side like a person who'd been shot in the skull. The crick in his neck would take a day to get rid of, at least. But despite the aching muscles, before he'd even managed to sit up all the way, he started reaching into the folds of the comforter for the hard lump of his phone.

He found it, turned the screen to him, and saw he had one new message from **Logan—your hero**.

He kicked the covers off, swung his legs to the floor, and ran one hand through his hair as if text messages had eyes that instantly connected them to the person who'd sent them.

A few swipes and then there was Logan's text message staring back at him.

It was a thumbs-up emoji.

For a while, Connor didn't move.

There were, in Connor's educated opinion, very specific uses for all of the emoji in existence, including the thumbs-up. It was meant to indicate you'd received an important piece of information, usually a specific request. That was about it. It was a more colorful, illustrated version of *COPY THAT* or *GOTCHA*. It was an emoji cousin to the letter *K*, a reduced form of *OK* used by those who felt themselves too busy or perhaps too subtly angry to reply with both letters of said two-letter word. The thumbs-up was most certainly not, however, an appropriate response to a specific question about one's well-being. It said, *I'd rather you didn't ask me* or *None of your business.*

Or, worse, you thought the question was an attempt to find out how the other person was feeling about the scorching hot make-out session you'd had the night before, and you were trying to communicate you felt nothing but remorse over it. Maybe because you'd had your ass dragged by the boss over it.

But if someone had seen them, if Rodney had reprimanded Logan, would he really have sent a thumbs-up in response indicating things were okay?

Pulse racing, Connor went to type a response.

Something clever and witty and teasing. Something that pretended like all the worst-case scenarios running through his head were outside the realm of possibility, so why not make a sheepish joke about them?

LOL. ROFLMAO. Teddy bears and hearts and maybe six hundred snakes to indicate the length of Logan's epic bulge.

But his fingers froze, and he found himself staring at the phone with a sick feeling in his stomach.

The phone felt like it weighed twenty pounds all of a sudden.

And only when he was in the shower, standing under the warm, dousing spray did he realize he'd put it down on the nightstand, undressed, and walked into the bathroom in a numb daze.

Logan's workout was a wash. All he could see was Connor's text and his own douchey response, so he'd quit halfway through and headed home. But not before pulling over and punching the steering wheel in frustration.

He could hear an episode of *Storage Wars* playing as he approached the trailer. No one was yelling except for the people on television, so his dad and Sally were probably dozing on the sofa. Good.

Just then his phone rang. It was Donnie.

"'Sup?" Logan answered.

"Oh, shit. What's wrong?"

"What do you mean?" Logan asked.

"You only answer the phone like a douche when something's wrong."

"I didn't answer like a douche."

"'*Sup*? What are we, frat bros?" Donnie asked.

"*Heeeeeeeeeeyyyyyy, queen!*" Logan squealed in the most effeminate voice he could manage. It didn't come naturally, but he'd enjoyed enough drag shows over the years to manage a pretty good impersonation.

"What is wrong with you?" Donnie asked.

"Nothing's wrong with me. Why are you asking me if something's wrong?"

"Luther called and said you were all messed up at the gym."

"Why is the manager of my gym calling you in San Diego?" Logan asked.

"Um, maybe because he's my old friend, and because I introduced you to him and took you to that gym to get you signed up." *Old friends* was Donnie's code for someone he'd had sex with on camera back when Donnie was one of gay America's favorite porn stars. Having retired out of performing at the ripe old age of twenty-six, Donnie now made a pretty decent living behind the camera working for Parker Hunter, a studio that specialized in guys who looked like they should be playing college football doing all the things to each other's bodies Logan had wanted to do to Connor's the night before. There was no real Parker Hunter. Like the impossibly good-looking models it employed, the name was meant to invoke all the unattainable and beautiful and mostly straight guys its customers probably lusted after in high school and college.

"Whatever," Logan said. "I'm fine."

"Luther doesn't agree. He asked me if you had a meth problem."

"And you told him no, right?" Donnie didn't answer. "Right?"

"I told him I'd investigate."

"Donnie, Friendship 101. When someone asks if your basically straight-edge best friend is hooked on meth, you tell them no. You don't offer to investigate."

"You're not straight edge. You're an uptight control freak. There's a difference. If you were straight edge, I wouldn't be friends with you. But we're tops, so controlling and uptight is kind of our job."

"Thank you for your Ted Talk on Gay Tops in America."

"Seriously, though, what's wrong?" Donnie asked.

"Nothing's wrong."

"Luther disagrees," Donnie said.

"Luther and I have exchanged three words in the six months I've been going to that gym."

"He's worried about you."

"He should have asked me himself then."

"He said it was like there were four different versions of you working out at once, and they were all fighting with each other."

"Well, that's fuckin' vivid," Logan snapped. "Luther should close the gym and take up poetry."

"Luther's gym is cheap as shit and clean. You really have lost your mind. Tell me what's wrong."

"What's wrong is that you're reacting to shit Luther said about someone he doesn't know."

"Well, now I'm reacting to you being an ass. Oh, and by the way, on the subject of *Friendship 101*, I got a top in the other room right now who can't get it hard even though he's been jerking off to his favorite porn for two hours. And in the other room, I got a bottom who's threatening to walk out because he says we always pair him with models who aren't into him. Never mind that sixty percent of our models are gay-for-pay because that's what our customers love. And in the midst of all this, I still found the time to call my best friend because the guy who runs his gym says he's been acting funny."

Donnie's lecture did the trick. They usually did. But only on certain topics. Following your heart, building confidence. The benefits of walking lunges versus goblet squats. The management of a small porn company. These were the areas where Donnie usually inspired him. Donnie's thoughts on music were best left undiscussed, especially considering Logan almost knocked him on his ass after he claimed Blink-182 were "the Beatles of their generation."

But in this instance, he was right.

Logan was seriously messed up. He wilted into one of the deck chairs that sat in front of the trailer.

Out came the entire story, every word of it, from the moment he laid eyes on Connor dancing, up through the scary-ass meeting with Rodney Harcourt, to the kinda douchey text he'd sent the guy that morning.

"Dude," Donnie said when Logan finished, and for a second, Logan thought he was going to make a porny comment about all the sexual descriptions Logan had included.

"What? Just say it, whatever you think."

"Dude," Donnie said again. "The owner's grandson? That's fuckin' risky, man."

"What happened to *the boner points the way to the heart*?" Logan asked.

"I said that once, and that guy was a gymnast," Donnie answered.

A silence fell, then he heard clicking sounds.

"What are you doing?" Logan asked. "Wait. You're Facebook stalking him?"

"I'm googling him. You have to actually be into somebody to Facebook stalk them. That's you, dude. I'm conducting some basic research."

"No, don't. I don't want to hear you say it. You always—"

"Oh, yeah, there he is. Yeah, totally. He's totally your type. He's got that grown-up Tintin thing you love."

"Will you *stop* saying that? It's disgusting, and it makes me sound like a pedo."

"It's true."

"Tintin was a boy. And what does that make me, the captain? That's fucking twisted, Donnie."

"Well, you don't have a beard. Yet."

"Why am I friends with you?" Logan asked.

"Relax, Murdoch. I said *grown-up* Tintin."

Neither of them said anything for a while, and in the silence that followed, he could hear TV sounds from inside the trailer.

"I don't know what you should do, man." Donnie cleared his throat, and from his huffing breaths it sounded like he was running his palms over his face. "That's a tough one."

The fact that Donnie, the king of jumping in balls first, was freaked out by the implications of what he'd done with Connor was certainly clarifying. But it made the weight in his stomach feel even heavier.

"He just texted you once, right?" Donnie asked.

"Yeah. And I thumbs-upped him."

"So maybe he got the message," Donnie said.

"Okay," Logan asked. "There's a message?"

"I don't know. You need to let this go, maybe? I mean, your job. Your health insurance. Your dad's bills. So the cave thing was hot, but is it really worth the risk? Like have you met a lot of really awesome rich people? 'Cause I haven't, to be frank."

Donnie had endured some painful experiences with successful boyfriend prospects who'd only seen him as their dirty little porn secret, something that only came clear once it was obvious they weren't willing to introduce him to most of their friends. It was bad and it was real, and it had happened more than once, but it also left him biased on the subject of guys in higher tax brackets.

"The party..." Logan said, but the rest of the sentence didn't come.

"What about it?"

"It said something about him. He could have made it about him, but it was about the guests."

"Uh huh."

"He's not some entitled spoiled brat is what I'm saying. At least he didn't seem that way last night."

"Yeah, anyone can seem like a saint when they're rubbing up against your boner," Donnie said.

"Yeah because that's what *saints* do!" Logan barked.

"Do you want my advice or do you just need to vent?" Donnie asked. "Honest question. I'm fine with either."

"Both."

"Be decent if he texts again. But don't play with Sapphire Cove, man. That shit with Rodney, he clearly wants you to rat on his nephew or something, and that's all kinds of trouble. The rest of this gig is good. The other options right now? Not good. Like really not good. Not with your situation. Bartending and bouncing come with zero benefits, and you won't clear enough to pay for your dad's surgery. You're perfect for law enforcement, but that's an uphill climb with a lot of training before you see the kinda benefits you need right now. And I'd put you on camera in a heartbeat if you were down, but as I always say, the money in porn's behind the camera, not in front of it."

"Thanks...I guess."

"All right, I gotta go. I think my two lovebirds are camera ready. Call me later. And don't work out for at least forty-eight hours."

"I'll be fine," Logan said.

"I'm not worried about you. I'm worried about the other people at Luther's."

"You're a prick, you know that?" Logan said.

"Yeah, but I'm your prick. Actually, scratch that. I make better choices than your prick."

That was debatable, but Donnie hung up before he could hear Logan's response.

"Mom, how are you with emoji?"

Her tuna-filled fork almost to her open mouth, Connor's mother glared at him through her librarian-chic eyeglasses, a look that told him he'd once more marred one of their regular Sunday brunches by posing a question unrelated to the sentence she was in the middle of. For a few seconds, the only sounds were the water gurgling from the lion's head fountain above the swimming pool and the puttering of a turboprop flying low over the sea of sloping Spanish tile rooftops that made up his parents' subdivision in Laguna Niguel.

Then she did what she always did when she was getting ready to read him—she pushed her eyeglasses up onto her forehead. Her hair was a great mane of gray locks with dirty blond highlights. She wore a loose khaki overcoat thrown over her flowing chartreuse peasant dress. It was her usual style, a combination of brightly colored, organic-looking fabrics around her ample frame topped off with a tasteful jacket of some sort that sent a sly message that she could afford fine clothes but preferred to dress for comfort.

"Connor, it was already abundantly clear you weren't listening. Do you have to make it so obvious?"

"That's not true." Connor set his fork down as if she'd accused him of trying to steal it. "I was absolutely listening."

"Oh, you were? Forgive me then. What was I saying?"

"More drama with your wine friends because you always insist your weekend gatherings have some sort of educational purpose."

"*Wine friends?* Lovely. Also, that seems like a very extreme reaction to Melissa's accusation that a true crime discussion club would be wildly *off brand* for us. Whatever that means. Honestly. How can people bring themselves to speak of other human beings that way? We aren't bottles of salad dressing, for Christ's sake. It's so superficial and materialistic. I mean, really. I expected more from Melissa. She used to do Agape."

"Crazy thought, Mom, but what if, instead of discussing a book or a movie or a painting, you all, just…" Connor spread his hands wide as if he had brought her the sun as a gift. "…*relaxed?*"

"Dreadful. What's next? Mah-jongg?"

His mother, like him, was a doer. A maker. She wrote out and bound her own cookbooks by hand. She'd organized all the many volumes in their home library according to the Dewey Decimal System. She had files for all her various projects, one of which was stuffed with pages torn from magazines on which people, mostly models, did things she might enjoy doing someday—a file she'd labeled *FUN*.

Fun that required a great deal of forethought and planning, apparently.

She routinely flew all over the world to dig wells and plant trees in countries many of her girlfriends back in Orange County would have trouble finding on a map. In other words, she'd been a hurricane with several different, shifting eyes ever since retiring from teaching high school after she married rich. Sometimes the contrast between her and her Orange County friends could make her seem like Eleanor Roosevelt trying to lecture the Rockettes on aging and self-esteem.

"You guys only argue when you try to assign some new educational value to the group. Wouldn't it be easier if you let that part go and had wine?"

"Fine," his mother groaned. "Relax into myself it is. I shall aspire to someday reach your level of authenticity and meditative calm. By the way, dear boy, when did you discover the writings of Siddhartha? Was it in between your twenty-three Diet Cokes a day, or when you and Naser were attaching pictures of every shirtless man on the Internet to your Pinterest boards?"

"I think this might be the end of our Sunday lunches."

"You say that every Sunday." She waved her hand through the air and renewed her attack on her salad.

"Can we focus, please?" Connor asked.

"On what you'd like to talk about, I take it. Yes, of course we can. You're my only child. So it's not like I have a choice."

"I have a serious question about emoji," Connor said.

"I support their right to get married. Next?"

"The thumbs-up one."

"Yes?" his mother asked.

"How do you interpret that when someone sends it to you?"

His mother chewed for a while. "I heard you, and I sort of agree, but stop bothering me."

Connor's face fell before he could hold it in place. His mother stopped eating and studied him in a way that told him despite their snarky rapport, her maternal instincts had been triggered by the flash of hurt in her child's eyes.

Brow furrowed, lips pursed so tightly they stung a little, Connor stared off at the distant, sparkling expanse of the blue Pacific beyond the sea of rooftops.

"I take it this is about a boy?" she asked.

"It is." Connor's sigh was heavy.

Connor shared most everything with his mother except for dessert. But no way in hell could he tell her about what had happened with Logan Murdoch the night before. She'd completely overreact, start stressing about some imaginary sexual harassment claim Logan might bring against him if they saw each other again and things went south. Connor was only twenty-three. He didn't even work at Sapphire Cove yet. He took up far too little professional space there to be the target of anything of the sort, he was sure.

But his mother had spent less time being wealthy than she'd spent struggling to get by on a teacher's salary. As such, she tended to focus as much on the liabilities and exposures brought by her husband's wealth as she did the benefits. But honestly, even if he was the owner's grandson, he wouldn't be supervising anyone when he started there in a week— including Logan. Connor would be an entry-level employee, for Christ's sake.

Answering to Gloria Alvarez, who I've known most of my life and who loves me like a son. Oh, and you're the owner's grandson, so it's not like you're going to wake up each day afraid of being fired. Oh, also, everyone will be afraid of you.

His mother was watching him closely, waiting, it seemed, for him to give some voice to his dark thoughts. But he didn't. Because they were twisting back on him in new and unexpected ways.

Maybe there were more risks to seeing Logan again than he wanted to accept.

Or maybe it was the reverse.

Maybe Logan's thumbs-up was a different version of the last words he'd said before they kissed.

I could get in a lot of trouble for this, you know.

Well, if that was the case, Connor could fix that problem easily. He'd prove to Logan he wasn't that kind of guy. He didn't hurt people. Didn't punish them. He'd never used his family connections against anyone at the hotel for any reason whatsoever. When it came to Connor, Logan Murdoch had nothing to be afraid of.

I'm a good person, and if he agrees to see me again, I'll be as good as I can be. For him.

He was trying to think of some way to phrase all that as a flirty text when his mother said, "And you're not going to tell me anything about this boy?"

"That's correct. It's too new, and sometimes you kill things before they bloom by breathing on them."

"What a lovely way to describe your mother."

"I wasn't talking about you specifically. I was using *you* in a general sense."

"I believe you're referring to the generic, impersonal, or indefinite you."

"Yes, Mrs. Harcourt. May I have a hall pass?"

"When do you head to New York to see Jaycee?" she asked.

"Eager to get rid of me, I see."

"No, I'm changing the subject since the last one isn't proving very fruitful."

"Two days." Connor had told everyone the trip was a mini vacation before he started his official job at Sapphire Cove.

But it wasn't.

It was a research trip. At UCI, his friendship with Jaycee had centered around their shared major, business administration, and their mutual desire to get paid for throwing fantastic parties guests talked about for the rest of their lives. So for a graduation present, rather than offer him a tourist's spin through the city that never sleeps, she'd offered him a few days of shadowing her at work, knowing full well he'd squeal with delight at the prospect.

And he did. Twice.

She'd graduated the year before, quickly decamping for an entry-level position at one of the top event planning firms in New York, if not the country. Tapestry handled everything from posh weddings in the Hamptons to elaborate bashes hosted by television studios. In a little over a year, her Instagram feed had gone from sunset pictures taken during her regular hikes through the Laguna Hills to selfies of Jaycee and her equally coiffed coworkers posing in front of floral recreations of the Empire State Building or the Taj Mahal, or striking a quick group shot on a beautifully lit dance floor in the Rainbow Room atop Rockefeller Center right before the first guests arrived. The magic moment Connor had described to Logan the night before, only her version culminated in the arrivals of former presidents and Brad Pitt.

"What fun things do you all have planned?" his mother asked.

"She's doing, like, three different huge events. I'm going to shadow her."

"So you'll be working?"

"I will be watching experts in my field working," Connor corrected her.

"What was that about relaxing again?"

Connor made a face like Pennywise staring through a sewer grate.

"Charming," his mother said. "I'm serious, Connor. We go, go, go in this family, and I think it's important you take some time to clear your head before you walk through the doors of Sapphire Cove as an employee and not a visitor."

"Rodney shut my party down early for no reason." Connor thought it best to just cut to the heart of his mother's concerns. She'd made no secret of her misgivings about his job-to-be—they all started with an R and ended with a T. With a lot of scotch in the middle. "He said he had to set up for a breakfast because there was a leaky pipe in the Seahorse Room, but I checked last night, and he was lying."

"Jerk," she whispered. "Do you want me to say something to your father?"

"No, no. I don't want to make waves right before I start."

"Connor, you *are* a wave."

"Is that a good thing?" he asked.

"It all depends on where you decide to break." She sighed as if he'd just doused her dress. Or maybe it was Rodney she was sighing over.

"How far are we going to follow this metaphor? Should I bring a surfboard?"

"I don't like the idea of you working for him." His mother stabbed a forkful of salad.

"I know, and I won't be working for him. I'll be working for Gloria, who's amazing."

"She is, and she works for him."

"Mom, we all know how the hotel runs. The staff works around Rodney because he only does the parts of the job that make him look cool."

"As if anything could make your uncle look *cool.*"

"Agreed."

"He does the parts of the job your grandfather and father don't want to do, and that's how he got the position. And it'll be his until you're qualified to take it."

"Sure," Connor said.

"*Sure?* That's your response to your destiny?" She speared a forkful of salad with so much force he was surprised the rest of the lettuce on her plate didn't try to make a run for it.

Connor sat back in his chair and folded his hands across his lap. "I'm lost. What are we arguing about?"

"We're not arguing, but I'm asking you. Plainly, for once, maybe because you're a college graduate now and days away from plowing headfirst into the family business, whereupon your Uncle Rodney will become a daily part of your life and not just a racist, drunken Thanksgiving embarrassment. Is a life at Sapphire Cove what you want?"

"I love Sapphire Cove," Connor said.

"But will you love running it?"

"That's a long way off, Mother."

"Precisely. So do you love it enough to answer to your uncle until then?" she asked.

"I knew you were concerned, but I didn't know you were this concerned."

"Connor, I'm only concerned about one thing. That you see this as a choice and not an inevitability. You have opportunities and privileges I never had, and I want it that way. Because you've earned them. You're not some lazy, rehab-bound wastrel we need to keep on a tight leash. You're my smart, beautiful, talented only child, and I want you to swing for the fences."

"I love Sapphire Cove."

His mother studied him, nodded, then chewed her salad like there was glue in the dressing.

But the words that followed him home that afternoon were *swing for the fences.*

Just another way of saying follow your dreams.

And while he knew it was too dramatic, even for him, to refer to

Logan Murdoch as a dream—dreamy, perhaps—Connor felt like his mother's exhortation to take risky choices with confidence might be precisely what he needed to get his finger tapping across the screen of his iPhone so he could turn Logan's annoying thumbs-up into something more promising.

He'd spent almost an hour typing absolutely nothing when the apartment door flew open and Naser screamed, "I'M A FILTHY WHORE."

"What is wrong with you?" Connor snapped.

"Call a priest," Naser moaned. "I need to be cleansed."

"You're Zoroastrian."

"My *mother* is Zoroastrian. But they have priests. Call them all. Every religion. I want to cover all bases."

"Well, apparently you did last night. With two pitchers."

"You shame me because the taste of my pain pleases you," Naser groaned into a sofa pillow, then he pulled it over his face and rolled over onto his back.

"And apparently it was a *Game of Thrones* themed three-way." Connor approached the sofa, channeling his best Dixie Carter at the end of a *Designing Women* episode, figuring it would effect the right change of tone. "Naser, enough. I'm not doing three-way shame with you again. I have only one thing to say about any of this. You need to stop trying to have a sex life that your mother will approve of. I can tell you right now there is no version of butt sex with another guy that will make Mahin Kazemi sit up and cheer."

Naser lowered the pillow and gave Connor a look like he'd let out a series of almond butter farts. "Did you actually put my mother and butt sex in the same sentence?"

"Don't deflect. They're linked in your mind, not mine, and that's why you always beat yourself up over harmless fun. Okay. Now that your problem is solved"—Connor held up a warning finger—"and make no mistake, I have *solved* it, Naser, I need you to shut up for like an hour and listen to what happened to me last night after you guys left."

"An *hour*? Oh my God, what did you do? Travel to Narnia?" Then Naser's eyes widened with recognition, and he shot up to a seated position. "Wait. Logan? Lovely Logan?"

"I think we agreed on Luscious Logan, but they're both terrible, so let's be done with them. Sit back. It's story time."

This time, he told the whole story. This time, he included all the nitty-gritty details, and by the end of it, Naser was glaze-eyed and slack-jawed.

"Text him, you idiot," Naser whispered.

"Wait, what?"

"Text him right now, Connor."

"He thumbs-upped me, Naser. What should I say?"

"I don't care. Text him an ass shot with the words OPEN 24/7 above it."

"*Naser Kazemi!*"

"Connor, this guy, the one you've described to me, a guy this hot and interested only comes around every seventy-five years. Like a gay Halley's Comet. You need to jump on this and ride it for as long as you can or you will regret it for the rest of your fucking life."

"A guy who gets awkward and tight-lipped after one kiss? That's not a comet, Nas, That's a light breeze off the ocean." Connor turned his back on Naser and made a beeline for the Diet Coke he'd been drinking when Naser burst into their condo on a cloud of self-hate.

"He's not blowing you off. He's afraid."

Connor sipped. "Do you think he got in trouble with Rodney over me? He didn't get fired. I know that."

"How?"

"I might have called the security department to see if he was on the schedule still."

Naser winced. "Okay. That's kind of stalkery and weird. And possibly an abuse of your position."

"I wasn't trying to track his movements. I just wanted to see if Rodney had fired him. I was after information, that's all."

"The information will come from texting him, Connor."

Connor slammed the Diet Coke can down so hard it spewed a few droplets onto the counter. "Not if he sends me another thumb!"

"In response to a two-word sentence. *Everything cool?* What are you, straight?"

"Don't be a heterophobe. We have straight people to thank for a lot of things. Like BBQ. Las Vegas. Tube socks. Merle Haggard."

"*Merle Haggard?* When have you ever listened to Merle Haggard?"

"Never. It's country, right? Is she any good?"

"*He* is dead."

"Well, so what? Did his music die with him?"

Naser tossed the throw pillow he'd been holding on his lap to one side. "Stop talking to me about Merle Haggard and go text Logan, goddammit."

"My head is spinning," Connor moaned.

"You love it when your head spins. It makes you feel alive."

"He made me feel alive, Naser."

"No baby voice, Connor," he whispered. "We talked about baby voices."

"We also talked about Bambi eyes, but you did them last night, like five times."

"Fine. Speak your truth, even if you have to whine."

"I wanted him to be dumb and married." This wasn't just Connor's baby voice. This was his hungry baby who'd fallen out of the cradle voice. "But he wasn't. He was so sweet. And when I told him about the things I loved, he listened. And he didn't, you know, when he heard my little gay voice for the first time, he didn't…"

"I know, sweetie. I get it too."

In the silence that settled over the room, Naser rose to his feet and shuffled toward Connor before curving a comforting arm around his back.

"And his dick was the size of a python," Connor whispered.

"You saw it?" Naser asked.

"I could feel it. There was no missing it. It was a giant, hissing python," Connor whispered. "An anaconda that had swallowed a python."

"Okay, don't go horror movie on me. You have thirty seconds. Then go in your room, sit down, dig deep and send him a text that describes everything you were feeling when you described last night to me."

Connor didn't move for thirty seconds.

Then Naser slapped him on one shoulder. "Go get that snake, bitch."

It wasn't the first time Connor had used a pen and paper to draft a text message, but it was the first time his hands were sweating while he did it.

One question. Boxers, briefs, or me?

Gross. No way.

Next try.

I can't stop thinking about you.

Better, but basic. People always said that like it was this big romantic compliment, but the list of things Connor couldn't stop thinking about also included the possible calorie count of his last meal and why one of his feet always looked smaller than the other. Logan belonged on a different, better list.

You blew my mind.

Dumb. And not ultimately very sexy. Who wanted to feel pride over somebody's brains leaking out of their ears during sex?

Are your fingers free this evening?

A dreadful, unnatural hybrid of his grandfather's sense of humor combined with a drag queen's desire to provoke.

Wear me like a condom you never take off.

This was a nightmare. He couldn't do this.

He was seriously considering Naser's ass shot strategy when the television erupted from the living room with the opening theme to *The Crown.*

"Nas, I'm working."

"Coming to your senses shouldn't be work, Blondie."

But to his credit, Naser turned the sound down. A bit.

Connor shot to his feet and went to the window and its view of the swimming pool at the center of their complex. Instead of the glimmering turquoise water, he saw the night dark surf pushing its way into the sea cave, summoning the memory of the ocean spray dappling his neck and cheeks.

The world didn't seem upside down. It seemed like it didn't have any walls anymore. College was over. All his friends except for Naser were leaving the OC in the dust. And his mom had basically implied flat-out that he shouldn't take the job that had been picked out for him since birth.

Why not take a risk?

Was he really afraid he might do something to endanger Logan's job?

Or was he more afraid of making an idiot of himself?

No pen, no paper.

Connor picked up the phone and typed.

"So I'm guessing this is a *Storage Wars* marathon?" Logan said as the ninth episode began.

"Oof, good thing I didn't drop you a bunch when you were a baby," his dad responded. "Wouldn't want to mess up that brain, Einstein."

While their living quarters were tight, Logan was proud of the job they'd done dividing up space. It comforted Logan to see his dad's sofa, worn in all the right places, on one side of the trailer's living room, and on the other, Logan's favorite easy chair.

"Maybe something else, Pop. Can we try Netflix?"

His father held up the remote, and Logan took one step across the tiny living room to get it.

He was scrolling through Netflix's eight-thousand-million viewing options when his dad let out a groan and straightened himself to a seated position with one arm on the back of the sofa. His metal crutches were resting against the arm of the sofa next to him. Logan watched them closely to make sure they didn't fall over. "Hey, son. No offense, buddy, but the Sally thing's not going to work out."

"Yeah, actually it's working just fine. It's not a fix-up, Dad. She's supposed to watch you."

"I know, but she's a troubled woman."

"You're a troubled patient, so it sounds like a match."

Logan's phone buzzed in his pocket.

Chip flinched, balled his hands against his stomach. "Probably Sally, busting me on my ice cream intake."

It wasn't Sally. It was Connor Harcourt.

"Just going to pop in my room for a second." Logan's voice sounded far away, and he was almost to his bedroom by the time his father answered.

"Yeah, sure."

He was determined not to read the text until he had some privacy, but his heart started racing when he saw how damn long it was.

Once he was leaning against his closed bedroom door, he sucked in a deep breath and picked up the phone and read.

Half of him was dreading some big, long apology that explained how last night was a huge mistake and he was sorry for doing anything that might get Logan in trouble at work, and the other half was expecting a raunch-filled sextathon finished off by an ass shot.

What he got was very different.

Hey. So I've tried like ten versions of this text and they all sound either trashy or basic. On my part, I mean. I was looking for the way to say I can't stop thinking about you when what I really wanted to say was I don't *want* to stop thinking about you. I was also going to say you blew my mind, but the truth is you joined my body with my mind for the first time, and they both went to a place they've never been before. So anyway, I know that's a lot and kind of intense, but not telling you how I was feeling today felt like a lie for some reason. Or maybe I just want you to know. Thanks for an amazing night, Lethal Weapon. Even if we didn't exactly finish. :)

Logan only realized how much he was smiling when his face started to hurt.

His response was already forming itself in his mind. A text about twice as long, a text about the things that had happened inside of Logan when he watched Connor dance, about how the room seemed to come to a stop around them the way it sometimes did for people in movies, the ache he'd felt when he'd had to leave the sea cave. He wasn't the biggest texter in general, but maybe Connor would turn him into one. This would be the beginning of a long and illustrious career of texting Connor Harcourt.

But somewhere along the distance from his brain to his fingers, this text—this perfect, desire-filled, honest, fearless text—died a sudden death. As he raised the phone and prepared to type, the walls of the doublewide seemed to close in on him, and all he could hear was Donnie's voice saying *Risky, dude.*

What he typed was, **Meet at Laguna Brew tonight at 6?**

4

Once the two of them stopped squealing, Naser agreed to help Connor get ready for his date.

Once Connor gave him a rough sketch of what that would entail, Naser's brow furrowed, and he got a faraway look in his eyes.

"Why do you need three hundred packs of Reese's Peanut Butter Cups?" he asked in a daze.

"Please drive me to Costco. I'm too excited to be trusted behind the wheel."

Costco had the peanut butter cups, but not the wire frame to which Connor planned to fasten them. It was also possible three hundred wouldn't be enough, so he bought an extra two hundred just in case. Then they needed a hardware store for the wire. Then it was time to buy some cowboy boots.

"Wait, cowboy boots?" Naser asked. "You don't wear cowboy boots."

"That's correct, and I'm not going to wear them tonight."

"Of course not. Why would anyone actually wear cowboy boots? They're so much better as condoms. What's going on, Connor?"

"Drive me to Spectrum and I'll tell you."

"So you're going to put the peanut butter cups *in* the cowboy boots. Then what?" Naser asked once they reached the crowded shopping mall.

"Naser. While I appreciate your curiosity, when a design concept starts to take shape, it's not possible for me to answer specific questions like this. It feels like an interrogation, and I know that's not your intention, but be patient with my process is what I'm saying."

"I see. Why don't I throw you into traffic instead for being pretentious and annoying?"

"That's fine, as long as you park near Nordstrom."

Eventually they found the perfect pair of boots, brown leather with tiny silver diamond designs flecked throughout the skin. Masculine with a hint of flash and sass. A perfect tribute to big, manly Logan and shiny, sassy Connor.

Then it was home to put his vision together, which he did on the kitchen counter while Naser routinely reminded him of what little time he had left to shower and get dressed before heading over the hill to Laguna Beach. But Connor was so lost in his work he only responded with dismissive grunts as he hot glued packages of peanut butter cups to the three stacked half chevrons he'd fastened out of wire. The first hot glue gun he'd hauled out of his crafting drawer had been jammed. The other five worked just fine.

The chevrons were fairly wide, so he took some time deciding how far apart to space the cowboy boots atop the bottoms of the three wires. He eventually opted to tuck them close together, adhering the side of one boot to the other so they looked like a gift underneath a soaring marquee of chocolate and peanut butter cups.

Naser started to speak. Connor held up a warning finger, which silenced his best friend instantly, then he began arranging packages of peanut butter cups vertically into both empty boots.

"If you rearrange those one more time, they'll unionize and go on strike," Naser finally snapped.

"Naser, I'm not really available for sarcasm right now."

"Well, are you available for some wine?" he asked.

"It's a coffee date," Connor snapped. "I can't have wine. He'll think I'm a drunk."

"Yeah, but you're not on the date yet, and you need to relax."

"I don't need to relax." In one hand Connor bunched up the peanut butter cups he'd stuffed into one boot so they were more visible above the top. "I need to focus."

"Connor, if you're going to manscape and douche in the next twenty minutes, you need to relax or you'll injure yourself. Also, I'm assuming you'll need your usual forty-five minutes to decide which blue polo shirt to wear."

"Is this more sarcasm? 'Cause I've issued a warning. This is an important moment for me."

"Maybe you should douche *with* wine," Naser answered.

Connor headed for his bedroom. "I need to go call my dad's driver. I texted him earlier, but he wasn't sure he could get the Rolls."

"Wait, a Rolls? Connor, it's a coffee date."

Connor spun to face his soon-to-be-ex best friend. "No, it will *start* as a coffee date, and then it will turn into something much, much better. Just like last night started as me thanking him for what he did at the party and then turned into something much, much better. I've already sent the driver a map of two different lookout points, both with views almost as good as Sapphire Cove's. We can go to the first one for preliminary chitchat, and then the second one has a trail where we can wander off to enjoy a repeat of our kiss from the night before. And maybe more."

"Outdoor make-out sessions, now with more rattlesnakes."

"I need to feel supported right now." Connor had almost closed the door to his room when Naser reached through the crack and gripped his shoulder.

"Blondie, wait," Naser said. "Look, I know you're all about having a plan. And it's great that you're such a detail-oriented person who owns six hot glue guns. But maybe you should, I don't know…show up for coffee and go with the flow."

"You're the one who said he might be afraid about the work thing. I have to bring my A-game."

"Connor, your A-game is *you*. It's not a rented Rolls-Royce."

"I can't leave any stone unturned," Connor said. "He's a gay Halley's Comet, remember?"

"I was exaggerating. I mean, we barely know the guy, right?"

"Oh, I plan on changing that real fast." Connor smiled, then gently pushed the door shut between them.

He had work to do. And Naser was right.

A fair amount of it would be in the bathroom.

The last time Logan had been this afraid, he was in the midst of a training exercise off the coast of Camp Pendleton a few months after a CH-46 had gone down during similar maneuvers, drowning a Marine he'd been buddies with in the process. When he'd looked out the open door of his hovering Black Hawk and realized the sparkling Pacific was a lot farther down than he'd first thought, his stomach lurched and his head spun, like they were both doing now. Combat deployments had brought with them their own sense of persistent anxiety, but the IED that had knocked him out of his Humvee he'd never seen coming, and the few times he'd been fired on had come fast and furious too. Neither incident compared to the sudden terror of that moment high above the Pacific, the dread that came with staring possible disaster in the face.

That's what he felt now as he rehearsed what he'd say to Connor.

Vertigo-inducing terror.

But he wasn't high above the ocean. He was sitting at one of the tables outside of Laguna Brew, the one farthest from the teenage girls who were texting like they'd lose money if their words-per-minute count dropped.

Then a car turned into the mini-mall's parking lot. Logan's heart lurched.

It wasn't just a car.

It was a big, gleaming silver Rolls-Royce.

The teenage girls stopped texting at the sight of it. The mother and her three kids who'd emerged from the yogurt shop next door stopped in their tracks, jaws agape.

The Rolls-Royce came to a stop, and Connor stepped from the back seat, looking as sparkling and perfect as the car itself. Dark blue, form-fitting designer jeans that plumped his perfect butt. A blue polo shirt with white trim on the collar and bicep-hugging sleeves. And the kicker: white leather shoes fringed with rhinestones that made it look like he was walking on air.

Baby blues and then some.

He looked like a shiny little piece of candy, and Logan wanted nothing more than to unwrap him.

Maybe that's why he'd stood up suddenly, like a shotgun had gone off.

Connor was walking toward him, his seductive smile lighting up his eyes. A draft of his citrusy cologne reached Logan before he did, inspiring a head-spinning memory of their perfect first kiss the night before. He'd styled his hair so that the sides were gel darkened, but the top was still light and feathery. Just enough for Logan to run his hands through.

Oh, God. I can't do this.

Connor took Logan's extended hand, using it to pull them into an embrace. Quick, but firm enough to cause a stirring in Logan's balls.

"Thanks for doing this on such short notice." Logan patted Connor's back three times in a row, like a coach congratulating his player.

Connor flinched. "Of course."

"Cool." Logan couldn't think of anything else to say. Pulling Connor's chair out for him might send the wrong message, and sitting down would bring them another step closer to the moment he was dreading.

But Connor took his hand suddenly, and just as suddenly Logan was struggling to keep his balance as the force of nature pulled him across the parking lot.

Oh, crap. He's trying to get me in the Rolls.

Before he could protest, Connor opened the car's door, which opened in the opposite direction from most normal cars. He knew the term for it, a suicide door, because mob guys couldn't take cover behind it before hitting the pavement and opening fire. Suicide might be exactly what Logan was committing if he stepped into the suddenly open space between him and the car's interior, but Logan entered it anyway. The display set up on the seat chased his breath away. Chocolate and peanut butter.

Cowboy boots. For line dancing, no doubt. It took a few seconds, then he recognized the shape the peanut butter cups were arranged in. The chevrons on a sergeant's badge. Connor had remembered he'd been a staff sergeant. And Logan had mentioned that, what? Once? Had he put this together himself or hired someone to do it? Did it matter? It was both too much and more than enough at once.

His heart was racing like it had when he'd peered out that open Black Hawk door. But instead of the ocean far below, he saw the fear and need in his former street fighter father's eyes the night before. A man out of options. Except for his only son.

"That's…" But Logan's voice left him.

"Oh, no. What? You don't like chocolate and peanut butter after all?"

"No, that's really amazing, Connor. I don't know what to say."

"You don't have to say anything. Just, you know, get in the car and I can show you some other places that are as nice as the ones I showed you last night."

Summoning all the resistance he could manage, Logan straightened, backed away from the car door, and when he finally turned to face the man next to him, he saw it happen instantly. Saw Connor recognize the fear and uncertainty on Logan's face and saw it dash something across the rocks inside of him.

"Oh." Connor wasn't pouting, but it was damn close. "I guess this was too much."

"No, no. This is amazing...I..."

What he wanted to say was *you're amazing*, but if he went down that hole, he'd end up tumbling into this gleaming, silver Rolls. Driving himself into Connor while the driver took them everywhere Connor wanted them to go. His head spun at the thought. But it wasn't a thought. It was a fantasy. And a guy like him, a guy in his situation, wasn't allowed fantasy.

Get on your fucking game, Murdoch. There's real shit at stake here. Take control. It's what you do.

"Let's sit." Logan gestured to Laguna Brew with one arm.

Pale, lips pursed, and glassy-eyed, Connor nodded and followed Logan back to the table. The previously texting teenage girls were watching their every move. He was determined to look Connor in the eye while he handled this, but it was hard. Hard because Connor Harcourt apparently didn't have a lifetime of trying to keep his emotions from showing on his face like Logan did, and there was so much confusion and pain—and embarrassment—there, Logan had to fight the urge to take the guy in his arms and carry him off to a place where the facts weren't what they were and they weren't themselves.

But a place like that didn't exist.

"I thought it would be better to do this in person," Logan said.

"Maybe once you tell me what *this* is I can agree. Or disagree."

"Last night was amazing." He steeled himself before he said what he knew he had to say next. "*You're* amazing. But it can never happen again."

"Oh." Connor cast his eyes to his lap and nodded, probably to hide how much this had wounded him. "Okay, then."

"I'm glad you understand."

"I don't, actually, but it didn't sound like a question so..."

"Okay. Let me explain. I didn't want to drown you in my family drama last night because I didn't want to come off like I was manipulating the boss."

"I'm not your boss."

"You're two steps removed. What I'm saying is my family situation is really serious. And I need this job. Badly."

"And you think I'd do something to endanger your job. In that Rolls-Royce."

"Or someone else would have an opinion about what we did in that Rolls-Royce and it would cause trouble for both of us."

"Did you get in trouble with Rodney last night?" Connor sat forward.

He thought of Rodney Harcourt's menacing smiles and smelly scotch. Saw spunky little Connor shouting at his uncle because Logan had repeated the contents of their meeting, the blowback coming down on Logan before Connor had a chance to rein in his temper. In short, he saw land mines everywhere he looked. Maybe this coffee meeting by itself was a terrible, dangerous idea. Maybe ghosting Connor altogether would have been safer for everyone. But he couldn't bring himself to do it.

And he was already doing this, so he had to see it through.

"No." It was sort of true, wasn't it? Rodney had made him a strange, passive-aggressive offer, a terrible offer. But he hadn't disciplined him. That might come later. If he rejected the offer.

"Does he know we went down to the caves?" Connor asked.

"No." This felt less like a lie than his previous answer. If Rodney did know, he hadn't let on.

"But you're afraid he'll find out and you'll get in trouble?" Connor asked.

"I don't know," he lied. "I don't know the hotel. I don't know your family. To be honest, I don't know you."

Connor's baby blues blazed with anger. "Well, I sort of thought that was the whole point of you inviting me here. So you could get to know me better."

"I don't know if it's worth it."

Connor looked as if Logan had thrown water in his face. "Oh, okay."

"Jesus. That did not come out right."

"No, I mean. It makes sense. A guy like you could hop on Grindr and find a dozen guys like me in a heartbeat."

"That's not what I meant, and it's not true."

"It is true. You're tall and gorgeous with a deep, manly voice and a huge…neck. You're like gay gold in the world of Internet hookups."

"Thank you…I think. But what I mean is there aren't dozens of guys like you out there. There's only one you, and that's why I ignored my best judgment and asked you to take me to the caves last night."

Connor chewed briefly on his lower lip and nodded in a more relaxed way. Signs Logan's sincere proclamation had mended some of the damage done by his careless words a moment before.

"Call me crazy," Connor finally said, "but I figured when a guy responds to a text like the one I sent with a meeting time and place, it's not because he's going to shoot you down." Then in a whisper, he added, "I worked on that text for an hour, by the way."

"It was a great text," Logan said.

"Yeah, it worked out really well."

"It's the way it is."

"So the way it is is that you're afraid I can't be discreet, or that I might try to get you in trouble if things don't work out?"

The temptation to unload about his dad's injury was still there.

No way. It wasn't fair to his dad, and it still might come off as some attempt to secure special treatment at work, which, if it got out, might have an effect as damaging as sleeping with the owner's grandson.

"You're the grandson of the guy who owns the place where I work, and your uncle is my boss." Maybe if Connor hadn't rolled his eyes, he could have stopped there, but Logan hated eye rolls. "Also, in all fairness, you probably have no idea what a guy like me has to do to get through a week."

"And I'm never going to find out, apparently," Connor muttered.

"I can't do anything to mess up this job."

"And you can't trust me not to, I guess."

"It's not about trust," Logan said.

"Okay. What's it about?"

"Priorities."

A coldness had taken over his voice, the coldness of a staff sergeant. The coldness of professionalism.

The chill of fear pretending to be strength.

When he saw the effect it had on Connor, a sudden weight pulled at his chest. The guy's embarrassment was gone. His hurt, it seemed, was also gone. Replaced by a fixed, stony expression that seemed to suddenly match the icy tone Logan had struck.

"All right," Connor said. "Makes sense, I guess. I mean, I can't expect to be one of your priorities after one kiss. That wouldn't be fair, would it?" When Logan didn't answer, Connor said, "So I guess I should go now. I wouldn't want somebody to see us together and get you in trouble."

Logan couldn't bring himself to answer. He didn't want Connor to leave. He wanted to transition this into some friendly outing or even awkward conversation that worked to put this moment behind them. But that would be impossible with the gleaming Rolls-Royce sitting a few feet away, a beautiful reminder of the amazing evening Connor had apparently planned for them both.

"No answer is an answer, I guess." Connor got to his feet and started for the Rolls.

"Connor!"

At the door to the absurdly luxurious vehicle, Connor spun, eyes widening a little when he saw Logan was right behind him. "You don't have to be afraid, okay?" he said. "Your job is fine. Everything at Sapphire Cove will be fine. I'm not going to say anything to my uncle or my grandfather or anyone. I won't even tell anyone you like dudes."

"They know I'm gay. I'm not in the closet."

"The point is, you're safe, Logan. You don't need to chase after me like I'm some terrible problem that's going to screw up your complicated life. And I'm sorry about whatever's happening with your family. I am. Truly. And I'm sorry you think I'd do anything to make it worse."

"Connor."

"What?"

"I need you to know something."

"Okay."

"The fact that I won't act on how I feel about you is not a statement on how I feel about you."

"Maybe. But the fact that I acted on how I feel about you makes me feel like kind of an idiot, so I need to go and just…get over it, I guess. Goodbye, Logan."

Logan wanted to block the door before Connor closed it, but that would be crossing a line. It left his arms with nothing to do, so he raised them above his head and then gripped his skull in a vain attempt to stop the headache that had started to pound as soon as the Rolls' engine started up.

He'd eaten twice that day, but as he watched the impossibly beautiful car pull out of the parking lot, his stomach felt empty and his face felt hot. And his throat felt like there was an apple lodged in it.

It was the right thing to do, a voice that sounded like one of his first commanding officers said to him. *And sometimes the right thing to do feels the worst.*

But when he returned to the table to retrieve his almost empty iced coffee and the car keys he'd stupidly left sitting there, the teenage girls who'd been texting up a storm earlier were glaring at him like he'd punched a kitten. They'd heard every word, apparently, and it looked like they had strong opinions about the ones Logan had said to Connor.

It was the right thing to do.

He turned those words into a mantra as he drove home. But he was only a few minutes from the coffeehouse when something caught his attention on the side of the road, something bright orange and rustling in the canyon winds. He pulled over and saw packs of Reese's Peanut Butter Cups attached to those half chevrons of wire Connor had affixed to a pair of cowboy boots.

Connor's gift. He must have pitched it from the Rolls on the way home.

As if some higher force had seized control of his body, Logan stepped from his truck, shook the dirt from Connor's meticulous handiwork, and placed the gift in the cargo bay. He told himself he was tying up a loose end. And cleaning up some litter.

It was the right thing to do.

He figured he'd leave it in his truck until the painful memory of their meeting had faded, but when he got back to the trailer, he found himself carrying the thing inside, with no plan for how he'd explain it if his dad or Sally asked him about it. But they were both dozing in the living room when he entered. As quietly as he could, he moved to his tiny bedroom. His cramped, one-room cell, as plain and unadorned as all the barracks he'd been housed in.

Once he shut the door, once he was alone with Connor's gift, he ran his fingers over the leather of each boot, noting the shiny little diamonds that flecked the rugged brown. Shiny and rugged. *Kind of like me and him.*

Kind of like what he and Connor could have been.

It was the right thing to do, he thought again.

Then he turned and punched one fist through the wall.

He couldn't face Naser.

Not yet.

Couldn't admit that Naser had been right about the Rolls and his itinerary for the evening and maybe even the gift. But since it was obvious

Logan had decided earlier that afternoon to drop the ax, maybe Connor shouldn't beat himself up over those gestures. It wasn't like they'd turned the night sideways. Also, Naser wasn't the *I told you so* type, but still. It would hang in the air between them and then Connor might do the thing he'd been trying not to do ever since he left the coffeehouse.

He might cry.

Which was ridiculous.

They barely knew each other. It wasn't like Logan was some epic loss.

But he felt like he'd glimpsed something between them the night before, something he'd never felt or seen with someone else. Potential. Not just the potential for something that would work—the potential for something extraordinary.

So Connor had the Rolls drop him off at his apartment, then he hurried into the parking lot and fired up his BMW before Naser might notice he was home.

He needed common sense. He needed someone he could trust, someone who could make a very good and very stiff drink.

He needed his mom.

But when he pulled up outside his parents' house, he saw Rodney's ridiculous cherry red Lamborghini parked next to the driveway, looking like a Red Hot someone had chewed up and spit out while high on cocaine.

Talk about the last person he wanted to see. If his mother was home, that meant she was sheltering upstairs to avoid his uncle's presence. So Connor parked a half block away and snuck into the kitchen through the back door.

He heard his uncle's voice in the living room and was almost to the back stairs to the second floor when he caught a glimpse of his grandfather in the living room. That was weird. His grandfather never dropped by for a casual visit. It was an unwritten rule that they always went to him, and Connor didn't remember anything about tonight being a special occasion. If Rodney and Grandpa Dan were here, that meant something was up. Something serious.

But since Rodney was clearly holding forth, he didn't like dropping in. Instead, he tucked himself against the wall while he eavesdropped.

"Wait, wait. Rodney, what does my son have to do with the history of Laguna Beach?" Connor's father asked.

"I'm using it as a comparison is all," Rodney said.

"Yeah, but I'm not getting it, though. If this is about scheduling, that's not really my—"

"It's not about the schedule. It's about the fact that Connor was hosting a gay orgy in the middle of the Dolphin Room."

"Rodney," his grandfather piped up. "Come on now—"

"Look, the point I'm trying to make about Laguna Beach is this. You hear all kinds of whining about how it's not as *colorful* as it used to be. Not as artistic. Now we all know what that's code for, and personally, people like me, people who drop a lot of cash when they go out, are pretty glad you can go down there for a nice dinner without getting yelled at by a pack of drag queens with cocaine coming out of their pores."

"There were drugs at Connor's party?" Connor's grandfather asked.

"I wouldn't be surprised, but that's not the point."

"What *is* the point?" There was barely any fight in his dad's voice. Rodney always wore his dad down. That's why he was the resort's chief pit bull.

"Look, we all know Connor's my successor—"

"Years from now, Rodney. Decades, even." His grandfather waved a hand in the air, indicating he didn't want to have this conversation.

"No, hear me out." Rodney cut them both off. "Look, I'm not a homophobe. But when someone's as wrapped up in identity politics as Connor, they're going to make choices that are about their agenda, not what's best for the business. And honestly, guys, what I got a glimpse of the other night in the Dolphin Room was a glimpse of Sapphire Cove's future with Connor in the events office. AIDS charities, gay weddings, drag queen dance parties. It's fine to hold your nose and do those things once in a while, but the more power Connor gets, the more that's going to be the life of Sapphire Cove."

"We've done significant marketing to the LGBT market," Connor's father said.

"Yeah, yeah, yeah. All the letters of the weirdo alphabet, I know. But the fact is, they're not the only market, and despite whatever people might say in public, this shit still makes a lot of people uncomfortable. And another thing…"

"What?" his father asked after Rodney refused to finish the sentence.

"We've got this new security agent. Really handsome guy. Former Marine. He's gay. That's fine. He keeps it toned down, reined in. But he was in my office last night because he was freaked out."

"Freaked out how?" his dad asked.

"He said Connor was showing him a lot of unwanted attention, and he wasn't sure how to respond because he's royalty. But it was clear Connor thought the fact that we hired a gay guy meant he had a right to him or something."

Connor suddenly felt like he was breathing through a straw. A straw buried in sand.

"Did this security agent say that or are you putting words in his mouth?" Connor's father asked.

"His words exactly. He said Connor made him uncomfortable."

Something inside Connor broke.

Broke the same way it did when Chester Bailey first called him a fag in third grade and Connor knew it was true. Broke like it had when Ken Frye, the first boy who'd ever truly kissed him—like really French kissed—went to school the next day and told all the other kids a lie that Connor had tried to force his hands down his pants during a sleepover even as he told him to stop. But Connor had thought these past breaks had caused certain muscles inside his heart to grow back stronger.

That which does not kill you and all that...

But now his head was spinning, and when he felt heat on his face, he realized he'd brought his hands to his mouth.

It was Connor who'd walked away from Logan when he thought he might be making Logan uncomfortable, and it was Logan who'd invited him back. Who'd asked him to show him the sea caves. Who'd made an alpha dog move with his flirty talk and slow walk and powerful kiss.

And now he'd lied to Rodney about the whole thing.

Is that why Logan had been so evasive on the subject of his meeting with Rodney? Had Rodney busted him after all and so Logan doled out this bullshit cover story to save himself? Or had Logan offered up the story preemptively, just in case? The same way he'd nipped their attraction in the bud. Logan Murdoch, it seemed, was a guy who liked to stay two steps ahead of risk.

Because *priorities*.

Because Connor, Logan had decided, was a terrible risk.

A risk that justified this awful lie.

Connor had been seconds away from bursting into the living room and giving Rodney a piece of his mind, but this detail had knocked him sideways.

"The point is, we need a plan to contain your son," Rodney said.

Say something, Dad.

But there was only silence from the living room.

Say something.

But it was his grandfather who spoke first. "I have to confess...I'm not the biggest fan of this *side* of Connor. Call me old fashioned, but I wish he'd marry and meet a nice girl, to be frank."

"Instead he's dancing like one and wearing pants so tight no real man should be seen in public in them." Rodney sounded excited to have his father on his side.

Connor felt the heat in his eyes before he felt the tears. It wasn't the first time he'd dealt with this kind of homophobia—slick, articulate, packaged for the folks who thought they weren't really prejudiced. In some ways it was worse than the knee-jerk bigotry of rural churchgoing folk who'd never spent any time with a gay person.

And he'd pretty much let his Grandpa Dan off the hook on the topic. He was from a different generation, and the fact that he'd never said anything awful to Connor about his sexuality to his face seemed like a blessing. Connor wouldn't have heard the man's thoughts now if he hadn't been eavesdropping.

His dad, though. Why was his dad being so quiet?

"You're not suggesting we don't give Connor the job," his grandfather said.

"No." It sounded like Rodney would be fine with that proposition, but for the purposes of this conversation he'd take what he could get. "We make a plan to contain him, that's all. So he doesn't turn our life's work into a low-rent gay bar. Because, trust me, if the travel community starts to see us as a niche destination for freaks, it'll only be a matter of time before we lose our status as the only family-owned resort on this coast. Our occupancy rates will fall until we've got no choice but to sell to Marriott International or Hilton Brands."

And there it was. The great Harcourt family fear Rodney always used to manipulate his older brother and father into doing what he wanted—the fear they'd have to sell to one of the big hotel chains.

There was another long silence.

His father broke it. "All right, Rodney. What's your plan?"

Connor felt the hot sting of tears in his eyes.

He was a problem, a freak. An agenda threatening his family's otherwise sound business plans. Even worse, the fact that he fell in love with men meant they might one day have to sell the damn hotel.

In his mind's eye, he was in the middle of the living room, giving his bigoted, lying uncle several piping hot pieces of his mind.

But what would he say to his grandfather? His father? It would be three against one. And from the sound of everything he'd just heard, it was going to be three against one for as long as he worked at Sapphire Cove. And not because he wasn't talented or dedicated or hard working. Because he was gay.

"You want us to have a talk with him?" his grandfather asked.

"No, I don't think that'll do any good. He'll call us all homophobes and a bunch of other millennial nonsense. What I need is for the two of you to help me stand strong against his more…childish side."

"Seems like maybe you're overreacting a bit, son, but I'll trust your judgment here."

"Sure. Okay, Rodney," Connor's father said.

Connor was outside, shuffling toward his parked car before he realized he'd peeled himself off the kitchen wall.

He drove all over Orange County that night. Down along the beach, through the canyons, then onto the 405 at Irvine and a little ways north. He pondered driving as far north as Los Angeles, but instead he opted for big, large meandering circles around the place he'd lived his whole life. A place of twinkling vistas and raw natural beauty where he'd spent his days in privilege and blindness. Blindness to the way people saw him, thought about him, talked about him when his back was turned. Blindness to whatever a guy like Logan had to do to get through a week. Like lie.

He drove for hours that night because he knew the minute he stopped he'd have to admit that something had been changed forever, and there was no going back.

Logan had assumed that after the terrible deed was done he'd eventually feel some relief. The relief of having taken a dangerous temptation off the table.

Two days later, no such luck.

Three days, same story.

Instead, he felt like a stranger inside his own body. Part of him was dead, the other part nursing fantasies of Connor confronting him at the hotel and doing some *Jerry Maguire* speech in front of the entire staff that sealed their fates together forever.

But in the long days that followed, Connor didn't show his face at Sapphire Cove.

And after a few nights of having his heart clench up every time his rounds took him past the spot where he'd followed the guy down the steps that hugged the cliff and toward something that had felt like a beginning and not an end, Logan made a deal with a coworker that got him out of nightly rounds.

For the time being, at least.

In the end, it wasn't much of a comfort. Whenever he was alone on duty or watching TV with his dad, Logan found a way to check his phone and stare at the blank screen following his last text to Connor. And whenever he had to check in on an event in the Dolphin Ballroom, he saw Connor dancing under its chandelier.

Eventually these feelings would go away, Logan told himself.

The whole thing had been a mistake. A messy, split-second mistake. For both of them.

If Connor didn't see that now, he would eventually.

Hell, eventually Connor might thank him.

Word around the hotel was that the prince had gone on a short vacation to New York before his job started. That was good. It would give them both time to brace for the initial awkwardness. In the beginning, they might have to ignore each other to keep things easy. Then one day they'd run into each other in the lobby during work hours— preferably daylight ones—and if enough time had passed, things would be all business, back to normal. Someday they might even tease each other about the crazy night they'd shared. By then, Logan would have a boyfriend who couldn't rent Rolls-Royces on a moment's notice, who knew what it was like to split a doublewide with your dad. And Connor would be engaged to some other Prince Charming whose idea of slumming it was flying commercial.

But a little more than a week after their last meeting at Laguna Brew, Sapphire Cove was shaken by a piece of news that inspired gossip from the front desk to the back offices of the security team.

The prince hadn't just taken a vacation to New York City.

The prince had found a job there.

And he wasn't coming back.

That night, Logan told the guy he'd traded late-night rounds with that they could go back to their usual schedules.

That night, Logan went down to the sea cave for the first time since he'd been there with Connor, only this time the surf gurgling through the rocks sounded like the whispers of ghosts. Something brief and bright and hot and magical had flared here briefly and then been lost forever. Swept out to sea.

Cast out to sea. By good sense. By responsibility.

By him.

"Some hero you are, dude," he whispered to the ocean winds.

Five Years Later

5

"Kiss me," the bleached blonde with zero percent body fat moaned.

Uh oh, Logan thought.

Logan had learned to keep lip-locks and cheap sex as separate as he'd keep a match flame and kerosene fumes. It was the only way to prevent overpowering flashes of the best kiss he'd ever shared with another man from wrecking his love life for good.

He'd had plenty of quick and dirty hookups with strangers since letting Connor Harcourt roll out of his life in a Rolls-Royce. But he'd told them all point blank that make-out sessions were not included. *Sorry, buddy. That's not how Sergeant Stud rolls.* So if they wanted to get their hands on the broad, muscle-plated chest featured in his profile photo or run their fingers over the globe and anchor tattoo on his right shoulder, those were the terms. Most guys were fine with it.

Not the ornery little dude writhing beneath him now. Apparently he'd experienced a change of heart. During their chat session that afternoon, he'd consented to Logan's conditions with a long string of thumbs-up emoji. But now that Logan had crossed the guy's threshold and entered the latticework of harsh sunlight cutting through vertical blinds the guy had only partially yanked closed, Blondie was determined to neck like a teenager on prom night. And if he didn't quit, Logan would have to politely bail, maybe head home for some quality time with his Xbox and a Heineken. Anything to avoid the memory of a name he still had trouble saying aloud.

This time around, he'd told himself he could spend a month on the apps, tops. A month of filling his spare time with quick, meaningless hookups in between heavy work weeks and visits to Donnie in San Diego.

Now he was well into month three, and the hamster wheel of anonymous, instant gratification Grindr offered was starting to give him a backache. And possibly a neck sprain thanks to a guy who wanted to share a kiss before they shared real names.

If they ever shared real names.

At least the dude wasn't a catfish. He was, in fact, the owner of the lean torso and chiseled eight-pack he sported in his profile photo, and the other far more explicit images he'd texted Logan earlier that day in an attempt to seal the deal. But now, after throwing the guy down onto his unmade bed, after playing the part of the big, tough former Marine to perfection while he roughly stripped the guy of his clothes, Logan was using every trick he knew to render his midday conquest boneless with pleasure, anything to stop the determined twink from zeroing in on his latest target—Logan's mouth. So far, nothing was working, and he was almost out of tweaks, nibbles, grips, thrusts, and twists.

He'd been clear as day during their three-hour Grindr chat. Would he have to say it again?

I. Don't. Kiss.

Would it matter? His man of the moment, whose peroxided hair made him look like a Q-tip dipped in tanning lotion, kept going for Logan's lips like a puppy, nipping and growling whenever he missed.

And, of course, as he'd feared, each failed kiss hit Logan with a burst of unwanted memory.

Memories of inviting shadows laced with ocean mist, of a head-spinning embrace inside a sea cave with a man who'd redefined Logan's ideas of strength and beauty. So what if these memories were half a decade old? They pulsed beneath Logan's desire like a second heartbeat.

Why couldn't the guy—who was a HaPyBtTm according to his screenname—be content with the rest of Logan's body? Chances were, they'd only end up spending about twenty minutes together anyway.

"Kiss me," HaPyBtTm growled.

Shit. He intensified his thrusts instead, tightening his grip on the undersides of the guy's lean, muscled thighs.

"Kiss me." This time it was a yip, like a lap dog.

Snippy, that's a pretty good nickname. His screenname didn't seem that accurate. There was plenty of bottoming going on, but not a lot of happy.

Snippy's brown eyes had filled with a predatory intensity. No sign of the submission he'd been promising Logan all afternoon.

When he asked a third time, Logan's eyes started to wander, looking for a way out. He caught a glimpse of his thrusting ass in the half-open mirrored closet door, then some framed pictures on the—*Oh, Jesus. Is that a boyfriend?*

"I said fucking kiss me, bitch!" A squeal this time, punctuated by a punch against the center of Logan's chest. A half-inch shy of the sore spot where he'd taken some shrapnel from an IED.

Logan hated it when bottoms punched him. Some did it for fun, to goad him on. Some did it when he went in too fast, which was maybe justified, but why not just ask him to slow down? Logan seized the guy's wrist before he could land a second blow. And that's when Snippy McFisty let out a defeated groan that told Logan the game was over.

Thank God.

Slowly, he pulled himself from inside the guy's clutching heat, careful to grip the top edge of the condom so it didn't slide off. There was nothing in it that might spill, but old habits die hard.

His first red flag should have been the guy asking to go bareback, even though Logan had already told him twice he was a condoms only guy. Didn't matter if Snippy was on one-a-day PrEP. So was Logan. There were other things to worry about besides HIV, he'd told him. The truth was, he was saving the intimacy of skin on skin, and all the trust that required, for someone more special than a Grindr hookup. But Snippy wasn't entitled to that information. There was a lot Snippy wasn't entitled to as far as Logan was concerned. Including a kiss.

If Snippy wanted boyfriend information, he should do boyfriend things.

And based on his nightstand, he already had one.

They were both on their backs now, staring up at the cottage cheese ceiling. None of that gasping or panting that indicated a good, sweaty session filled the room. Instead, their breaths were low and even, the silence awkward.

It was an awful feeling when the reality of an anonymous hookup closed in around you. A lot of things could do it. Mostly environmental factors you hadn't anticipated—glacier-sized piles of dirty laundry you had to step over to get to the bed, suffocating litter box smells, surprise drug paraphernalia. Strange scratching sounds from down the hall that suggested either a roommate or a prisoner. Maybe the last guy who'd made the mistake Logan had.

But Snippy's insistence had stirred something else. Unwelcome memories of a guy whose big blue eyes had stopped Logan in his tracks the moment he'd first gazed into them. A guy he'd briefly slow danced with to the sounds of crashing surf, a more intoxicating and fulfilling experience than any sweaty, naked tumble Logan had enjoyed in a stranger's bedroom since.

"What happened?" his host asked, sounding wounded and nothing like a guy who'd just punched Logan for holding to the boundaries he'd established before he'd come over.

"Look, I don't mean to be a jerk, but I was super clear. No drugs, no fisting, no water sports. I don't bottom, and I don't kiss."

Snippy let out a whiny grunt and pulled a pillow across his chest defensively. "I know. I thought I'd be the one, though."

The one what? Logan thought.

"Hey." Snippy rolled over to face him. "Why don't you hang out until my boyfriend gets here? He likes it rough and dirty. I'll watch while I make dinner."

"Actually, I think I'm going to jet. I got some errands to run. Nice to meet you, though."

Logan swung his legs to the floor, slid the condom off, and dropped it in the nearest wastebasket.

"Well, shit," the guy said. "There goes twenty bucks."

"Say what?"

Standing, Logan hopped up and down as he tugged a sock on to one foot, not the most comfortable way to get dressed but with every new sentence out of this guy's mouth, the more Logan wanted to get the hell out before the aforementioned boyfriend burst in and chloroformed him.

"You know, you're kinda famous around these parts." Snippy had raised himself up on his elbows in a way that made his abs pop, but his wild bedhead didn't match the sultry pose.

"This building?"

Had he hooked up with someone else in this apartment building? It was possible, but he doubted it.

"No, silly. The OC. As in Grindr Orange County, Sergeant Stud."

Logan felt a flash of embarrassment at having his screen name repeated out loud. He was pretty sure the guy across the room from him wouldn't want to be called HaPyBtTm in polite company. But there was no polite company around, so what was the big deal? Still, neither one of them included their faces in their profile pics, only their shirtless, muscled torsos, some teasing glimpses of naked waistlines. That said something about a mutual desire for anonymity.

"Oh. Alrighty, then." Logan punched one leg through his jeans and then the other.

"Come on. Don't get all butthurt. If you don't want guys comparing notes, you shouldn't hook up with every dude who's into dudes in Orange County. Expand to LA or something."

"What's this about twenty dollars? I don't get it." He knew he should get out of there and fast, but he couldn't resist asking.

"Oh. My friends and I had a bet going that I'd be the one who could get you to kiss."

"By punching me?" Logan asked.

"By asking nicely."

"Awesome," Logan whispered.

"The punching was my idea."

"Got it."

"So what's your deal anyway?" Snippy asked. "You straight? Married? An assassin?"

"You going to enter it into my file with all your Grindr buddies?" Logan pulled his T-shirt over his head—the tight, plain hunter green one he wore mostly to hookups to make a good front door impression because his biceps popped in it. Now it felt sweaty and confining.

"Don't get offended. You're a memorable guy, Sergeant Stud. Even if you are over thirty. But with your height and that body...shit. You can keep at it for a while. Come thirty-five, though, you're going to want to transition over to Scruff or else you'll get autoblocked by twinks like me."

Like you're such a treasure, Snippy, Logan thought.

"Wait," Snippy asked, looking panicked. "You're not over thirty-five, are you? 'Cause that's like a rule with me."

"Is it?"

Logan was thirty-two, but he'd rather let the ageist douche twist in the wind than say so.

Having tied the laces on both of his sneakers in record time, he buckled his belt. Usually, unless the meeting was a complete disaster, he compensated his hookups for his no kissing rule with a light peck on the forehead on his way out the door. This hookup, however, qualified as a complete disaster. Almost as bad as the guy he hadn't realized was a tweaker until they were both undressed and he suddenly said he just needed a minute to check the oven and see if there was still a witch inside of it. Logan had gotten out of there fast.

"Have a good one," Logan said. "I'm going to head out before you drown me in integrity."

"I'm wearing Cool Water. But thanks, I guess?"

"Not talking about your cologne, Happy Bottom. You take care now. And don't punch people."

"Men love a mystery, Sergeant Stud!" the guy called after him as he booked it down the apartment's single hallway.

Logan answered by shutting the front door behind him with a firm thud.

It was so hot outside the air hit him like another punch from Snippy, this one in the face.

The Santa Anas were blowing desert winds over most of Southern California, lighting wildfires as far north as Kern County.

As Logan drove back to his apartment, he saw a thick plume of dark brown smoke crawling skyward from the dry, brown mountains to the west. Apparently it was Orange County's turn in the barrel. No surprise. They'd had some terrible fires here over the years, and with the weather forecast predicting high eighties for the next two weeks, this one better get knocked down quick.

He'd try the dating thing again, he told himself as he drove.

Maybe expand to San Diego and LA. Not to rack up more quick and meaningless encounters like Snippy had suggested. He'd find quality guys who might be worth having coffee with, or God forbid, dinner. Guys he might feel comfortable kissing once they got to know each other.

Maybe Donnie could set him up with someone again.

It wasn't like the Army guy had been a total fail. They'd had the whole military thing in common, and some fun dates. But as soon as the guy started telling stories of his hard partying ways—all-night dance parties, so much Molly he was having memory issues—Logan could see the burning bridge from a mile away.

He'd kissed the guy though. Once or twice. During sex.

And both times he'd thought of Connor Harcourt. Hadn't just

thought of him. Had seen the pain in his eyes the last night they'd stood across from each other.

Which was fucking ridiculous.

How could he still be haunted by a five-year-old make-out session that might have cost him his job?

Maybe because he wasn't making enough of an effort to get Connor out of his head. He was still saving all those write-ups his events were getting on New York style blogs. And reading them over and over again. And he could always delete the fake Instagram account he'd opened so he could follow Connor's. That always led to no good.

Logan was pulling into the parking lot of his sprawling apartment complex when a phone call from his security director lit up his cell.

It chapped his ass that Buddy Haskins had gotten the promotion Logan had put in for, but given he'd been at the hotel much longer and was best friends with Rodney Harcourt, it made sense.

He popped his earpiece in.

"How can I help you, Buddy?" He managed to sound both professional and cheerful.

"So what's this about an incident yesterday?"

"What incident?" Logan stepped from behind the wheel of his truck.

"Something about you messing up the camera system."

It was such a twisted and inaccurate version of what had happened Logan needed a beat to figure out what Buddy was actually talking about. "No, no. I never touched the system. I never got the chance. I needed to review some footage, and Pete got up in my face and started yelling at me about how I didn't have access, and I asked him since when and said if it was anyone's call, it was yours or Rodney's."

"All right, well, I'm calling. So why did you need access?"

Logan stepped into his apartment, thanking his stars he'd left the AC on by mistake.

"Some guest was bullshitting us, claiming he stepped in wet paint outside the north hallway exit on the way to the pool. He wanted meal vouchers, two free nights, free parking for his car, which had been in valet for, like, six days. So I checked out the spot and the reason the signs were down is because the paint was dry, and maintenance said it'd been dry for a day at least. But when I went out front, I saw they were doing some curb painting in the motor court, so I figured if I looked at the footage, I'd see the guy stepping in the paint out there on purpose so he could rip us off."

"Christ, dude," Buddy muttered. "That's a lot of work over some meal vouchers."

"And two free nights in a king guest room, and six nights of free parking. I was protecting the hotel, Buddy. The guy was a fraud, man."

"All right, well, Pete says you really disrespected him."

"Yeah, well, I'm not used to guys who've been there three months telling me how to do the job I've done for five years." Logan tried not to slam the refrigerator door now that he'd pulled a Heineken free. He failed.

"We've got new procedures with the camera system. Pete got told, you didn't. Don't bite the messenger's head off."

"Okay," Logan said, feeling like he was being shoveled some heavy bullshit. "So what am I supposed to do when I need access to footage?"

"Go through me."

"All right, well, watch out for Pete because he's pretty damn possessive of the thing."

"Logan, enough, man. Enough. It's a hotel, all right? Not a war zone. A hotel. Sometimes you come at stuff too hard and you make headaches for everybody. Headaches I don't need. Like, I know Steve liked all your emails, but Rodney didn't, so cool it."

It'd been a while since Logan had sent upper management an email recommending various tweaks to their security procedures. He'd always been careful to phrase them in a diplomatic manner, and always careful to offer his own services, sometimes after hours and for no overtime, to execute the little fixes he suggested. Steve used to welcome his emails, but after he left and Logan was passed over for his job, it sounded like his suggestions weren't going over so well. Especially the one questioning the install of the new camera system.

"Just asking how I'm supposed to do my job, that's all," Logan said.

"Your job is to stand at the lobby doors and look as dashing as you always do. That's why Rodney wants you on so many days. The lady guests love you, and some of the guys do too, which I know really works for you. So, you know, stay in your lane and don't make my life harder."

"All right," he said. "Warning received. I'll stay in my lane."

To vent his frustration, he popped the top off the beer bottle against the side of the counter using the side of one fist.

"Good. But I'm sorry, Logan. I'm going to have to write you up."

"For what?" Logan bellowed before he could stop himself.

"This is an issue with you, man. This getting up in people's faces thing."

"I didn't get up in anybody's face. Pete got up in mine."

"Still, I need you to figure out how to de-escalate this kind of stuff when it happens. You're a big guy, and you freak people out. I don't need someone like Pete turning all *Me Too* on us."

Logan pulled so hard from his beer he was afraid he might down half the bottle in three gulps. But he was afraid if he dropped it, he'd put his fist through the wall.

Me too? What the hell was Buddy talking about? Was he implying there'd been an element of sexual harassment in his quarrel with Pete the day before? The whole thing was insane. Logan hadn't been written up in five years of working at Sapphire Cove. The fact that he was going to be now, over trying to do his job, and with a thread of homophobia running through it to boot, was too much to swallow at once. So he swallowed more beer instead. In this moment, there was no winning. An argument with Buddy on top of an argument with Pete, who was apparently Buddy's new favorite, would make the whole thing worse.

"Do what you have to do, Buddy." Despite his best efforts, he'd said it like, *Come at me, pal. I dare yah.*

Buddy didn't bother with a goodbye.

At least he didn't ask me to apologize to that prick, Pete.

Worse things had happened in his time at Sapphire Cove than Buddy Haskins becoming security director, but sometimes Logan forgot that fact.

No, the worst thing without a doubt had been the death of Dan Harcourt a few years ago, an event that had left the long-term staff members, folks who'd worked there since the place had opened in the sixties, emotionally gutted.

Martin Harcourt's death a few years later didn't level Sapphire Cove's staff in the way the loss of his father did. People were sad, of course, but Martin had been more hands-off with the hotel's day-to-day operations, hadn't nursed the long-term relationships with the hotel's senior workforce that his father had.

Crashing either man's memorial just to get a glimpse of Connor felt gross.

Hoping either tragedy might have caused them to bump into each other also felt kinda gross. So he'd kept that hope to himself.

Still, Connor had slammed the door on Sapphire Cove so fast it was hard for Logan not to suspect their last meeting had something to do with it.

As he showered away the sour smell of cheap sex, which somehow smelled worse when it didn't remind you of anything fun, he kept wondering why Pete, a guy who'd been there three months, had been told about a new procedure with the cameras and not Logan. And he kept wondering how Pete could have felt so damn confident about his newfound knowledge, getting up in Logan's face like he was a bouncer and Logan a guy trying to crash the rope line. And he kept wondering why Buddy didn't seem to give two shits about some asshole trying to cheat the hotel with a fake claim. Rodney had lost his shit over less.

Then there was the fact that Logan had never been written up in five years of working there and happened to be the only security agent on staff with actual fight and self-defense training, and yet Buddy, a guy whose idea of strength training was letting out several loud farts in a row, had been promoted over him. By a general manager who thought Logan looked so great in his uniform he'd practically turned him into an art installation in the lobby.

None of it made any sense.

And all of it left him debating a larger and more important question.

What the hell was going on at Sapphire Cove?

He tried to watch TV, tried reading for a bit. Texted Donnie to see how the porn awards show he was attending in LA was going and got back blurry shots of porn stars making out in a hotel ballroom. After a while, he felt the familiar call, the one that made him excited and nervous at the same time, that had him opening his Instagram account, Palm Tree Guy. Technically, it wasn't a fake account. There were only four pictures on it, but Logan had actually taken them, and they were all of very real palm trees on the grounds of his very real apartment complex.

Connor's profile, on the other hand, was mostly shots of the amazing events he'd been throwing in Manhattan for five years. Soaring floral centerpieces. Gorgeous ice sculptures. Backyards in the Hamptons transformed into stylish wedding chapels. But every now and then Connor was in one. Posing before an empty dance floor, or with a team of New York hipsters who'd helped him execute the festivities in question. Five years had sharpened some of the angles in his face, and most of the time now there was a serious look in his baby blues, and his outfits were a bit more muted and grown up but still stylish with glimmers of flash.

Maybe New York had toughened him up a bit.

Or maybe Logan had.

Yeah, right, dude. He's got a big, fabulous life in New York City. He's not thinking about some dumb jarhead he made out with five years ago.

None of that mattered. What mattered was the minute Logan laid eyes on those baby blues again, his hand went to his zipper, exposing his hard cock to the cool air, and in no time the blend of memory and fantasy—imagining what Connor would have looked like riding him, what it would have felt like to feel the guy's arms and legs wrapped around him, wondering if every inch of him would have tasted as delicious as his neck, wondering if he smiled right before he came—had Logan dazed and stroking.

It worked like clockwork, and it always ended in an eruption that made him feel emptier and more sated than he ever had in some strange guy's creepy apartment, the kind that left him lying on the sofa for a while because cleaning himself up meant leaving his fantasy of what could have been with a guy he'd thought about almost every day since they'd first met.

6

It was the champagne that did it.

One second, Connor Harcourt was toasting a successful event with his team. The next, he was knocked backward in time to the night of his college graduation party, when flutes like the one he held now had circled the Dolphin Ballroom at Sapphire Cove and a gorgeous security agent had barged into his life without warning.

It wasn't the taste or even the buzz, but the particular golden shade it could adopt in the right light. Inside this former Midtown Manhattan cathedral turned banquet venue, the glass in Connor's hand had turned the same color as those sparkling flutes he'd carried through the grandest ballroom at his family's resort. A resort he hadn't set foot in for half a decade.

A different lifetime, a different Connor. A naïve kid who hadn't yet built a real life for himself. Now he had a career divorced from his family's money and all the entanglements it brought.

Nothing in his life was more important than work. Work had saved him when his old life and dreams collapsed. Work would save him if the shit hit the fan again.

And this afternoon, work had been a triumph. Together with his team, he'd helped make The Center for Diverse Fiction's annual awards dinner a glittering success.

His team was basking in the afterglow.

The organizers had already dropped by to thank him. A single handshake and a cursory smile toward the end of a party meant unhappy clients they'd be hearing from on Monday. But this afternoon, they'd lingered, bright eyed and cheerful and not nearly as harried as they'd been at the outset, talking through their favorite aspects of the lighting and the meal.

Jaycee must have heard from them too. Busy with another event across town, she'd already texted him heart eyes and "thank you" hands. And the guests, seated as they were at floral-festooned tables amidst the beautifully uplit columns of the old, deconsecrated cathedral, had broken out into small pockets of low but excited chatter as the final winner of the evening accepted her award. Above them, the vaulted ceiling was covered with Tapestry's special surprise: vivid projections of all the book covers of the nominees, which swam and shifted around each other like a sluggish school of brightly colored fish. A similar design to what he'd used to project his classmates' pictures onto the walls of the Dolphin Ballroom the night of his graduation party.

Stop thinking about that night. Stop thinking about Logan Murdoch and his lies.

The stakes had been high with this one. It was only the second event under Tapestry United, Jaycee's nonprofit wing of the company, devoted to securing funding for struggling charities working to foster social justice and racial inclusion. Thanks to Jaycee's extensive contacts list, organizations like The Center for Diverse Fiction, which had moved their offices out of Manhattan a year before to avoid skyrocketing rents, were able to throw lavish fundraisers, honoring their guests and potential major donors with a level of luxury and style typically reversed for the .01 percent.

Champagne toast concluded, it was time for another Tapestry tradition.

Connor tapped his flute with a fork to draw them away from their individual conversations.

"Now, Sarah, as the newest member of our crew, you might not be familiar with this little ritual, so allow me to explain. At Tapestry at the end of an event well worked, which basically means one where the roof didn't fall in and people didn't die of anything besides natural causes—"

"Should we maybe raise our standards?" Sandra Paulson, his most senior coworker, always phrased her instructions as questions.

"Someday," Connor answered, "but the point is, at the end of each event the team leader goes around and recognizes what is, in their opinion, the most outstanding contribution each member made to the night's proceedings—"

"They used to be called the Tapestries," Sue Lofton cut in, "and we had little trophies we made up, but Alan said they added too much to the budget."

"At some point, I'm going to be allowed to finish this, right?" Connor asked.

There were some nods and some grunts, but nobody acted like that was a sure thing.

"Okay. Sue, once again, you showed amazing facility with the lighting coordinator, and I want to commend you for your excellent execution of the ceiling projections we treated the client to this evening."

As Connor pointed to the cathedral's ceiling, Sue did a half bow while taking a sip from her champagne. "Thank you. Follow me on Insta," she said as if addressing her many fans.

"Chad, you did a great job of charming the office manager at the sound coordinator's warehouse when she was refusing to send a replacement amp for the main podium."

"What can I say?" Chad stretched his muscular arms as if he was hugging the world. "I'm charming."

"Well, if you keep saying that, the charm might wear off," Connor continued.

Chad put both hands over his heart as if he'd been shot through with an arrow.

"Sandra, every night this week I will replay the simple, polite, but devastatingly effective speech you made to the building manager about fire safety, how electricity actually works, and how short our lives might have been if we'd actually plugged all of the stage's power cords into the one power strip he bought for us earlier today, even though we told him, three weeks ago, exactly what our electricity needs would be. I was a particular fan of the graceful hand gestures you used to indicate a conflagration capable of wiping out a city block."

"Thanks. I minored in large-scale conflagrations in college." Sandra fluttered one manicured hand through the air as if to indicate a river of fire.

"And Sarah," Connor continued.

Sarah, their newest member, with her Kewpie doll face and adorable chipmunk voice, braced herself as if for a physical blow. "Oh, God, me? No, not me. I was horrible today."

"Wrong turn onto the Queensboro Bridge and the resulting panic attack notwithstanding, you demonstrated an amazing amount of sticktoitiveness after our idiot ice sculpture artist lied to us about having a delivery van, which manifested in your willingness to go completely outside of your comfort zone to get the job done."

"And Manhattan," Chad muttered.

Connor raised a warning finger. "Even if, I'm sorry to say, through no fault of your own, you brought us the wrong ice sculptures."

"*What?* No!" Sarah lunged at the gap between the columns next to Connor so she could see the melting ice sculptures towering over the now depleted raw bar. "Oh my God. They're supposed to be two globes. Those are…people."

"No, they were never people. They were always ice," Sandra said.

"Ice *people*, I think is what she's saying," Sue offered.

"Indeed," Connor answered. "I did some research, and apparently the one close to us is Ivan Hirschbaum, and the one farther away is his wife, Eva. They celebrated their fiftieth wedding anniversary this afternoon in Greenpoint. With our ice globes, apparently. However, since the sculptures were packed in dry ice when you picked them up, this is once again the complete fault of our idiot ice sculptor who we will never use again because tomorrow he'll be dead and floating in the East River with Jaycee's handprints around his neck."

"Also," Sandra said, "I passed by the raw bar earlier, and it sounded like everyone thought they were the Greek gods of art and literature or something, so I think as far as the guests go, we're fine."

"They don't look Greek to me," Chad said.

By this point in the event, they looked like monstrosities out of the *House of Wax,* but the point was Sarah should get credit for what she had managed to accomplish.

"All right, everyone. One glass of champagne and then once they start the exit music, you're at your breakdown stations. Nothing stays. It's one of those, so stay on your vendors to pack up so we can get out of here before midnight."

The group dispersed, leaving Connor alone to study the twinkling sea of banquet tables, the precise shafts of lighting that divided the stage without obscuring the massive projection of the center's elegant logo onto a white tapestry draped over what had once been the cathedral's altar.

Then he made the mistake of looking down at his own flute, and the sparkling shade within made him five years younger, five years dumber, and a few hours away from suffering a rejection that had lingered ever since.

7

If Logan could bottle the energy that filled Sapphire Cove's lobby on Sundays, he'd savor it in sips each morning. It was caffeine blended in something sweet. The excitement of new arrivals blended with the bittersweet farewells of satisfied departing guests.

The checkouts were always the most boisterous. They shouted nervous questions to each other about who'd packed what as they trundled their carry-ons across the marble floors, which sparkled with a new shine after the recent renovation. They either sought out the bellmen or ignored their help to avoid doling out one last tip. But the envious looks they all gave Logan as they passed into the motor court said the same thing: He was surrounded by this beauty all year long, and for this, he was a lucky man.

Sunday check-ins sent the same message. They were mostly conference attendees, wide eyed and grateful as they realized their sterile offices would be replaced for a week by Dale Chihuly-inspired chandeliers and panoramic views of the Pacific. The vacationing couples and families, they'd arrive later in the week, and with them a sense of stress and entitlement, a desire to make their three days perfect. If Logan could give them any advice, it was let your trip happen to you and not the other way around.

But until then, Sunday mornings were a chance for Logan to remind himself of the pact he'd made for himself—never take Sapphire Cove's beauty for granted. He was lucky to have this job, lucky to spend his days in this gorgeous place. Lucky the place had given him the stability he'd needed to help turn his father's life around.

The latest renovation had only amplified that beauty. The old gift shop that once bisected the lobby had been swept away, replaced by an open seating area that allowed an uninterrupted view from the lobby doors to the wall of plate glass windows in the restaurant overlooking the coastline. The lobby seating areas were now clusters of square, wicker love seats and chairs with deep cushions of aqua and coral beneath chandeliers that looked like sea anemones. The potted plants were spare, slender, and artfully arranged in their tiled ceramic pots so as not to block the view.

Inside Camilla's, where the holdouts tried to drink in as much as they could of the cliffs and ocean before checkout time, the once gaudy gold furnishings had been replaced by glass and metal tables and chairs that seemed to float against the ocean's blue expanse.

And yeah, Rodney Harcourt could be a prick, and Logan was still sore he'd been passed over for the security director gig, and Buddy's plan to write him up still had him gritting his teeth every time he thought about it, but Logan took some pride in the fact that the general manager thought he was a fixture worthy of these surroundings.

The fact was, he loved this place, loved that it was still a scrappy, family-owned business on a coastline peopled by posh corporate outposts. Even if the family had its issues and its tragedies.

And he loved the kids. The ones who'd wander away from their parents and hide behind potted plants, engaging him in a game of peekaboo that soon became their whole delighted world. Logan had a sixth sense for the presence of the little tykes, and he'd always manage to scoop them up in one powerful arm before they slipped outside or ran too far from Mom and Dad. He'd refused more than one unnecessary tip from a parent grateful to have their toddler returned. There were things you should tip for in a hotel—protecting a young child's life and limb wasn't one of them.

That's what he was doing when about fifteen federal agents came barging through the doors from the motor court, and the shit, as they like to say, hit the proverbial fan.

All eyes went to the exposed gun holsters on their belts. They were all men, mostly white, wearing khaki pants and running shoes and a blend of dress and golf shirts under their FBI windbreakers. Several split off in the direction of the front desk, and several more split off in the direction of the management offices. And one, snowy-haired, a rigid side part, and a brawn that suggested a football background, made a beeline for Logan, locking him in the sights of his intense chestnut eyes as Logan handed off the still wriggling child to a mother who'd already started retreating from him in horror.

Logan was trying to watch the approaching agent, but he couldn't help but notice how the dawning wave of recognition was sweeping the lobby. Heads everywhere had turned to the front doors. Guests were already asking questions of the front desk staff, their voices rising with concern.

The FBI was raiding Sapphire Cove, their presence like a slick of oil threaded through sun-kissed children and well-dressed vacationers. The guys who'd gone for the front desk knocked hard against the employee door. The minute the door was opened by Gloria Alvarez, the assistant manager, they pushed their way through without further invitation. One of them raised a paper in one hand—a warrant, Logan realized. *A goddamn warrant.*

"You Logan Murdoch?" the snowy-haired agent asked. They were nose to nose now.

"I am. Everything okay, sir?"

"What's going to happen right now is you're going to stay right here with me, and you and I are going to talk a bit, and I'm going to ask you not to get distracted by what's going on around us."

"All right, anything I can do to help." Logan's mouth felt dry, and his throat even dryer.

"You work in the security department here?" the agent asked.

"That's correct."

"You've been here five years?"

"Yes, sir."

"And your direct supervisor is Buddy Haskins?"

"That's correct."

"And above him is the general manager, Rodney Harcourt. Is that also correct?"

Down the nearest guest room corridor, from the direction of the nondescript entrance to the back of house management offices, came two federal agents. And between them, in handcuffs, was Buddy Haskins, white as a sheet and staring at the floor as he walked.

"Woah," Logan said.

"Yeah, it's going to be that kind of day, Mr. Murdoch."

"This is fucking *bullshit*," a familiar, very angry voice shouted.

Logan watched as a handcuffed Rodney Harcourt was walked along the same path through the lobby that Buddy and his accompanying agents had taken seconds before. When he saw the staring faces waiting for him, Rodney let out a furious groan and bowed his head, cursing under his breath about how the hotel had a back exit and was all this nonsense really necessary.

"These are the easy questions, Mr. Murdoch. They're about to get harder, and I'm going to need a place for us to talk other than the lobby. Eyes on me, if you can."

Summoning his Marine Corps discipline, Logan obeyed. Then he saw two more agents emerge from the management office, and his discipline collapsed. The agents wore gloves and were carrying a stack of the components that made up the brains of the hotel's new and improved security camera system.

And something started to make a very strange and disturbing kind of sense.

8

Every Sunday, Connor took a long walk through lower Manhattan, no matter the temperature. It was a great excuse to make regular visits to Hudson River Park so he could close his eyes and pretend he was back at Sapphire Cove, enjoying cool breezes off the Pacific. It rarely worked. The river usually smelled like New York's special blend of car exhaust and kitchen refuse, and there was always an ocean of noisy traffic right at his back. If the preceding weekend had been packed with hard work, he'd silence his phone for an hour or two so he could catch his breath.

That's how he missed fifteen text messages from his mother and twenty from Naser.

A block from home, he clicked on Naser's first text, a series of exclamation points followed by a link. A CNN webpage opened, and a video started to play. Frantic valet parkers at Sapphire Cove advanced toward the camera, their arms outstretched, their expressions stunned, trying to push back a tidal wave of reporters. He had to read the blazing chyron at the bottom of the screen several times before it sank in: **ORANGE COUNTY RESORT AT CENTER OF BLACKMAIL RING THAT TARGETED CANCER PATIENT, MANY OTHERS.**

Then the screen filled with a studio portrait of his uncle from much younger and more telegenic days, purloined from the hotel's website. Then it cut to archived footage of what had to be a perp walk. His uncle and that guy Buddy, who'd actually worked his graduation party long ago, being walked out of the lobby in handcuffs. Buddy?

What the hell had his uncle been up to with that jerk Buddy?

The present and the past were colliding in ways that threatened a migraine and a martini.

When he answered his mom's call, he heard a rushing noise that made it clear his mother was traveling in a car. Fast.

"Mom?"

"Connor?"

"I see it…I'm watching it. I'm watching the news."

"It's bad, Connor. It's real bad. Your uncle used the security camera system at the hotel to blackmail the guests. The *guests*. I can't believe it. I can't *believe* that man."

"I know, but what can we do? We don't have anything to do with the hotel."

"It's not that simple, sweetie. Listen, I'm sending a car to your apartment in an hour."

"What? Where are you?"

"I was in LA for a conference, but I'm headed down to Orange County now. I'm not going to stay at the resort because the place is chaos now, but I'll be nearby at Jan's in Corona del Mar."

"Okay, but *me*, Mom. Where is this car taking me? I don't understand what's happening."

"Teterboro. I got you a flight."

"Teterboro?" he asked. "What airline?"

"It's a private plane, Connor. The last commercial flights for the West Coast were all booked. I can't risk putting you on standby. We need you here for a meeting first thing in the morning. This is an all-hands-on-deck situation."

Needs. Meetings. All hands on deck. In Connor's mind, those words didn't fit alongside Sapphire Cove.

"Mom, I'll provide you with any support that you need during this, but I have nothing to do with Sapphire Cove, and neither do you, to be frank. We should steer clear of this. This is Rodney's mess."

"It's not that simple, Connor."

"I'm listening."

"Look, a lot of things changed while you were gone. A few years ago, your grandfather amended the rules of the family trust that owns the hotel. They inserted a morals clause for the GM position."

"For Rodney."

"Precisely. And a criminal allegation with charges filed at this level—

it's a blatant violation of the clause. It doesn't matter if Rodney's innocent. It doesn't matter if he's eventually exonerated, and it doesn't matter if he goes to trial and prevails. Rodney will never run Sapphire Cove again as of today. His lawyer just got a letter to that effect from the trust manager."

Fired, he realized. His mother was telling him that his shitbag uncle had basically been fired.

"Who will?" Connor asked.

"You will, Connor, or it will be sold to an outside company."

In a daze, Connor almost stepped off the curb and in front of a speeding cab by mistake. The cab whizzed by, and he barely flinched from the backdraft.

He had a vague sense that he was standing, but he could no longer feel his legs.

"Mom." It was more like a gasp.

"I know. It's a lot. And to be frank, God love Grandpa Dan, but I didn't approve of this because I knew the position it would put you in. But heavens above, I never expected it to go down like this. Or this damn soon."

"Mom." There was more breath in it this time, but he still sounded like he'd run a marathon.

"One step at a time. Pack a bag, get some things together. Try to throw down some food or something before the car gets there. I don't know if they'll have food on the plane. To be honest, for the price I'm paying for this thing, they should feed you a milkshake that adds fifty years to your life."

"Pack a bag?" Connor asked. "Pack for what? I mean, you're asking me to walk away from my life?"

"No, Connor, I'm not. I know it may seem like that, but I'm not. I'm asking you to make a choice. And it will be *your* choice. But I need you to make it in an informed way, and I need you to make it in consultation with the attorneys and financial advisors who manage the trust. Can you do that for me?"

He tried to answer, but he couldn't find his voice.

Sold. As much as he'd tried to divorce himself from Sapphire Cove, the idea of it being sold to an outside company still made a part of his soul feel hollow.

"Connor, please. This is about your father, your grandfather. Everything they built. I'm not saying it's the right choice for you to step up and do this. But we can't let Rodney wash away their entire legacy in twenty-four hours without so much as a meeting with the lawyers. We can't. I need you home now."

"Of course," he said. "I'm on my way."

Which seemed like a silly thing to say since she was the one who'd already sent a car for him.

And a plane.

Connor had never flown on a private jet before. When he was a kid, he used to ask his dad why they didn't fly private since the other kids thought they were rich.

His dad said they weren't that kind of rich.

When Connor asked what kind of rich flew on private planes, his dad answered, "The kind of rich that doesn't stay rich."

Now a dream he'd had when he was seven had finally been realized, but he couldn't bring himself to enjoy it. For most of the flight, he paced the narrow, carpeted, cosseted cabin and chewed the nuts they'd offered him. Occasionally the one flight attendant would stick her head in and ask him if he needed anything. After the second time he asked her to rewind the hands of time to the day before, she stopped asking.

He monitored the flight's path on the digital maps that filled the screens on either side of the cabin. He tried some stretches and breathing exercises he'd learned from Jaycee.

Then, somewhere over Illinois, he broke down and popped open his laptop and watched more of the disaster unfold.

He couldn't handle much of the TV news clips that were being refreshed and added to by the minute. The familiar motor court turned into a media circus. The drone and helicopter shots that floated in over the resort's expanse atop its green promontory as a reporter's bombastic voiceover made clear this pristinely beautiful oasis had become a den of moral rot and criminality. These images were too painful to bear.

But the FBI press conference was all hard facts, and that, for some reason, he could stomach.

So he watched it twenty times.

The case, it seemed, was solid, almost six months in the making. It rested on testimony and wiretap evidence gathered after two victims of the scheme had broken down and alerted the authorities. One of them, the wife of a cancer victim who'd apparently spent the last months of his life mailing substantial checks to Rodney Harcourt to keep him from telling the board of his company that he was dying and getting his treatments privately in one of their villas.

Then, just a week ago, Rodney Harcourt, Buddy Haskins, and three other security agents—who were identified as Pete Roman, Willis Devon, and Scott Springer—all collected blackmail payments from three different victims, each one of whom was wearing a wire for the FBI. With the exception of the now deceased CEO whose deathbed letter had cracked open the scheme, the FBI refused to comment on the nature of the secrets these additional victims had been blackmailed over, despite dogged and invasive questions from the reporters present.

Somewhere over Kansas, Connor decided that this was all his fault.

If I hadn't left…if I'd stayed and fought.

By Colorado, he decided this was both arrogant and ridiculous, and as the plane turned southwest toward Orange County, he'd formulated a mantra.

Here to support my mom. I'm here to support my mom, that's all.

By the time they'd landed at John Wayne Airport, he'd whispered it, chanted it, even sung it to a strange sing-songy melody. Then he was watching the passenger planes parked at the main terminal slide by the windows as the Gulfstream taxied to the far end of the tarmac.

And there, standing next to a parked SUV, was a familiar figure that brought a much-needed warm feeling to his heart. About Connor's height, even though he usually lied and said he was five foot six, with a bit more gym-built brawn than when they'd been college roommates and considerably more facial hair and an adult confidence in his otherwise rigid steps. Naser.

Right now, there was no one Connor wanted to see more, and as they approached each other on the tarmac, his eyes misted.

Three months. That's how long it had taken Naser to stop visiting their favorite hangout spots and texting Connor a picture of the place where he used to sit, stand, or chill, and accompanying the photo with a maudlin quote on loss and grief from literary sources ranging from Tolstoy to Rumi. Finally, Connor had enough and responded, "Bitch, I moved to New York, not Antarctica. And you currently make more in a month than I'll make this year. Get your gay ass on a plane and come visit me."

Things were a little better after that. But Naser's first visit, he was still a scared puppy. He never opened up easily. He made few friends, but the ones he did make, he made deeply and well, and the loss of Connor in his daily life had hurt him harder than Connor had expected it to. But there'd been another darker emotion lurking under Naser's pain, and it only surfaced after the fourth or fifth visit.

Connor's best friend had blamed himself for everything that had happened with Logan Murdoch.

It took a long time to convince Naser that the factors that drove Connor to chuck it all on a moment's notice and move east were more complicated. Maturity helped with perspective. The older they got, the more they realized life didn't always center around great dick.

Sometimes it did, but not always.

And the older you got, the more you realized that if the guy attached to the dick wasn't great then the dick couldn't be considered great either.

"Gurl," Naser groaned as he opened his arms. "Most of the time my East Coast friends come home it's for something tedious like rehab. But you had to go be all scandal ridden and dramatic."

"Nothing's funny right now." He fell into Naser's arms. "Seriously, I can't deal."

"Oh, I know, sweetie. It's terrible. I had to fly cross country on a private jet all by myself once and I'm still having nightmares about it."

"Where's my mother?" Connor allowed Naser to pull him toward the waiting Suburban with one arm curved around his back.

"In the car. On the phone. It's been a lot of phone calls. Are you drunk?"

"No, why would I be drunk?"

"If I had a private plane all to myself during a time like this, I'd be drunk."

"I don't even know if they had liquor," Connor said.

"Did they have Wi-Fi?"

Connor nodded.

"Were you watching any of it?" Naser asked.

"The FBI press conference, but not any of the other videos. I couldn't take seeing the hotel like that."

"Good."

"So it's bad?" Connor stopped walking, as if Naser's answer might force him to run back on board the plane.

Naser clearly didn't want to tell the truth, but Connor would bust him if he lied, and he knew it. So he did what he always did when asked an uncomfortable yes or no question. He gave specifics. "Sylvia Milton, the wife of the cancer victim, is going on CNN tomorrow. She spoke to reporters outside of her house this morning. She's..."

"What?"

"She's a good interview. Looks like a trophy wife, but far be it from me to judge. However, she *was* about twenty years younger than her husband, and I did some googling and apparently she was a fashion model when they met."

"Doesn't take away her right to be pissed," Connor said.

"Not saying that." Naser pursed his lips and gave Connor a once-over, his usual routine when he was about to tell Connor something he didn't want to hear. "She's good with the cameras is what I'm saying. And bad for the hotel. But hey, how's this for a perspective shift?" Naser took him by the elbow and started walking them toward the idling SUV. "Now the entire world knows what we've known for most of our lives."

"And what's that?" Connor asked.

"Where most humans have a soul, Rodney Harcourt has a pile of shit with a stick of lit dynamite in it."

"Yeah, and I think the dynamite blew," Connor said.

"Indeed. Also, word to the wise. They let us park on the tarmac because there's media outside the gate. They're gonna yell crazy shit at us through the windows. *Were you in on the blackmail ring? Do you have any of the money?* Don't freak. It's not what they're actually reporting. It'll be designed to get a rise out of you. So just nod and smile until the driver gets us through."

"Want to stay on as my media consultant?"

"One of the partners at my firm got busted for embezzling from a client last year. The rest of us got some on-site training in crisis management."

"*Connor!*" It was the urgent and determined tone his mother always used when she wanted his arms around her.

He threw his arms around her and leaned into the welcoming expanse of her body, loving that she always smelled of Chanel No. 5, loving the firm, determined kiss she always gave him on the cheek. Like she wanted to give him more but figured he'd only allow him one, so she had to make the most of it. In this crazy moment, he'd allow her as many as she wanted.

Next thing he knew they'd piled into the Suburban, Naser in the front, and he and his mom in the back. The minute the security guard for the private terminal opened the car gate, flashbulbs erupted, and television cameras with blinding light rigs advanced toward them. Connor did as Naser instructed. Raised his hand in a royal wave and kept his smile tight and contained. A pose meant to say, *I don't look guilty because I'm not guilty. But how nice that you've all come to herald my arrival.*

"Do you have numbers?" Connor asked his mother once they were clear of the melee.

"Yeah. Fifteen percent," she answered.

"Occupancy's down fifteen percent?"

"No, sweetie. Occupancy's *at* fifteen percent. They think tomorrow afternoon the hotel will be empty."

"You're not going back there, son," Chip Murdoch said.

For the third time.

Logan ignored him. Again. He'd overslept, and he needed to find his jacket and shoes so he could get back to work. He'd tossed them somewhere in this spacious, cluttered office before crashing on its leather sofa the night before.

The morning before.

That morning, he corrected himself.

It had been three a.m. by the time he got to the Chip's Kicks in Irvine for an emergency meeting with his new lawyer and his dad. That's how long it had taken to quell the shit storm at Sapphire Cove. Quelling was a generous way to describe it. Corralling the media behind the legal property line had meant multiple calls with the city and the sheriff's department to establish where the legal property line actually was. Then he'd had to recruit some maintenance guys to track down all the reporters who'd snuck on the property as guests. Then there were the real guests themselves, who cornered him in hallways, demanding to know why they shouldn't check out. Demanding refunds if they already were checking out.

Then came the death threat phone calls that lit up the hotel's switchboard as the news went international, reducing two of the hotel's operators to tears. Even though he was sure the calls were cranks, he'd sat with the operators until two in the morning and brought in some plywood to cover the inside of the call center's single window to make them feel safer. The whole thing had been a nightmare, forcing Logan to put off his scheduled sit-down with his lawyer hour by hour as the night raged on.

Finally, knowing full well he was about five hours late to his meeting, Gloria Alvarez had insisted Logan leave the premises, and even then Logan had protested. But Gloria had been adamant, her refusal to leave her post no doubt fueled by the decades she'd spent with the hotel.

And now time was of the essence.

He found the jacket lying on the floor behind the sofa, his shoes pushed against the wall. Christ. Had he spontaneously combusted?

For the first time since jerking awake, he noticed his dad was standing with his arms thrown across the office door. Outside he could hear the pulse and throb of the morning workout crowd.

"You need sleep," his dad said.

"I got sleep." Logan punched his arm through one sleeve of the rumpled blazer he'd worn the night before. All day before, now that he thought of it.

"Sleep, my ass. You took a three-hour nap, and you were talking for most of it."

"What did I say?" Logan asked.

"Something about Tom Holland that sounded personal. I tried not to listen."

"That's nice of you. Is there press here?"

"No," his dad answered.

"Then why are you standing against the door like that?" Logan asked.

"'Cause I'm serious as cancer. You're not fucking leaving."

"You want me to stay in your office all day? Do some filing?"

"You're not going back to Sapphire Cove."

"Dad, there's no security staff. Do you understand what that means when you've got media like that out front? On top of that, anybody who works at the hotel who was worried about their immigration status hightailed it out of there the minute the cameras showed up. It's a shit show, and we need everybody we can get until we figure out what's next. This is not the time for a day off."

"Ever. You're not going back there *ever*. You hear me? You're done with that place, and it's done with you."

"What are you talking about?"

"You heard what your lawyer said."

"He said if the FBI had anything on me they would have arrested me yesterday. They know I'm innocent."

His father growled and looked to the floor between them.

"*You* know I'm innocent, right?"

"Aw, come on, son. Of course I do. That's not the point."

"What's the point then? I need to go."

"Bullfinch said you're going to be a target with your coworkers."

"For Christ's sake, Dad. It was a throwaway comment. I'm not thirteen. I can take it."

"After the shit that place has put you through? No raise in five years. Passing you over for that idiot Buddy Haskins. I'm sorry. Idiot and *criminal* Buddy Haskins."

"Yeah, and the health plan that allowed you to turn your life around."

"You have more than paid them back for that, and they haven't given you shit in return. In fact, now it's *only* shit. You're the last man standing in a corrupt department, so now you're going to get dragged through Rodney's mud and Buddy's mud. Alone!"

"Maybe not." Logan reached behind his dad, grabbed the knob, and pulled the office door open enough to knock his dad forward off his feet. The morning regulars all turned their heads. "Hey! What's up, guys?" he shouted. "Anybody want to go to work at a hotel today? It's a beautiful place, great benefits. We just got a little problem with the media right now."

He was answered by a chorus of *No thank yous* and *Not on your lifes,* which told him they'd been following the story closely, maybe thanks to the bank of televisions above the row of cardio machines. When Logan saw only two out of the five were broadcasting Sapphire Cove coverage, he was relieved, a fact that was testament to the madness of the past twenty-four hours.

"I appreciate your concern, Dad." Logan shoved past him and into the gym. "But I've got a job to do."

"Work here."

Halfway across the gym, Logan stopped in his tracks and turned to face his father.

They'd had this conversation before. And it hadn't sounded like this.

His dad ran a chain of successful businesses now.

If you'd told Logan five years ago that would be the case today, he would have laughed in your face. But the path there hadn't been a straight line.

It started with the clinical depression that formally settled over his dad after he could no longer deny that he'd never work a construction gig again. Then Logan spent several months trying to get him into therapy and saving up the funds to pay for it. Then, after finally letting the therapist crack his shell and talking about his difficult past, his dad had started posting YouTube videos.

Which Logan had thought was absolutely nuts.

His grouchy, hard-as-nails dad talking into a camera about his difficult life like some teenager? What drug was that therapist giving him? But he'd made a pact with himself that he wouldn't second-guess the therapist's advice, no matter what. Convincing his dad to go in the first place had been hard enough.

And the vids, it turned out, weren't just emotional confessionals about where he'd been and what he'd suffered. They were essentially self-defense and fight tips he'd learned on the streets and then fine-tuned through training later in life. Chip Murdoch was good at talking about that kind of stuff. Chalk it up to a life spent trying to impress women in bars.

When his dad came running to him claiming a video on Chip's Kicks had a million views, Logan was sure he'd read the counter wrong. Sure enough, when Logan checked the channel's page, he saw the views on all of his dad's videos were north of a million five. A few were closing in on two million and higher. After that, the numbers kept growing. Something about his dad's story—the tough background and the late in life injury that felled him—combined with his dad's grouchy, no bullshit sense of humor had turned Chip Murdoch into a standout YouTube fitness celebrity in a sea of guys who usually looked like Logan and ladies who looked like Jillian Michaels.

The ad revenue wasn't going to buy a house on Newport Harbor, but it wasn't something to sneeze at either. Then came some strategic partnerships with other YouTube fitness personalities, and within another year, and with Logan's help, the first Chip's Kicks opened in Fountain Valley. A year later, another location followed in Tustin, then a third in Irvine. They were small, humble gyms where the real stars were the trainers, kickboxing diehards drawn by Chip Murdoch's Internet fame and love of the sport. Each had a healthy roster of members, most of whom showed up each day, constantly hoping Chip himself would walk in with the camera crew that followed him around as he filmed demonstrations with his favorite staff.

If Chip couldn't kickbox anymore, he could talk about it at least, and he'd found an audience that was eager for him to do just that.

The fact that his grouchy, balding, and now paunchy dad was making serious bank off a platform where the biggest earners were usually teenagers opening boxes of new makeup or playing Minecraft for hours on end seemed like one of the world's best surprises.

"You don't want me working here," Logan said. "We talked about this."

"That was before."

"Six months ago."

"You were mad about getting passed over for Buddy, and I didn't want you to make the choice just 'cause you were pissed."

"What would I do? Mop the floors?" Logan asked.

"Aw, bite me. Of course not. We'd figure it out. You got mad skills. You're smarter than I am. Always have been. Pisses me the fuck off sometimes, to be frank. But we'd make it work. But maybe that's not what it's about."

"What's it about?"

"You helped me get back on my feet when I was down." Chip averted his eyes like he was making an embarrassing admission, or a scary one. "Maybe it's time I help you get back on yours."

Logan was so startled by this offer, so startled by his grumpy dad's sudden sincerity, he wasn't sure what to say. He let his eyes wander the gym, saw all the eyes glued to the two of them.

"I love you, Pop, but I gotta go back. I love Sapphire Cove, too. I spent eight years of my life in combat zones where nobody wanted us around and most of us didn't even know why we were there. And then I ended up in a place everybody wanted to be, day after day, and most of them left happy, or they forgot about their problems while they were there. So call it stupid, or call me a big baby, but I like being part of that. And the people who work there, they're our friends, our family. You know them. You've been to Gloria Alvarez's house for Thursday potluck."

"I love Gloria. I asked her out. She totally freaked on me, though."

"She's married, Dad."

"I didn't know when I asked. She didn't have a ring on."

"She was cooking. The point is, Dan Harcourt, Martin Harcourt, they were good men who took care of their employees. They gave better benefits than most of the resorts on the coast. They didn't find a way to force you out because you sprained your ankle or gained a few pounds, and Rodney and Buddy, they can't ruin all of that. They're not that powerful. I won't let them be. And I won't watch this place go down without a fight. It's more than a hotel to me."

His dad threw up his hands.

Logan's temples were throbbing. He felt like he had a massive hangover even though he hadn't had a drop of hard stuff the day before. Even though he'd wanted to down half a liter of Stoli like it was water.

Then he saw something on one of the flat screens that caught his attention. A familiar face captured in an inferno of flashbulbs and bright lights. A beautiful face. A face he'd jerked off to two nights before. Again. A face that had once radiated boyish innocence before unleashing mischief. But there was confidence in his eyes now.

Connor. The logo beneath his chin said the footage had been taken last night, and the wide shot of the car speeding away revealed a glimpse of John Wayne Airport.

Funny how the name suddenly felt like a relief, when a few days before, it would have triggered embarrassment and a sense of defeat. Now it felt like something else. Something warm and familiar, something emerging from a time before Sapphire Cove was a hotbed of scandal.

Connor was back.

Connor was coming home.

And he was probably headed to Sapphire Cove.

Finally.

"I appreciate that, Pop. Really. I do. But I'm still on my feet."

"Fine, but just so you know…if you get knocked down for good, I'll be here."

He wanted to hug the old man, even if it freaked him out a bit. But if he did that, he might break down himself. Because he was tired. That's all. Tired. It wasn't like his dad had made a moving, life-changing offer. An offer that also showed gratitude for all the sacrifices Logan had made for him five years before.

He started for the exit.

"Son!"

"I gotta go, Pop."

"I know, I know. You're a man of honor and integrity, and you honor your commitments because that's the Marine Corps way. But you stink, son. You stink *hard.* You stink like the towels at this gym when they've been in the hamper for two weeks. You haven't had a shower and you're wearing clothes you wore all yesterday. And no son of mine is going back to that shit show smelling like a landfill. There's enough there that stinks already."

Logan was about to check his pits when he caught the eyes of a woman standing a few feet away with her trainer. They were both nodding gravely. "Sorry, hun, he's right," she said softly. "We can smell you from over here."

"And it's a gym, dude," her trainer added.

"Go shower," his dad said. "Get yourself some Chip's Kicks merchandise on the house, then wrangle up a new uniform once you get to the hotel. Look at it this way, it's not like there's a general manager who's gonna get on your ass for not dressing to code."

Deep down, the Marines had made Logan good at following orders.

But the shower in the end became an excuse for one thought to circle through his head again and again, like a plane that couldn't bring itself to land.

Connor's home.

9

Sylvia Milton looked like she slept each night in an isolation tank and spent several hours every morning in the company of skincare experts she had on retainer. She was that indeterminate age extremely wealthy women arrive at shortly after forty and never seem to leave. On camera, her cascade of platinum hair shimmered, and her big blue eyes were as radiant as they'd been when she modeled for a living.

Crap. Nobody's going to be able to look away from this woman.

He figured the interview had been filmed in her backyard. According to what he'd been able to learn about her online, it was a big backyard attached to a ten-million-dollar estate in Scottsdale, Arizona. And yet, Sylvia was positioned in front of a humble-looking patch of hedge. Was the TV crew trying to conceal that off to her left was enough space to play polo in? It was anyone's guess. At the moment, in the eyes of the camera, at least, Sylvia Milton wasn't rich or poor or somewhere in between. She was a victim of Sapphire Cove.

"Are you satisfied by the arrests yesterday?" the interviewer asked.

"Satisfied? I'm not sure I'd use anything like that word in this instance. My husband's final days were ruined by Sapphire Cove. They were simply *ruined*. Marching a bunch of people in front of some news cameras isn't going to give us back the last year of his life."

"But in all fairness, those people were the very individuals the FBI believes are responsible for this scheme."

"This scheme, this *plot,* is bigger than individuals. It went on for months. It netted millions, and in the process Sapphire Cove violated the promise all hotels make to their guests. Security, privacy. Respect. Deference. A commitment to making their dreams come true."

"This is not a woman who's ever had to find a bargain on Hotels dot com," Connor's mother grumbled from the seat next to him in the shadowed conference room.

"You can't blame me for thinking," Sylvia said, "that this is about a place, a *culture,* an environment that allowed these acts to flourish."

"Will you be bringing a civil suit against the hotel?" the interviewer asked.

"I can't comment on any legal action at this time. All I can do is share my experience, my late husband's experience, and offer it as a warning to anyone who dares set foot inside Sapphire Cove before there is a change of management or a change of ownership."

As the camera held on Sylvia's intense stare, the reporter's voiceover cut in, explaining that a change of management was indeed underway, if not a change of ownership. Given the intensity of the woman's anger, Connor doubted it would satisfy her.

An assistant pressed a button. Shades covering the wall of glass to his left started to rise with a hum, revealing a stunning view marred by a cobra's hood of dark smoke rising from the mountains on the western horizon.

Somehow Connor had missed the wildfire during his descent last night, probably because he'd been too busy chewing his nails and staring at his feet.

The opposite wall of glass looked out onto their law firm's expansive office, but right now, a second wall of shades protected them from the prying eyes of other assistants with exposed desk carrels.

Their old family lawyer, a tall, broad linebacker of a man named Harris Mitchell, was seated across the table, but the manager of the family trust that owned Sapphire Cove was unfamiliar to Connor—Lois Penry, a stocky, no-nonsense woman with a pageboy haircut and thick-framed glasses.

To his astonishment, Connor had actually managed to get some sleep the night before, probably thanks to the time change. So he couldn't blame this raw nerve feeling on pure fatigue. Now that the conference room was flooded with sunlight, he was once more having trouble looking away from the copies of the *Los Angeles Times* and the *Orange County Register* someone had laid out on the table. The hotel's scandal was front page news on both.

The *Register's* headline was particularly chilling. **IS IT SUNSET FOR SAPPHIRE COVE?**

"Something tells me this isn't going to be the last we hear from Sylvia Milton," Connor's mother said.

"Late last night someone started a Twitter account called Stop Sapphire Cove," Lois Penry said. "As of the interview this morning, it has about four hundred thousand followers. The hotel's social media channels were so deluged our digital marketing firm suggested we disable the comments feature on all of them. I gave the go ahead. I hope that's okay."

With a start, Connor realized they were all looking at him. Of course they were. Technically, he was the new GM, and so it had been his decision to make.

Impossible, he thought. *This is all completely impossible.*

"And we think the Twitter account is her?" his mother asked.

"We can't prove it, but it would make sense."

"Stop Sapphire Cove," Connor said. "What's she trying to stop us from doing? Firing the people who blackmailed her husband?"

"Booking rooms, it looks like," Harris Mitchell said.

"So she's trying to cancel us," Connor said.

"Indeed," his mother said. "Speaking of which, how are we doing on the cancellation front?"

"They're constant," Harris said. "Two conferences have opted to pay the fee rather than proceed. Two more have decided to hang in, but they've made it clear that if anything else bad comes to light between now and their dates, they're out. And if we try to charge them the fee, they'll hit us with lawyers. And bad press."

"So let's say Sylvia Milton doesn't let up and they cancel too," his mom said. "How long can Sapphire Cove operate?"

"If occupancy stays where it is now, which is pretty close to zero," Lois said, "we can operate out of cash reserves for about three months."

"Assuming I do take the GM position, solely to prevent a sale, how long do I have to stay in it before I can hire or promote someone else?" Connor spoke.

"A year," Harris Mitchell answered.

"Jesus Christ!"

"Connor," his mother said softly.

"Look, I'm sorry, but I don't understand any of this. I didn't run off to New York to find myself, guys. Two weeks before I was actually supposed to start working at this hotel, I overheard a conversation between Rodney, my father, and my grandfather where they made it clear they thought my being gay was going to damage the business they'd built. I'd have to be contained. Those were their words."

"Those were Rodney's words, Connor." His mother was studying him as if everyone else in the room had vanished.

"They discussed me as if my very existence was a liability, Mom. And this was at the prospect of having me in the events office. To say nothing of actually running the place. So I left and I broke my back making a life for myself, a career, where I wouldn't pollute their precious Sapphire Cove. And now I'm being told that if I don't step up and take the reins, everyone who works there is going to be out of a job in three months or less. I'm trying to keep it professional here, folks, but this is a lot to take in."

His mother rested one hand gently on the side of his arm. "Connor, if you don't want to do it, they'll find other jobs."

"How, though? *Hi, I worked at a hotel where the staff was involved in blackmailing the guests. You got any openings for me?*"

Nobody said anything for a while.

"Connor, with all due respect," Harris said softly, "the fact that your first thought in all this is for the people who work there actually recommends you for the position."

"I can't believe this is what Grandpa Dan really wanted. I don't believe it's what my father really wanted."

"I can assure you they were of sound mind when they rewrote the trust," the lawyer said.

"They knew, Connor." Everyone fell silent at these words from his mother. But she waited until he turned to her.

"You told them, didn't you?" Connor asked. "You told them I heard them."

His mother studied her lap.

"Mom, I asked you not to."

When she saw whatever expression was on his face, his mother said, "Folks, if you wouldn't mind, I think this just became a mother-son conversation."

Quietly, with heads bowed, the lawyers and bankers rose without collecting their papers and briefcases. In what felt like an instant, Connor was alone with his mother, their stunning view of the distant wildfire beneath a blue and cloudless sky, and the echoes of the bombshell she'd dropped.

"Mom, why did you do that?"

"Because I'm your mother, and it's my job to not listen to you. Especially when you're very wrong about something. And you were very wrong about that."

"I wanted to let it go."

"No, you wanted to pretend like it never happened, and it did. And they deserved to feel bad about it, and that's why I told them."

"So I guess this is them feeling bad about it, huh? Drop everything and dive headfirst into a business I have no experience in."

"Connor, you've thrown weddings for actual princesses. For daughters of former presidents. Events that needed to conform to Secret Service protocols while involving national media. You can handle Sapphire Cove, my darling boy. Even right now. They knew that. You didn't run off to study dance or medicine. Your life is about making order out of chaos and crowds, and making sure it's beautiful to boot. That said, whatever decision you make here, I'll support you fully. The hotel was never my dream. It was your father's. And speaking of which..."

She started digging into her handbag. When she drew her hand free, she was holding a manila envelope, and written on the front, in his father's familiar block print handwriting was his first name, *CONNOR*.

"In case of a moment like this, he wrote this for you. Told me I had to give it to you if he wasn't around."

"What does it say?" Connor asked.

"I don't know. I haven't read it. Never opened it. I could make a guess, but why not read it yourself? Let's let your father speak for himself. Then you and I can talk through all of this."

There was already a lump in his throat at the idea of his father writing him a letter like this, something to be saved and protected until the time was right. Their relationship during those last years of his life had been consistent and cordial, and in his own way, Connor had forgiven him. Mostly by shuttling his resentment toward Rodney. But now it seemed like he hadn't really dealt with those feelings at all. Rather, he'd stowed them on a high shelf in a deep closet, the same place where he'd put parts of himself before he'd been ready to come out.

His hands shook as he opened the letter.

Hey Buddy,

If you're reading this, it means I've left the picture. I can only hope it happened in a manner that spared you and your mother any undue pain or suffering. But that's me, trying to manage the worst-case scenarios even from the great beyond.

If you're reading this, it means something else too. It means your Uncle Rodney's best self has lost the battle with his worst self, and he's done something to violate the morals clause your grandfather and I installed in the trust after you left.

I won't dwell too much on this now, but I do want you to know this, regardless of whatever Rodney has done to trigger this unfortunate event, there was goodness in my brother once. There's still goodness. But his relationship with your grandfather was a complicated one. They quarreled and fought in ways your grandfather and I never did. In some sense, they were two halves of the same person, and each one of them felt like he got the wrong half and was madly jealous of the other. Your grandfather wishes he could be more a pit bull like Rodney. And Rodney wishes he could be more loveable like Dad. But neither one of them quite knows how to pull it off, and so they fault themselves for what they lack and resent the other for what they possess.

If your mother's the one who gave you this letter, then she's probably told you that your grandfather and I figured out you overheard us talking about your graduation party that night. Shame doesn't come close to describing how I felt when I learned this. And an apology will never suffice. That's why I didn't bother with one. And that's why I want this moment to be something more.

Let me come clean about a few things.

Part of me didn't want you working at Sapphire Cove. Not because you're gay or because of any of the things you heard Rodney say that night. I didn't want you to go through what I went through for years and suffer with Rodney as I'd done. There are things about Rodney you didn't know. Maybe they've surfaced now and that's why you're in an office with a bunch of lawyers asking you to run the hotel. These things involved drugs and various other crimes your grandfather found a way to cover up over the years. The point is, I didn't defend you during that meeting because part of me thought this was going to be your chance to get free. Free of a family conflict that had made me so unhappy in my later years, more unhappy perhaps than your mother ever realized.

So why didn't I call you and apologize to you?

Simple. I was in awe of you. The whole family was. When you threw off the shackles of our money and struck out in New York on your own, when you made a career for yourself on your own, out of your own natural talent and skills, it was one of the most impressive things I'd ever seen. And so I made a choice, possibly the wrong one. I thought if I apologized, I might pull you back into our orbit and away from the challenges you were facing in New York. I didn't want you to abandon your glorious path, even if it was anger at me that kept you on it.

You may have gone all these years thinking I didn't want you to run Sapphire Cove, and your grandfather didn't too. Nothing could be further from the truth. We both wanted you to run the hotel someday, but we didn't want Rodney to tear you down before that day came. So we came up with this solution. If Rodney somehow turned into the person we always feared he might become, then you were in, or the Harcourt name would no longer be associated with the hotel at all.

So there's the whole story.

I hope you'll forgive me for doing it this way. But I also know I don't have any right to your forgiveness. Just know that you were my pride and joy. That when I first held you in my arms in the hospital I felt a sense of completeness rivaled only by the day I married your mother.

Know that you could never disappoint me, not then, and not now, whatever you decide. There are two memories that have brought me more happiness than any other in life. The first, when we opened the doors of Sapphire Cove and let in the first guests. The second, when I held you in my arms for the first time.

Please accept the gift that comes with this letter. Back when we first opened, every room had a brass key. When we finally switched over to a card system, I saved the first one we ever had made, always intending to give it to you on the day the hotel became yours. And it's still yours, even if you decide not to take the job.

But know before you do, that we wanted you to have this opportunity, dreamed of you having it. Not because we need for you to make us proud. No, son, we're offering you Sapphire Cove so that we can make you proud.

Love,
Your Dad

He won his fight against the tears until he'd managed to shake the brass key, with its bronze tag bearing the hotel's original and groovier logo, into his palm. Then, to cover the coming burst, he handed the letter to his mother so she could read it while he walked to the plate glass windows, cupping the key in his hand, and cried before his own reflection.

When his mother was done, her sigh was deep. "That man." He heard the tears in her voice. "That strange, wonderful man. You know he proposed to me like this? In a letter. With bullet points about all the ways he thought he could make me happy for the rest of my life. I have to say, it wasn't the romantic proposal I'd always dreamed of, but by the third time I read it, I realized no man I'd ever been out with had ever spent that much time on the topic of how to make me happy. I'm not sure anyone had ever given it that much thought."

She was next to him now, curving an arm around his back.

"I should have said something," Connor said.

"You didn't need to, darling. I think that's the whole point of this. Sometimes it's a parent's job to know, and to get out of the way."

"But he died thinking I was mad at him," Connor said.

"No, he didn't, honey. He died thinking you were happy, and that's what mattered to him most. He died proud of you. Nothing will change that ever. No matter what you decide to do now. Same goes for me."

For a while, he rested in her comforting embrace until the sniffles subsided and he could breathe normally again.

"Maybe we should get something to eat, talk things over."

"Or," Connor said, "I could just go save the hotel."

She would have been fine either way, he knew. But this way brought joy to her expression.

It was amazing, Logan thought, that so many of the remaining guests were still honoring traditional checkout procedure.

True, some stormed out the front doors lugging their suitcases, preparing to unleash all manner of verbal hell against Sapphire Cove as soon as the cameras reached them.

But a surprising number of them were lining up at the front desk. Probably so they could demand refunds and other special requests, which Gloria Alvarez was granting pretty much across the board. So long as they didn't involve stealing furniture from the guest rooms.

The more he thought about it, the more he realized he shouldn't have been surprised by this unexpected formality. These were, after all, guests who'd stayed through the night, so it wasn't the FBI raid that had driven them off. It was the constant presence of the media just outside the entrance to the motor court. Maybe they figured the cameras would leave after twenty-four hours, but so far, no sign of it. And with Rodney's arraignment not scheduled until Monday morning, he doubted they'd be gone anytime soon.

Whatever the case, the result was a logjam at the front desk unlike any he'd ever seen.

The drinks, both hard and soft, and hors d'oeuvres being passed through the crowd by the restaurant staff were definitely making things easier, a perk made possible by the restaurant's complete absence of customers.

"So does this gig come with a gun?" a familiar voice said into his ear.

When he saw Donnie had gone to the trouble of wearing a blue blazer like the one Logan had stolen from the locker of an arrested coworker, Logan practically threw his arms around the guy. But his best friend hadn't gone completely formal. His sandy blond hair was still rumpled from the baseball cap he'd probably torn off his head right before he walked in. His light scruff matched his hair, and against his tan skin, carefree attitude, and blue bedroom eyes, it always made him look like a sun-kissed beach bum who'd just woken up from a nap in a hammock, cradling a Corona on his stomach.

Standing a few feet away were three good-looking guys. Familiar-looking guys. Instead of blazers, they each wore different types of dress pants. But the pants fit. That was all Logan cared about. Their polo shirts weren't exactly formal, but they'd each tucked them in, which not only highlighted their muscular physiques, but made them look like tough guys who'd been strong-armed into attending their fancy little sister's birthday tea.

"Man, I am glad to see you," Logan said.

"And don't forget my backup dancers here." He gestured for his three friends to step forward. "Logan, this is Brandon, Scott, and J.T., and yes, those are their real names."

Each one stepped forward in turn and gave Logan a firm shake, as if they'd practiced.

Brandon was taller than Logan, which was saying something. Olive skinned, with a chiseled face and a Caesar cut of jet black hair and giant arms. Next to him was Scott, with a gymnast's compact body and a bleached high-top fade that contrasted with his dark skin. He came up to about Logan's stomach but looked like he could probably do a triple backflip across the lobby on a moment's notice. Logan wasn't worried about the guy's height. He'd met enough Navy SEALS over the years who could kill a man in three quick moves despite being five foot, four inches. And then there was J.T., with corn silk blond hair in a conservative side part, big chestnut eyes that made him look eager to please, and milky skin the same shade as the sunscreen he probably needed to keep from burning to a crisp the second he stepped outside.

"Nice to meet you, gents, and I appreciate you stepping up today," Logan said.

"Seriously, though," Scott said. "Do we get guns?"

"Yeah, no, we don't do guns here. Too much liability."

"Okay, good, 'cause I don't have firearms training," Scott answered.

"I do," J.T. said in an adorable Southern accent Logan figured was either Tennessee or one of the Carolinas. "I can shoot a beer can off a rock at fifty feet."

"Good to know. I'll keep that in mind. But yeah, we don't have many shootings here at Sapphire Cove."

"Just blackmail, right?" Donnie landed an affectionate punch on Logan's shoulder.

Logan grabbed Donnie's hand and drove it down to his side with enough force to make his wrist hurt. "Not funny, dude," he growled.

"Come on, man. It's a little funny." Donnie's winning smile had melted hearts as hard as Logan's over the years. Not this time.

Logan heard a familiar voice shout his name from across the lobby. It was Gloria. She rarely raised her voice, even when she was angry. Working her way up from the front desk through the events office to one of the assistant general manager positions had given her an encyclopedic knowledge of the hotel that kept her calm under the worst of circumstances. This one was testing her. And even though she'd been awake for almost twenty-four hours, her thick black mane was neatly held in place by a barrette tie-back. She eyed the gaggle of handsome new arrivals as she approached, gave them polite nods and smiles, then she pulled Logan away from the group by one arm.

"Could I have a moment?"

Logan knew it wasn't a question. He followed her away from the group.

"We have a news bulletin from our friends at the bank. They're on their way over with our new GM. And it's Connor Harcourt."

"Holy shit."

Gloria turned, startled by his reaction. "You've met? He hasn't been here in five years."

"No, I mean, I was worried you'd be upset," Logan lied.

"Why would I be upset?"

"Makes sense to promote you, doesn't it?"

"Thank you for volunteering me during one of the worst episodes in this hotel's history."

"I was trying to give you credit. You deserve a promotion."

Gloria crossed her arms over her chest and studied him with a raised eyebrow. "Logan, I've been awake almost thirty-six hours, and a few days ago, before my world ended, I invited my daughter and her three-year-old to move in with us while she regroups after her divorce. The last thing I want now is more responsibility added to my plate. Now, please tell me. What is your actual issue with Connor Harcourt?"

"We've met," Logan said.

"When?"

"Five years ago. My first night here."

"Okay."

Logan stared at her.

"Logan, I'm really tired. Out with it."

"We had a moment," Logan said.

"A disagreement?"

"Like a my tongue was in his mouth and his tongue was in my mouth moment."

"On this planet we call that kissing."

"Yeah, well, it didn't end that great. He had feelings. I had feelings. I told him how we couldn't act on them because of my job, and he didn't take it so well. Look, I'm just telling you because if he suddenly shows me the door, that's why. I don't want you to think I wasn't willing to stay and fight."

"I've known Connor since he was a boy," she said. "He's a good man. He'll do right by this place. He'll do right by you."

Logan pulled her in and gave her a quick peck on the forehead, seeing a swell of gratitude in her eyes. "You're out of here by five. I don't care what anyone says. You need a break and a real meal."

"I'm fine," she whispered and then she was gone.

Logan smelled his best friend's familiar woodsy cologne, felt the guy give him a light punch in his lower back. "That was one smooth disclosure, buddy. You got this hotel shit licked."

"Shut up."

"You excited for the return of Tintin?"

"I swear to God. There's so much going on in this hotel right now, I could deck you right here in the lobby and no one would notice."

"Yeah, but then you'd be down a security guy. Speaking of which, we better go get suited up. Didn't you say some guy was waiting for us in the office to get us in uniform or something?"

"The way you're dressed is fine. You need to get set up with earpieces and walkie-talkies. I've got to meet our new GM's entourage, so head on back. His name's Emmanuel. You can walk in. No one's going to stop you."

Donnie gave him a thumbs-up and headed for his three handsome team members.

Logan reached out and grabbed his arm, letting Donnie's friends get some distance away. "Those guys are all porn stars, right?"

"*Former* porn stars. Looking for a new career path, and you know how I like to be there for my guys when they age out. And honestly, they're shit cameramen so I gotta find something else for them to do."

"All right, then."

"Is that a problem, Murdoch?" Donnie asked, clearly prepared to ream Logan's ass if it was.

"Not at all. Thank you for being a friend."

"I'm your original golden girl, and don't you forget it."

Donnie gave him trigger fingers, which didn't seem very Bea Arthur or Rue McClanahan or Betty White. But it was very Donnie.

The lawyers begged off Connor's first official visit to the hotel as GM. Lois Penry, however, thought it was essential she accompany him and his mother in their hired SUV.

She rode up front, sorting through a stack of files on her lap she'd probably hand off to him once they reached Rodney's office.

My office, he reminded himself.

"Has anyone addressed the press?" Connor asked.

"Lawyers released a statement last night while you were flying in." Connor's mother was swiping through headlines about the scandal on her phone. "But it was basic. We're horrified. Rodney's been terminated. Our hearts go out to the victims. Full cooperation with the FBI investigation. That sort of thing."

"Do you know Gloria Alvarez?" Lois asked.

"I was supposed to work for her. I love Gloria," Connor said.

"Great. She's been on duty since the storm broke. The FBI questioned her briefly yesterday and wanted nothing to do with her, so we figure she can be trusted. Also, she's been working for about thirty-six hours straight, but she's still on her feet somehow, so she'll meet us in the motor court."

Gloria had been promoted? That was one of the better pieces of news he'd received today.

Lois continued. "And she'll be joined by the one security team member who wasn't arrested yesterday. We recommend promoting him to acting security director, but that's obviously your call."

"What's his name?" Connor asked.

"Logan Murdoch."

"Are you kidding me?"

His outburst so startled his mother she almost tossed her phone into the air. Lois spun in her seat and gripped the back of her headrest to try to get a better look at him. At least he hadn't frightened the driver off the road.

"Connor Harcourt, watch your tone!" his mother cried.

"I'm a grown-up, Mother."

"All the more reason to act like one."

"I apologize, Lois," Connor said.

"Yes, Lois, he apologizes for his completely preposterous outburst."

"Obviously my justified and totally not preposterous anger was not directed at you, Lois. I'm just shocked that a stone-cold liar like Logan Murdoch still works at Sapphire Cove. But maybe I shouldn't be, given the way things have gone under Rodney."

Lois stammered. "I'm sorry, Connor. I wasn't aware of any history."

Connor sighed. Loudly.

"Do you want to tell us what this is about, young man?" his mother asked.

"He's been here five years? Continuously?"

Lois flipped through the files on her lap. "I don't know when he started..."

"I do. He started five years ago. I want to know if his employment's been uninterrupted since then."

Lois flipped more pages.

His mother glared at him until he stuck his tongue out at her.

"Charming," she whispered.

"It's been continuous since then," Lois said. "Would you like to see his file?"

Connor took the folder from her. "And we're *absolutely* confident he had nothing to do with the blackmail scheme?"

"Our lawyers are assuring us there's no way the FBI would have come in with a dragnet like that if they were planning to arrest people later. Now there's the possibility that someone they've got in custody could implicate someone currently on staff during questioning. And they said they'd consider giving us a heads-up before they arrest that person. But it wasn't a promise. Just a consideration. Whatever that is."

Connor flipped through Logan's file and saw confirmation of the details he'd shared with him five years before. Yes, he'd been in the Marines. Yes, he'd been a staff sergeant. And his work record was spotless. But who'd kept this record? A disgraced security director currently sitting in a jail cell?

"Do you want to tell me what's going on?" his mother asked.

"I am making my first decision as general manager that is for the good of the hotel even though it turns my stomach."

"And what would that be?" his mother asked.

"I need someone in the security department with experience, who knows Sapphire Cove. And that's why I'm not firing Logan Murdoch. Yet."

"I take it you don't want to promote him to acting security director?" Lois asked.

"I would rather be eaten by a shark." Connor snapped Logan's personnel file shut.

Suddenly the crush of reporters gathered outside the motor court's entryway was racing toward them, a chorus of shouts and footfalls and TV news people jostling to get close to the windows.

The next thing Connor knew, the driver had somehow managed to inch through the crush, and his mother was sliding out of the back seat. In their wake, two attractive guys in too-tight polo shirts were directing the media back behind the dividing line of the motor court's entrance. Maybe Connor was just out of it, but the guys looked very familiar.

Oddly familiar.

Suddenly there was nothing but space between him and the powerful, veiny hand that had extended itself in greeting. Not just in greeting, he realized. The guy was offering to help him down out of the SUV with fingers he'd once run through Connor's hair and an arm that had once held him in an embrace so powerful Connor had foolishly thought it would never end.

"Welcome back to Sapphire Cove, Mr. Harcourt," Logan said. And as Connor stared into those dark eyes that had once bored into his with consequences, Logan added, "We've missed you."

10

It seemed like the right thing to do, extending his hand. It wasn't that he wanted to steal a touch of Connor's soft, smooth skin, or get close enough to find out if he still wore the same citrusy cologne. Those things would have been nice, sure. But they weren't his priorities. The SUV was up high, and Connor was the same height as when they'd last seen each other. A little help down was a respectful gesture. A welcoming gesture. And anyone who might have had a homophobic reaction to it was long gone. Arrested, in fact.

So when Connor refused Logan's offer of assistance, giving his open hand a blank stare before walking straight past Logan and into Gloria Alvarez's arms, Logan explained it away by saying maybe the gesture had been a bit too much. A little inappropriate, even. And maybe the familiar comfort of Gloria's embrace had called to Connor more than any awkward memories of his last encounter with Logan.

Gloria's expression pulsed with raw emotion as she hugged their new boss.

She needed the hug.

So, fine, it was for the best, even if Logan felt slighted.

"Janice Harcourt." Connor's mother thrust her hand at Logan as if to distract him from how badly he'd been ignored. Logan returned her handshake. "I don't believe we've met."

"We haven't. I'm Logan Murdoch."

"I know. Just so we're clear, you didn't do any blackmail stuff, right?" she asked. "Sorry. I used to teach high school so I can be pretty direct."

"I have never participated in any criminal enterprises during my employment at Sapphire Cove."

"Just before, right?" Janice cackled.

Logan smiled. "No, not then, either."

"Great." Janice smiled and clapped her hands together as if the entire matter had been settled in an instant.

Meanwhile, Gloria and Connor spoke to each other in intimate tones, their words indecipherable. Outside in the sun, Gloria's exhaustion—her bloodshot eyes, her drawn features—were impossible to ignore, and since they hadn't made a plan for Connor's arrival, Logan decided it was best if he take the lead.

"Mr. Harcourt, there's been a major renovation since you were here last, so we thought it would be best if we started with a tour of the premises so you can—"

"Let's have Gloria lead the tour." Connor kept his back to him. "Since she's senior. You and I can discuss security issues separately."

Senior? Really, dude? Logan thought, but what he said was, "Sure, makes sense. But before we leave the motor court, I wanted to point out our strategy for managing the media. We've got—"

Connor turned, revealing an expression icier than Antarctica. "You're not managing the media. You're containing the media. There's a big difference. Getting a bunch of reporters to stand behind a property line isn't going to do anything to control a story of this size. As I said, we can discuss security concerns separately."

The man's look was more angry, more focused, more determined than any look he'd given him outside Laguna Brew five years ago. And Logan's only thought was, *Really? Five years and you're still not over it? It was one night. Grow up, Prince.*

They filed into the lobby in awkward silence. Logan felt matching aches on both sides of his jaw, a sign he was grinding his teeth. As they did their best to veer around the checkout melee without being noticed, Logan made a mental list of all the things he'd done on the hotel's behalf these past twenty-four hours that went way beyond the call of duty.

He did his best to memorize it, fully prepared to rattle over every item aloud if Connor Harcourt decided to make this as difficult as humanly possible.

With Gloria in the lead, they passed through the lobby, which seemed far more vast and open than when Connor had last visited. "We're demanding key card access from everyone, so it's keeping out the stealth reporters with camera phones."

Maybe, Connor thought, but Gloria looked exhausted, so he didn't want to question her.

Logan Murdoch, on the other hand, better be ready to answer for the thoughts and deeds of every housefly that flew in through a cracked window.

"When did the renovation finish?" Connor asked.

"Beginning of this year," she answered.

Connor found the changes to be a relief. Otherwise, the flood of memories would have overwhelmed him.

The corner of the restaurant where he'd sat for hours with Grandpa Dan was still there, but the booths were gone, replaced by spindly metal chairs and glass tables. And the big puddling draperies around the hotel's ocean-facing windows, behind which he'd hidden from his mother during games of hide and seek as a little boy, were also long gone, replaced by slender boxes that ran along the ceiling, concealing automatic window shades. Gone was the bright pink carpet that had covered most of the halls the night of his graduation party. Its replacement was muted, cream colored, with bright slashes and checks of pastel colors here and there that matched the sofa cushions on the wicker furniture in the lobby.

Gloria did her best to rattle off the changes, but her voice was strained and muted. Either her heart wasn't in it or she needed rest. Besides, Connor could see the improvements, the fixes, and a few design misfires without her pointing them out. Not because he was familiar with the hotel's new guise. Because he'd been so familiar with the old one.

In the Dolphin Ballroom, Connor realized he was standing in about the spot where he and Logan had first met. And Logan was glaring at him in a way that suggested Connor's dressing down of him out front had sent its intended message.

I don't like that you're here, and I'll deal with you when I'm ready. Hope that doesn't make you uncomfortable, *Staff Sergeant Murdoch.*

The ballroom's carpet was different, a similar, more muted style to the guest room hallways. The old art nouveau smoked-glass wall sconces were gone, replaced by flaring organic shapes in various shades of blue that looked like pieces of coral growing out of the walls. Also gone, the old traditional crystal chandeliers. They'd been replaced by a single giant one that looked like an inverted sapphire coral reef growing downward from the ceiling, its larger tubes stuffed with bulbs that glowed with such radiance it was impossible to see their individual shapes.

"My sea caves are still open, right?" his mother asked.

"Yes," Logan answered.

Connor did his best not to look in Logan's direction.

"Good," his mother said brightly, then to Logan, "That was a special project of mine. All the placards and the boardwalk. I wanted there to be something educational about the place. Never managed to sell Grandpa Dan on boat tours of the coast, but it wasn't for lack of trying. You can take the teacher out of the classroom, but you can't take the classroom out of the teacher."

"I've heard," Logan said. "And I think it's a wonderful thing you did, Mrs. Harcourt."

"Well, aren't you a nice young man," his mother proclaimed.

"You go to the sea caves often, Mr. Murdoch?" Connor asked before he could stop himself.

"No." Logan's look was mostly blank, but his one raised eyebrow gave off a flash of defiance. "I've only been inside them once. A very long time ago."

Connor smiled. "That's a shame. It's a good place to hide out from unwanted attention."

"Sure, I guess. But I don't do a lot of hiding on my job. Unless I'm scoping someone I think is trying to rob a guest room."

The only way out of this awkwardness was to get back to business, and for that he needed to focus on Gloria. But when he turned to her, he saw she'd raised one hand to her forehead and was staring down at the floor as if a strange message were written on it.

"Gloria?" Connor moved to her swiftly.

"I just...I need..."

That's when Connor saw one of her legs bend. Sideways.

He caught her by one arm before she went down, and by the time he'd guided her into the nearest chair, Logan had her other arm.

"I've got her," Connor said.

"We've both got her," Logan said. "She's on the chair. Set her down."

Once Gloria's nearly dead weight settled into the chair, Connor saw that she was pale and sweating. "Where are your glucose pills, sweetie?" he asked.

"Handbag. My office."

"I'll get it," Logan said.

"No, I'll get it, you stay." Janice hurried from the ballroom before Logan could protest.

"What have you eaten today, Gloria?" Connor asked.

"Some bread and juice... Trying to keep it up so I didn't...crash."

Gloria wasn't just diabetic, she was insulin dependent, which Connor had learned when they'd worked his graduation party together. He'd been present for one of her low blood sugar episodes before, but it hadn't been quite this severe. She was stressed and overworked, and given the contents of her most recent meal, hungry.

"Gloria," Connor whispered, taking her hands in his, hoping to both steady and warm them. "I need you strong, gurl. I need you to get some rest."

"I couldn't leave, Connor." Her eyes were full of tears. "I couldn't leave your grandpa...your dad."

A blood sugar crash could sometimes cause delusions, but it mostly caused a slight, drunken slurring of words, and Connor figured that's what he was seeing now. But Gloria's tears were real. Piercingly real.

"This place," she whispered, "this place gave me everything. I couldn't leave thinking it wouldn't be here when I got back."

Fighting tears himself now, Connor brought their foreheads together. "I need you to go home and eat a nice big meal and get a good night's sleep. And if you do those things for me, I promise you, Sapphire Cove will be waiting for you when you're ready and back on your feet. We'll all be here waiting for you."

"Got it!" His mother's hair was a flyaway mess and her chest was heaving, but she clutched a handbag.

Her hands still shaky, Gloria was able to get the glucose pills to her mouth.

"There we go," Janice said. "Perfect. That should get us to rights."

Blinking back tears, Connor stood. Gloria took a deep breath and smoothed her skirt back into place.

"I'm sorry," she whispered. "I'm so sorry, guys."

"You have nothing to apologize for." Connor helped Gloria to her feet. "Do you need us to get you a ride?"

"I can call my daughter. She's been trying to get me to leave too."

Now that she was standing, Connor gave her a hug.

Gloria gently held the flaps of his blazer. "Maybe this is how it was supposed to be. I mean, it shouldn't have happened like this, I know. But you running Sapphire Cove. It's what your dad would have wanted."

Connor had assumed he'd cried himself out at the lawyer's office, but Gloria was bringing him perilously close to a second round.

Janice took Gloria's elbow in hand. "Come on, sweetheart. I'll walk you to your office. We can call your daughter from there."

The rest of them fell silent as the two women left the ballroom, slowly and arm in arm. Then, groping for his most businesslike tone in order to push away the emotions Gloria's episode had brought to the surface, Connor turned to Logan. "All right, Mr. Murdoch. Tell me why I should believe the FBI."

"About what?" Logan asked.

"About you."

"That I'm innocent, you mean?"

"Are you innocent?" Connor asked.

"Yes."

"You're the only member of the department that wasn't in on a criminal conspiracy?"

"Correct."

"How's that possible?" Connor asked.

"Well, for starters, none of them liked me."

Imagine that, Connor wanted to yell.

"Why's that?" Connor asked.

"Because I was good at my job. Better than most of them. And I can be a hard-charging asshole who doesn't put up with other people's stupid mistakes."

"You got any evidence of that?" Connor asked.

Logan gave him a sly grin as he slowly closed the distance between them, aggression coming off in waves. Waves that did things to Connor that confused his brain. And other parts of him he wanted to stay out of this exchange.

"If you check the hotel's server," Logan said carefully, slowly, "you'll find several emails over the years from me to management suggesting changes in procedure and repairs to different systems that I thought would make the hotel safer and more efficient. Including an indictment of the camera system and how improperly it was installed. You'll also see that after Steve Wasserman, the last security supervisor, left, nobody responded to those emails. Because they weren't well received. By Buddy Haskins or your uncle."

"I'll be sure to look."

"Also, one other thing. If they'd asked me to take part in their blackmail scheme, I would have said no. Because I'm a good person."

"You got any evidence of that?" Connor asked.

Logan laughed silently, shaking his head, his tongue making a lump under his upper lip. But his dark eyes were glassy. Angry. And Connor could feel his pulse beating in his ears, his neck. His sweaty palms. "Well, for starters," he said, "I don't hold grudges."

"When you're *comfortable*, that is," Connor growled.

"Huh?"

"Gentlemen." Lois Penry slapped her hands together as she tried to move between them. "I don't really know what's going on right now, but what I do know is I have a text saying the department heads are all gathered. So why don't we take all of this really *interesting* energy and shift it in the direction of Seal Rock II. Because that's where they're waiting for us."

"Let's do it," Connor said.

"Sounds like a plan," Logan said.

Prick, Logan thought. *Arrogant, entitled, spoiled, immature prick.*

Ironically, growing up, striking out on his own and building his own career had turned Connor into everything Logan had feared he'd be five years before, and that meant the decision Logan had always regretted had been the right one.

The goddamn roof was falling in on their heads and the prince had the nerve to walk in here bent out of shape about a kiss from yesteryear, raking Logan's ass over the coals.

What the hell was wrong with him?

Maybe he was stressed out and exhausted and Logan should give him the benefit of the doubt, or at least twenty-four hours on the property to adjust.

But still, as if anything about the way Logan had treated Connor back then had suggested he'd join a criminal conspiracy based in secrecy and lies. If anything, Logan had been unfailingly, bracingly honest. Even when he didn't want to be. Even when it had embarrassed and hurt him.

Except for the part about what Rodney had said to him in that scary meeting.

Or his family situation.

Still, the last thing he'd wanted to do back then was throw water on the flames of desire that had sprouted between him and Connor, but he'd done it directly, and to Connor's face and in words that felt honest and true. The omissions were about protecting his dad, protecting his job. And to some extent, protecting Connor from a blowup with his uncle.

He'd done it right, goddammit, and now Connor was treating him like a criminal.

They walked side by side because it reduced their chances of having to look each other in the eye. Lois tailed them, gawking at them like they were both growing third arms.

Finally, Logan broke the tense silence. "There's something I need to say."

"And you're confident now's the time to say it?" Connor asked.

"Yes."

"Go ahead."

"I need to lead this meeting," Logan said.

"You do? Why's that?" Connor asked.

"Because you're about to jump into a shark tank feet first. And your feet are bleeding."

"Do you always speak in pedicures, Mr. Murdoch?"

"I'm serious, Connor. This isn't the Shapiro wedding. You need to—"

Logan realized his mistake as soon as Connor's eyes widened and his eyebrows jumped. He could feel his cheeks flushing, and suddenly he was having trouble swallowing.

Idiot. You fucking idiot. He started to talk again, but it was mostly word salad, a grasping attempt to try to spit out the words that had been on the tip of his tongue before his colossal fuckup.

"The Shapiro wedding?" Connor said. "How do *you* know about the Shapiro wedding?"

"I saw something online."

"Where? It was a small wedding for sixty people in Greenwich. We did it as a favor for a friend of our boss. He's a dentist, not a Kardashian. Where did you read about the Shapiro wedding on the Internet? Melinda

Shapiro's Facebook page?"

"Can we focus, please?" Logan asked.

"I am. On the Shapiro wedding. Which you brought up."

"Look…"

Fuck fuck fuck fuck fuck fuck, Logan thought.

Connor was beaming suddenly, then he was laughing, and Logan could feel what was coming like the approach of a locomotive. And his feet were wedged under a crossbar.

"Are you Instagram stalking me, Mr. Murdoch?"

"I'm trying to help you here," Logan growled.

"By taking over my first department meeting," Connor said.

"That's not the right way of looking at it."

"Oh, and telling me how to look at it, apparently."

"They will eat you alive. Trust me. They're terrified of losing their jobs. They don't know what's coming next. And now you're going to walk in there and start ordering them around, and you're Rodney's blood relation to boot. I, on the other hand, know these people. They respect me. And I've got a ton of leadership experience."

"From the Marines," Connor said.

"I was a staff sergeant."

"And in the zone for gunnery sergeant. I remember."

"Yeah, I know, I remember that you remember."

"Glad we had this moment," Connor said.

"I should lead the meeting, Connor. It's for the best."

"Because you were a Marine."

"Because you have zero experience with this hotel and the hotel industry in general."

Logan expected an eruption, but instead Connor let out a throaty grunt and crossed his arms over his chest and furrowed his brow as he nodded, as if Logan's suggestion was complex and required careful contemplation.

"Okay." He gestured to the conference room door next to him. "Go ahead. Lead the meeting. It'll allow me to get a feel for everyone's temperament."

"I'm glad you see it my way," Logan said.

"Uh huh, sure."

Fearing a sudden change of heart on Connor's part, Logan nodded and pushed past him into the room.

Holding the tip of his tongue between his teeth, Connor followed Logan into the conference room. The revelation that Logan had been checking in on his life via Instagram had him supremely amused.

Maybe a little too amused, given the gravity of the situation.

He also had a pretty good idea how Logan's power move was going to play out. So rather than ripping the guy a new asshole over his condescension and insubordination, he decided to let the whole thing unfold.

Everyone gathered around the conference table stopped talking the minute they entered. Logan suggested the department heads all introduce themselves round-robin style, which they did. Connor noticed a few familiar faces in the group.

"Hi, guys." Logan walked around to the far head of the conference table so Connor could take the opposite one, closest to the door. "So this has been a really intense—"

Lois Penry cut in quickly. "Sorry, one note before we begin. We're missing Jolene Tomas, head of housekeeping. If you don't know, the Palm Fire tripled in size overnight, and she's helping her mother evacuate."

Logan cleared his throat. "Folks, it's been a rough twenty-four hours. And for most of it we've been in the trenches together. Now in the Marines we have an old saying that goes—"

A hand went up and Logan fell silent. It belonged to Jonas Jacobs, who'd introduced himself as head of the events office. He had the prim and proper air of a man who cleaned his toothbrush by hand before brushing his teeth with it. Impeccably dressed, he looked to be in his late forties, bald, with a strong jawline, hazel eyes that blazed against his dark skin, and a goatee beard that looked sculpted with a ruler.

"Logan." Jonas didn't wait to be called on. "No offense, but a pep talk? Really. From you? I mean, I don't mean to speak out of turn here, but I must ask. Perhaps a question and answer first? Did you really have no idea any of this was going on? We're being told everyone in your department was in on it."

"As I just told Connor, they didn't like me."

Logan's cheeks flamed when he realized he'd admitted to being interrogated by their new boss.

"But Logan—" The man who spoke now had introduced himself as Arthur Ruiz, the maintenance manager for the entire property. "You were in charge of the cameras, and they were recording audio. That's illegal unless you've got notices everywhere, and no one ever told maintenance to post a notice. That's all they were talking about on NBC this morning."

"I *wasn't* in charge of the cameras, Arthur. I tried to pull footage three days ago from an incident, and they wouldn't let me. Probably because they didn't want me to find out about the audio recordings."

Now the shouts came fast and furious, too fast for Logan to keep up with. So Connor decided to show the guy some mercy. Even though he'd been waiting—and maybe a little excited for—exactly this. He wrapped his knuckles on the table a few times to get everyone's attention. When they fell silent and looked his way, he stood.

"Logan," Connor said, "now that I've got a feel for everyone's temperament, why don't you let me take this one?"

Both sides of his jaw tensing, Logan sank into his chair with a small, angry nod.

"First up, before we go any further, nobody's getting fired," Connor said.

There were one or two audible sighs.

"If the FBI doesn't think you were part of this," Connor continued, "then I trust their judgment, and I'm going to proceed as if you all have the best interests of the hotel at heart. Because the fact is, I need you. All of you. And I need everything you can bring to this. So if you're worn out, if you're afraid of what's to come, or for whatever reason, you've had enough, let me know right now and I'll let you go with three months' severance. Otherwise, let's batten down and buckle up."

Lois Penry cleared her throat in a manner suggesting she'd just done some quick calculations around Connor's severance promise and funds had come up short.

He ignored her. He was taking a risk, and he knew it.

Nobody would accept the offer, he was sure.

He was right.

Nobody moved. Nobody stood up. Nobody looked away when he looked into their eyes.

He summarized the situation for them as best as he could, felt the energy of the room soften as they listened intently. He emphasized they were in a media war over the hotel's name, and no one should speak to the press. But they should also feel free to speak to him about any concern, no matter how big or small. And right now, what he needed from them most was honest and candid situation reports about their various departments. He emphasized again that it was a new day. That he and his uncle had not been on speaking terms, and he said diplomatic and slightly veiled things indicating his awareness of his uncle's abusive tendencies. By the end of his speech, he had them all in the palm of his hand.

After an initial moment of hesitation, they started to go around the table in the same order in which they introduced themselves. Connor suddenly realized he should be taking notes, and that he didn't have a pen. He was about to rise and look for one when suddenly a pad of hotel stationery and a pen hit the table in front of him, and he looked up to see Logan had brought them to him. With a bowed head and a chastened expression.

Connor was surprised. And maybe a little touched.

A little.

The reports seemed candid. They were certainly detailed. No sign of the spin he'd feared, maybe thanks to the candor with which he'd started the meeting.

Together with this information and the financial disclosures he'd been given back at the law office, it was clear the hotel hadn't been in dire straits before the raid. It looked like Rodney's hideous criminal scheme was entirely for personal profit and that before the bomb blast of the FBI raid, Sapphire Cove had been functioning fairly well.

After he thanked them all and commanded them back to battle stations, he expected them to hurry from the room. Instead, they lined up to each shake his hand.

There was one person who hadn't lined up, however. Logan. He was standing against the far wall, hands shoved in his pockets, staring glumly at the floor.

Once everyone departed, they were alone together for the first time in five years.

Logan stayed standing.

Connor took his seat again, studying Logan.

Logan studied the floor.

"So what was that about an old saying in the Marines?" Connor asked.

Logan's smile was bitter. "I guess you enjoyed that part."

"A little," Connor lied. He'd really, really, really enjoyed that part.

"I guess I overstepped."

"A little."

Logan lifted his gaze to Connor's. "And I guess I should quit."

Connor's anger had him sitting forward suddenly. He hadn't been expecting this, but a mature part of his brain was telling him he shouldn't be upset about it. Should welcome it, even. But no way. No way was Logan walking out of this exchange this easily.

"Well, that's convenient," Connor said.

"You know, Connor, maybe you should decide what it is you actually want."

"What I want? Okay. What I want is to turn the clock back twenty-four hours to a time when a provision in a trust I didn't know about suddenly demanded I walk away from a life I built for myself and take the reins of this place for a whole year or else it gets sold to an outside company. That's what I want, Logan Murdoch."

"I meant with me, Connor. What do you want with me? You want me to leave as punishment for the fact that I was either in on this thing or should have known about it? Or do you want me to stay so you can make me miserable over a five-year-old kiss?"

"A five-year-old kiss?" Connor shot to his feet before he could stop himself, blood rushing to his face. The evidence of his anger didn't deter Logan, however. The guy was approaching him slowly, matching him almost step for step, a solid wall of defiance and so many other hard things Connor wanted to squeeze and touch and do other things to that made him hate himself. "A five-year-old kiss? You think that's why I'm pissed at you?"

"Of course it is. You don't think I'm really involved in this and still standing here, do you? Hell, if I was guilty, I wouldn't stick around to get arrested later. I'd be off in Mexico spending my blackmail money."

"How would I know? I don't know you, remember? I didn't get the chance. It was too dangerous."

"And there it is!" Logan threw his arms out and let them slap to his sides.

"No, I'll tell you where it is. It's in Rodney's office, the night of our five-year-old kiss when you told him I'd made you uncomfortable. That I'd subjected you to unwanted attention. That I'd acted like I had a right to you because you were the new gay employee. I brought you a gift bag and made conversation. You're the one who flirted me down to the sea caves then offered me a slow dance with your tongue."

Logan was so visibly stunned, Connor's words left him, then his breath.

"I never said those things to Rodney. Never." His voice was low, like thunder. And when he pressed one hand into the table next to him, it was balled into a fist. A fist, Connor realized, that would have landed square on Rodney's face if he'd been in the room at that moment. "Not one goddamn word."

For a while, neither one of them spoke, just listened to the sounds of their breaths growing heavy as realization washed over them both. There was no arguing with Logan's conviction, with the way he held Connor's stare and the way his anger caused his massive chest to rise and fall.

"When did he tell you this?" Logan finally asked.

Connor was too startled by the sincerity of Logan's refusal to respond. But after a breath or two, he found his words. "He told my family you said it. He didn't use your name, but I knew it was you. He said there was a new handsome gay employee I'd done all those things to."

"Did you ask him who it was?"

"I couldn't."

Logan raised an eyebrow. "Why not?"

"Because I was eavesdropping."

"I see. So you never asked him about it and he never said my name?"

Connor's self-righteousness had turned to a flush of embarrassment that swept him head to toe, making his clothes feel sticky.

"Well, it wasn't me because I never said those things." Logan clearly wanted to gloat. Instead, he clasped his hands behind his back and gave Connor a vaguely satisfied stare.

"Well, then who was it?"

"It was *no one*, Connor, because Rodney was lying."

"Did you say anything to him about me at all?" Connor's voice was shaky, shaky from the fact that a foundation of anger he'd rested on for years had been pulled out from under him and now he felt like he was floating in space.

Logan took a deep breath, stretched his neck out, then stared at some spot above Connor's head that was helping him access the memory. "He called me into his office that night because he wanted dirt on you. He's the one who used the words *unwanted attention*. Not me. It was like he was implying he wanted me to set you up, entrap you, so he could accuse you of being inappropriate. And I was scared shitless, to be frank. Because I needed this job. Bad. We didn't know if my dad was ever going to walk again without crutches. His career in construction was over. He didn't have any skills or savings. He'd sold his house. I'd ditched my apartment. We'd moved into a trailer and still we couldn't afford everything. Without the benefits I got from this place, we would have been screwed."

"So what did you say, Logan?"

Logan nodded, cleared his throat, as if he thought Connor might not be prepared to hear it. "I said, 'I think your nephew is amazing. The party he organized was off the charts, like something you'd see in a magazine. And he made everyone there feel like they were the guest of honor. I saw him treat the staff with respect I didn't expect out of him. And he was ready to handle the security incident himself before I intervened. I've never met someone as impressive as him.' That's what I said."

Connor struggled to stay standing, struggled not to clear his throat because he was afraid to do so would unleash a series of exhausted and miserable sighs. Struggled not to imagine what every inch of Logan looked like under his blazer and dress pants. "Are you sure? I mean, it's like you memorized it."

Say it again, Connor thought, *naked.*

"Yes, I'm sure," Logan answered. "I ran it back and forth in my head a thousand times after that night because I was sure I'd lose my job over it. And if you still don't believe me, I'll say this. After everything you've learned about your uncle today, how could you still take his version of that night over mine?"

It was like the wind had been knocked out of him and replaced with sand.

Finally, Connor said, "I won't. I won't take his version of that night over yours. I just…"

But Connor couldn't finish the sentence because all possible conclusions threatened to drag him even further from the realm of the professional and into the complicated, the haunted, the lustful. If anything, Logan was being too easy on him. He'd known more than enough about Rodney before today to render him skeptical of any words out of the man's mouth. And yet, on the night when his uncle had spouted all manner of lies about his graduation party, for some reason, Connor, eavesdropping from the other room, had decided to take his lies about Logan at face value.

Because for some reason it had been easier to hate Logan for all these years than to admit to all the other feelings that surged inside of him whenever he thought of the man's name, remembered the firm grip of his hands, the woodsy, musky scent of him. The way he looked into your eyes when he smiled like he wanted you to know you were the reason he was smiling.

And now they were staring at each other like idiots.

And neither one of them was smiling.

Logan broke the silence. "Thank you. And I didn't know that about the trust. That's intense. I'm sorry."

"Thank you. It is. Intense."

"And it's probably another reason I should quit," Logan said.

"How's that?" Connor asked, panic flaring in his gut.

"I'm a distraction. On every level. You don't need distractions right now. You need help and support."

"Shouldn't I be the one to decide if you're any help?" Connor asked.

"Maybe."

"Do you want to leave?" Connor asked.

There was pain in his eyes, or at least what pain looked like on Logan Murdoch. Lips tensed and slightly parted, eyes narrow, but the strain visible in the muscles of his neck and the tense set of his jaw. Pain made worse by a man trying to hide pain. "No. I love it here. I loved it enough to put up with all the shitbags I worked with who've brought hell down on this place. But to be honest, even though I didn't do what you thought I did, I would leave before I'd hurt you again."

"It was just a five-year-old kiss," Connor lied.

"Apparently not."

Connor's heart thrummed, and Logan stared into his eyes with an intensity that made the back of Connor's neck feel caressed, held, gripped. Supported.

"If you want some time to—"

"I need you." The words came from Connor before he could stop them.

Logan went very still.

"I need someone in the security department who knows this hotel. Especially in the middle of all this. I need you to stay, Logan. Will you stay?"

"Absolutely."

"All right. It's settled then. Great."

"Right," Logan said.

"So obviously we need a new security department."

"Already underway," Logan said. "There's one catch, though."

11

Donnie grunted as he affixed the power drill to the metal bolt in the ceiling directly above his head. "So what you're saying is that you were a huge dick."

He fired the drill into action before Logan could defend himself, leaving Logan no choice but to glare up at the man from the base of the ladder he was holding in both hands. "Not sure I'd put it exactly like that, *best friend*," Logan said once the squealing stopped.

"That's all right, buddy. I did."

After he'd introduced Connor to the new security team, Logan and Donnie had started removing security cameras from the guest room corridors. Now that the FBI had made off with the system's nerve center, the cameras didn't connect to anything, but their redundancy and visibility was a blatant reminder of Rodney's crimes to all who passed. They needed to be gone. Now.

Logan held the ladder. Donnie worked the drill.

As Logan had feared, Connor had recognized their new security agents Brandon, Scott, and J.T. from their previous work as Parker Hunter models. Contrary to his fears, however, Connor wasn't remotely bothered by their work history. He'd shaken hands with all three men, then laughed under his breath as he and Logan walked back toward the lobby, suddenly more cheerful than he'd been since his arrival. "So my uncle said I'd ruin this hotel one day with all my various and sundry gay agendas. Now he's in jail and I've got a security staff gay America used to jerk off to. That really works for me."

Logan had laughed, and the tension between them had eased even more.

Now Connor was making calls to introduce himself to the organizers of the conferences that had decided not to bail.

Logan wanted to be there, but he hadn't been invited.

Right now, after the dizzying moment of their swift and unexpected reconciliation, Logan kind of wanted to be everywhere Connor was.

And that, he realized, might be a very big problem.

"Okay, let me say it then." Donnie reconnected the drill bit with a large bolt. "You were a huge dick, taking over the meeting like that."

"Yeah, well, it didn't actually work out in my favor. So I learned my lesson."

"Which he probably saw coming. Which is probably why he let you do it." He let out another piercing shriek of the drill, then gave up. "*Motherfuck,* did they weld these things in here?"

"He's good," Logan said. "Way better at this than I thought he'd be."

"At unscrewing these fuckers?"

"No. At managing the hotel."

Two guests walked by dragging suitcases, a middle-aged man and woman dressed for the beach. Holdouts, perhaps. Or maybe they'd waited until they'd found a room or flight before heading to the checkout desk.

"Kinda late for that, don't you think?" the man muttered as they veered around Donnie's ladder.

"Would you like a bellman to assist?" Logan called.

"No, thanks. I don't want him going through my watch case," the man barked.

Donnie scaled half the ladder, then hopped the rest of the way to the floor. In one fist he held the remains of the camera they'd dismantled. "Get used to it. It's going to be like that for a while."

"For as long as we have guests. Which shouldn't be very long," Logan grumbled.

"Ooof. Touché. Here you go."

Donnie handed him the camera's lens and battery backup pack.

"I can handle it from the guests, but my coworkers…" Logan said. "I figured they'd have more respect for me."

"They probably do. They're just afraid. And people are dumb when they're afraid. Give 'em time. So are you director of security yet?"

"Yeah, it didn't seem like the right moment to jockey for a promotion."

"I thought you said you and Connor had a good talk," Donnie said.

"We did, but we're not going to clear all the air between us in an afternoon."

"It was one kiss. Five years ago. Get over it. Move on."

Logan fell silent.

"What?" Donnie asked.

"I jerk off to his Instagram," Logan whispered.

"Aw, shit, dude."

"It's not even that thirsty either. It's, like, him fully dressed, holding a bunch of flowers."

"Maybe you're jerking off to the flowers," Donnie offered.

"I'm not, Donnie. I'm not jerking off to the flowers."

"Sexuality is a spectrum. I wouldn't judge."

"I'm judging myself," Logan said.

"Well, maybe this isn't a good idea," Donnie said quietly. Which meant he was serious. "You working here. With him."

"I told him."

"You told him you jerk off to his Instagram?" Donnie barked.

"Shut up! *No.* I told him maybe I was a distraction and he should let me go."

"But you put it back on him," Donnie said. "Made it his decision."

"Yeah."

"'Cause you don't want to quit."

"Kinda, yeah," Logan said softly.

"'Cause you want to work here. With him."

"Pretty much," Logan whispered.

"But do you even like this place anymore? With all this shit going on?"

"I love this place, always have. And even with all this shit going on, I love it even more now that he's back."

"Hoo, boy," Donnie whispered. "Oh, by the way. Bad news. You've only got me for twenty-four more hours. Our Mexico shoot got moved up because of some bullshit with the rental house."

"Crap. Can you get me some more people?"

"Yeah, not sure they'll have the curb appeal of the last three, though. Those guys. The metrics we used to get on their scenes back in the day. Through the roof, man."

"*This* job's not about curb appeal. Unless we're talking about the actual hotel. It's about confidence and strength. And I'd love people with some basic self-defense or fight training, but I'm not going to be picky."

"Good to know. Let me make some calls."

"After we get the rest of the cameras," Logan said.

"How many are left on this floor?" Donnie asked.

"Five."

"Jesus Christ." Donnie studied the length of the corridor as if every foot contained a piece of Rodney Harcourt's rotten soul. "Was he going to blackmail every room?"

"Looks like it, yeah."

Connor managed to get through to the executive director of the Lighthouse Foundation right away. The national literacy organization's networking conference was still on the calendar in three weeks, and they'd bring the hotel's occupancy to around fifty percent. Nicole Richter was professional, but frosty. She repeated the same conditions she'd expressed to the hotel's lawyer. They reserved the right to bolt if any more disclosures came to light. In response, Connor did his best to distance himself from Rodney, to declare it a new day at the hotel and make clear he'd been brought in after an absence of five years without admitting fault outright. His next call was to the Southern California Patent Attorneys' Alliance, who were set to occupy almost sixty percent of the hotel two weeks after the Lighthouse Foundation attendees vacated. Their executive director's tone was similar. But he wanted dirt. Connor did his best to walk the line between discretion and keeping a curious, and very important, client happy, mostly by alluding to his own difficult history with and contempt for his uncle.

Once he hung up, he took a moment to breathe, studying his uncle's absurdly big cherrywood desk. It had been swept clean of its contents by the FBI, save for some water rings left by the rock glasses Rodney favored for his morning, early-afternoon, late-afternoon, early-evening, and late-night cocktails.

He gave himself four seconds an inhale and eight seconds for the exhale, hoping the breathing exercise would relax him. It did. A little.

But the only thing that would make the phone calls sting less was throwing himself into another urgent task. So he turned to his laptop and logged into the hotel's server, using the instructions the front desk staff had given him. A few keystrokes later, he found what he was looking for.

Logan's emails.

Long, detailed, and diplomatic essays outlining shortfalls and room for improvement in their various security procedures. Proposing solutions that touched on areas from parking and event management to shift scheduling. Logan had pitched a more efficient system for receiving and tracking guest packages after a shocking number were lost in a single quarter, a pitch that had apparently gone ignored. He'd proposed better fortification for a staff entry door on the lower part of the hotel, which, sure enough, a few months later, an abusive husband used to try to track down his wife after she checked into the hotel under an alias. They'd caught the guy before he got to her, but by then he'd been within a stone's throw of his terrified wife's room and sending her menacing texts. If Logan's warning had been heeded, the bastard might never have made it onto the property.

His emails, overall, were smart and informed, never hostile or accusatory. But they were specific and detailed and always laid out a clear plan of action. In short, Logan should have been a shoo-in for security director. And yet, after a while, just as Logan had said, management had stopped responding to him. Maybe because one of the more recent emails was a detailed indictment of the new camera system, which he described as "possibly excessive and unfocused in its installation."

It was all there as Logan had said it would be, and it painted a multi-year picture of Logan as a natural born leader who'd never been given a shot.

The FBI had seen it.

And now Connor had seen it too.

Naser dropped in to review the books, which they both realized would include finding the books, which Naser agreed to do. Once Connor was alone, he realized he still had a call to make, to his head of housekeeping, who'd missed the department meeting because she was evacuating her mother from the Palm Fire. To Connor's astonishment, Jolene Tomas answered the phone, sirens wailing in the background. He got his message out loud and quick. Introduced himself in three seconds, let her know her job was waiting for her and she should take the time she needed. When he asked her if she was okay, she apologized for not being back already, said she'd planned to bring her mother to the newly opened shelter and then hurry back to work, but she'd been advised the shelters were not always the best place for single, elderly women and so they were taking her to Jolene's apartment even though there was almost no room for her there. When Connor told her again she could take all the time she needed, Jolene exploded into tearful thank yous before whoever was with her demanded she get off the phone. It sounded like they were practically trying to outrun the flames.

Connor was exhausted by the time he hung up. Not by Jolene, but the brief and overwhelming glimpse of chaos and fear the tumult of sounds all around her had given him.

For a while after he hung up, the sounds lingered.

And then, suddenly, he had an idea.

It could be a terrible mistake.

But the biggest mistake, it seemed, would be to do nothing.

There was no rule book for this, no plan. And if his father and grandfather disapproved, they were welcome to manifest before him now and give him some words of warning. That kind of stuff happened in movies all the time, but so far, this seismic life change had been entirely ghost free.

He should discuss the idea with someone, probably lawyers. But first, he needed to assess the immediate impact it would have on the hotel. His assistant general manager was getting some much-needed rest. That left only one person he should talk to.

A few text messages later, there was a resounding knock on his door.

He opened it, and in stepped Logan.

Suddenly they were alone in Connor's new office, without the spacious conference room to give them the buffer of distance or the presence of others to give them somewhere to look besides into each other's eyes.

"Should I?" It took Connor a second to realize Logan was asking if he should close the door. Part of Connor, the part that felt as if the ground underfoot always sloped in Logan's direction, thought it was a terrible idea. But the more professional part knew that what they were about to discuss needed to stay top secret. For now.

Connor nodded. Logan closed the door.

"How'd the calls go?" Logan asked.

"Fine, I think."

"I'm sure. You did a great job in the department meeting."

"The meeting you tried to take over, you mean?" Connor asked.

"Yeah, I guess I should apologize for that. Officially."

"I'll save it for later. Maybe cash it in when I screw something up. Which I might be about to do."

"I doubt that," Logan said. "You're taking to all this better than I thought you would."

"Thank you. And I found your emails. They were excellent. A real manager would have seen that."

"Thank you."

For a second, Connor thought they might stand there awkwardly thanking each other all day. Then he found his voice again. "I have an idea, but I think it might be batshit, so I'd like your feedback."

"Shoot."

"I think we should start taking in evacuees from the Palm Fire."

"How many?" Logan asked.

"As many as we can house. We lost one hundred guests total since the story broke, and fifty since this morning, and it's not showing any signs of slowing down. Pretty soon we're going to be empty."

Connor could sense a struggle in Logan's silence.

"Obviously, this is about PR as much as it's about helping people," Logan finally said.

"Absolutely. And clearly you have some concerns, so let's hear 'em."

"It's more about the security side of things. We're really low on manpower right now."

"Well, maybe it's the *man* part that's the problem. Should we recruit some women?" Connor asked.

"I'm down, as long as they're comfortable going into tense situations alone. We don't have the heads to buddy people up. And to be honest, the guys Donnie brought seem solid, but they're former sex workers, and that could be an issue."

"Not with me it won't."

At first, Connor wasn't sure why Logan was smiling and chewing his bottom lip. Then it hit him—*not with me you won't*. With one exception, they were the same words he'd whispered to Logan in the sea caves that long-ago night, right after Logan expressed fear he'd get in trouble for making out with Connor.

Connor's cheeks got as hot as they had the first time Logan called him Baby Blues.

"Sorry. That was unintentional," Connor said.

"It's fine." But Logan, it seemed, was blushing too, and that made

Connor's heart race. "Anyway, I'm worried about what happens if some reporter figures out we've got three former porn performers working for us."

Or Sylvia Milton, Connor thought.

"I wouldn't fire them," Connor said. "The blackmail palace has no right to take a puritanical attitude toward perfectly legal sex work."

"I appreciate that, and I'm sure they would too. But if they're being harassed, they might quit, and then we'd be down three guys."

"A valid point," Connor said.

"But I'm only bringing this up because in a normal situation, if we're talking about housing a bunch of evacuees who might be boozing pretty hard to deal with the stress, I'd recommend we double the number of guys on the graveyard shift in case someone has a late-night freak-out. Right now we can't. We don't have the people. So basically, my response is, it's a lot of unknowns when we don't have a lot of security."

"We'd be prioritizing at-risk evacuees they're worried about housing in county shelters. Apparently that's a lot of elderly women who live alone."

"Anyone who doesn't think a bunch of old women can get rowdy should visit a bingo hall."

"Are you a bingo hall regular, Mr. Murdoch?"

"Volunteer with my dad at least once a month."

"Well, aren't you a good boy," Connor said.

"I try. I'm getting better."

There it was. Logan's signature smile. Wide-eyed and direct and inviting, and impossible to look away from. The fact that he was also leaning casually against the closed office door, as if trying to seductively bar Connor's escape, only made it harder for Connor to look away.

Dear God, it's me, Connor. Please tell me why you've invented a man who can make my butt clench with his smile.

"Are we talking about bingo because you think I shouldn't do this?" Connor asked.

"No. But I think we need to beef up our security staff pronto. When are you thinking of starting?"

"Tonight." Connor punctuated this announcement with a brusque nod.

"Tonight?" Logan stood up straight. "Woah, okay. Well, I won't be able to hire a bunch of new people by then."

"And you don't think I should do it until you can."

"It's not really my place to tell you to hold off," Logan said.

Well, we've sure made progress in the hour or two since you tried to hijack my meeting, Connor thought, but he figured the comment would pick at the scab rather than help it heal.

Connor rounded the edge of the desk until only a few feet separated them. "I'm making it your place. I'd like you to be my security director."

The silence between them was electric. It was, if his emails were any indication, a position Logan had wanted for years. Would sexual tension with Connor be his reason for not accepting it?

"I'm not sure how your other department heads will feel about that," Logan said.

"I'm not asking them."

"And you."

"My feelings on the matter have just been made clear." Connor crossed his arms, a gesture that was starting to feel like a method for hiding his feelings for Logan from Logan. He was pretty sure it wasn't working. And he wasn't sure he wanted it to.

Logan studied him head to toe, then studied the floor at his feet, then cleared his throat. "I just…want to be sure that you're not…that our history doesn't…"

"What part of our history, exactly?"

"Not what happened in the caves… Just… What I'm saying is…"

"Are you usually this resistant to a promotion, Mr. Murdoch?"

"I don't know. I haven't had one in years. I'm out of practice."

"Fair enough. Let me be direct then. I'm giving you this promotion because you deserve it. Your emails made clear you know the lay of the land here better than anyone except Gloria. And yes, our history does play a role. But not in the way you think."

"Oh, yeah?"

"Five years ago I assumed the worst of you based on almost no evidence and a very unreliable source. Now I've been presented with ample evidence to the contrary, so you deserve for me to assume the best of you."

Logan looked into Connor's eyes as if he was savoring these words but didn't want to let him know how much pleasure they'd given him. "Thank you, Mr. Harcourt," he finally said.

"Now's the part where you promise not to let me down."

"I promise not to let you down."

"Okay. We need to shoot for a press conference by this evening.

Before then, we need to reach out to all the county offices—"

"Wait. A press conference? Seriously?" Logan asked.

"Yes. I don't mean to sound cold blooded, but we're doing this to separate the hotel's name from Rodney's actions, and so we need to roll this out now, loud and hard. Sylvia Milton's posting new hate tweets every few hours. His arraignment's tomorrow morning, and then he'll be out and talking to press. I want to own the story before then."

"I just…who's going to give it?" Logan asked.

"I am."

"Connor…"

"You don't think I can handle it?"

"No, I know you can handle it. After the way I saw you handle the department meeting, I'm pretty sure you can handle anything, but I…"

"I don't remember you being this tight-lipped, Logan."

"It's been a few years."

"I meant since this morning," Connor said.

"Yeah, well, I was a jerk, and I overshot the mark, and I'm trying to dial it back and let you do your job."

"I appreciate that," Connor said. "But it doesn't explain why you're opposed to the idea of a press conference."

"I don't want you to get hurt."

Logan flinched, as if he hadn't meant the words to sound so unguarded and emotional, so full of need. And it was the second time in a few hours Logan had mentioned the prospect of Connor being hurt as something that might hurt him as well.

"Hurt?" Connor asked.

"They're aggressive. And kind of nuts. And when they first showed up yesterday they were shouting insulting questions at everybody."

"Yeah, I know. They did it at the airport last night when we landed."

"I'm sure, but it's your first day, Connor, and it's been a hell of a day already, and you're doing great, and I don't want you to get torn apart by a bunch of bloodthirsty reporters before you get a breath."

Connor felt like wilting into Logan's arms over these words, but he stayed standing. As straight as someone as gay as him could be expected to stand.

"I appreciate your protectiveness," he said. "And if it helps you feel better, I'd like you to stand next to me during it."

"During the press conference?" Logan asked quietly.

"Yes. I'll be the new face of the hotel. You'll be the new face of the security department. That should send a message to any of the other staff who might have the nerve to doubt my choice given I didn't fire any of them. Are you comfortable with that?"

"Of course I am," Logan whispered. But he was studying the floor, and his Adam's apple bobbed a few times, and goddammit if he didn't look like he was about to cry.

Connor waited and waited. But no tears came.

"Great, then," Connor said. "Let's start making some phone calls."

"Yeah. I just…let me take a minute. I gotta run to the restroom."

"Logan…"

"I'll be right back," he called.

But Logan was already gone.

He totally went to the bathroom to cry. Which left Connor feeling better about all the choices he'd made in the past half hour. They were all steps in the right direction, each one the best choice for the hotel, even if each one was sure to leave him so sexually frustrated his fingernails would be chewed down to nubs by nightfall.

The media outside had assembled in an orderly fashion for the first time since Connor's arrival, a few paces away from the podium the hotel had wheeled out about twenty minutes ago. When Logan saw the nest of microphones clipped to it, some bearing logos of news stations familiar to him since childhood, his heart vaulted up into his throat.

The sight was almost as nerve-wracking as the one that had greeted him and Connor as they passed through the lobby—most of the staff members had been retreating into corners of the lobby, huddling around their smartphones as they prepared to watch live feeds of whatever Connor was about to say to the world.

When he saw the several feet of asphalt between his feet and the podium, Connor seemed to freeze up like a dog next to a glass floor. Before he could think twice, Logan reached out and gripped Connor's shoulder briefly. "You got this, Prince." It was a low and commanding whisper that left little room for doubt.

And it worked.

The next thing Logan knew, Connor was at the microphones, staring into the blinding glare of the cameras, Logan beside him, trying to look impassive and cold, but his heart racing until the first nervous shake left Connor's voice and his remarks hit their stride. They were professional and articulate and scripted in concert with the hotel's attorneys.

The talking points were predictable. The hotel was fully cooperating with the FBI's investigation. Rodney Harcourt had been terminated. And so on and so on. In fact, the remarks were so predictable, some of the reporters were starting to look bored, even making phone calls. Logan assumed they were talking with their control rooms about whether or not they should cut away from their live shots.

Then came the big announcement.

"As many of you are aware, the Palm Wildfire tripled in size overnight and concurrently, the evacuation zones were significantly widened early this afternoon. We will be providing accommodations to the first wave of evacuees until they are cleared to return to their homes."

New currents of energy had shot through the crowd before him. Connor had their full attention.

"We will be prioritizing the elderly, single women, and families with small children, all groups which face elevated risk in public shelters. At no time will Sapphire Cove seek any form of compensation from any individual evacuee or any state or local agency. Furthermore, we will not simply be sheltering them. We will be providing them with all the services of the hotel, including three regular meals a day. In essence, during one of the most difficult times in their lives, we will be making the full extent of our services and the skills of our incredible staff fully available to them until their nightmare comes to an end. This is, at its core, the job of a resort like Sapphire Cove—to remove its guests from the trouble of their daily lives, to offer them a mental and spiritual rest. For those forced from their homes by this terrible fire, it is our humble honor to do this free of charge."

Now it was time for Connor to utter the words that made Logan want to take the guy in his arms and shield him with his body.

"I'll be happy to take a few questions," Connor said.

During the eruption of shouts, Connor pointed to a newscaster crouched down in front of the crowd. Due to the glare, he could only see her silhouette, but her voice was TV ready. "Mr. Harcourt, what are you going to say in response to people who claim you're simply using the victims of a natural disaster to distract from this scandal?"

"I'd say the only people who can answer that question will be the evacuees themselves. When they're free to return to their homes, ask them directly, and if they say they felt used during their time here, then I will have failed to live up to the promise I made today. But my goal and the goal of everyone who works here is not to use their status as victims, but to make them forget it for as long as they're sheltered at Sapphire Cove."

"Mr. Harcourt," another voice in the crowd shouted. "Have you put a timeframe on how long you're going to allow them to stay?"

"For as long as they're unable to return to their homes. That's the timeframe. Next?"

The next questions were the ones they'd anticipated—mostly attempts to get details of the FBI investigation the hotel didn't have and wouldn't share if it did.

Then came the one they'd feared most.

"Mr. Harcourt," another voice shouted. "Earlier today, Sylvia Milton, the widow of one of your uncle's alleged victims, had this to say about your hiring this morning, and I quote 'It remains to be seen how swiftly installing the nephew of the perpetrator of these crimes will do anything to purge Sapphire Cove of its culture of criminality and corruption, especially given the young man seems to have no experience in hotel management whatsoever.' What do you have to say to that?"

Logan waited for Connor's face to flush or his jaw to clench, but instead, their new general manager cleared his throat and spoke with the steadiness of a seasoned politician. "Yes, it's true I have no experience in hotel management. I have experience in event planning, which those of us in the business like to say is managing one crisis after another. And hotels, for the most part, are a series of contained crises. Like this one.

"Five years ago, my family expected me to take a position at this hotel. Rodney Harcourt, however, believed my homosexuality would damage this hotel's brand, and so he waged a campaign to convince my father and grandfather of the same thing. Rather than allow my family to be further divided by his homophobia and abuse, I chose a different path, which is why I spent the last five years working in New York City as an event planner.

"I'm back now because it was the wishes of my late father and grandfather that I take the reins should Rodney Harcourt's troubled past bring charges of this nature against the business they'd spent decades building. And so it's now my responsibility to ensure the FBI is unimpeded in their investigation and to ensure that those staff members who had nothing to do with this alleged scheme are given the opportunity to keep their jobs. Jobs, I might add, that they've performed so well over the years that Sapphire Cove has been the recipient of multiple awards and accolades from the travel industry. And in a very short time, it will also be our responsibility to care for some very frightened people who are in need of shelter, comfort, and a respite from troubles that make ours here at Sapphire Cove today pale in comparison. Thank you for your time, but I need to get ready for our new guests. That's all for today."

There were more shouted questions, but most of them drowned each other out.

Once they were standing in the lobby, Logan and Connor were greeted with smiles and enthusiastic nods and even a thumbs-up or two from the staff members who'd watched the press conference on their devices. A sign that maybe, just maybe, it had been a success.

"How'd I do?" Connor asked.

"Most excellent," Logan said.

"Are you sure?"

"Most sure," Logan answered.

Naser appeared next to them. "While I'm not sure the lawyers will agree with the extent to which you dragged Rodney's ass back and forth over hot gravel until we saw bone, I certainly enjoyed it and will probably be re-watching it several times before bed."

"All right, well, excellent," Connor said. "We've got some guests to prepare for then."

When Connor gave him a heart-melting smile, Logan tried to smile back in a way that wouldn't make clear to everyone in the lobby that Connor Harcourt made hard parts of him melt and soft parts of him hard. Also, he was relieved that no one, especially Connor, had figured out how long he'd spent in the bathroom fighting tears after he'd been granted the promotion he'd wanted for five years. And on a day when he thought he might have to say goodbye to Sapphire Cove forever.

12

Most of the evacuees arrived in school buses. Bright yellow, shockingly out of place as they rounded the ornate French fountain in the center of the motor court. The dazed passengers they disgorged carried plastic milk crates and bulging duffel bags and anything else they could stuff with their most prized possessions before the fire department had ordered them out of their homes. Most cats were in carriers. Most dogs on leashes. The buses made things easier for the hotel, made it easier to match names of new arrivals to the lists the city officials had provided.

Others clearly weren't comfortable leaving their belongings-stuffed cars behind at the city shelter parking lots, so they came in their own vehicles turned mobile storage units, some blackened by the smoke and grit of quick escapes from the flames, their back seats piled high with boxes and suitcases. They came quickly and eagerly, spurred on by city officials desperate to free up shelter space as the fire grew and grew. A nursing home was within its sights next. After that, an apartment complex.

Some evacuees, to Connor's astonishment, were actually smoke-blackened themselves, the whites of their eyes shockingly bright as they stared up at the hotel's pastel façade as if they thought they'd reached heaven after a long trudge through hell.

The last thing he wanted was a crush in the lobby that made these poor people wait any longer for a good rest. To say nothing of how bad it would look to the cameras outside. Reception had fanned gateleg tables across the lobby's width, the kind they used for conference registrations, and the staff had rolled out a remote check-in system they only used during peak periods to take pressure off the front desk. Instead of credit card information, they took names and driver's license numbers and printed room keys with handheld readers. Families of more than three were given the first available villa or suite, groups of three or less were given regular rooms.

With Naser at his side, Connor circulated through the crowd, listening closely for any sign the headcounts provided by the city officials were off. If they ran out of rooms, this would be a disaster. But so far, so good.

For the first time that day, the lobby was full of people whose expressions betrayed no harsh judgments or irritation or sick fascination. Given what they'd endured over the past two days, watching orange rims of fire creep over dry mountainsides toward their homes, it was doubtful they knew anything about the hotel's scandal at all. They were people on the cusp of losing everything they'd owned, and now they were close to a shower and a comfortable bed and surrounded by soft, warm light and cool air conditioning, and to them that was all that mattered.

It was amazing to watch this dance between the single-minded need of the arriving evacuees and the collective sense of purpose with which the staff rose to meet it, staff members who'd been in fear of losing their jobs hours before. In essence, it was unfolding exactly how Connor had described it to the reporters outside. This was an act that uncovered the fundamentals of what a place like Sapphire Cove was supposed to do for all who stepped through its doors. Provide for them, anticipate their needs, make them forget the world outside.

As they worked, Naser scrolled through coverage of the press conference to see how it had gone over. Every now and then Connor shot him a look, and Naser gave him a thumbs-up that said whatever he was reading was largely positive.

At some point, his mother showed up with his suitcase. Apparently, Logan had already taken the penthouse suite out of the registration queue so Connor could stay there. A little presumptuous, maybe, but also incredibly convenient and logical given Connor didn't plan to leave the hotel anytime soon, and he'd already started worrying about when he'd get his next shower.

In a way, it's kind of like he read my mind.

Logan appeared next to him suddenly.

"Did you get all the cameras down?" Connor asked.

"Every last one."

"All right, riddle me this," Connor said. "How are we going to get all these people to eat? We told them dinner's at eight when they checked in, but most of them are so dazed I doubt they'll remember."

"We can knock on their doors," Logan suggested.

"That's a lot of doors. Do we have the staff for that?"

"I'll tell you this. First thing they're doing when they get to their rooms is turning on the TV so they can see if their house burned down. If there's not a TV within sight, we're not getting them to go anywhere, including a nice buffet."

"Can we get the food to their rooms?" Connor asked.

"All at once, it'll take forever. They'll be starving."

"I'm thinking we should get some TVs to the Dolphin Ballroom, otherwise these people will never get any food down. Can we do that?"

"On it," Logan answered, then, when he was a few steps away, he turned and winked at Connor in a way that made Connor's breath catch a little.

When Connor and Naser made it to the ballroom after the second wave of folks were checked in, there were flat screen televisions studded throughout the tables, all tuned to wildfire coverage. The food hadn't been laid out yet, but some of the evacuees were gathering so they didn't have to watch in suspense alone.

Logan was correct. Right now, nothing was more important to these folks than TV access. When Connor caught his eye from across the room, Logan gave him a thumbs-up and a smile.

With so many guests gathering in the ballroom before the food was served, they had more than enough staff to remind the latecomers. By the time the buffet was out of food, not a single person had complained about missing a promised meal. Still, Connor ensured there'd be kitchen staff on hand late into the night to prepare a sandwich or a salad for anyone they might have missed.

Goddamn, we did it, he thought as he flounced down onto the love seat in the penthouse suite, his new apartment. The truth was they'd done something, something good. Whether or not it could be classified as *it*, however, remained to be seen.

The minute the crowd started filtering back to their rooms, Logan took Connor gently by the arm as Naser walked next to them, scrolling through his phone for the latest press conference coverage. Now the three of them were alone, and it was time to hear the results. Connor was exhausted, but not so tired he couldn't get anxious all over again.

As if he thought they all might need some air, Logan opened the doors to the suite's terrace, filling the room with a warm ocean breeze that rustled the sheer drapes and the matching orchids on the love seat's side tables.

"All right, let's hear it," he said.

Naser plopped down into a chair at the black lacquer dining table. "Okay. For the most part, great. I mean, you've got a few people accusing the hotel of exploiting the tragedy, but they can't get very far with it since the hotel's not charging anybody."

"Are we going off Twitter right now or the news?" Connor asked.

"The news. Even the cable news stations covered it. If you were looking to shut the whole story down, then linking the hotel to the wildfire probably wasn't the best way because the Palm Fire's also national news. But you weren't looking to kill the story, you were looking to *change* the story, and you've done that in spades."

"Because of the wildfire?" Connor asked.

"And because of what you said about Rodney at the end," Naser added. "That's definitely given a new element to it."

"What kind of element?" Connor asked.

"The soap opera kind. CNN's already got two hot take op eds about it. One accuses you of playing the victim card and using identity politics to distract from your uncle's crimes. The other holds you up as an example of how marginalized people always bear the brunt of the horrible mistakes of straight white men. The fact is, it's put you and Rodney on opposite sides of the story, and that's made for a conflict they're sinking their teeth into."

"Well, that's good, right?" Logan asked, but he was looking warily at Naser, as if he thought Connor's best friend might take his arm off for speaking out of turn. "If you're on the opposite side from Rodney and you run the hotel now, that means it's a new day at Sapphire Cove."

"Any word from our friend Sylvia Milton?" Connor asked.

"Nothing official," Naser said, "and the Stop Sapphire Cove Twitter account looks quiet for now."

"Probably still figuring out how to respond to the press conference," Connor said.

"Or giving up, maybe?" Logan asked.

"Yeah, I doubt that," Connor said. "Did they get rid of the mini bars? I could use some almonds or something."

"No, you need an actual meal," Logan said. "I'm having food brought up."

"Well, okay… You didn't even ask me what I wanted."

"I called your mother and she told me what you liked." There was a knock at the door. "There it is right now. Crab cakes and Dover sole with beurre blanc."

"Woah," Naser muttered. "That's a lot of breading."

"Lecture me about carbs right now and I'll eat your face instead. It's all protein except for the Botox."

"On that note," Naser said, "I must depart, as my mother saw me on the news a few hours ago and is totally freaking out about it. My presence has been requested at a family meeting, the third this week, by the way. And even though I am supposedly tonight's topic, no doubt my sister will turn it into a discussion of the low returns for her new dress line. Good night, everyone."

Naser rose from the table and stepped into Connor's hug. "You did excellent today, Blondie."

"Couldn't have done it without you."

"Possibly, but probably not." Naser turned to Logan. "And you, sir. Keep it up and I'll finally be able to sell that plot of land where I always planned to bury your body."

"I want to be cremated, so that's cool."

Logan followed Naser out to make sure he'd shut the door all the way, and then they were alone. Connor was about to take his first bite when he realized the open terrace doors were allowing in not only the gentle breezes, but also a sweet, soothing sound: the sound of children laughing and playing in the swimming pool. He was on his feet and out on the terrace in the blink of an eye.

"You're not gonna eat?" Logan asked, appearing next to him.

"In a minute."

Connor had been drawn to the open deck door like a moth to a flame. Voices echoing on the ocean winds. The nighttime sounds of a full hotel.

He felt a presence next to him, turned, and found himself staring into Logan's eyes.

"The magic moment," Logan whispered.

And suddenly it was five years ago and they were standing next to the balustrade four stories below, and his grandfather and father were alive and the world seemed free of death and scandal and full of promise, and everything between him and Logan seemed exciting and new.

And now they were here. Together again, but changed. Older and wiser, but also exhausted and scared.

Logan must have seen that Connor was about to pull a Gloria Alvarez because he said, "Oh, hey now," and the next thing Connor knew he was in Logan's arms, blinking madly to hold back the tears. It started as Logan trying to keep his legs from going out from under him, then, quickly and easily, it turned into something else. Something more tangled and intimate, something that brought the side of Connor's face to Logan's hard chest. A mirror image of the near-dancing pose they'd assumed in the caves five years before, only now Connor was swirling with so many emotions it was impossible to count. Lust was one, for sure, but there were others. Grief and relief made the most potent blend of the bunch.

"I was so afraid it would be quiet," Connor said. "I was so afraid we'd get to the end of this day and my grandfather, wherever he is, would see that I let his hotel go empty. That I took away his magic moment."

"But you didn't." The rumble Logan's voice made in his chest tickled Connor's ear, bathing his neck in delicious chills, just like that night in the sea caves when they'd slow danced in the mist.

"We didn't," Connor whispered.

Slowly, Logan started walking them across the room, and for a split second, the idea that he might be walking them toward the bed made Connor's head spin. But when his butt bumped into the edge of the love seat, he realized they were headed in a different direction. The dining table. A second later, Connor was sitting in front of his food. Logan bent down over the back of his chair and drew the plate closer to him, maybe because the position gave him an excuse to keep them close. Or maybe he really did think Connor should eat.

"You need to eat," he said softly.

"And you probably need to go," Connor said. "Have you slept at all?"

"A little."

"How much?" Connor asked.

"A couple hours. On a couch. In my dad's office."

But Logan didn't move. He was still leaning forward, arms around the chair, hands holding to the edge of the table, mouth so close to Connor's ear that if Connor turned his head even slightly, their lips would be inches apart and temptation would take over for sure.

"Are you sure you don't need anything else?" Logan asked.

All the ways Connor wanted to answer that question would have made an HR rep run screaming from the room and Logan's buddy Donnie raise a camera to film the proceedings.

"I better eat before I pass out," Connor said.

"Sounds like a plan."

Logan went for the door.

"Wait, Logan." When he turned, Connor stood.

Logan looked relieved he'd called out, relieved to be held in place on the suite's threshold, and that was tempting. Dangerously tempting.

I named my favorite dildo after you, he thought.

"Next time you can cry in front of me," he said.

Logan's tongue made a lump under his upper lip, then he nodded, laughing. "That obvious, huh?"

"Kinda."

"Yeah, well, why break a trend?" Logan seemed to regret his words the minute they were out of his mouth.

"A trend?" Connor asked. "What do you mean?"

"It wasn't the first time I wanted to cry in front of you. And didn't."

It took Connor a second to realize he was talking about that night at Laguna Brew. "Since we're talking about it, can I say something else about that night? I promise to keep it professional."

"Sure," Logan said.

"Whenever I think about that gift, I cringe."

"The boots?"

"And the peanut butter cups. In a half chevron."

Logan's smile said he'd thought about the gift often, hopefully with feelings as warm as the ones radiating from him now.

"It was a lot," Connor said.

"It was a lot," Logan said with a smile.

"And ridiculous."

"And adorable. It was adorably ridiculous."

"I'm crafty. What can I say?"

"That and a lot of other things," Logan said.

"Good things, I hope."

"Very good."

Now it felt like there was a live wire connecting them, and Connor kept expecting Logan to break eye contact. To look to the floor or offer a polite but brusque nod, but for a moment that felt like an eternity, they stared at each other across the warmly lit, carpeted distance. *This is already hard, and doing it with him might make it even harder.*

"I should go," Logan whispered, but he didn't move a muscle. In his mind's eye, Connor saw them grappling across the plush carpet to the bed. Or maybe that was his penis's eye. Or maybe the fact that penises didn't have eyes was why they always got men into so much trouble.

Did Logan see it too? Is that why he swallowed and nodded and slowly, ever so slowly, backed out of the room and drew the door shut behind him, all without breaking eye contact?

For only the second time in his life, Logan was fighting a stubborn erection while in uniform. Once more thanks to Connor Harcourt.

It was his smell that did it, the same smell he'd inhaled that long-ago night in the sea caves, the one that emerged from under Connor's cologne, strong and potent enough to compete with the salty ocean air, a smell like freshly baking bread with a hint of sugar and a trace of masculine musk. There was also the snug and perfect way Connor had fit inside of Logan's embrace, the heat that had come off him.

Logan hadn't requisitioned the penthouse suite for Connor because he thought he'd need it. He'd done it because Connor deserved it. But yeah, there'd been a small part of him that had fantasized they'd finish off this day together in its king-sized bed. And they'd come close. Damn close. And if Connor had asked him not to leave, if he'd so much as gestured to the comforter, Logan would have laid him flat and spent the rest of the night finding out if every inch of him tasted as good as he smelled.

But it was better this way, he reasoned. Better to finish off the night with a long hug and the nice little accomplishment of serving Connor one of his favorite meals. These things had done as much to push their painful history away as their conference room showdown.

God, had it really been that afternoon?

It felt like a week ago now.

He'd been sure he'd bone down by the time he reached the management offices, but no such luck. It was the smell that was doing it. The delicious, intoxicating smell of Connor Harcourt all over his clothes.

He needed to brief J.T. and Scott on the basics of the graveyard shift. He had a text that said they were waiting for him in the security department's locker room, where they'd also set up some trundle beds so they could take nap breaks. Under normal circumstances, one security agent was enough for most overnights. But the hotel was currently filled with emotionally strained people who weren't exactly there for a romantic getaway, so Logan thought it best to make sure security was beefed up. The stress of worrying about their homes might cause some of their guests to lash out in crazy, unexpected ways. Especially if they'd brought their own booze.

But he couldn't talk to the guys in this condition. With his khakis tented, all blinking and dazed with lust.

He needed to hit the head. He ducked into the private bathroom right off the management offices to catch his breath. Braced his hands against the counter, bent forward to avoid his own crazy expression.

Memories of combat. A bad car accident he'd once seen on the 5 Freeway heading into LA late one night. Puppies. None of his usual boner shrinkers did the trick. He was bowing his head, that's why, and bowing his head brought his nose close to his shirt, and that's where Connor's smell was.

Jesus Christ, am I really doing this?

But the Logan who controlled his limbs wasn't listening to the Logan who'd posed this question. The former Logan had already unzipped his trousers, freeing his cock into the bathroom's cool air. That Logan was already leaning against the wall, bringing the patch of his shirt that smelled most like Connor to his nose, close to his lips. Smell, he'd read somewhere, was connected to memory in the brain. And these memories were supercharged. Firing across a distance of five years, meeting up with the fresher memories of their recent embrace and Connor's sultry look, unleashing thunderous pulses through his chest, his head, his balls.

The Mr. Reasonable voice in his head kept reminding him that he hadn't done something like this since he was a teenager. Beating off in secret in a semi-public place. Choking breaths back to keep from being heard. But Mr. Reasonable was apparently not on the guest list for this adventure. That, or Mr. Reasonable, like the ocean air inside the sea caves so long ago, wasn't strong enough to overpower the scent of Connor Harcourt.

A quick, furtive wank like this usually resulted in furious strokes, but his hand moved steadily and expertly across his shaft, lingering briefly over the head at the top of each stroke. He'd only been at it for a few seconds and already he was at the edge of eruption. But his hand wasn't to thank for that. For that, he had Connor's smell and his tempting, dangerous proximity a few floors away.

He was building toward a climax more satisfying than any he'd managed in the messy bedrooms of strangers these past few years.

He gritted his teeth and punched the wall when he came. A crazy move, but it kept him from roaring so loud they'd hear him in the lobby.

He crumbled against the wall, eyes closed. Wishing he was crumbling onto Connor, their bodies tangled in the sheets of the penthouse suite's big, creamy bed. Hard bodies floating on a heavenly cloud dappled with their mingled sweat.

You better cool it, dude.

Mr. Reasonable was back, sounding all measured and adult as usual. Maybe Mr. Reasonable was a scared little boy playing dress-up in adult clothes, and it was time to make fun of the fact that his glasses were five times too big for his face.

"Dude, you okay in there?" It was J.T., the Southern sweetheart, no doubt drawn by the sound of Logan punching the wall.

"Yeah, I'm fine, thanks, buddy," Logan croaked.

"Sorry, man. I know it's been a tough day."

Oh, you have no idea, brother.

An hour later, Logan walked through the front door of his apartment to find the lights already off. Donnie was sawing logs on the sofa, and Brandon was passed out on an air mattress on the floor. Until things quieted down, whoever was off duty would crash at Logan's to avoid making the commute from San Diego.

Once he was locked in his bedroom, he opened his closet to make sure the cowboy boots Connor Harcourt had given him five years ago were in the same corner where he'd kept them ever since moving into this apartment.

13

In the assistant general manager's office, directly behind reception, Gloria Alvarez and Connor were having their first extensive conversation since his return. The office was spacious and had a window looking out on to the motor court that allowed in a warm spill of sunlight. Unlike their former general manager, Gloria didn't need the privacy of a windowless office to day drink and orchestrate criminal conspiracies.

After beginning things with a long hug, their meeting had focused mostly on the state of the hotel for the last five years, but as Connor had expected, it turned into a long overdue catch-up that veered in and out of pleasant reminiscences of the old days, of Connor's father and grandfather.

In short, it was the deep breath they both needed after the chaos of his return the day before.

But there was one topic Gloria had studiously avoided until now.

"So," she said with an air of finality. "Logan."

"He told you."

"Some. I don't need the details. That's not why I brought it up. I just hope you both can get past it is all."

"We'll do what's best for the hotel."

"Good," Gloria said. "Because I'll be blunt. You need to. Both of you. He's one of the best people who's ever worked here, Connor. I heard how they ganged up on him in the department meeting. If I'd been there,

I would have had his back."

Connor was about to respond when there was a harsh knock. He opened the door and saw Donnie looking back at him, pale and wide-eyed.

"We got a visitor who's really shaking things up out here," Donnie said.

"Who?"

"Your uncle."

The last time Connor's pulse had roared in his ears like this he'd done a Barry's Bootcamp class first thing in the morning with only a Diet Coke in his stomach.

By the time he reached the lobby, there was sweat under his collar, and his throat had gone raw in that way that told him he was dangerously short of breath. He'd expected Rodney to retaliate, of course. But through the press. Not with a surprise appearance at the scene of his crimes.

Rodney wasn't alone. A tall, bespectacled man in an expensive-looking charcoal suit was next to him, and behind them both, a cameraman and the blond television reporter who'd shouted questions at Connor during the press conference the day before.

"I'm sorry, man." Donnie matched Connor step for step. "They walked up the hill so no one saw his car coming. He said some things to the reporters, then he grabbed that one there and asked if she'd come inside with him. We asked them to leave, but they're talking all kinds of shit."

The fact that Rodney had grabbed the reporter at the last minute suggested this wasn't a well-coordinated invasion. A small comfort, but a comfort nonetheless.

When Rodney saw Connor approaching, he turned and raised his arms. "The prodigal son returns!" he bellowed.

To Connor's increasing distress, his uncle had dressed like he was coming to work. Blue blazer with a bulging white pocket square and pressed khakis, along with spit-shined black dress shoes.

"Rodney, this is not a good choice." When the camera was shoved in his face, Connor was tempted to order them out as well. But the media could still be his greatest asset if he played this right. "I'd be happy to grant you a walk-through and a sit-down interview later today, but I'll need you to set up a time with one of our assistant general managers. They'll be happy to—"

"No." Rodney raised a trigger finger and swept everyone with it.

"They're with me. I'm giving them access."

"No, Rodney. You can't do that."

Rodney stepped forward and clapped a hand on both of Connor's shoulders like he used to do when Connor was ten and he was trying to steer him out of the room. "Yeah, yeah, real cute, big man. Look, fact is, all the wrong people got to you before I did, and that's why you're all confused. Tell you what. I'll let bygones be bygones, and we can call your little press conference yesterday water under the bridge. Come back to my office, we'll take a load off. Talk this out. You can fill me in on how things have been going while you've been playing your little game of hotel."

Connor tried not to let his rage enter his expression, but he couldn't quite manage a smile. "That's not going to happen."

"Oh, okay." Rodney's eyes were bloodshot, maybe from the same stuff Connor could smell on the man's breath. "Well, you can hightail it back to New York then and let me do my job, sport."

"It's not appropriate for you to be on the property right now. I need you to leave. I'm sorry."

"Yeah, no. See, you don't tell me when to leave *my* hotel."

"It's not your hotel. It's owned by a family trust. And the trust fired you two days ago."

The lawyer stepped forward. "Yeah, we'll have some things to say about that."

Connor met the man's glare with one of his own. "Good. Say them in a law office or a courtroom. Not the lobby of this hotel an hour after your client was arraigned on charges of blackmailing guests here."

Taken aback by the look in Connor's eyes, the lawyer gently gripped Rodney's elbow and tried to pull him away, a sign his commitment to this scene was wavering. If it had ever been much to begin with. "All right, Rodney. Why don't we let them have some—"

"Fuck that! I'm not going anywhere." Rodney shook his lawyer's arm off. "You think you're going to litigate our family's dirty laundry in the press? You think that's how the hotel game works, kid? How about I walk out there right now and tell them what your dad said to me when he found out you were gay? That he felt like he'd been kicked in the teeth and wished he'd had a daughter instead?"

Connor felt like he'd been slapped. "Go ahead. I'll take the mic right after you and read the letter my father wrote me before he died. The one where he explained why he and *your* dad had to rewrite the trust because they were afraid one day your criminal behavior was going to run this place into the ground."

At first, Connor thought the sudden pressure at his chest was a new surge of anxiety. Then he realized it was coming from Rodney's hand. His uncle had grabbed the lapels of his jacket with enough force to knock him off balance. Rodney's heaving breaths were whiskey rancid.

The cameraman backed up to get a better angle on them both, but the center of Connor's world had become his uncle's bulging eyes. Over and over again the lawyer said Rodney's name, but Rodney didn't seem to hear that, or anything else. He was deafened by his own rage.

"I don't know who the fuck you think you are, you little faggot, but if you don't—"

And then Rodney was gone.

He'd been whipped away. There were no other words for it. The tension at Connor's chest was also gone.

An impact shook the floor and rattled the vases of flowers on the console table nearby. That's when Connor saw that Rodney had been slammed into the nearest wall by a tidal wave of force. A tidal wave of force named Logan Murdoch.

The breath went out of Rodney in a stuttering series of gasps. Logan gripped the man's throat in one hand with a force that rendered Rodney's limbs limp and useless. To top it all off, Logan didn't even look winded by his efforts.

"You ever put a hand on Connor again and I'll break it," Logan said in a voice like low thunder. "And you ever call him a name like that again, I'll knock you into next week and wear the assault charge like a badge."

Rodney responded with a wheeze.

"You've got two choices, Mr. Harcourt. There's not a third. You can hold your chin up, walk out of this hotel and straight past those reporters without saying a damn word. Or I can throw you out so you land flat on your face and give them all the photo op they're waiting for. You've got ten seconds to pick. Or I do. And I gotta be honest, I'm leaning toward face plant."

Logan released Rodney's throat, giving him a second to regain his balance.

Pale and breathless, Rodney stumbled forward from the wall, avoiding the stunned stares of everyone in the lobby. Including Connor's. The camera swung to follow him as he shuffled through the lobby doors.

The lawyer turned toward Logan, his lips parted. The expression on

Logan's face made the lawyer blink several times, turn, and follow his client out of the lobby.

Outside, Rodney took option one. Even as they advanced on him, he didn't raise his head or say a word to the cameras. He must have realized the terrible mistake he'd made, dragging a reporter into the hotel to film him acting like the very villain Connor had described at the press conference the day before.

"Would you like to set up an interview with Connor later?" Connor heard Gloria say to the reporter.

"You know, I think we might have everything we need," the reporter said. "Thanks."

But their voices seemed far away.

All Connor saw was Logan. Big, beautiful Logan who'd unleashed a display of swift and focused power. And he'd done it without knocking a single hair of his own out of place. Gloria asked Connor if he was all right, maybe because he looked like he was in shock. He was in a way. But not from Rodney's outburst. From what Logan had done. Grabbing a force for malevolence in Connor's life and silencing it with one hand and a solid wall and threats he'd uttered with cool confidence.

Their noses were almost touching.

Logan's fingers were at Connor's neck, grazing his skin.

"I should probably get a closer look at this," he said. "See if there's a bruise."

"Yeah, totally," Connor whispered.

Connor wasn't bruised. Physically, anyway. But right now, being alone with Logan seemed like the treatment for every ailment he might ever have.

"My office." Someone else said these words, not Connor.

They walked together, side by side. Like coworkers. Like professionals. But all Connor heard were Logan's footfalls next to his, a metronome for his wild, uncontrollable desire.

When they reached their destination, Connor stepped inside first.

He turned, half expecting to see a puzzled or remote look on Logan's face that said Connor had imagined the rivers of pure desire flowing between them after Rodney stumbled out of the lobby. Instead, he saw fire in Logan's eyes, saw Logan reach behind him and slam the office door with one powerful arm, lock the deadbolt with a swipe of one fist. Saw Logan advance on him, the focused fury with which he'd incapacitated Connor's uncle turning into feral lust. A hunger that drove Connor's back to the wall as Logan advanced, ready to claim the territory he'd just defended.

Logan gripped the side of Connor's face, reached up with his other hand, and ran his fingers through Connor's hair, as if the feel of it between his fingers satisfied a long-denied craving. The silent, deliciously torturous dance sent a single message—all the power and force he'd used to drop Rodney like a rock, he could also use to send Connor into ecstasy. And he was willing to do it right here, right now. On top of his uncle's desk.

"My hero," Connor whispered.

Suddenly, their mouths were locked, but it was like they were flying. That's how powerful Logan's embrace was. Every inch of Connor's body that fell outside the radius of Logan's devouring kisses felt vaporous and free, spirit floating above skin.

When his kisses met Connor's neck and found the special spot he'd discovered years before and neglected ever since, Connor's back arched. His desperate moans turned to hungry, pleading whines.

"My hero," Connor whispered. When Logan heard these words a second time, he growled, spun Connor to face the wall, unbuckled Connor's belt, yanked his briefs down with a single, powerful tug, releasing Connor's achingly hard cock, exposing his ass to a blast of cool air quickly followed by Logan's heat. Deliciously exposed, Logan's fingers traced the crack of his ass, gently, teasingly.

"One kiss isn't going to be enough to satisfy me this time," Logan said.

Logan's fingers gently caressed his bare crack, sending cascades of pleasure up his spine, forcing desperate moans from him.

"You too, it looks like. Someone's very sensitive down here," Logan whispered.

There was a shifting and rustling behind him.

"Very, very sensitive." Logan's voice sounded like it was coming from a different place. Literally. The man had dropped to his knees behind Connor's exposed ass, and the fingers he'd been using to caress were now gripping Connor's cheeks, spreading them slightly.

Oh my God. Is he really about to—

Before Connor could finish the thought, Logan bathed the most sensitive part of his body with his tongue. Shock, alarm, and pleasure crashed into each other inside of Connor, forcing him to bite down on one clenched fist he'd pressed to the wall above his head, like a man getting arrested by desire. Logan's licks were long, hungry, and fearless, leaving Connor slick, exposed, and trembling, telling him no part of his body was shameful or off limits. That not an inch of him would escape Logan's long-delayed desire.

It was too much. It was everything. It was perfect, and it left Connor whispering curses against the wall like a man watching his every shred of reason leave him.

Then Logan's mouth was at his ear. "So what do you say, Mr. Harcourt? Do I stop? Because if I don't, I don't care if God knocks on that door, you don't leave this office until your cum is on my hands."

"Don't stop."

Logan let out an appreciative growl, then he dipped his middle fingers in between Connor's lips. With a leap in his chest, Connor realized what was to come and left them slick with spit even though he was fighting the urge to suckle them just so he could taste Logan. But the man had work to do. Logan used his lubed-up fingers to probe at Connor's entrance, letting out a surprised grunt when he felt almost no resistance. Then, slowly, working, probing, he found the seat of Connor's pleasure. Grazed it, stroked it, applied pressure all while working Connor's throbbing, leaking cock with his other hand, his mouth at Connor's neck.

As Logan intensified his ministrations, Connor straightened, rocking back until he was almost standing and riding Logan's fingers up and down. Reaching back, his hand found Logan's muscular neck and held on for dear life. He couldn't decide if he was leaving his body on waves of pleasure or being driven so deep inside of it he was discovering a place where pleasure reigned supreme. A place where there was only Logan's all-consuming embrace, powered by a reckless and relentless finger-fuck coupled with expert strokes of Connor's cock.

He was close, perilously close. In danger of crying out so loud they'd hear him in LA.

He rocked forward, releasing Logan's neck, bracing himself against the wall with both hands and clamping his mouth around the arm of his jacket, muffling the cry that was already tearing from him. He expected Logan to shush him, or at least ask him to be quiet, but the man only quickened the thrusts of his fingers and the strokes of his other hand. He was watching Connor's face, studying every change in his expression, using them to guide his probing, his stroking, his determined finger-fucking.

So often when he was alone, with only his hand and fantasy to guide him, Connor's orgasms were prolonged but stuttering. As if they fought their way through his entire body in stages, each new rush forcing another series of startled cries from him. This was an unstoppable eruption that swept him from head to toe. It wasn't a series of cries that tore from his throat, but one long moan muffled into the spit-dampened arm of his jacket.

He rocked back against Logan's body.

Logan slowly withdrew his fingers from within Connor's heat and wrapped that same arm around Connor's stomach, holding him upright while he lavished his neck with more kisses.

The combined sense of being emptied and supported made Connor feel both boneless and airborne.

"Breathe," Logan whispered. "Just breathe."

Connor was doing his best. But it was hard.

"Told you I'd finish."

And when Logan raised the hand he'd used to stroke Connor to release, his fingers were coated. For a second, Connor thought the quick search for a tissue would bring an end to their lustful reverie. But Logan didn't release him.

This time, there was no crackle of voices in Logan's earpiece. No hasty escape. This time he steered Connor to the sofa, letting him stay rag-doll limp in his arms as he settled down onto the cushions, allowing Connor to wilt against him, face down, shielding his exposed cock and balls between his legs. Once Connor was settled, he gently pulled a tissue from the box beside the sofa, using it to clean his hand. But slowly, as if he didn't want the business of it to distract from Connor's lingering bliss. The air-conditioned air still kissed his exposed ass, but Connor didn't want to move. Couldn't move. Didn't care that the distant sounds of the hotel were penetrating the office, driving home the recklessness of this act.

A moment that had started five years ago had finally come to a blissful fruition, and every orgasm Connor had experienced since had been a warmup for this one. And now, if either one of them tried to run, there'd be a lot more to run from.

But neither one of them was running. They were lying in each other's arms as if they never planned to run again.

14

"I have something to confess," Logan finally said.

Connor's head shot up from where it had been resting against Logan's chest for several peaceful minutes now. "Now? *After* the finger banging?"

"Maybe I should have said something earlier," Logan said.

"That depends on what it is."

Connor, Logan could tell, was three seconds away from being pissed. If Logan didn't pull this off quickly, it wouldn't be any fun.

"I made up a fake account so I could follow you on Instagram."

Relief brightened Connor's smile. His laughter warmed Logan's heart. "I knew it."

"I wanted to see what you were up to," Logan said.

"My account's not private. You could check it out anytime you wanted."

"Yeah, but I didn't want to miss anything," Logan said.

"What's your profile name?"

"Palm Tree Guy."

"And that means what exactly?" Connor asked.

"It means the only things on my account are pictures of the palm trees I took outside my building really quick. Every few months I'd add another one. I actually have followers. They must be really into trees."

"I love it."

"Don't gloat just because I was obsessed," Logan said.

"I'm not gloating. It's cute. You're like, all, Mister Manly Marine Guy, and then you're Instagram stalking me like some high schooler."

"Well, I have to confess," Logan said. "I was pretty pumped there was never a boyfriend in the pictures."

"Yeah, well, there weren't any. Not really."

"Not even one?" Logan asked.

"There were opportunities. None of them panned out."

"Opportunities. Wow. How romantic. Did they come with dental?"

"Let's just say I keep my Instagram work focused, all right?" Connor said. "What about you?"

"I'm not officially on Instagram, remember?" Logan tightened his embrace around the man he'd longed to lie with like this for years.

"I meant boyfriends, silly."

"None, but I do have a couple of wives and a bunch of kids sprinkled all over Southern California. The holidays are nuts."

"Logan."

Logan thought of glacier-sized piles of other people's dirty laundry and strange litter box smells and guys who talked to him like he was either a piece of meat or an obligatory inconvenience. "No boyfriend. Just the apps."

"Ah, I see."

Maybe Connor was jealous at the thought of Logan banging random hookups, but if so, he was keeping it to himself.

"What did you think I was going to say?" Logan asked. "When I said I had something to confess?"

"That you were hooking up with that guy who works out on the pool deck."

"Which guy?"

"The one with the floppy blond hair and the pretty blue eyes. I haven't met them all yet."

"Spencer Chase? That guy's like a feather. I'd snap him in half."

"He's pretty, though," Connor said.

"You apparently think so."

"I don't. I just…I don't know. I guess it seemed like you two would have chemistry. Or compatibility, at least. Close quarters and all that."

"What kind of chemistry? The guy's so…gentle. I like 'em sassy and mouthy and relentless." To emphasize his point, Logan stopped running his fingers through Connor's hair and gripped his head, giving it a little shake. "Besides, I don't play around at work."

Connor's eyebrows arched. "Oops."

"This isn't playing around." Logan cupped Connor's chin in one hand. "I'm not, at least."

Connor's gaze softened, a brightness coming into his eyes. "I'm not either. But technically, we're in the post-sex-glow period where people say all sorts of stuff they…haven't thought through, so let's catch our breath before we try to figure out what we just did."

"Technically, *you're* in the post-sex-glow period because I didn't cum."

"And trust me, I would love nothing more than to rectify that injustice. But if we stay in this office any longer, the staff of this hotel's going to figure out you aren't just consoling me." Connor sat up, trying to pull himself together.

"Well, I was. But in my own special way."

It looked like Connor wanted to give Logan a consoling pat on the chest. But he wasn't paying attention to where his hand went, so it landed atop the bulging tent Logan's cock made inside of his jeans. Connor turned his head quickly, like he'd touched a snake that had coiled quickly around his wrist and he couldn't move to get away.

As if against his will, he started stroking Logan's khaki-encased cock.

"Just a peek," Connor whispered, unzipping Logan's pants. "Just one little peek to see if…" Logan's cock emerged into the cool air, veiny and achingly hard. "Oh my God. It is. It so is. Wow." Stroking it gently, he looked right into Logan's eyes. "You're so much bigger than your dad."

"What?" Logan sat up so quickly he forced Connor into the other arm of the sofa. He managed to stuff his cock back inside his pants as he wrestled Connor to the cushions. Meanwhile Connor was cackling like a hyena, his cherubic cheeks flushing bright red.

"I'm sorry, I'm sorry," he gasped. "I don't have time to blow you and I totally want to, but we have to get back to work, so I thought I'd find another way to make it go down. Also, it really *is* an amazing dick, and I don't want you to get a big head about it, so I thought I'd throw you off center a little."

"How's this for off center?" Logan attacked Connor's stomach with tickle fingers.

"No. Don't. Tickling makes me pee."

Logan stopped. "All right, well, we're still learning things about each other, I guess."

"Yeah, like how hot your dad is," Connor said.

"Stop talking about my dad!"

Grinning, Connor nodded as if he was taking this proposal under consideration but wasn't sure he could commit yet. God, the guy was adorable. The more he gazed up into Logan's eyes, his devilish sarcasm faded, replaced by a look of vulnerability that made everything inside of Logan want to protect him. Again. And again.

"What are we going to do about this, Logan?" Connor asked.

"Are you experiencing regret, Mr. Harcourt?"

"Let me rephrase the question. What are we going to do about the fact that we're going to do this again and again and again? I hope. And work together."

"I've added a new professional responsibility."

"All right, now, let's be clear. In case HR's listening in, you do not have a professional responsibility to have sex with me."

"Connor, at the rate Sapphire Cove's going, our HR rep is probably human trafficking people."

"You know what I mean. Sex with me is not a requirement of your job."

"I do, and that's not what I meant."

"I'm listening," Connor said.

One arm around Connor's shoulders, Logan settled back against the sofa, forcing Connor to do the same. Connor turned to look at him until they were nose to nose, the little gap of distance they'd managed to keep between themselves these past twenty-four hours now permanently abolished. "I just pissed off a very angry criminal with nothing left to lose, and he's about to get destroyed in the media over that incident in the lobby. I also happen to have it on good authority he owns several firearms. So until he's either done something stupid enough to land himself back in jail or his lawyers and the hotel reach some kind of agreement, you don't leave my sight, Baby Blues. You're a high-value target now. And that means you're under my constant protection. Twenty-four seven."

"Well, isn't that convenient." Connor was grinning.

"Indeed. For both of us. And in light of all that, it would be reckless for us not to act on our feelings for each other, because to not do so might drive us apart. And right now, we simply can't be separated. And therefore, we're going to need to constantly...vent these feelings, hopefully in a more reciprocal fashion so the frustration doesn't drive us apart either."

"Should we put all that in writing?" Connor asked.

"Hell, no."

"All right, well, I'm not sure I can let you follow me for every step," Connor said.

"Good luck stopping me."

Logan bent down and kissed him long and hard, fighting the desire to tear Connor's clothes all the way off this time. Connor's hand traveled to the bulge in Logan's crotch, but lightly, as if he was saying goodbye. For now. Which was a perfect opportunity for what Logan was going to say next.

"Oh, don't worry about that. I'll have Spencer Chase take care of it down in the sea caves."

"Logan!"

Rage lit up Connor's eyes as he closed his hand around Logan's bulge.

"Stop, stop," Logan bellowed. "I was just getting you back for the dad thing."

They were seated upright now, noses touching.

"I guess I deserved that," Connor said.

"Kinda, yeah."

"But Logan, what you did in the lobby…I mean, I've had a good life, but that's the first time anyone's ever really stuck up for me like that."

Logan kissed him again, gently this time. "Yeah, well, there's plenty more firsts where that came from."

Then, before either of them could get in another wisecrack to deflect from the gravity of their feelings, Logan slipped free of Connor's embrace.

"Wait here," Logan said. "I'm going to go make sure the lobby's really clear and see if there's been any fallout."

"All right, after that, I'm going to visit the guests who lost houses last night."

"We're going to visit the guests who lost houses last night."

Connor grinned. "Wow. So you're really serious about this security routine."

"As serious as that orgasm you just had." With a half bow, Logan stepped carefully from the office and pulled the door shut before Connor could protest.

15

For a solid two hours, the visits went surprisingly well. It helped that Connor and Logan arrived with two room service waiters bearing trays of cookies and tea services from a well-stocked rolling cart. Less enthusiastically received was the news that mental health counselors were already on site and willing to talk to the grieving guests individually. And no one seemed interested in the larger group meeting scheduled that evening for those who'd lost homes.

One woman, a single mother with three young children, actually threw her arms around Connor when he told her they were moving her to a larger villa until she figured out her next housing option. Connor accepted this attention with the restrained dignity of a seasoned politician. And Logan, matching him step for step, felt like his Secret Service detail. Which Logan loved. It allowed them to stay close, turning their moment of frenzied passion into something steadier and constant.

No running this time, no awkward text messages giving way to a half decade of silence and obsession. No hovering in the open door of a Rolls-Royce wondering what might have been.

But aside from enjoying their nearness, Logan was checking entrances and exits, stepping silently between Connor and the sliding glass doors in each room, shielding him from whoever might be lurking outside. He hoped he was overreacting, but he'd seen something terrifying in Rodney's eyes when he'd held the man to the lobby wall. Something that reminded Logan of his fellow vets who'd treated their PTSD with a combination of booze and harder things. Men who'd convinced themselves they had nothing left to live for.

But Logan didn't regret defending Connor. Not for a moment. Rodney's insane spiral was well underway by then, from the moment he thought it would be a good idea to show up drunk, ready to begin a day's work at a place that had fired him.

And it made him happy, truly happy, to watch Connor claim the position his uncle had tried to deny him.

After two hours, there was only one name left on the visit list. A woman named Donna Langdon. According to some of the staff who'd talked with her the night before, she was a widow and a retiree, and along with her home, she'd lost a painting studio full of her canvases. She wasn't in her guest room when they knocked. A few texts with the front desk and the waitstaff inside Camilla's and someone finally reported her sitting outside by the pool. Alone.

They found her on one of the lounge chairs nearest the cliff's edge, giving the beautiful ocean view a thousand-yard stare. It was clear she wasn't seeing sparkling blue water and whitecaps rolling toward shore, but the smoldering ruins of a decimated home she hadn't yet been cleared to visit. She had a proud, hard profile, and her hair was a great gray mane she'd tied back with a scrunchie. In younger years, it had probably been blond, making her look even more like a lady Viking than she did now.

At first, she didn't react to their approach. Logan sensed, right away, that this visit wouldn't be as easy as the others, and his protective feelings for Connor surged.

Connor took the tea tray to her himself. When he set it down on the lounger next to hers, she waved a hand at him without looking at him. "Yeah, yeah, yeah. You've had your big show with us. There's no need, really. And I hate tea. It tastes like half of something."

Connor took a seat beside the tray, as if he too wanted to stare meditatively at the view. A few paces away was where Logan stayed, mostly because he didn't want the hostile woman to feel crowded. Also, it gave him a better view of their surroundings. The pool wasn't quite as crowded as it had been after breakfast. But it had plenty of side entrances through which a drunken Rodney could emerge in search of Round Two.

"Seriously," Donna Langdon said, "you can drop the whole nursemaid routine. It's not my first time at the misery rodeo."

"We have coffee too," Connor offered. "And Diet Coke. And

whiskey."

"I'm fine."

"I'm sorry it feels like a show."

"Isn't it?" she asked. "I mean, no offense, but after my house burned to the ground, it wasn't like I was going to keep watching wildfire coverage. Like, here's Donna house. Still burned to the ground. So I looked up this place. Your uncle's an ass, by the way."

Connor nodded. "That he is."

"But still, I don't appreciate being used like this. I mean, that's what this is, right? You brought us all in here yesterday in front of the cameras, and now you're coming to ask me to leave."

"No."

"What then?" she asked.

"I'm going to move you to a much bigger room until you have your housing figured out, and I'm going to offer you free spa services for as long as you're here. Along with the three meals a day and everything else."

Donna Langdon seemed genuinely surprised. "For how long?"

"As long as you need a place to stay."

"You say that now…"

"I'll say it three months from now if I need to."

"Why?" she asked.

"Because you lost your house, and it feels like the right thing to do. And you came alone, and no one's been to visit you yet."

That he'd gone to the trouble of finding out this additional personal detail caused her to flinch and look back out to sea. "Why you, though? I mean, come on, this whole thing is about making this place look good."

"Maybe. In part. Or maybe it's bigger than that."

"How?" she asked.

"Maybe it's about this place actually *doing* good. Maybe in a place where people did very bad things, the ones who're left behind, the ones who are innocent, need to do a really good thing, to clear the air. Kind of like burning sage."

"Really? A burning sage reference to a woman whose house just burned down?" But she was smiling when she said it. She was a salty one, this Donna Langdon.

Connor sputtered with laughter. "Granted. Not the best choice of words."

"You sure had a lot of empty rooms," she said. "You must have lost a lot of business over all this."

"We did. We are."

"I guess I can't blame you then. You're trying to keep from losing what's yours."

There was a catch in her voice, but she didn't cry. Connor gave her a moment. Maybe he thought she was about to start.

"You know, to be honest," he finally said, "this place has been a colossal pain in my ass over the years. I can't remember a time when my family wasn't worried sick about it. When they felt like it wasn't good enough, wasn't doing well enough. How The Ritz was going to eat our lunch, and then the Montage was going to wipe us off the map. Honestly, when it comes to Sapphire Cove, I'm not sure I'd be that sorry to let go of it. It'd be a hell of a lot more profitable to sell it, rather than trying to keep it open when it's this wounded."

Part of Logan was shocked to hear this, but another part of him—a part that was getting to know Connor better and better with each passing hour—figured he was heading someplace unexpected with this speech. "But it's my dad, you know. And my grandfather. They're both gone, and this place is them through and through. When they died, we weren't on the greatest of terms, and there was a lot of stuff we probably should have said to each other. Losing this place, it would be losing memories of them I can never get back." He looked over his shoulder and met Logan's gaze. "And some other memories I don't want to let go of."

Because he was well within Donna's eyeline, Logan tried to keep his expression professional, but he failed. He could feel it in his cheeks. But it didn't matter. Donna was watching Connor closely, hanging on his every word.

"In the end," Connor said, meeting her stare, "places are about the people, right?"

Donna Langdon didn't say anything for a while, but she didn't look at the ocean again. She looked at Connor, studying him, gauging his sincerity. Her stare was glassy-eyed, and it was starting to gain a sheen.

"I lost my son," she finally said. "A year ago."

Connor nodded.

"He hit his head surfing. I mean, how fucking California is that, right?" Donna tried to crack a smile, but it didn't quite take, even though Logan was pretty sure she'd used the joke countless times to defuse her grief. "Most of my pictures of him, they were in my studio at the back of the house. I couldn't get them in time. I waited too long. Because of my *fucking* lemon trees. Every month, those damn people from the city were by, telling me I had to cut them back because of fire danger. I didn't tell them why I couldn't bring myself to do it."

"Because your son used to do it," Connor said.

Donna nodded, and that's when the tears finally came, and that's when Connor reached across the space between them and took one of her hands, and she yielded it without protest.

"You're right," she managed. "It's not the house, it's the people. It's the memories."

Connor stood up slowly and shifted to Donna's lounger so he could put his arm around her back.

Logan figured it was the woman's first good hard cry since she'd gotten the news.

"I'll take that whiskey now," she finally said.

If they'd planned it, Logan would have felt weird about it. But they didn't, so when the photo a guest snapped of Connor with his arm curved around a weeping Donna Langdon went viral later that day, it seemed like a just reward for all the efforts the hotel was making on behalf of the Palm Fire's victims. If anyone wanted to question the photo's authenticity to his face, Logan would be happy to describe the candor and vulnerability Connor had mustered to create that genuine moment, and the fact that they'd both sat with Donna for an hour and ended up gently convincing her to talk with one of the counselors on site.

No doubt the emerging image of Connor Harcourt as a compassionate hero was also being aided by his depiction as a victim. After its first airing on a midday LA newscast, video footage of Rodney Harcourt slurring and assaulting his nephew had been reposted and condemned by every marginally famous LGBT person with a social media presence, and a bunch of the straight ones too. Logan, the hunky hero, as several meme makers had already named him, was also coming off pretty well. There were already Photoshopped images of him pinning various villains from history to the wall of Sapphire Cove's lobby. He was particularly fond of the one that put a digital version of Adolf Hitler convincingly in Rodney's place.

Meanwhile, the Stop Sapphire Cove Twitter account seemed to be struggling for a toehold. The night before, it had managed to get some late-night traction over allegations the hotel was manipulating wildfire victims for its own PR purposes, but Rodney's meltdown that morning had thrown cold water on this fresh outrage. The account's latest tweets asserted Rodney's scene in the lobby had been staged, but they weren't getting much traction, maybe because some of the evacuees currently being housed at the hotel had started responding with statements about how well the hotel was treating them.

"Are you going to tell me what happened in his office earlier or not?" Donnie asked.

Logan was standing guard outside Connor's office when Donnie snuck up on him from behind.

"Nope," Logan said.

"Later then." Donnie nodded as if it wasn't a question.

"Maybe. If we can have a judgment-free zone."

"Oh, shit. You fucked him, didn't you? God, you're so dumb. You're going to end up working for your dad and you guys are going to yell at each other for the rest of your lives until one of you chokes on a sandwich 'cause you're trying to get the last word in."

Logan looked to Connor's closed office door. Inside, Connor was meeting with Jonas Jacobs about the two upcoming conferences poised to save the hotel's bacon. The low murmur of their voices continued, indicating they hadn't heard Donnie's accusations.

"I didn't *fuck* him, okay?" Logan said. "So relax."

"Aw, that's so sweet. What'd you guys do instead? Snuggle and write your initials inside hearts?"

"I'm sorry, fuckhead, but do we live on a planet where you've never slept with one of your models? 'Cause I don't remember you having some huge dividing line between sex and work, porn star."

"I don't sleep with my models."

"That's right. You wait until at least two days after their last shoot with you."

Suddenly, Donnie grimaced and grunted at the same time. "Crap. Listen. Tell your dad I'm sorry I can't make his thing tonight. Before the Sapphire shit storm here, I thought I'd have time to pack all the gear for the Mexico shoot today, but since I was here I didn't—"

"His *thing*." Logan gripped his forehead. "Dammit, I totally forgot."

Every year on the anniversary of opening his first Chip's Kicks location, his dad got some of their close friends together for a celebratory dinner. Tonight was that anniversary. The crowd wasn't supposed to be that big: two of his dad's closest friends, Jed and Petey, who'd both helped him knock out drywall at his first location; the woman Jed had started dating a few weeks ago, who was meeting the group for the first time; and Donnie, who was technically Logan's obligatory plus one, given his dad still referred to him privately as Porn Donnie or Your Porn Friend. There were other bigger dinners and parties throughout the year for the gym's management and staff, but tonight's was about the people who were in his dad's life when it changed course for the better. A tiny group, and any absence, especially Logan's, would be hard felt.

"Connor'll let you go," Donnie offered.

"I'm not letting Connor out of my sight."

"Dude. It was one hookup, and he's been back a day. Maybe slow your roll."

"No, man. Rodney's out there off his damn rocker, getting his ass handed to him in the press. I'm not letting him walk around unprotected."

"Also, you're banging him," Donnie said.

"I'm not just banging him. I'm picking up where we left off. Finally."

Donnie stared at him. He was either holding back a smart comment or trying to come up with one.

"All right," Logan finally said, "tell me what you really think. No bullshit."

"You don't have to tell me that he's the one you've never been able to get out of your head. Believe me, I know. I'm the one who's there when you bring him up as this perfect guy who got away. And honestly, I'd always hoped something like this would happen. I mean, not like this, but that he'd come back. And to be *really* honest, I kind of thought that might be the only reason you stayed here after they passed you over for the promotion."

Maybe it was. But only in part, and Logan didn't want to butt in to argue nuance when Donnie was giving him real talk.

"It's also why I stopped trying to set you up with anybody. I knew a part of you froze over after him, and you were either going to have to see him again and realize he wasn't what you remembered or get another shot. And I want this to be a second chance for you guys. I really do. But it's only been twenty-four hours. Don't lose your head yet."

"Okay."

"And figure out the thing with your dad tonight."

Connor and Jonas emerged from his office. Jonas smiled and nodded in their direction, then gave Donnie a quick once-over. Jonas was perhaps one of the most private employees at Sapphire Cove. The idea that he might be familiar with Donnie's work was new information, indeed.

Then Jonas was gone, and Donnie was approaching Connor with one hand extended. "Well, Mr. Harcourt, as much as I'm grateful for this exciting peek into the hospitality industry, I'm afraid I must now return to the hallowed halls of man-on-man on-camera action."

Connor sputtered with laughter as he shook Donnie's hand.

"I take it we've replaced you with someone with a comparable personality," Connor said, but it was directed at Logan.

"I'm not sure that's possible," Logan said. "The personality part, anyway. But we've got coverage."

"Now remember the rules when it comes to Logan, Mr. Harcourt."

Logan took a step toward them. "Donnie, let's just—"

"Don't feed him after midnight. Don't insult the United States Marine Corps. Don't make fun of his tattoo, even though it's dumb. And do not, under any circumstances, let him pick the music in the car, because he's got garbage taste."

"Says the guy who showers to Blink-182," Logan grumbled.

"I'll make a note of all that." Connor was clearly charmed.

Donnie turned to Logan and gave him an aggressive bear hug, which, it turned out, was designed to bring his mouth to Logan's ear. "He still looks like Grown-up Tintin. Have a blast, Cap'n," he whispered.

"I fucking hate you, dude," Logan whispered back. Then he grabbed the back of Donnie's neck in one hand and turned him toward the nearest exit.

Once Donnie was gone, Connor's smile faded. "Can I see you in my office, please?"

Worried Connor had overheard their chitchat, Logan did as instructed, braced for an uncomfortable conversation. Instead, Connor threw the door shut with almost as much force as Logan had used that morning and gave him a kiss that made Logan's head spin.

"As much as I'd love to do more, this kiss couldn't wait until we're alone," Connor said.

"We kind of are alone," Logan pointed out.

"We need a bigger radius than this. Believe me, I'd love to hit my knees and prove that half of what my uncle said about me this morning is absolutely true, but we have to maintain some sense of decorum at work."

"Sounds sensible. Just let me go jerk off in the head real quick."

Connor palmed Logan's crotch. "I will take very good care of this one later. I promise." Connor withdrew, took a seat at his desk, and popped his laptop open. "But right now I have to figure out if it's worth the effort to try to corral the guests who lost their homes into meeting with these mental health counselors. So far, they haven't exactly warmed to the idea of therapy."

The office phone's intercom tone chimed.

Connor answered. His expression turned grave.

"Sure. We'll be right out," he finally said, then hung up.

"Not Rodney again," Logan said.

"Not quite. It's the FBI."

Logan's heart hammered. Were they about to endure more arrests?

The FBI agents who'd interviewed Logan briefly on the day of the raid were waiting for them by the front desk, but without their battalion of friends in FBI windbreakers.

Connor introduced himself, shaking the hands of both agents, and Logan did the same. Then they all stared at each other awkwardly for a beat. "Are we going to need lawyers for this?" Connor finally asked.

"No," Agent Ward said, "but we might need someplace private."

A few minutes later, the four of them were in one of the conference center's smaller meeting rooms. The one in which they'd held yesterday's staff meeting had been converted into a daycare and playroom.

"Mr. Harcourt, have you had any further contact with your uncle after this morning's altercation?" Agent Ward asked.

"None. Why? What's going on?"

"What about you, Mr. Murdoch?" Ward asked.

"Not a peep. And I'm not expecting one."

The agents exchanged a knowing look. Logan's heart dropped.

"Your uncle broke the law when he visited the hotel this morning," Agent Ward said.

"I haven't had time to file a restraining order," Connor said. "Or charge him with assault."

"A condition of your uncle's bail was home confinement. He was under orders from the court to proceed directly to his residence after his arraignment and receive an ankle monitor. He did neither of those things. Instead he came here. And he hasn't been seen or heard from since."

"Have you talked to his lawyer?" Connor asked.

"His lawyer quit."

"That's rich," Connor said. "His lawyer was with him this morning."

Logan took another step toward Connor, thanking his lucky stars they were in a meeting room with no windows. "They also left together," he said. "I confirmed it with our staff. Where did the lawyer drop him off?"

"He's saying they had a physical altercation as well, and he had no choice but to eject Rodney from his vehicle before they reached Rodney's house."

"Cute story," Logan said.

Agent Ward closed his eyes and nodded, as if he didn't believe it either.

"So nobody knows where Rodney is," Connor said.

"We're currently unaware of his whereabouts, and we thought you all should be advised," Agent Ward said.

"Don't suppose you're going to help us with any protective measures here at the hotel," Logan said.

"We're keeping an eye on the hotel. Don't worry."

If the agents hadn't been present, Logan would have taken Connor in his arms right there. After some brusque goodbyes and the departure of both men, Logan did just that.

"Shit," Connor whispered into Logan's shirt.

"Like I said, you don't leave my sight."

"I take it we've changed the locks at this place," Connor said.

"All the exterior doors are key card access. We changed the codes for those as soon as the trust told us he'd been terminated. Inside the perimeter are some manual locks. We'll have locksmiths out tomorrow. And the install of the new camera system starts in an hour. We can both supervise. But in the meantime, like I said—"

"I know." Connor lifted his face from Logan's chest, staring at him with those big blue eyes that made Logan want to carry him to the penthouse suite and call it a day. "I don't leave your sight. I promise. But do you really think Rodney's going to come back here?"

"It's not the hotel he'd be after. It's us. But luckily, I've got skills."

"That you do."

This kiss felt more daring and electric, maybe because they faced the risk of someone walking in at any moment. Which reminded Logan that the door was unlocked. He gently pulled away from Connor, moved to it, and locked it.

"Oh, wow," Connor said. "Round two? Really?"

"As much as I'd love to, I'm securing the room while we're in here. I've got to call my dad, if that's okay." Logan tugged his phone from the inside pocket of his blazer.

"You think he's in danger too?" Connor asked.

"No. He has a thing tonight, and I need to tell him I won't be there."

"A thing?" Connor asked.

"It's a dinner. It's like an anniversary for his business, and I'm supposed to be there."

"Logan, I don't want you to miss that. One of the other guys can stay with me."

For the first time, Logan realized that prospect would mean leaving the guy he was crazy about under the protection of gorgeous former porn stars he'd recognized upon their first meeting. Wanting to seem protective instead of jealous, Logan swallowed the thought.

"The other guys are ripped, but none of them have fight training. I've got some interviews lined up for the morning that will hopefully change that."

"Bring them here," Connor suggested.

"The interviews are here," Logan said.

"No, your dad and his crew, I mean. How many people is it?"

"Five now that Donnie can't go," Logan said.

"Okay, well, I'm not exactly comfortable wining and dining with family and friends in the middle of the hotel right now, but we could set it up in my suite. The table in there seats six. Room service can cater. God knows they've got the food. And it's pretty good food, right?"

"I don't want you bankrupting the hotel for my dad."

"It's six people, Logan. It's not going to bankrupt the hotel. Everything else I'm doing, *that's* going to bankrupt the hotel."

"Yeah, but…"

"But what?" Connor asked.

"My dad is an acquired taste," Logan said.

"Like spinach?" Connor asked.

"Spinach isn't an acquired taste. I love spinach."

"Let's stay focused. You're warning me about your dad. Why?"

"He's intense. He makes up nicknames for people, and they're not always appropriate. And he says stuff about me to people that's embarrassing."

"Oh, I see. So *you're* the one with the embarrassing dad?" Connor asked.

"He's a little rough around the edges is what I'm saying."

"Okay. I think I'm getting it."

"I don't know if you are," Logan said.

"No, your dad's a salt of the earth kinda guy, and I flew here in a private plane, and you're afraid we won't get along."

"You flew here in a private plane?" Logan asked.

"It was nothing. My mom panicked because she thought she couldn't get me here in time. She'll do this sometimes."

"Fly you places in private planes?" Logan asked.

"No, drop five million in one swoop on something ridiculous, and then she'll go back to living like a pauper for a year."

"Oh, yeah, I know. My dad does that all the time. He'll be sitting there on the sofa and then all of a sudden it's, like, should I have some Cheetos or spend five million dollars?"

If any more sarcasm had dripped from Logan's tone, it would be puddling on the floor at his feet, but Connor seemed amused.

"So this is the issue, isn't it?" Connor asked. "You're afraid your dad and I are from different worlds, and we're going to tear you down the middle like a *West Side Story* thing."

"He says crazy shit that's kind of right on the line, Connor. He's a grumpy fuck."

"Like what does he say?" Connor said.

"Like he says that my type of guy always talks like he's about to burp glitter."

"I always sound like I'm about to burp glitter?" Connor asked.

"Not to me, but to his crazy mind, maybe."

"Okay. Don't ever tell Naser that because he will never stop with it."

"Naser wouldn't dare. He sounds the same way."

"Oh, so, Naser's your type too?" Connor asked.

"Listen, since we're doing this whole thing on fast forward anyway, can we fast forward through your baseless jealousies? I didn't spend five years crying to Donnie over too many beers about how *Naser* was the one I let get away."

"You cried over me?" Connor asked.

"A little. Now and then."

"Cool," Connor said with a smile.

"All right, now."

"Okay, seriously, then," Connor said. "I have to ask. Was this whole *different worlds* thing in your head five years ago? Or were your dad's medical bills the only issue?"

"Maybe. I don't know. But this is a fact, Connor. My dad is seriously a pain in the ass. And you've got a lot of pains in your ass right now already."

"Well, I can think of one I really want to add later."

Logan closed the distance between them and gripped one of Connor's shoulders with the hand that wasn't holding his phone. "And you will get it, Mr. Harcourt. I promise you. But in the meantime, I'd like to maybe start a new trend and have conversations about sex with you that don't mention *my dad*. Like at all."

"Deal. We can test that tonight when you bring him here for dinner. Does that work for you?" Connor asked.

"We're going to find out. Once you spend an hour with my dad…"

"Well, we'll have to see what the city officials say. It might not be a full hour. I might be in and out coordinating stuff."

"Then *we'll* be in and out," Logan corrected, "and he'll have to understand."

"Sounds like a plan."

Logan smiled.

"Would you like some privacy?" Connor asked.

"Stay right there," Logan said as he put a bit of distance between them. "Don't move an inch."

Connor dropped his arms to his sides and sucked in a deep breath, as if he planned to stay wherever Logan told him to for the foreseeable future. And that fact made Logan happy in more ways than one.

16

It took twenty minutes of discussion, a fair share of which bordered on heated, but Logan finally agreed to let Connor set up for the dinner party alone in the penthouse suite, with Joel, who Logan had promoted from maintenance, standing guard outside the door. It helped that Joel was a former college football player who dabbled in mixed martial arts on the weekends and had a glare that could stop a train. But Connor's assurances he wouldn't leave the room until Logan got back sealed the deal.

When he'd called to propose the change of venue earlier that day, Logan's dad had agreed, but in a guarded, neutral tone, using phrases like "If that's what you need."

Logan knew the signs. His dad would find a way to punish him later.

Later, it turned out, was immediately upon his arrival at Sapphire Cove that evening.

Chip Murdoch stepped from the driver's seat of his buddy Jed's Nissan Sentra wearing a suspicious scowl. As for the rest of his outfit, he wasn't dressed in what he would've worn if they'd stuck to their original plan to visit his favorite steak house, a circa 1950 hole in the wall where you could still smell the cigarette smoke from days of yore and the red leather booths seemed to sprout fresh holes before each visit. Blue jeans, maybe a braided belt and one of his nicer polo shirts, possibly a Chip's Kicks baseball hat if he didn't feel like running gel through his hair.

Instead, he'd run gel through his hair. And dressed in his one unbleach-damaged pair of black jeans and a red and green plaid dress shirt he hadn't donned since Logan was in high school, possibly for Logan's graduation. Someone had even ironed it. Not Chip, because he didn't know how.

And that's when it hit Logan for the first time.

Sapphire Cove intimidated the hell out of his old man.

"It's so pink," Chip said by way of greeting.

"Good to see you too, Pop."

"Has it always been this pink?" the man grumbled.

"They didn't paint the outside during the renovation. You've never been here?"

"No, you never brought me here," his dad said.

It sounded like an accusation.

Because it was.

Before Logan could respond, Jed Frye, all six foot five and three hundred pounds of him, was pumping Logan's arm and introducing his new girlfriend, Linda, a mature silver-haired beauty, who'd gotten a nice blowout for the evening. Her silver and white floral print midi dress had billowy sleeves and rhinestones studded through the flowers across the chest. She gave Logan a nervous smile as they were introduced. But the way she kept studying Chip suggested she was somewhat relieved she wouldn't have to deal with the scrutiny of being the group's new addition now that Logan's dad was being ornery.

Petey DiGiovanni stepped forward next, the Laurel to Jed's Hardy, about the size of Connor, with thick glasses and a spray of salt and pepper hair tumbling from underneath the fisherman's hat he never went anywhere without. Both guys had been his dad's friends since they were practically teenagers. Guys he'd run with, done construction gigs with, drunk way too much Wild Turkey with until they all came to their senses. Now both men worked low-stress jobs for Chip's Kicks that allowed them to live lives with the pace of retirement. And their shared history meant they knew to ignore the old man when he acted like a grouch.

Chip turned to watch the valet drive off with Jed's car, as if he thought the guy might be stealing it. Then, as if nobody had introduced themselves to Logan or even spoken, he said, "You'd bring me to the employee Christmas party, but it was never here, and when I asked you why not, you'd say who wants to go to a holiday party at the place they work every day."

"Is that really how I sounded?" Logan asked. "In this conversation I don't remember having?"

"Someone's kinda hungry," Jed said under his breath.

"Or *crungry,* as I tell my kids," Linda offered. Then, nervously, she extended a hand in Chip's direction. "Not that you're being childish, Chip."

"Don't feel bad, Linda," Logan said. "He's totally being childish."

Jed patted her on the back. Linda's smile became a grimace as she looked at her feet.

"I'm not hungry because I already ate," Chip said.

"Seriously?" This pissed Logan off. "You ate before your big dinner? They're knocking themselves out in the kitchen for you."

"Yeah, well, I don't know what kind of food they have at this place. It's probably all snails on a bed of baby blankets or something."

Logan turned to Chip's crew. "Do me a favor, folks. Follow me but walk like ten or twelve steps back."

All three of them nodded, relieved to be distanced from their friend's sour mood, if only for a few seconds.

As they entered the lobby, Logan's arm firmly wrapped around his father's upper back, Chip flinched at every sudden movement, studying each passing guest as if he thought they might throw paint on him. When he saw the lobby wasn't filled with couture-clad swimsuit models and their wealthy European husbands but harried evacuees and their children and pets, he seemed to relax a little. But just a little.

"What's going on with you, Pop?" Logan asked.

"I don't know. Being here's weird," Chip said.

"Why?" Logan asked.

"This has always been your world," Chip grumbled.

"Since when is my world not your world?" Logan asked.

"Since you never brought me here," Chip answered.

"You never asked to come here."

"Because it didn't seem like my kinda place."

"Which means you didn't want to come," Logan said.

"No, it means I thought I'd feel out of place if I came, and I do, all right?"

"Why? I mean, Christ, a dog just peed over there," Logan said.

"Oh, okay. So I'm on par with the pissing dog. Thanks, son."

"Dad, I swear to God with you right now."

"I...I don't know, it feels weird here. The floor's so shiny and nice, I feel like we're going to get charged for walking on it, and this shirt. Why am I wearing this damn shirt? I haven't worn it in, like, fifteen years. It smells like closet."

"Actually, it smells like Polo," Logan said. "A lot of it."

"That's because Petey went Rambo on me with the cologne bottle when it came off the hanger smelling like mothballs." Petey threw up his hands and rolled his eyes, which Chip didn't notice because he was still too busy suspiciously studying their surroundings. "It's your damn cologne, by the way. You left it at my place when you moved."

"It's fine," Logan said. "I don't wear Polo anymore."

"Oh, yeah, no. You probably switched to something fancier now."

Logan stopped and turned his father toward him. "Old man, you either knock off this routine or I'm going to pitch you headfirst over the cliff."

"Oh, you have cliffs here too. You have *everything* at Sapphire Cove."

"We're trying to have a special night for you," Logan said.

"We were going to have a special night at The Scarlet Inn," Chip whined.

"The Scarlet Inn is a shit hole. They have a *B* from the health department."

"Ah, whatever. That's 'cause they didn't bribe the guy."

"Right. 'Cause they were too busy giving him ptomaine."

Chip looked at Logan like he'd kicked a puppy. "It's my place. How can you talk about my place like that?"

"It's not your place. You just make us eat there because the hostesses treat you like a rock star."

"Yeah, well, maybe that's what I deserve on my special night."

"Logan." Petey spoke up from behind them. Amazing that his Jersey accent had not dimmed in the slightest even after decades on the West Coast. "Don't pay attention to him. He's just being Chip. You go ahead and take us to whatever froufrou, fancy pants, hot pink dining room with big sparkly flowers you've got picked out for us. Who cares if it all looks like a Barbie car?"

"All right, don't you start too, Petey," Logan warned.

Petey shrugged in a manner suggesting his choice of words wasn't meant to be confrontational, something he also did when he innocently called someone he hadn't meant to start a fight with a stupid fuckface.

"Is anything here *not* pink?" Chip asked.

"Or white?" Jed asked.

"Boys," Linda chided.

"Okay." Logan waved his hands in the air. "Okay, here's what I propose. Dad, you're right. It's your special night. We should do what you want. So the deal is this. Connor and I thought we'd be stuck here 'cause there was a chance we'd have to rearrange some rooms if they reopened parts of the evacuation zone. But we found out a few minutes ago that's not happening tonight. So technically, we're free to leave. So why don't I go tell him? Then we'll call the hostesses at The Scarlet Inn and get your reservation back. Which they'll do in a second because they love themselves some Chip Murdoch."

Nobody said anything for what felt like an eternity.

"Nah, I'm good," Chip finally said.

"Okay. Are you really? Because this is a one-time opportunity. Once we get in that elevator…"

"Yeah, I don't want to disappoint this Connor Harcourt guy."

Logan glared at him, sensing the approach of another dig.

"Especially since you're probably boning him," his dad added.

"Dad! I swear to God. You're really lucky I respect old people."

"*Elders*. The word is elders, son."

"Honestly."

"What? You think I'm an idiot. You practically sprouted wood the other day when you saw him on TV."

"Okay, here's the deal," Logan said, practically bringing their noses together. "If you want to live through your special night, you and I don't say another word to each other until we've both eaten a meal. A full one."

Linda, a natural mother, it seemed, stepped forward. "I think that sounds like a wonderful idea, boys."

"I already ate," Chip grumbled.

"I haven't," Logan growled through gritted teeth.

"All right, the nice lady has spoken," Chip said, indicating he was agreeing to it because Linda had approved it, not because Logan had suggested it.

Nobody else spoke as they rode up in the elevator.

Nobody spoke as they walked the long, carpeted corridor toward the double doors to the penthouse suite.

He texted Connor they were on their way when really what he wanted to text was, **Run like hell. I'll meet you in Mexico.**

Joel was standing guard outside the suite as Logan had instructed. He nodded and stepped aside so Logan could do his special knock. The door opened, and he gestured for the group to step through ahead of him, which they did, one after the other. Heads bowed, arms at their sides, like new convicts entering prison for the first time.

When he stepped inside the room, he realized their collective silence had shifted from awkward to stunned.

The penthouse suite was filled with flickering candles, the dining table set with the hotel's most formal place settings. Two white-tux-clad servers stood at the ready, and the terrace doors were open to the warm night. The same hot winds that were fueling the fire to their east made for a gorgeously clear, starry sky above the ocean outside. But it wasn't the room's décor and illumination that had stunned the group silent. It was the fact that somehow Connor had managed to get ahold of the original, framed sign for the first Chip's Kicks, the one that typically hung in Chip's office, and he'd hung it on the wall above the credenza, in a spot formerly occupied by a bland watercolor seascape. But the old sign wasn't the only addition.

All the artwork on the walls had been replaced with framed mementoes Connor had somehow managed to obtain from Chip's office and Logan's apartment, the latter probably thanks to the fact that J.T., Brandon, and Scott all had keys. The pin lights that once sent halos of warm light across sailboats on wind-tossed seas, seashells, and other beachy scenes now illuminated framed photographs marking the growth of Chip's Kicks. Logan was in some of the shots, but mostly they featured his dad posing with various trainers and clients over the past five years. And if all that weren't enough, atop the credenza and flanked by two vases bulging with roses, was the most special photograph in Logan's life, a framed picture of his mother and his dad, beaming as they cradled a newborn Logan.

And there, standing at the head of the table, beneath a miniature cloudscape of mylar balloons, beaming with pride, was Connor. Above his head, the largest balloons were letters spelling out *CHIP'S KICKS*.

In a daze, Chip walked toward the framed photograph on the credenza, magnetically drawn to the sight of Logan's mom. He picked it up and gazed at it. All traces of the ornery bastard from the lobby were gone. After a few moments, Connor stepped toward him, hand extended.

"Congratulations on five years, Mr. Murdoch."

Still stunned, Logan's dad shook Connor's hand. "This is really something, kid." There was a catch in his dad's voice. "You really did a thing here."

"How could I not?" Connor asked. "It's your special day."

"Well, shit. Now I feel like crap 'cause I was a huge dick to Logan on the way here."

"Well," Connor said, "if it helps, he didn't actually know I was going to all this trouble."

Chip barked with laughter. It proved infectious, claiming Jed and Petey and Linda too.

"Is that true, son?" Chip asked. "You didn't know about all this?"

"Not the pictures, no," Logan answered.

"All right. I feel half as shitty then."

Logan felt about as far from shitty as you could get.

He knew. Connor had read his mind, sensed the bruise on Logan's soul. He'd been able to tell that Logan had soft pedaled the whole different worlds thing during their talk about tonight's dinner earlier that day. He'd sensed how much their different backgrounds, the gulf between their so-called worlds, had frightened Logan five years ago. And how to a more muffled, but still painful extent, it still frightened Logan now. And so he'd thrown open the doors of his special world to make Logan's grumpy dad feel as welcome as he could, but first he'd taken care to place Chip Murdoch himself, his achievements, his survival story, all through it.

Trying to impress his dad with a lot of elegant theatrics would have been one thing. Putting him on the walls of Sapphire Cove as if he belonged here was another, far better thing.

From across the room, Connor caught Logan's look. He smiled and shrugged, as if all this was the least he could do.

The next thing Logan knew he was sinking down into the chair next to Connor's, the one Connor had pulled back from the table for him as if next to him was somewhere he'd always belonged.

There were no interruptions, no crises that called Connor and Logan away from the table. The meal proceeded in dreamlike fashion, and it felt to Logan like fate had brought them all together for this exact purpose. To share wine and stories and laughter and be kissed by warm ocean breezes and give Logan's dad some of the credit he deserved for turning his life around five years before.

They'd just finished the entrees when Connor said, "What was she like?"

It took everyone a second to see he was staring at the photo of Chip, Logan's mom, and baby Logan, the one he'd placed between the roses. The question was meant for Chip, who'd already entertained them with several harrowing stories about the night of Logan's birth—a sixteen-hour labor, a breech birth, all resulting in an eleven-pound baby with so much face fat its eyes disappeared if you tipped it slightly forward in one arm.

"Lucy?" Chip asked. "She was like her son."

"Gay?" Logan asked.

There was a ripple of laughter around the table. Chip smiled, but it looked like his heart wasn't in it. His heart, it seemed, was in memories of Lucy. "Nah, she definitely wasn't that. Or if she was I sure as hell converted her." Petey and Jed both guffawed.

"That's not how it works, Dad. There are no conversions. That's not a thing."

"I know, I know. I'm only messing with you."

"How was she like Logan?" Connor asked.

Chip paused, sipped his wine. It didn't seem like he was offended by the question, more like he thought any question relating to his late wife required careful, thoughtful, honest answers.

"She was strong," he finally said. "We used to joke an aneurysm was the only thing that could take her because it was so quick, you know? Anything else, it would have had to sneak up on her and she could have whacked the shit out of it before it got her brain. But it wasn't just physical. She had a sense of obligation. Loyalty. Like he does."

"And you do," Logan offered.

"Meh. I've had my moments, but yours aren't as few and far between."

"That's not true, Pop," Logan said.

"It is true." Chip was looking down at his plate. "I never defended my country like he did. And no offense, Mr. Harcourt—"

"Connor, please, Mr. Murdoch."

Chip smiled. "No offense, Connor, but if I was him, I would have quit this place forty-eight hours ago when the shit hit the fan. In fact, I even tried to convince him not to come back. But no way—"

"Dad—"

"Relax. It's all good." To Connor, he said, "The speech he gave me. About this place. About how happy it made him to work here. I shoulda written it down. You could have put it on the brochure."

"Good thing he came back then," Connor said. "'Cause I don't think any of us could do this without him."

After they finished the crème brûlée, the evening ended with a round of hugs, during which Chip pulled Connor off to one corner of the suite to say things to him under his breath with a grave expression on his face, their foreheads almost touching. Logan texted Joel to come guard the door while Connor helped the catering staff break down the setup. His dad's little tête-à-tête would have made Logan nervous if Connor hadn't looked like he was about to bust out laughing the whole time.

Then Logan walked his dad and company down to the lobby at a leisurely pace.

They'd left the elevators and were approaching reception when his dad turned to him and patted him on the chest, like he was proud of him.

"What?" Logan asked.

"You did good."

"With the dinner?" Logan asked.

"All of it."

Chip gestured to their surroundings like Logan had built the place. But Logan knew what he meant. Sensing a private moment between father and son, the rest of the group wandered deeper into the lobby.

"All right, out with it," Chip said.

"Out with what?"

"Come on. I saw the way he looked at you. And the way you looked at him. Whatever it is didn't start yesterday. How come you never told me about this guy 'til now?"

"This whole thing kind of gave us a second chance," Logan said.

"What happened to the first chance?" Chip asked.

"It wasn't the right time."

"When? When wasn't the right time?" Chip asked.

"Five years ago." Logan could see realization dawning in his father's eyes. There was no turning back now. "I didn't want to mess things up here."

The devilish smirk left his dad's expression. "Because of my accident. And the bills."

"It was my first day."

"Holy crap. That night you put your fist through the wall. Was that about Connor? You told me you'd OD'd on caffeine."

Logan cleared his throat, grunted, shifted on his feet, then finally nodded.

Chip was nodding too, studying the floor. God, how he hated the look of shame that could sometimes come into his father's eyes when he thought about the past.

"I should've saved," his dad said. "I should've planned better."

"Come on, Dad. You don't have to do this now."

"Nah, it's true. I thought I was invincible. Not perfect. But invincible. And I thought that made up for being really not perfect. But sometimes you had to pull the weight for both of us. You deserve this place, sport, even if it's more than I could give you."

"Old man, what you gave me could fill Orange County," Logan said.

"Maybe," he said. "She could have given you a lot more, though."

"Maybe just different things."

"Great things," his dad said, "because she was pretty damn great."

He threw his arms around his dad before he could think twice about it, and his dad returned the hug for as long as he was comfortable doing so. Which wasn't very long. When he stepped away, Jed was headed for them. "Hey, Logan, is it all right if we hang out in the bar for a bit?"

"Yeah, sure," Logan said. "Spend lots of money while you're at it. Then maybe we can all keep our jobs."

"Good. I didn't know if it was wildfire victims only," Jed said, then taking Chip by the shoulder, he added, "What do you say, Kickstart? You ready to knock off or you want to tie one on? Remember, I'm designated driver." It was an inside joke—Jed had been clean and sober for ten years.

"Sure, why not?" Chip said.

His father was about to turn toward his awaiting friends when Logan spotted Donna Langdon sitting by herself at one of the bistro tables in the Sapphire Lounge. The bar was otherwise full of evacuees, and at first, it tugged at his heart to see her all alone. Then he noticed the large sketchpad on the table in front of her and saw her furiously at work, surrounded by the crowd. Given how many canvases she'd lost to the fire the night before, that seemed like a sign of recovery.

"Hey, Pop."

His father spun away from the group. When Logan beckoned him over, he complied.

"That woman over there, the one sketching," Logan said. "Her name's Donna. Go talk to her."

"She looks like serious business. You setting me up for a date or a flogging?"

"Some of both, I think. She'll give you a run for your money."

"I never understood that expression," his dad said, but he was already tucking his shirt in and adjusting his sleeves and running through all the other gestures he performed right before approaching an intriguing lady for the first time. "Who wants to run for their money?"

Logan patted him on the back, like he was a runner leaving the starting mark. If Chip got the joke, he didn't let on, because his eyes were already on Donna Langdon as he and his friends moved toward the bar.

Once he was back upstairs and heading for the door of the penthouse suite, Joel gave him a sad look. A guilty look. Logan read the signs immediately.

"Where is he?" Logan asked.

"Don't be mad."

"I told you not to let him leave the room."

"He's my boss, dude. I can't order him around. He said to give you this."

Something about the phrasing set Logan back a bit. Technically, Connor was Logan's boss too, which meant technically Logan shouldn't be ordering Connor around either. But they'd made an agreement, and this wasn't it.

Was it an agreement, though? Or an order. An order he didn't seem to mind.

Joel handed Logan something orange, something familiar.

"Besides, Brandon's with him," Joel added.

A pack of Reese's Peanut Butter Cups. And there was a little drawing taped to it. A pen sketch of the balustrade right outside the Dolphin Ballroom, one of the many drawings of scenic spots on the property they included with the stationery in each room. And the spot where they had their first real conversation.

"He said don't keep him waiting," Joel added.

"We'll talk about this later." But he was having trouble sounding like a hard ass, thanks to Connor's gift.

"He's my *boss*, dude," Joel whined.

17

When Logan reached the balustrade, there was Brandon, standing at the exact spot where Logan and Connor had enjoyed their first conversation five years before. Even though the guy was Logan's size, he wore a hangdog, sheepish expression as Logan approached.

"Where is he?" Logan asked.

"He wouldn't let me go all the way, I'm sorry. And he said to give you this."

It was another pack of Reese's Peanut Butter Cups. This one had a drawing of the sea caves taped to it.

"Where is he?" Logan asked.

"The caves."

"You let him go all the way down to the caves by himself?" Logan barked.

"I had to. He's my boss."

"And he reminded you of the fact, I take it," Logan said.

"Like twenty times."

"You're lucky I need you guys."

"Come on, Logan. He's my—"

"I know. He's your boss. I get it."

Heart racing, Logan descended the steps toward the crescent of beach below, alone this time, but headed to something better, surer. Something he'd thought he'd lost.

The gate to the boardwalk was closed and locked. He opened it with his key and walked through the dark yawning cave entrance.

Connor was in the exact spot where they'd first kissed.

"You are in serious trouble, Mr. Harcourt," Logan said.

"That sounds promising."

"What did I say about not leaving my sight?"

"I don't know, but you said it in that grumbly voice you get that makes me want to dry hump your leg."

"Your safety is my priority."

He hadn't chosen that word on purpose, but he saw the effect it had on Connor. On that fateful night at Laguna Brew, priorities had been Logan's reason for not bringing them back to this very spot a second time. And now here they were. Fate had made Connor his priority, and he didn't mind one bit.

"Prove it," Connor whispered.

Logan pulled him close, but he wasn't willing to grant him a kiss. Not yet.

"Or maybe you were helplessly drawn by the irresistible scent of chocolate and peanut butter. Feel free to thank me for the dinner party at any time, by the way."

"I loved the dinner party. It was an amazing dinner party. But you're going to get punished before you're thanked."

"Well, that sounds like a party on top of a party, if you ask me."

Those bright, twinkling eyes, that smile. Logan gripped the back of his head and brought their mouths together. Felt the yield, the hunger, the warmth, the sense of Connor's body rising into his. Arm curling around his back. Taking his time, tasting Logan's lips, his tongue.

When they finally broke, Logan was breathless, and his pulse and the surf seemed to be competing with each other to drown out the nagging voice of every worry he'd ever battled.

He spun Connor toward the guardrail, forced him against it, and savored the pleasurable groan that escaped him at this quick little display of brute force. He'd gone instantly swaybacked, driving his ass into Logan's crotch as Logan deftly unbuttoned Connor's pants with one hand. He left the guy's belt in the loops so it wouldn't slide free and into the water. He kept his other arm looped around Connor's stomach, holding him in place as he made quick work of undressing him from the waist down. The idea of breaking their reverse embrace, right now, with Connor's smell filling his nostrils and the taste of his skin fresh on his lips, was intolerable. Even if it meant it would take longer to get Connor naked. Or mostly naked. Or just naked enough.

When the misty ocean air hit Connor's exposed thighs, he actually cooed, and when Logan peeled his white briefs down his waist, then traced his fingers gently along the underside of his stiffening cock and his tightening balls, Connor's groans became hungry and throaty. Rich, pleasure filled.

He'd had to back up slightly to push Connor's underwear down, but even after relieving the pressure of Connor's body against his crotch, Logan's throbbing cock was still pressing painfully against the inside of his zipper. But the mouthwatering sight of Connor's suddenly exposed ass distracted him from the little jabs of pain, which in and of themselves felt like a sweet form of torture. Creamy white, full of invitation. Connor leaned forward as if there was a magnetic pull between his backside and the throb inside Logan's khakis.

Logan felt a burning urge to free his own cock, but there was something so delicious about undressing Connor and staying clothed himself. Yes, it was power. And he liked using power to give pleasure. But he loved the sense that he was unwrapping Connor, revealing more of his essence, taking his sweet time savoring the sight of every flushed and naked inch of him. Connor yielded so totally to this, his surrender didn't just feel like a gift. It felt like a blessing.

He's giving himself to me now. In this moment. Which seemed impossible a short while ago.

"Shoes and pants off, now," Logan said. "That's an order."

Logan's dominant tone seized control of every muscle in Connor's body. Suddenly, Connor turned around, bent forward, pulling off his shoes one after the other. Logan wanted to let him do all the work himself so he could savor the sight of every fresh inch of exposed skin coming into view, but he couldn't resist. He sank to a crouch and pulled Connor's puddled pants out from around his ankles, the cell phone in one pocket thudding hard against the boards. But now that he was down here, he couldn't resist raising his hands to Connor's hips, caressing the smooth skin there, leaning forward and giving a teasing lick to the underside of Connor's balls, then a long lick to the underside of Connor's shaft that made Connor grip the rail behind him, clenching his teeth while he gasped. His fingers found the smooth and once forbidden crack of Connor's ass. He stroked his hole, savoring its heat, prepared this time for the sensitivity there, the way it made Connor shudder and chew his lower lip and take deep hungry breaths through his nostrils. Logan got to his feet, abandoning Connor's jerking cock, bringing their mouths together, drinking in the speed with which Connor's lips yielded to his. He kneaded the hardness in Logan's crotch, then started digging for the zipper pull.

"Logan…"

"Yes?" Logan asked between powerful kisses.

"Please…"

"Please, what?"

"Your cock. Give me your cock."

"Hmmm. Not sure you've waited long enough."

"I have, though. I even named my favorite dildo after you."

"Oh, so you're making me compete with a sex toy?"

"Not at all. When someone names his favorite dildo after you when they only rubbed against you for a few minutes five years ago, that's, like, the highest praise a power bottom can give you."

"Is it now?" More long, lip-tugging kisses.

"Please, Logan. Please don't make me wait any longer."

Logan laughed under his breath and gripped the back of Connor's head so he could draw his face away enough to gaze into his hungry blue eyes.

"Where do you want it?" Logan asked.

"Everywhere," Connor whispered.

One hand on Connor's shoulder, Logan pushed him to his knees, something he'd done a dozen times with a dozen different guys, all of whom had wanted him to play the tough, commanding Marine. But he'd never been so dazzled by the sight of someone's bare ass sticking out as he hit the debauched prayer position that meant Logan was about to get serviced. He'd never run his fingers quite so deeply and thoroughly through the hair of anyone who'd ever taken him into his mouth. Never felt a partner's body become a presence, a force. A name and a feeling and a history and a possible future.

Connor gave Logan's pants a hard tug, then several shorter, teasing ones as soon as they cleared the target area. Slowly, Connor ran one hand over the furious bulge painfully encased in Logan's briefs, then with a look of delight in his eyes, he pulled the briefs down, laughing gently when Logan's achingly hard cock plopped free of its prison, revealing the kind of throbbing, unstoppable erection Logan hadn't given rise to since he was nineteen. When Connor gripped the base of Logan's shaft, shivers raced through Logan's body, then, at Connor's first skillful strokes, his legs tremored.

Connor took his time discovering Logan's length and his girth, expertly, slowly. It looked like he was marveling at it, which made Logan feel both hungry and proud. Connor traced the veins with his fingers, his nose, then, finally, mercifully, his tongue. He'd had no idea Connor was this leisurely a lover. Before they'd been rushed, and before that, interrupted. Now time was theirs. The cave was theirs. The night was theirs.

In almost no time, with that male intuition and familiarity that can make sex between two men earth shattering, Connor's tongue found the most sensitive spot on Logan's cock, on the front and underside of the head. He focused his ministrations there, slow and studious, suckling as he worked the shaft with one hand. Logan didn't want to tear his eyes away from the sight of Connor's beautiful work, but it was so intense, his head rolled back on his neck despite himself. Amazing the way Connor managed to give so much pleasure with moves that looked so leisurely and gentle. Sometimes a blowjob, no matter how active and skillful, felt like the other person fulfilling an obligation. Rarely did it feel like your cock was being savored, consumed. *Loved.*

The pulse of this word through his mind stiffened him further, but the rest of his body felt like he was turning boneless thanks to Connor's soft lips, expert tongue, and stroking hand. And he realized it wasn't those things melting him inside, it was the thing that united all of those things— Connor's hunger set free. Connor worked Logan's body the same way he did everything else: with fearlessness, dedication, and passion.

The surf pounded outside the cave's entrance. The ocean gurgled under their feet and into the cave around them, and along with Connor's devoted passion, all these elements combined to make him feel like he and Connor, in this moment, at least, really were the only two people in the world, something he'd never felt during sex in his entire life even though he'd heard plenty of songs about it.

It wasn't the cave of his memories. It was the cave of now, of here, of yes.

"Connor…" he heard himself say.

Connor rose to his feet, lips meeting Logan's gasping mouth suddenly. He ran his hands up under the flaps of Logan's untucked dress shirt, undoing buttons until he had Logan's right nipple in between thumb and forefinger. He twisted it until Logan's back arched from the rush of pleasure. His cock jerked and bobbed in response.

"There we go," Connor whispered.

Connor bent down and closed his lips, then his teeth, around the nipple he'd turned into a hard bud of pleasure. Sucked it, then bit down gently until he got the same response from every nerve in Logan's body and more quick throbbing growth in Logan's cock.

"There we *go*," Connor said again, sounding even more excited this time.

This time he lavished the nipple with his tongue, alternating between sucking and biting. Kissing his way over to the other, repeating the same actions, producing the same blissful result. He released Logan's cock, devoting both hands to the fireworks show he was setting off in Logan's chest. "Someone's got sensitive nipples," he said.

"Someone's doing things there no one's ever done before."

"I doubt that, baby. You seem like a man with experience."

"I have experience with the moves," Logan whispered, saw the intensity in his tone had silenced Connor, and brought his eyes to his again. "But you're giving me a lot more than moves."

"How's that?" Connor whispered.

"Because it's you." Logan kissed him back, gently this time. "You're giving me you."

Connor's surrender escaped in a stuttering, throaty groan, then he gave a lingering kiss that Logan tried to return. Which was difficult. Connor's expert nipple work was making him gasp for breath.

But it was a reward, this kiss, so Logan worked to receive it. A reward for keeping the vow he'd made to himself with all those meaningless hookups. He'd reserved this intimacy for the one he truly wanted to share it with, and now, as a result, Connor's lips tasted sweet and precious.

They were both breathless now, so Connor smoothed Logan's hair from his forehead, studied him closely through the moonlight, and traced the bridge of his nose with a finger.

"You go back down there, and I'm gonna cum," Logan said.

"That's my plan, Lethal Weapon."

Connor hit his knees.

Maybe a mistake to tip his hand the way he did. To let Connor know how close he was to the edge. Because now Connor seemed determined to take them over it, hard and fast. One of his hands traveled up Logan's chest, searching for a nipple, no doubt. Wild with desire, Logan seized Connor's reaching hand and brought Connor's fingers to his mouth, sucking them, tonguing them. He'd never done anything like it before, but it made him feel joined with Connor even with him down on his knees and wreathed in the cave's shadows.

"Connor."

The word erupted from him with that note of pleading and anticipation and a bit of fear that told him it was going to be a ball-churning, toe-curling event. And when it came, suddenly Logan felt skinless and owned, as if his entire body had been reduced to something raw and stripped of its defenses, something Connor now held in both of his stroking hands. He had emptied himself countless times, but never had the piercing bliss made him feel this vulnerable, this exposed and yet cradled in the same instant.

The shudders. The gasps. The drawn-out release, not nearly as stuttered as if he'd done the deed himself. And a twinge of worry that his chesty bellows had been audible all the way at the top of the cliff. Then Connor was slowly crawling his way up his body as he stood. He'd tilted his face to one side, and Logan was pretty sure why, so he gripped Connor's chin gently, saw some glistening threads of his eruption had landed on his beautiful cheek, and with a growl, he licked them up. Carefully. Methodically. One by one. Drawing lustful cries from Connor in the process.

"That was a really good punishment," Connor whispered.

"Oh, no, baby. Your punishment's next."

Connor's laugh was low and throaty, as if nothing could please him more.

Logan couldn't remember the last time he'd actually giggled, but that's what he was doing now as they slipped from the cave and snuck back into the hotel. Then, once they crossed the threshold into the penthouse suite, their lips locked again, and they were stumbling toward the bathroom like dancing partners drunk on lust. It was Connor who undressed Logan this time, hands exploring his hard body in the marble bathroom's warm, honey-colored light. And Logan realized it was the first time he'd been totally naked with the guy. When they stepped into the shower big enough for two, Connor was tasting, licking, nibbling, giving himself free roam of Logan's hard expanse of muscle, searching for the spots that made Logan twist and gasp.

As the spray hit them, Logan was also ready to explore. He turned Connor's face to the wall, soaped his hands with the hotel's signature body wash—a blend of vanilla and eucalyptus and mint that he knew he'd forever associate with the taste and feel of Connor from this night on. He covered Connor's ass with it in wide, smooth circles, all so he could subject its glorious crack to suds-filled bliss. Connor's moans became something else, something breathier and throatier and full of increasing, building need. In every inch of Connor's body, Logan found the surrender he'd craved for years.

Time melted away, maybe because it was the first time they had so much of it. So much of it to spend in hot and hungry kisses. They couldn't make up for five lost years in one night, but they could sure as hell have fun trying.

Once they'd exhausted their lips and exploring hands, Connor brought his head to Logan's chest, letting his body go limp inside his powerful embrace.

"I have a theory," Connor said. "It's kinda nuts and it's not all that scientific, so you have to kinda go with me on this."

"I'm all ears." But more accurately, Logan was putty in Connor's tender embrace.

"So you know how sometimes people feel weird after sex. Like, they'll freak out or…I mean, I'm not freaking out, I just want to tell you my theory."

"Sure." Logan reached up and smoothed Connor's damp bangs back from his forehead.

"Okay, so, evolution."

"I've heard of it," Logan said.

"Back in the caveman days. Cavepeople days. Whatever. There wasn't a lot of shelter, so if you were going to do the nasty, you probably had to do it outside. And it's very distracting, doing the nasty. As we learned, it can feel incredible. Like mind blowing."

"Mind blowing is an excellent description," Logan added.

"But it can also completely take you out of yourself. Which, back in those days would have been a problem because…" He arched his eyebrows, indicating Logan should fill in the blank.

"Because people smelled terrible?" Logan ventured.

"No. Because of animals."

"Animals?" Logan asked.

"Right. Wild animals could be stalking you. So if the minute you finished sex, you didn't sit up right away and look around and get worried, you might get eaten."

"And not, like, how I ate your ass this afternoon eaten," Logan said.

"Nowhere near that amazing. Like torn limb from limb eaten. Which meant you got taken out of the gene pool. So that's why there are a lot of people in the population today who get worried and freaked out after sex. Because they're descended from the ones who were always anxious a saber-tooth tiger might get them after they got laid."

"What are you worried about, Connor?"

Connor blinked up at him. "I'm not worried."

Logan tightened his arms around Connor's back. "Fine. What's your saber-tooth tiger's name then?"

For a while, Connor didn't speak, which gave Logan a chance to gaze into those baby blues he thought he'd never see again. Logan expected some concern about the hotel or workplace complications, or maybe longing for New York now that the realities of the job were settling in, but instead, Connor took a deep breath. "I almost let you cum in my mouth. Because I really wanted you to."

"How is this a problem?" Logan whispered.

"It's kind of soon. And maybe a little risky."

"Ah, I see."

"And maybe this is a question I should have asked before now, but things are moving pretty fast for us."

"After five years of waiting, that is."

"True, but you know what I mean," Connor said.

"I do. And I'd never let you do something that put yourself at risk."

"Even if it felt really good?" Connor asked.

"It wouldn't feel good if I knew you were at risk."

"That's a really good answer, Logan."

Connor graced him with a gentle kiss.

"I haven't been a priest," Logan said. "Far from it. But I haven't been reckless either. I've been on PrEP since it came out. But I didn't ditch condoms."

"Same here," Connor said. "So we'll be using them?"

"For the time being, yeah."

Connor's eyes lit up, lit up at the prospect of a commitment between the two of them that might include scheduled STD tests, loosening layers of protection. Safety. Commitment. Trust. And the time to acquire all those things. Together.

"Good," Connor said. "'Cause I'm ready for my punishment now."

Logan smiled.

Then, suddenly, he stepped from the shower, looked back to see Connor giving him expectant, puppy dog eyes. Logan continued with his withholding act, passed a towel back to him, which Connor took, pouting now over the tiny bit of distance Logan had so quickly put between them. Maybe he thought it was a denial of his request.

Hardly. It was just the beginning of it.

He leaned against the edge of the bathroom counter as Connor stepped out of the shower, watched Connor dry himself off with sudden cold remove, as if surveying Connor's body, coldly calculating his weak spots. It made Connor suitably nervous, which was its design. When Connor stepped from the stall and started for him, Logan reached up and gently took Connor's chin in his hand. At the first sign of disciplinary force, Connor's eyes blazed with hunger.

"And what exactly should you be punished for, Mr. Harcourt?" Logan asked in the tone with which he used to grill his recruits.

"I don't know," Connor said quietly. "Lots of reasons. I've got a sassy mouth, that's for sure."

"That you do." Logan reached up and slid a finger into the corner of Connor's mouth, which he immediately suckled. "It's pretty, though."

"Yeah, well," Connor whispered, "maybe that distracts you from what comes out of it sometimes. Maybe you need to do a better job of making sure I"—he sucked Logan's finger quick and hard—"watch my words."

Logan spun Connor around so quickly Connor let out a small, delighted yelp. He clamped an arm across Connor's chest and brought his head back until his ear was at Logan's lips. With his other hand, he reached down and gripped one of Connor's ass cheeks with force, shaking it hard. "Oh, so you think this pretty little ass distracts me from making sure you don't mouth off like some spoiled brat?"

"Maybe."

"And when exactly have you mouthed off to me, Connor Harcourt?"

As Connor considered his answer, Logan sought to distract him by tightening his arm clamp around his chest, drawing Connor's ass back against his cock, which was once more swelling from the sound of Connor's teasing, kittenish tone. "Maybe that night at Laguna Brew. I could have been more…understanding. Of your predicament."

"But you weren't," Logan growled. His cock was upright and hard now, cupped in the crack of Connor's ass. "Because you knew, deep down, what I really wanted to do was toss you in that Rolls-Royce and fuck you until you couldn't remember your name because you were so busy screaming mine."

"Uh huh. And that was bad of me. Very bad of me to play with you like that, Logan Murdoch."

"Well, okay then."

Logan released Connor and took a step back, leaving Connor standing alone and naked in the middle of the bathroom as if he'd been placed in a sudden timeout. Of course, Logan's ragingly hard cock was a dead giveaway this was all role play, but Connor's eyes seemed far more riveted by the sight of Logan's mock stoic expression.

"Bed. Face down."

"What's my—"

"Shut up."

Connor fought down a smile, took a deep breath, and pressed the bathroom door open with one hand. When Connor was within a few feet of the bed, Logan gave him a focused and firm shove on his upper back that sent him face first into the comforter. He watched the impact closely, looking for signs of resistance that said the shove had been too hard, or Connor might be all talk when it came to his desire for rough play, in which case Logan would dial back and readjust. Instead, he saw total submission, arms that bent and seemed to wilt into the silken bedding, a mouthwatering ass that actually rose up in response to this loss of control.

Perfect.

Logan straddled Connor's back and grabbed his flushed neck. Quickly, without warning, he reared up and leveled a single, hard slap across Connor's ass. He'd planned to start lighter, with a little test. Something that didn't leave his cheeks flaming. But the shove onto the bed had served that purpose, and this strike had hit a perfect target, causing Connor to moan with pleasure and arch his back like a cat.

"You've led a very privileged life, you know that, Connor Harcourt?" Logan growled.

Again.

"And sometimes a boy like you needs a little discipline." He waited a few seconds and unleashed three hard spanks in rapid succession, just so Connor couldn't get used to the rhythm. Connor's moans became hungry whines through clenched teeth.

"A little focus," Logan growled.

His cheeks aflame, Connor was grinding his crotch into the sheets. He was a beautiful little bitch in heat, and he was all Logan's. And there was no denying the thrill Logan got from venting his frustrations from that long-ago night, from the sense that joy had slipped through his fingers, and the boy who drove him wild couldn't bring himself to understand. He understood now, and he'd orchestrated this delicious fusion of anger and pleasure for that exact purpose.

"A little pain might be what you need," Logan whispered.

Gently, Logan rubbed Connor's flaming cheeks. He was feeling for resistance or fatigue, but Connor's back was still arched as if seeking out the pleasures offered by Logan's punishing palm. Still, Logan couldn't crank it up a notch without permission, so he bent down and brought his mouth to Connor's ear. "Have you learned your lesson, you little brat?"

"Not yet, Mr. Murdoch," Connor whispered. "I think I might still see you as nothing more than a big sexy hunk of man flesh who only exists for my pleasure. You better take control and teach me otherwise."

The beast he'd kept mostly caged since the first night they met kicked the door off and burst out into the night. Logan unleashed several hard blows in quick succession. The blend of hunger and surprise Connor moaned into the sheets seemed to strengthen the power in his hand.

A subtle hint of Connor's taste had been on his lips ever since their tumble in his office that morning, leaving him semi-aroused all day long. Like the scent he'd left on his shirt the night before, it was a trigger. More than a trigger, a brand. A brand that would call him to do forbidden, nasty things whenever it reached his senses.

Logan unleashed a lustful, slick attack on Connor's sensitive crack with his tongue, and Connor's surprise met with pleasure, riding an underscore of wildness. It had always been one of his favorite things, rimming. Done right, it could turn the biggest, strongest alpha man into a whimpering mound of pleasure. But with Connor, it was like Logan was accessing the very core of his desire, and in a way that said his ass was the seat of infinite pleasures for them both. Connor grabbed fistfuls of comforter, his mouth gasping against pillows. Biting them even, which made Logan let out a satisfied laugh.

God, he tasted good. Still shower clean, but also that delicious baked bread smell spiced with masculine musk.

He tasted his thighs now, teasing him. Tricking him into thinking he'd moved on before swiftly and forcefully returning to his spit-slick crack, biting those perfect cheeks.

"Please," Connor moaned.

Logan grabbed the back of Connor's neck again, using the new leverage to drive his humming, throbbing cock in long, slow strokes along the crack of Connor's ass.

"Please what?" Logan growled.

"Please fuck me, Logan." Four words spoken in a desperate whisper. Four words that meant a total loss of composure, a total surrender to desire. Logan rewarded it by kissing that special spot on the side of Connor's neck that made him writhe. And at the unbridled, hungry sounds that came from Connor in response, Logan had to stop driving his cock along Connor's ass or he was going to erupt before he was ready.

Suddenly, Connor rolled over. With a jolt, Logan felt one of the guy's hands around his throat. In the moonlight, he could see Connor's rock-hard cock jerking against his pale stomach. He'd been in danger of cumming, no doubt, and that's why he'd flipped himself so quickly. But the grip on Logan's throat said something else. It was a reminder that in the end, it was the bottom who had the power. The power to grant entry. The power to say yes and no and when.

"Now," Connor purred. "Fuck me, *now.*"

When Connor pointed one hand toward the nightstand drawer, Logan realized he'd prepared for this moment. A tug on the drawer and a box of condoms and a bottle of Swiss Navy slid into view.

Such a resourceful guy, this gorgeous angel I'm about to fuck into heaven.

Connor scooted backward onto the pillows until his upper back was resting against the upholstered headboard. He gripped the undersides of his thighs, spreading his own bent legs. Logan had never seen anything like it, the focus and determination, the eagerness with which Connor positioned himself for him, rendering himself even more submissive in advance of Logan's invasion.

Logan started to rush through the tasks before him, tasks he could do in his sleep, but which in this moment seemed more significant than ever before.

A thread of lube poured along his exposed cock. A few strokes to spread it. A pinch on the top of the condom to make sure air didn't get captured, then several strokes to roll it down his shaft. He knew he was big, always had been, and that meant he needed to exert extra effort in this department. Make sure the condom was both snug and as far down his shaft as it would unroll.

He was so turned on, so damn hard, he was worried these quick tasks might make him blow for the second time in two hours.

But he held on, held on until he was gripping the top of the headboard with one hand, lowering himself down over Connor's heat. Connor's eyes were wide and wild, sweaty chest heaving with breaths, as Logan guided his cock into him. Slowly, carefully. There was the first wince, the first gasp, sounds that usually took him briefly out of the moment because they meant pain and adjustment. But coming from Connor, they meant something different entirely. They meant, *Finally.*

"Logan." A note of surprise in the way he said his name. As if Logan pressing into him revealed an entirely new dimension of the man he'd already extensively explored with his fingers, lips, and tongue. Connor rocked his hips back, raising more of his ass to meet the long, slow penetration. When his hands went to Logan's chest, Logan thought he might be trying to slow him down, but Connor wasn't. His fingers found Logan's nipples instead and went to work. The rocking motion in Connor's ass, Logan realized, was about taking him in deeper, swallowing even more of him.

"You're so big," he whispered, "you're so fucking big, and I want all of you."

"Good, 'cause you're going to get every goddamn inch."

Chewing his lip, Connor grunted, but Logan could tell he needed more time. More time to adjust, to connect, to relax around him. That Connor was this tight, that Connor needed the time delighted him, filled him with proprietary hunger.

Logan, it seemed, was one of the biggest men he'd ever taken, if not the biggest.

And the last, and by God, I'm going to be the last.

Connor's eyes fluttered open, his breaths becoming steadier and deeper. He grabbed the hand Logan was using to brace himself against the pillows and brought Logan's fingers to his mouth, kissing them, sucking them. All signs the initial pain of entry was receding, allowing desire to surge.

"You ready, baby?" Logan asked.

"So fucking ready," Connor whispered.

And then it was the slow build, the magical build. And the sounds Connor made, stuttering groans blended with soft cries, indicating pain giving way to the satisfying scratch of a profound and hard to reach itch. Connor rocked his hips back further, surrendering totally now. His nostrils flaring, his breaths were now as deep and hard as Logan's strokes.

It was clear Connor had given himself over to him, lost himself completely in the fuck. All resistance had left him, and Logan's powerful thrusts were jostling his seemingly boneless body against the tangle of soft, silken bedding. It was as if Connor Harcourt's spine had melted, and the center of his poise and his power now came from Logan's thrusts.

Even though Connor went silent, Logan could feel its approach. Could see its imminent arrival in the way Connor's bright pink cock jerked wildly. Could sense from the sudden, deceptive calm that settled over Connor that he was trying to pull himself back from the brink. But the long, throaty groan that slipped from his mouth indicated he was failing.

"Logan, I'm going to cum." He said it quickly, painfully, as if ashamed.

"Damn right you are. Damn right you're going to fucking cum, Connor Harcourt."

"Logan." A cry now, a cry that had a trace of almost every emotion Connor was capable of.

That's when Logan realized what was really driving Connor's sense of astonishment tinged with alarm. The first gush of seed seemed like a spill, then it was followed by several quick jets, and all of it erupted from Connor without him lifting either of his balled fists from the bed. Logan had never seen this in real life—in porn films once or twice—but never with his own two eyes. It was the stuff of legends. A hands-free orgasm. And it was happening to Connor. It was happening to Connor because of Logan.

Maybe Connor always came this way when he was getting fucked, or maybe Logan had truly done something rare and often impossible, something no man had ever done to Connor before. The question alone swamped Logan in a wave of pleasure that made his vision blur. Even as he kept thrusting, even as he kept studying the delicious sight of Connor's blissful thrall, Logan realized he was about to have a first of his own.

He was erupting inside of another man for the first time.

He didn't have to pull out first. Didn't have to whip the condom off and do the obligatory jerk session as they both tried to make it feel hot and inspired, and not like the utilitarian finish it would have been. He was emptying himself inside of Connor, filling the condom with heat, bellowing as he did so. A feeling so intense that when he finally caught his breath, he had to look down to be sure he and Connor hadn't flown apart into a pile of limbs.

But Connor was gazing up at him, his satisfied smile drowsy with bliss. When he opened his arms, Logan sank into him slowly, and for a while they lay together. Exhausted, emptied, blissfully entangled.

"Don't move," Connor whispered. "Please, don't move. Need to feel this."

Logan felt something brush against the small of his back, realized it was Connor lacing his ankles together and resting them there.

"You're still hard," Connor whispered. "Still feels good, 'cause you're still so hard."

Logan tried to say something back but couldn't find words as powerful as his urge to taste Connor's lips. And he loved that. Loved that Connor had emptied him of words and cool, rational thoughts.

"It's going to hurt to walk tomorrow," Connor said, "and I'm going to love every step."

Connor remembered a quick trip to the bathroom to clean himself up, then sliding back into bed to discover that Logan had turned down the covers, shut off most of the lights, and was waiting to pull him into a drowsy embrace with one powerful arm. He'd snuggled into Logan's comforting bulk, preparing to summon some intimate, gentle words that conveyed how thoroughly and wonderfully fucked he felt.

Then suddenly it was six in the morning, and the first golden light of dawn was streaming through the sliding glass doors. Neither of them had pulled the drapes the night before. Better, he and Logan hadn't moved an inch from where their blissful post-sex exhaustion claimed them.

"Good morning, sky." He traced a finger up the center of Logan's bare chest, but his hero didn't stir. "Good morning, sun." He grazed the underside of Logan's jaw with the tips of his fingers. Logan groaned gently and pulled Connor tightly to him. "Good morning, little things that run." Connor ran his fingers across Logan's chest like the four legs of a skittering mouse.

"Seriously," Logan grumbled, closing one hand around Connor's tickling one.

"You don't like morning songs?"

"I think it's little *winds* that run," he said.

"Nah uh."

"Yeah, huh. It's a poem. We learned it at school."

"Well, the camp counselors used to say *things*, so…"

"Wait, *camp?*" Logan asked, opening one eye. "You've been camping?"

"It was a summer camp."

"Yeah, but outside?"

"I go outside."

"In a tent? Overnight?"

"We had cabins," Connor said.

"Cabins or chalets?"

"There are sides of me you don't know about yet, Staff Sergeant Murdoch."

"Lies. I got to know all of them last night." Wearing a drowsy smile now, Logan kissed Connor's forehead.

"I'm serious, Logan. I am not the pampered, spoiled prince you seem to think I am."

"So you figured out a way to get facials in the woods?"

"No. But I still had a good time. In the beginning. I was great at skit night."

"Oh, yeah?" Logan asked. "So how long did you stay at this alleged camp?"

"Oh, you know. A bit. Right up until I wrote a strongly worded letter to the owners about how there seemed to be no provisions in place in the event of simultaneous, coordinated mountain lion attacks and asked them how they could sleep at night knowing the blood of so many children might end up on their hands."

"And then you decided to leave," Logan said.

"Oh, no. *They* decided I should leave. You see, it was less of a letter and more of a petition, and apparently I upset a lot of the other children. But they signed it. So it shows you they agreed with me. Who cares if there was absolutely no historical precedent for such a scenario? The world needs to be prepared for a mountain lion uprising."

"Connor, if mountain lions were capable of a mass uprising, I don't think they'd be as endangered as they are."

"Oh, what are you, the mountain lion whisperer?"

"Also, wild guess here," Logan said. "You never wanted to go to this camp and this was your strategy for getting sent home. Probably so you could spend the summer working here."

"You know me so well," Connor said.

Suddenly it seemed as if the comforters were alive, shifting all around him, getting ready to devour him. And he didn't mind. What it really meant was Logan was moving, and it was a reminder of how big and all-consuming the guy was. The next thing he knew, Connor was on his back, Logan above him, all tan, smooth muscle and tousled black hair, and eyes that looked even sleepier than they were thanks to his heavy, dark eyebrows. He held Connor's wrists to the pillow on either side of his head. The sight of his lips so close was a reminder of all the sweet words he'd said these past two days, all the wickedly wonderful things he'd done with his mouth that had made white hot arcs of pleasure shoot up Connor's spine.

"I don't want to get out of this bed," Logan said.

"Me neither. But we have a hotel to save."

"True."

"Also," Connor said, "rest assured. You're coming back to it. Tonight. With me."

"Good to know."

"You had other plans, mister?"

Logan kissed Connor on the forehead. Connor was disappointed by this until he remembered a thing called morning breath. It had been a long time since he'd spent the night with someone, a long time since he'd woken up in anyone's arms. Especially arms like Logan's, arms that seemed like they could carry him through a storm.

"Nope," Logan whispered.

"Well, good, because keeping me under watch twenty-four seven was your idea."

"I don't remember you complaining." Logan moved his kisses to Connor's neck.

"I'm not," Connor whispered. "I'm simply figuring out the housing arrangements involved."

"But, Mr. Harcourt," Logan said, effecting his best Southern belle voice. "People will *talk*."

"Well, yesterday all they did was sing your praises over what you did to Rodney in the lobby. They might be letting you off the hook, Murdoch."

"Here's hoping. In the meantime, we need a shower."

Again, the gentle kisses on his neck that worked their way to his special, most sensitive spot. "Who goes first?"

"Didn't you hear?" Logan said. "You're under my protection.

Whenever we shower, we shower together."

Before Connor could catch his breath, he was rising into the air, and that's when he realized Logan, also naked as the day he was born, had hoisted Connor up into his arms just like all the brides that had probably been carried across the threshold into this very suite.

"I'm hoping this protection will continue even after my uncle goes to prison," Connor said.

"Definitely my plan," Logan said before kicking open the bathroom door with one foot. "Until then, let's get you nice and clean."

Nice and clean left them both spent and gasping under the spray and clinging to each other until the last few seconds before they knew the day's work could no longer be ignored. But making up for lost time took a lot of work too.

18

The breakfast buffet for the wildfire victims had gone off without a hitch, so Connor and Logan headed to the management offices for another day's work.

Logan had filled his morning with interviews for potential new security agents, which he planned to conduct within sight of Connor's closed office door. Connor had his daily check-in call with Lois Penry.

Even with a closed door between them, knowing Logan was watching over him was a comfort, like a low, vibrating current connected to all the delicious aches Logan had left throughout his body the night before.

What Lois suggested a few minutes in startled him so much he had to stammer his way into a response.

"Is this a suggestion or a recommendation?" he finally asked.

"Neither. A possibility. If it makes sense to you."

"Gotcha." Connor felt like he should say more, but he couldn't. Lois's suggestion had shocked him.

"Look, the way the trust is written, it gives a lot of latitude to the GM position. And so there's rarely going to be anything we can force on you. What I mean is, if I bring up an idea like this, please don't feel threatened. I just…when I saw the tension between you two the other day, I figured maybe we needed to think outside the box."

"How much would bringing in an outside security firm add to the budget?" Connor asked.

"Some. But we'd no longer have to carry liability insurance for the security team. So there'd be some reduction in costs that might offset the firm's management fees."

His face hot, suddenly feeling as if Pacific Crest Bank might have hidden cameras in this office, the sea caves, and the penthouse suite, Connor measured his next words carefully. "I appreciate your sensitivity, but Logan and I have had some extensive discussions and things have worked out."

"Oh. Okay, then," she said.

"Actually, I think the security director thing is going to be permanent."

"Oh, okay," she said.

"He's got a lot of experience here, and I found some items on our email server that attest to his commitment to the resort."

"Yeah, well, we reviewed his work history before I recommended him to you the other day, and it was pretty spotless. So I'm not surprised. But my sense was, *your* history with him went back further than that."

Oh, shit.

Connor swallowed. "All water under the bridge."

And water streaming down my naked body as he stroked me into soapy heaven this morning.

"I guess that's good news then," she said, "so long as you have a security director you can trust."

"We have established trust. Yes. I can say that for sure."

And so many other things that have me hurting in all the right places, for a change.

"Okay. There's also the matter of the rest of the department. I'm not sure if all the positions have been filled, but we can bring in an outside company for that too. Even if they're only temporary hires."

"I think we're working on that as we speak," Connor said. "But if we don't turn up anything good, I'll let you know."

"All right, well, great. Security at Sapphire Cove is going a lot better than I thought it was."

"Well, it had nowhere to go to but up."

Lois moved into some formalities intended to end the call when suddenly a thought occurred to Connor. "Before you go, Lois. I just thought of something. About this whole outside security company thing."

"Yes?"

"Is there a world where we bring in an outside firm and Logan keeps his new position?" Connor asked.

"Of course. I mean, we'd be doing the hiring, not the other way around. So we could make whatever arrangement with the company we wanted to."

"Could we make an arrangement where they answered to *you*?" Connor asked.

"Who's *they* in this scenario?" she asked.

"The security department."

"So the security department would answer to an outside firm, and we here at the bank would manage the outside firm."

"Correct," Connor said.

There was a brief silence. "And as GM, you wouldn't. Am I understanding you correctly?"

"Yes."

"Which means you'd no longer be Logan's boss."

"Right," Connor said.

There was silence from the other end, silence that left Connor short of breath. It was a question he had to ask, but he was pretty sure the asking had tipped his hand to the woman who held almost as much power over the resort as he did.

"The loss there would be for you," she finally said. "I mean, you'd be ceding your management control over the security department. And in light of recent events, some GMs would see that as a frightening proposition."

"Well, given how badly the last GM abused the department, maybe the change in oversight makes sense in the long term."

"That's definitely a compelling argument."

"It's something to think about, at least. I was curious, that's all. Let's table all of this for now and then come back to it, maybe in a few days."

"Sure," Lois said.

Then they said their goodbyes, and Connor hung up and stared at the blank wall for a while, feeling like an idiot.

Did forty-eight hours of passion really justify changing the management structure at Sapphire Cove? Was he getting ahead of himself, like the person who brought a U-Haul on their second date? Or should he immediately start working to make sure he was no longer Logan's boss based solely on the fact that he and Logan had slept together?

There was no corporate office to answer to. No board of directors.

Only a bank responsible for ensuring a document his grandfather had written years ago—and amended fairly recently—was enforced and that the hotel remained financially viable. There were lawyers, of course, all of whom would probably shit a brick if they knew Connor and Logan were sleeping together.

But still, would altering the hotel's chain of command have damaging consequences down the road? Was it a selfish choice based in fear and hormones?

Logan's special knock rattled the door.

When Connor opened it, the man's tense, stony expression set him back on his feet.

"We've got a problem," Logan said.

"Rodney?"

"No. Missing kid."

"Oh, no. How old?"

"Three," Logan answered.

"Oh my God. How long?"

"Parents woke up this morning and he wasn't in their room. They've been looking *themselves* because they were too embarrassed to say anything because they're not paying guests."

Connor gasped.

"Stick with me during this," Logan said. "We've still got You Know Who to worry about."

"Absolutely." But Connor's thoughts were full of images of three-year-olds wandering alone down beaches and along cliff's edges and into dark caves.

His heart was suddenly beating harder than it had in days, and all things considered, that was saying something. The boy's mother was so panicked she could barely get words out, and the father was pacing next to them like a caged tiger. Apparently, in this family, wanderlust was genetic. The boy's name was Benji. No developmental disabilities or language difficulties to be aware of. Just a problem staying put, which they called "the explorer's bug." On the three-acre property they'd been evacuated from, he had a tendency to roam and very little fear of encountering wildlife.

The sheriffs were called. Pictures of the boy—an apple-cheeked redhead—emailed from the mother's phone were printed out by front desk staff and handed out to anyone within range of the lobby. And that was an ever more inclusive group, Connor noticed, as guests were drawn by the tense energy and sense of alarm radiating from Benji's already exhausted and traumatized parents.

Logan took control, drawing Connor and all the security guys on duty into a quick huddle. There was someone there Connor didn't recognize, a linebacker-big Pacific Islander. Connor realized the man had been one of Logan's interviews that morning. Now he'd been sucked into the action of the day, a sign he'd been hired or really wanted to be.

"All right, gents. Biggest surface area we have to cover is the east hill, so Brandon, I want you to get anyone who looks sharp and capable out there. You'll need to sweep uphill and down, and parts of it are steep, so no one with any movement issues or bad shoes. Also, we're talking about a three-year-old who's been uprooted in the middle of a disaster, so if he can figure out which direction home is, he might be headed that way, and that's east."

Brandon nodded. "What kind of search, Logan? Like a grid search?"

"Do you know how to do one?"

"No," Brandon said.

"That's fine. Try to space everyone out about ten feet from each other and have them walk straight downhill and then up again. Now, tons of people are going to want to help who are older, maybe not with the best vision. Keep them *inside* in the hotel. But honestly, a little boy who wants to explore is probably outside, not in. Still, there's a chance of anything, and we don't want anyone to go to waste.

"J.T., I want you back on the cameras pronto. Keoni, organize two groups to walk the entire perimeter on top of the promontory, not the hill. Leave that to Brandon's crew. One group starts making the circle in one direction, the other in the other. That way you've got different sets of eyes going over the same territory. You're looking under bushes, trees. I also want you searching the cliff's edge but from *behind* the balustrade, got it? The balustrade's there because not everything on the other side is 100 percent stable. Scott, you're coming with me and Connor down to the beach."

"Isn't the beach closed?" Scott asked.

"I'm not counting on a three-year-old to read the signs."

Before Logan could pull away from Connor, he seized his arm. "Logan, the caves. If I left the gate open—"

"You *didn't* leave the gates open last night. But we'll check to be sure. Because we're going to check everywhere. Because we're going to find this kid."

As cries of Benji began to echo down all the hotel's corridors and reverberate through its public spaces, Connor took the beach stairs three at a time.

Once they hit sand, Logan and Scott started checking under the row of mini catamarans, and Connor, his heart racing, went straight for the gate to the sea caves.

It was locked. Thank God.

Just in case, he opened it with his key, raised the flashlight Logan had given him, and set about a search of the caverns he'd explored as a boy, calling out the name Benji over and over. The only response was his own echoing voice and gurgling water and the nearby roar of the surf. Dread tightening his chest, he angled the beam into the frothing water next to the boardwalk. The tide was so much higher than it had been the night before. If the boy had somehow climbed the gate and wandered in here and been… He couldn't finish the thought.

Connor emerged from the cave, squinting in the sunlight, and made his way to the bend in the boardwalk that hugged the cliff's face. Here he had a good view back toward the sand. And that's when he saw a bright spot of red at the far side of the beach, yards from where the opposite cliff plunged to the sea.

"*Logan!*"

Connor was running now, sand punching into his shoes as he went. His cry and speed had landed Logan and Scott on his tail.

The opposite end of the crescent-shaped beach had no cave structure, but a series of jagged offshore rocks that turned into a shrunken cityscape of tide pools at low tide. Now it was high tide, and clinging to one of the rocks was a terrified three-year-old boy in bright red pajamas, sobbing his heart out. Connor saw immediately how it played out. At low tide, the mound of rocks probably looked like a perfect castle for a curious little explorer. Then the tide had started to come in, and a toddler's hesitation had turned into fear and then paralysis, and soon the castle became a buoy amidst a vortex of roiling seas channeled by the jutting rocks on both sides.

Connor had experienced one full-on panic attack in his life, on a flight that lost power in one engine and had to make an emergency landing.

This was worse.

Logan ordered Scott to call the fire department and request a Coast Guard rescue, then he joined Connor at the rocky edge.

"Benji!" Connor called.

The boy jerked in response to his name, and Connor thought he might slide free of the spray-slick rocks he clung to, and only then did his precarious position become clear. He was so small, so afraid, and clinging to the rocks as the waves came in again and again would require an adult's poise and steadiness at least. He had neither.

"Connor." Logan sounded so cool and calm for a second Connor thought he might be hallucinating. He turned to him and saw that he'd removed his coat. He wasn't sure why because in his head he was still seeing Benji's tear-stained baby cheeks and his agonizing grimace. Logan closed the distance between them, grabbed the back of Connor's neck, and looked straight into his eyes. Connor was too startled to make sense of what he was doing. "Whatever happens, whatever comes next, promise me something."

"What?"

"Don't go in the water."

"I promise, but—"

But before Connor could finish the sentence, Logan planted a hard kiss on his lips, turned, and dove headfirst into the waves.

Drowning was fighting.

Drowning was exhaustion.

So Logan gave himself completely to the violent sea, made the current his ally. Summoned his hours of training at the Marine Corps Water Survival Course on Coronado Island where he'd played both rescuer and panicked drowning victim, learned well the tricks water and its omnipresent threat can play on the body and the mind. He'd timed his dive to coincide with the incoming wave and felt a surge of triumph when he realized it was pushing him inward toward the cliff's base. Now it was a matter of letting the retreating current slam him into the rock rather than pull him out to sea.

He thought he was on track when his head broke water and he saw the little boy several feet ahead of him, between the wave that was drawing him out to sea and the shore. He'd missed.

No choice but to let the wave draw him back, farther and farther. No mad strokes, no exhausting kicks. Floating. Breathing where he could.

Waiting for the next surge. Mother of God, it was taking its sweet time. The boy's wide eyes got farther away, his wails swallowed by the surf sounds that were right at Logan's ears. His back. His life.

Then everything around Logan started to rise, so fast it plugged his nostrils with stinging salt water. But it was lifting him, working with him, serving him. He'd made the sea his bitch.

He hoped.

And then his stomach slammed into the rock at what must have been fifteen miles an hour, and the wind went out of him with a sound that would have made people laugh during a cartoon. But he had his arms around the rock.

Now he had no choice but to fight the sea, holding on for dear life as the wave that had lifted him surged away from him. It dropped the sea level enough for him to hoist his foot up onto a rock ledge. Then another, and suddenly he was free of the water.

Free but soaked and dripping, crouching atop the rock. Little Benji was below him, staring up at him, still gasping but not crying quite so hard now that he was no longer alone. There was just enough surface area on top of the rock for the two of them, but he'd risked his life to get here because it was clear the boy was too young and too terrified to hold on by himself. Now he could hold on to Logan, and Logan could hold on to the rock.

"How you doing, buddy?"

Incomprehensible words blended *mommy* and *daddy* and *sorry* into a language known only to terrified toddlers. Logan rolled onto his back, lifted the kid up onto his stomach, and buried the guy's face in his chest so he could pretend the scary things had gone away. But they hadn't gone away. When he risked a look back toward shore, he saw Connor down on his knees, terror in his eyes, and his hands to his face.

Later, if I survive this, I'll throw my arms around him and tell him how much he looked like that kid from Home Alone.

But instead, Logan lifted one finger and twirled it to indicate the rotors of a helicopter. Scott pointed to his phone to indicate he'd made the call. And then it was a matter of waiting.

"Well, your mom's sure right, little buddy. You are an explorer. But right now, I need you to stay still and hold on to me 'til help arrives."

He braved another look back at the shore, but the sight of Connor's fear tugged too many strings in his heart at once. It had been instinctive, reflexive, diving into the water the way he had. And his greatest fear hadn't changed: Connor was the same guy who'd been ready to charge party crashers who were twice his size. Would he risk his life by diving into these waves if things went south?

Logan prayed help would arrive before the question could be posed.

Finally, a Coast Guard helicopter swept low toward them across the bright blue water. The waves around them were so loud he could barely hear the Sikorsky's massive rotary blades. Logan had enough training strapping Marines to spinal boards that he'd figured he'd be a crackshot at dealing with whatever rescue device they dropped from the chopper's side door. But what emerged was not just a platform, but a Coast Guard officer attached to a cable. Logan repositioned himself as best he could, until he was sitting up with Benji on his lap. The boy clung to him for dear life. But then it was like the Coast Guard guy was sitting next to them on the rock, even though he had a connection to a world of safety and rescue Logan currently lacked. All Logan had to do was pass the kid into his arms, then the little boy was belted in several places to the officer's bright orange suit.

"I'm coming back for you!" the Coast Guard officer roared.

Logan gave him a thumbs-up, and then they were rising into the air. The boy's eyes went saucer wide and his mouth a silent O.

Logan was relieved—so relieved he didn't see the wave that swept him off the rock.

Connor screamed so loud it felt like his throat was on fire. The next thing he knew Scott had his arms around him, forcing him to keep the promise he'd made Logan.

But plunging headfirst into the waves was the only thing that made sense when Logan vanished under them. Almost every fiber of his being felt pulled in the direction he'd last glimpsed the man of his dreams. The rest of them were screaming.

So fast. Gone so fast.

He went as close to the edge as he could, the waves sending spray onto his face, looking for any signs he could find. The helicopter still hovered overhead, and now some sort of Coast Guard boat was slicing toward shore. They'd save him, for sure. They'd save him. They had to. Maybe he'd do what he'd done last time, go limp and let the waves carry him where he wanted to go. But he'd been struck hard and fast, and it hadn't been planned, and how much water did it really take to fill a person's lungs? How many drops to drown them?

Connor tried to take a deep breath, but sobs ripped from him, refusing to be held in. Sobs of panic and despair. Sobs of terror and hurt and anger. Sobs that said, *Am I really going to lose another man I care about to this place?* Then something pulled on him from behind, and he thought it was Scott again, but the pull was too strong, too hard, too familiar.

"What the hell did I tell you about going in the water?" a voice growled in his ear.

Connor spun and stared into Logan's eyes. His chest was heaving, and his uniform shirt was torn in some places, blood-spotted in others. There was even a bruise on his right cheek and something on his forehead that looked like it might turn into a welt. But he was here, on dry land. He must have been slammed into the lip of jagged rock against the cliff's face and pulled himself out while Connor had been searching for evidence he'd been swept out to sea. But Logan was here, alive, and holding him. And there was no way to resist the urge that took over, the urge to bring their lips together, to cup Logan's face in his hands to make sure he was real and not some vision spewed forth by an angry sea.

For a while, Connor couldn't bring himself to let Logan go, and Logan, it seemed, couldn't end their embrace either.

"Uh, guys," Scott said. "I'm not sure if, uh, you wanted this to be a private moment, but it's not."

They turned and saw Scott pointing to the guests who'd massed on the beach behind them. Their raised camera phones had recorded everything about the rescue, including the fierce kiss that had followed it.

But if any of them had a problem with it, there was no telling, because they were too busy applauding.

19

Once the doctor disappeared through a curtain that did little to blot out the chaotic sounds of the ER beyond, Logan looked up at Connor with puppy dog eyes made more pitiful by the effects of Vicodin. "Are you mad at me?"

"Nope. Now that you've agreed to a CAT scan, I'm happy as a clam."

"You're mad at me. For going in the water."

"How could I be mad at you for saving that boy's life?" Connor asked.

"I didn't say it was justified. I just said it was what you were feeling."

"Oh, okay. Thanks for creating this safe space for you to tell me what I'm feeling."

"You're mad. I knew it."

"I'm not mad. I'm just freaked out that you almost drowned."

"I didn't almost drown."

"It looked different from where I was standing."

Logan laughed. "You kinda looked like the kid from *Home Alone.* Your hands were on the sides of your face like…" Logan tried to imitate the classic Macaulay Culkin pose, but it pulled on muscles still singing with pain.

"That's funny. 'Cause I felt like I was in *Jaws.*"

Logan studied him, eyes going glassy from fatigue and possibly the pain pill they'd given him a while ago. He reached out as far as he could, and Connor took his hand.

"It was scary," Logan said.

"I'm sure."

"Not the waves. I mean, the waves were scary. But I was prepared for that. The scary part was knowing you had to watch, being afraid you'd jump in to try to save me."

"You're hot, but you're not that hot."

"Is someone using humor to deflect?" Logan asked.

"Is someone feeling the pain meds they gave him a few minutes ago?"

"Maybe a little."

Logan pulled him in for a gentle, lingering kiss. Connor couldn't bring himself to draw back, and suddenly their foreheads were touching as their hands stayed linked. "This is what I do, Connor Harcourt. I act. I fix. Or I try to, at least. And maybe after the night we had it scares me to think you might not be okay with that."

"You really think I'm going to complain about falling into bed with a hero?" Connor asked.

"Heroes get hurt. Sometimes that's too much for the people waiting for them to come home. My buddies in the Corps, I watched some of their marriages end. They'd say it was the distance, but it was the worry. It was the fear. I never had to deal with it. I was always single. I could take risks. All I had to care about was me and my Marines, not somebody waiting at home."

"Your dad was worried about you, I bet."

"My dad shared more feelings with me last night then he has in my entire life. You know what I mean. When I saw the look on your face when I was out on that rock, it was a first for me. And the fact that I might hurt you felt worse than drowning."

When Connor looked away without meaning to, Logan reached up and gently raised his chin until they were looking into each other's eyes again. "Tell me what was in your head when I was out there."

"It feels stupid," Connor whispered. "And dramatic."

"You're not stupid, and today's all about dramatic. So out with it."

"I didn't want to lose another man I cared about to Sapphire Cove."

Logan nodded, but his eye contact didn't waver. "See, that's it, though. I would have done all that even if I was a guest. Or if we'd been on some other beach. And I guess I want to know if you're okay with that. Or if you can be."

Connor thought of roaring waves, saw Logan vanishing under the water. Then he saw a little boy being lifted to safety, felt the sudden embrace of Logan behind him, the sight of him injured, dripping but alive, heard the applause of the people who'd watched it all from the beach. And before he could think twice about it, before doubt could creep in, he brought Logan's hand to his lips, kissed it. "I don't want to be with someone I'm not afraid to lose."

Logan smiled. Then suddenly the curtain was pushed back, but instead of the doctors, it was a familiar chubby-cheeked little boy being carried by his mother. The mother looked far more relaxed than she had that morning in the lobby, and her son looked clean and happy. When he recognized his savior, he threw his arms across Logan's big chest and held on, this time out of love instead of fear.

"Should Logan really be giving TV interviews while he's high on drugs?" Gloria Alvarez asked.

They were standing in the motor court where she'd been updating Connor on the mood of the hotel after the morning's rescue. Now Connor followed the direction of Gloria's gaze to where Logan was holding forth before a cluster of news cameras not far from where they'd held the press conference a few days before. He definitely seemed a bit more hand gesturey than usual, and maybe his eyes were a little wide, but the reporters seemed to be eating it up.

"He's not high on drugs. They only gave him one pill before his CT scan came back clear."

"Yeah, I hear they can pack a lot into one pill these days," Gloria said.

"Hey, as long as they aren't talking about my uncle, he can go on all afternoon."

"Are you sure about that? He's been describing the curriculum at the Marine Corps Water Survival Course for twenty minutes, Connor."

Now that Connor gave them a closer look, some of the reporters did look bored.

"I'll get him."

When Connor was within earshot, he could hear what Logan was saying. "And when I say PT, it's not water aerobics, now, okay, you hear me? We're talking a crawl stroke that doesn't involve the legs. Then once you reach the other end of the pool, you hoist yourself up out of the water with both—"

"Guys, thanks so much, but we need to get Mr. Murdoch off his feet."

He took Logan's arm and guided him away from the cameras.

"I should really tell them more about my training because we don't want people who saw the news to just dive into the water when—"

"Or you should get off your feet for the rest of the day like the doctor said."

One of the reporters shouted after them. "Hey, how 'bout that kiss, guys? Any comments on that?"

"Indeed," a familiar voice said from several steps away. "How about that kiss?"

Connor's mother was standing right next to Gloria, in the very spot Connor had occupied seconds before. Had she been holding back and waiting to strike? No doubt she'd seen the video of the water rescue, but her crossed arms and pinched brows said she had a lot more to say about the lip-lock that followed. Her hair was pulled back in a ponytail, and she was dressed entirely in canary yellow. Which was always bad news. Ponytails and monochromatic outfits were Janice Harcourt's code for *I have serious work to do today, most of it on you.*

"Connor, I have a table reserved for us out on the pool deck," she said.

"I'm kinda busy right now, Mom."

"That's correct. You have a meeting with your mother."

Logan cleared his throat, trying to seem way more sober than he looked. "Mrs. Harcourt, given Rodney's actions, we need to make sure Connor—"

"I'm aware of the new security directive, Mr. Murdoch. And I have Brandon watching over the table for us and Scott ready to escort you guys up to your room before he takes Connor back to the pool. To meet with me." She leveled Logan in a glare that had once been capable of blasting a confession out of the most difficult of high school students. "That is where you're staying, isn't it, Mr. Murdoch? In Connor's room?"

In the tense silence that followed, Gloria actually winced.

"When he's not saving three-year-olds from drowning," Connor said.

"Uh huh. I'll be waiting," she said, and it sounded like a threat.

Logan turned to Connor. "Let Gloria take me up, and then go with Scott."

"Are you sure?" Connor asked.

"Yeah. I don't have any experience with moms, but that looks serious," Logan said.

"Okay. I'll be up in a bit. Stay off your feet like the doctor said."

"Yeah, yeah."

"No, not, *yeah, yeah*. If you can't bring yourself to follow the doctor's orders, follow mine."

"Well, you are my boss."

It was a joke Logan might not have made so directly if he hadn't been chemically altered.

Logan leaned forward, and when he dropped his voice to a whisper, the effect of the pain pill was even more pronounced. "Okay, fine. But only if you promise to ride me like a cowboy later."

"Okay. You're a little altered right now, so that might be a consent issue."

"I consent," Logan growled, waggling his eyebrows. "I consent. I consent. I consent."

By the third *I consent* he was rocking his hips back and forth like he was getting ready to line dance.

"Go upstairs."

But Logan was swaying back and forth to a new tune only he could hear. "I consent. I *conseeent*. I *caaaan seeeeense*, that cowboy's going be our preferred position until my shoulder stops hurting. Hey, that's clever."

It wasn't clever, but Logan was cute when he was high. "Go upstairs, Gay Will Rogers," Connor said, trying to fight his smile.

"Give me a kiss first," Logan slurred, lips pursed.

"Yeah, we've had our one public display of affection for the day."

"C'mon, they're waiting for it."

Connor looked over his shoulder and saw the reporters were, indeed, waiting for it.

He gave them a wave, grabbed Logan's hand, and pulled him toward the doors.

The kiss, and other things, would have to wait.

He had an angry mother to deal with.

Families splashed in the sunlit pool. Before a backdrop of bright green coastal hills, a group of wildfire victims were being led in a yoga class on the rolling lawn nearby. To the casual observer, the pool deck made it look like the hotel was back to its pre-scandal routines, if you didn't notice that the guests were more diverse than usual and their outfits not as desperately trendy or needlessly expensive. His mother had not only reserved a table, she'd cordoned off an entire corner of the deck that met up with the glass wall for Camilla's. Brandon stood nearby, rigid as a centurion. He gave Connor a polite nod as Connor approached.

His mother had ordered them both iced tea, her preferred drink for moments of *Be quiet and listen, this is serious.*

"I figured you'd rather do this in private," he said, slurping tea.

"I figured out here we'd cut down on the possibility of a tantrum."

"I don't throw tantrums."

"Except for the other day, and on the subject of the very man you were kissing on television just this morning."

"Okay. We were not kissing *on* television. People filmed us kissing on the beach and then took their footage to—"

"I'm aware of how camera phones and social media work."

"Well, then stop making it sound like we went on *Good Morning America* to make out."

"At this rate, I wouldn't be surprised if they asked you to. That's how much attention this is getting."

"Nobody at the hotel seems to care."

His mother leaned forward and dropped her voice to a whisper. "Good. Because I don't care about this hotel."

"You care about this hotel, Mom. Come on."

"The only thing I like about this hotel are the views and the senior staff. I hate what it did to our family. I hate the power it gave Rodney over all of us. And I would have fully supported your decision if you'd decided to sell it. And make no mistake, I would have married your father if he was a CVS clerk."

"You say that now, but you've spent *a lot* of his money since then."

"Mind your tongue, Connor Harcourt!"

"Just saying," he muttered, and he figured the best way to mind his tongue was to give it some more iced ginger tea. This stuff was the bomb.

"What I care about is my son," she said. "And you're now on film making out with your security director."

"We wouldn't be the first people to fall for each other at work."

"You don't just work together. He's your subordinate."

"Yeah, that's not how it plays out in the shower," Connor grumbled.

"I need you to be a grown-up about this."

"Oh, believe me. They're very grown-up showers."

"Being crude is not going to throw me off my game here."

"Oh, come on, Mother. You taught high school for twenty years. A plane could crash into you and it wouldn't throw you off your game. You have to at least let me try every now and then."

"Not now, and not over this."

"Maybe I'm not in the mood for a lecture right now."

"And you know exactly how this works. Stop interrupting and it will go by quicker."

"I get it," he finally said. "You don't trust me to handle this relationship in addition to everything else."

"How long has this been going on between you two?"

"That's…such a complicated question."

"Good. Give it a complicated answer. I'm all ears. And I'll know if you leave something out, so don't even try."

And so he started at the beginning, and by the time he was finished, his mother's anger had softened into something that seemed more complex and more confused. He was jittery about his closing, but he knew he couldn't live with himself if he didn't give voice to it.

"And I'm sorry to put it like this, but you owe Logan an apology, Mom. He saved a child's life this morning, and you treated him like he's the Whore of Babylon."

"On one condition. Find a way to make it so that you're no longer his boss," she said.

Connor felt his heartbeat thread. "You're not telling me to fire him."

"No."

"What are you saying then?" Connor asked, thinking of Lois Penry and outside security firms and how his mother's schoolteacher's mind always had a sixth sense for unpleasant but often essential solutions.

"Move departments around. Work with the bank. You run this place now. You're smart. I'm sure there's something you can figure out."

"You really think what's going on between me and Logan will damage the hotel?"

"I don't give a damn if it damages the *hotel*, Connor. Sure, I want you to have a shot at saving this place. But if it doesn't work, and he is who you say he is, I want you to have a shot at Logan too. Especially if Rodney was the reason you didn't the first time. And just a few more days of being his boss in this pressure cooker, you'll both be kneecapped before you can take to the field."

He saw the logic in her argument. But he wasn't sure if he believed her. Something was working between Logan and Connor, something that was larger than their kisses and their orgasms. They were building something, saving something, together, and this might be the glue for whatever was developing between them.

But when it came to his mom, he knew how to recognize a win when he saw one.

"Mom, I've got to meet the new security agents Logan hired this morning. I don't mean to cut this short, given the canary yellow. But I am actually quite busy."

When Connor stood, it was mostly a test to see if his mother would object. She stared at him, a blend of frustration and what might be guilt in her expression.

He bent down and gave his mother a kiss on the forehead. "You're a tough old broad, Mrs. Harcourt."

"Watch who you're calling a broad. Old I'll take. Old means you had the strength to stick around." As he went to stand up again, she gently gripped his hand and looked up into his eyes. "But remember this, my son. You will always be more important to me than this place. Always."

Connor figured that earned her a kiss on the cheek instead of the forehead.

Movie Night had originally been scheduled for the pool. But after that morning's near drowning, the prospect of a bunch of kids bobbing up and down on floaties while they watched *Finding Dory* no longer seemed like a pleasant diversion. So Jonas had relocated the event to the hotel's biggest ballroom where the staff had carted in spare mattresses from rollaways and dressed them in vaguely coral-looking formations using bright sheets and blankets and any other beachy party favor they could find in storage.

All of it seemed like the perfect way for parents to keep their kids occupied while they nervously checked for fire updates on their phones. And when Connor checked in, it looked to be working.

The latest updates about the Palm Fire were encouraging. The winds had shifted, sparing the nursing home that had been in the fire's sights and driving the flames toward a less populated area.

They were wheeling in the popcorn machine as Connor made a quiet exit.

J.T. escorted him to the penthouse suite, all Southern charm, his cornsilk hair in its usual, enviably perfect side part.

Connor opened the door gently and saw most of the lights were off except for a few dim ones in the seating area. Resting on the dining table was a bright gift bag, swaddled in the ribbons Connor recognized as the signature of his mother's favorite gift wrap service. He read the name on the card.

A gift from his mother to Logan. This pleased him far more than a gift with his name on it.

Or maybe he should wait to see what it was first.

And where was Logan?

Connor turned, and the sight that greeted him brought out a gasp.

Logan was asleep, a soft spill of warm light from the bedside lamp falling on his Greek statue of a profile, making a slender river of gold along his smooth, hard chest, stopping right below one of those dark nipples Connor had tasted for the first time the night before. He'd roused Logan quickly that morning so he hadn't taken the time to drink in the sight of the gorgeous man at rest. His lips slightly parted with each breath, his eyes closed, his face relaxed and devoid of the tense, ready-to-respond energy that lit up his muscles whenever he was awake. Silent and slumbering, his size was somehow more noticeable. And this leisurely glimpse of Logan at rest felt more intimate than any moment of shared nudity they'd enjoyed the night before.

Slowly, Connor went to the bed and sank down on the edge of it.

Logan stirred. His smile was instant, pure. Boyish, even. Then his eyes widened as memory seemed to strike. "Oh God. What did I do?"

"You have a really interesting reaction to pain meds."

"Crap," he groaned. "I shouldn't have taken it. I can't handle that stuff."

"I think it's fine as long as you don't interact with humans for at least twelve hours."

"What did I do, Connor?" Logan moaned.

"Where do I begin? I think your crowning achievement was when you joined us for an evacuations update with Gloria on FaceTime."

"Oh, yeah?"

"Yeah. It was going all right until you told her to take off the boa constrictor around her neck because it was distracting you."

Logan winced. "I'm guessing there wasn't a snake."

"Not even a scarf. You passed out after that. Gloria had her sister, who's a nurse, come to check on you, and she said your vitals were fine, you were probably having a mental reaction."

"You can say that again. What else?"

"You tried to kiss me in front of the reporters outside."

"I sort of remember that."

"Also, the reporters basically know everything there is to know now about Marine Corps Water Survival training."

"I remember, and I still think that's important. What else?"

"You told me we'd be doing it cowboy style until your shoulder felt better."

"My shoulder does feel better. But I still want to be your Trigger." Logan's smile blended seduction and youthful lasciviousness into a combination that made Connor's breath catch.

"Definitely on the agenda," Connor said.

Their lips met. Logan's hand went to the back of Connor's neck, found its by now familiar grip that started out gentle and then got harder the more Connor went boneless under it.

Suddenly, Logan broke their kiss. "Wait. Your mother. I remember your mother. Was she actually wearing all yellow or was that like the snake?"

"The yellow was real. Very real."

"And she was angry," Logan whispered.

"Ish."

"Did you guys talk?" Logan asked.

"We did."

"And it turned out okay?"

Connor sat up and lifted the ribbon-strewn gift bag in his other hand. "She sent over a gift."

"Oh, that's nice."

"It's for you."

"You're kidding." Logan pushed himself to a seated position, which caused the comforter to tumble farther down the parade of defined muscles that was his torso.

"Open it carefully," Connor said. "It was a...complex discussion."

Logan stared down at the bag on his lap as if he thought its inhabitant might jump out and bite him. Then he started gently fingering his way through the blue tissue paper inside. He pulled out what was clearly a wrapped hardcover book, but no sooner had he torn a single strip away then he gasped.

"Chesty Puller," he bellowed.

"Who's that? A stripper?"

Logan tore the rest of the paper off, revealing the cover of a book called *Marine! The Life of Chesty Puller* by Burke Davis. The rendering of the title character featured a man with a deeply lined face, outfitted in green camouflage with binoculars hanging from his neck and what looked like a green baseball cap shading his lantern-jawed face.

"He's only one of the most famous Marines who's ever lived," Logan said. "He's the most decorated Marine in Marine Corps history. Fought all over the world. He was a lieutenant general by the time he retired. He's like the father of the modern Marine Corps."

"Is there a stripper who's named after *him?*"

"All right, now. Don't be smart. I get real serious about Chesty."

"I can see that. I'll read the book."

Logan flipped open the cover and read something on the opening pages. "Yeah, no you won't. This is a first edition. And it's signed. Nobody's ever touching this again. I'll get you a paperback."

Logan opened the nightstand drawer and dropped the book inside.

"Yeah, right next to the lube?" Connor said. "Not sure that's a good plan, soldier."

"Marines are not called soldiers." Without taking his eyes off Connor, Logan opened the top drawer, pulled the book out, then dropped it in the drawer below. "We're called Marines."

"Glad to see your shoulder and your ego are on the mend."

"Yeah, there's nothing a few hours of a narcotics-fueled coma won't fix. This is an amazing gift. I'm going to have to thank your mom. I guess your talk went really well."

Connor grunted and got to his feet, walked to the end table next to the double doors, and started emptying his pockets onto it.

"Or not," Logan said.

"I think there's a condition attached to that gift," Connor said.

"Oh, yeah?"

"Are you hungry?" Connor asked.

"No. Are you avoiding something?"

"Maybe."

"Turn around, Connor."

"You sure you're not hungry?" Connor asked.

"What is it? What did she say?"

"Okay." Connor turned to face the bed. "Look right at me."

"I am."

"Now, answer honestly. Do you see any reptiles clinging to my person? Because I want to make sure you're completely of sound mind before we discuss something complicated."

"When have things between us ever not been complicated?" Logan asked.

"The question has more to do with your mental state."

"I'm good," Logan said. "I see no reptiles." He swept his hand through the air as if he actually had spotted a few but had somehow managed to make them vanish with sheer force of will.

"Okay, good. Let's order some food."

"Connor."

Connor sighed. "I suggested to my mother that her treatment of you earlier was maybe not befitting someone who'd just saved a child from drowning."

"Well, that's all right. I can't remember how she treated me earlier."

"It wasn't all right with *me*. And I think after we talked she saw the error of her ways. And agreed to apologize." Connor gestured toward the nightstand that now contained her gift. "With one condition."

"I'm listening."

"She wants us to find a way for me to no longer be your boss."

Logan's brow furrowed. "You have to be GM for at least a year or the hotel gets sold. Isn't that how the trust works?"

"Yeah."

"Is she suggesting I stop working here?" Logan asked, voice tight, gaze level.

"No. She thinks there are changes that could be made to the management structure so that I'm no longer your superior."

"She thinks it's unprofessional that we're…"

"Sleeping together."

Logan's eyes shot to his. "It's a lot more than that, isn't it? I mean, were not just sleeping together…right?"

"Beyond right," Connor said, acting blasé, but feeling relieved Logan said it first. "And she thinks so too, apparently. Or at least wants us to have a shot at whatever a lot more than just sleeping together is. And she thinks we won't if I have to be your boss during this stressful time for the hotel."

Logan's expression softened, and the first signs of a smile came to his lips. "Well, that's kinda nice. So how would this work? This management change, I mean."

"Well, I had an idea, but I didn't want to talk about it with her before I talked about it with you. Basically, we'd bring in an outside security company that would answer directly to the bank, and you'd keep your position but with the new company."

Logan nodded, thinking this over. Didn't fly off the handle. Didn't throw his legs to the floor. Didn't leave the room or freak out or any of the other nightmare scenarios Connor had dreamed up during the hours leading to this one.

"And then you wouldn't be my superior," Logan said.

"Yeah, but I mean, there're a lot of unknowns."

"Sure, but there always are. We'd figure it out."

"So you're not upset?" Connor asked. "That you'd have a new boss for the second time in a few weeks."

"Not if it means I can spend more time in bed with my current one."

"We're spending plenty of time in bed together now," Connor said.

"Why would I be upset?" Logan asked.

"I don't know. I thought maybe..." Connor lost hold of his words and took a deep breath.

"You were really nervous to talk about this, weren't you?"

"Kind of, yeah," Connor said.

Logan cocked his head.

"Okay. A lot," Connor added.

"Why?" Logan asked.

"It makes it sound like we're in a relationship and it's not just a fling. And it's happened really fast and been really stressful, so I don't want to force you—"

"I just told you this is more than just sleeping together," Logan said.

"Yeah, but a fling is, like, one rung up from that."

"Okay. Well, I'm feeling, like, several rungs up from that."

"So am I." It felt like these three little words required all the breath in his lungs.

"Good. We're on the same page then. Or rung. Or ladder. Or whatever."

"Yeah."

Logan's intent gaze pulled Connor's lips to his. When their long, leisurely kiss ended, they were staring into each other's eyes. "Connor?"

"Yeah."

"Take your pants off." A clear, confident command delivered with laser-like focus.

"Only my pants?" Connor whispered.

"And your underwear." He reached up and gently smoothed Connor's bangs back from his forehead. "Anything that's going to get in the way of me fucking you."

It sounded like an order, and when Logan gave him orders, Connor had no choice but to comply. Especially if the order was to undress. His cheeks flaming, his hands shaking with anticipation, he stepped to the side of the bed, undid his belt buckle, and let his slacks fall to the floor.

"Slow," Logan said.

Connor wedged his fingers under the waistband of his white briefs and pulled them down gently until the tail of his white dress shirt was teasing the cheeks of his ass in a way that made his balls ache. There was something delightfully obscene about the sight of his own thickening cock rising between the dangling flaps of his shirt and the hungry smile it brought to Logan's face.

"Come here," Logan said.

Connor closed the distance, unsure of exactly what Logan had planned.

When he was within easy reach, Logan reached out and cupped Connor's tightening balls. Then, in an instant, Logan had swallowed Connor's cock to the root, sucking him the same way he'd fucked him the night before—hard and thrusting, confident and intense. Only then, amidst the head-spinning, bone-melting bliss, did it occur to Connor they'd been together many times now and this was the first time Logan had taken Connor into his mouth. Perhaps the natural result of Connor's submissive nature, of his yearning desire to hit his knees when aroused. Or maybe he'd secretly feared Logan would be averse to the act in some restrictive, top-only way. He wasn't. Not in the slightest. There was a moment when Connor thought Logan might finish him off right there, Connor standing next to the bed still half dressed, with Logan on his side, mostly naked beneath the sheets, as if Connor had furtively snuck into the room and been overtaken by a bedridden patient whose movement restrictions didn't apply to his mouth and arms. And desire.

Logan released Connor's cock, letting the head slip free of his slick lips with a proud little pop. "Get on me."

Again, no growls or overdone playacting. Just a series of firm commands.

Connor went to unbutton his shirt.

"No," Logan said, "get on me. Now."

Logan drew back the sheet and pushed down his boxers, exposing a giant cock that had been brought to fullness by the taste of Connor's pre-cum. Connor straddled him, easing back onto Logan's hardness until it was sandwiched between his cheeks, and savored the delicious feelings of those veins, that skin. Dreamed of the day when he could have it without a barrier between. Dreamed of what that would mean. Several more rungs above just sleeping together, several rungs above a fling. A ladder leading to a heaven Connor had glimpsed years before, a heaven stolen by his bastard uncle.

With one arm, Logan opened the nightstand drawer. With his other, he reached up and cupped Connor's chin in his powerful hand.

"You're going to look into my eyes while I fuck you," he said.

An easy, confident proclamation that brokered no question, no doubt. No hesitation. Connor felt his entrance clench in delicious anticipation. No other man had ever been able to induce a response down there with his voice, with his words. With hunger-filled instructions.

Connor nodded as much as he could in Logan's grip. He wanted to wait, to give Logan all the control, but he couldn't stop himself from sliding his ass slowly up and down Logan's throbbing, pre-cum slickened cock, the rhythm of his abandon taking control of his hips, his thighs, his entrance. A groan escaped him.

"The minute you look away, I stop," Logan said. "Because I want to see everything that's going through your head while I'm inside you. All of it. So if you want it, you have to look into my eyes."

He was so wildly eager to have Logan inside him, Connor signaled his consent by bringing their noses together, staring into Logan's eyes from inches away. He listened to the familiar shred of foil wrapper, the squirt of lube. Then Logan's slick fingers arrived at his entrance, steadily probing him, opening him, prepping him. Going deep, finding the right nerves. Grazing, stroking, prodding. As he did all of it, Logan met his own challenge, gazing into Connor's eyes as he made him helplessly ready.

Then it was time.

Only when the moment of entrance came did Connor realize what a challenge it would be. Letting someone enter him had always required a retreat to some private mental space, especially someone as big and powerful as Logan Murdoch. A place of deep breathing and maybe some fantasy too, all of it meant to distract from the initial, fiery pain. But this time, he had Logan's dark eyes to anchor him, Logan's fearless, adoring stare. His absolute commitment to drinking in the sight of every emotion coursing through Connor's expression, adjusting in response. The familiar sensations came in quick succession—the initial spasm of resistance that always seemed to suggest he'd never yield, intensifying, worsening, burning, and then, miraculously, the first moment of give—a moment Connor could never experience without letting out a high-pitched, unguarded, and more than a little feminine cry. And a moment, which, in the past, had always made Connor feel briefly and utterly alone, even when he was wrapped in someone's arms. Before now, all sex had been like that. The entry was an isolating event, and the eventual union, the coupling—the true connection—required a gradual return brought by the first steady thrusts of his partner.

It wasn't that way now. It wasn't that way with Logan. He was here with Logan for every stab of pain, every spasm of surrender. Logan was watching him, caressing him, learning him. Offering no judgment or commentary on what this blissful and wanted invasion required of Connor's body, of his mind, of his spirit.

"That's it, baby," Logan whispered. "That's my boy. That's my prince."

At these words, a sudden blend of gentle and firm, both radiuses of resistance inside Connor gave way, and suddenly he was full of Logan. Speared and anchored.

Logan began to thrust, once, twice. Then Connor rocked back to meet his thrusts, and Logan seemed to realize it was better to let Connor take control, let Connor's rocking draw them toward the blissful edge. Now it was Logan's face that transformed, Logan's expression that became a storm of emotions. Hunger turning to bliss. Aggression turning to submission. The top becoming the slave to the bottom's passion.

Connor knew he wouldn't last long. Not in this position, and not given Logan's size. Both these things conspired to hit all the right angles inside of him. Pain had turned to a throbbing heat that consumed his thighs, his knees, his lower back. Soon it would sweep his entire body. But he kept his promise, gazing into Logan's eyes. There was recognition there, a realization that Logan's commands had ultimately given Connor more power over him than he'd expected.

"Logan…"

"Yeah?"

"Not going to last…much longer."

"Good. I want to see it. I want to look into your eyes while you cum."

"Logan…"

Logan sensed it, felt it, knew it was coming. He kept his hand on Connor's chin, and with the other he reached up and gripped the top of Connor's head. He must have been remembering how Connor had thrown his head back during his moment of ecstasy the night before, and he wanted to secure it in place as they approached another. Logan Murdoch wanted to be damn sure that even in the midst of a wild orgasmic thrall, Connor couldn't look away.

"Can I?" Connor asked breathlessly, unable to finish the sentence. Logan glanced down and saw Connor had seized his own cock in one hand.

"Yeah, baby. You can. You can as long as you look into my eyes."

Connor obeyed. Staring, gazing, revealing. Stroking.

The cry that tore from him was multi-octave, prolonged. Maybe because he couldn't thrash or flail as it surged. Directed it right down at Logan as he erupted across his bare chest and stomach. Logan's eyes lit up with delight, his teeth clenched in desire behind his smile. Grunting as he drank it all in, the sight of Connor's bliss channeled and unleashed, and so very close. His mouth a perfect O, the last of his groans stuttering. And then his gasping mouth met Logan's, and Logan caught it in a wet and hungry kiss.

And for a moment, they were still.

"Do you need me to stop?" Logan asked.

And for a second, Connor thought that might be the case. In any other circumstance, with any other man, riding so hard and fast would have required a reprieve. But Connor felt purged, swept, and boneless.

"No," he whispered into Logan's muscular neck. "I need you to cum."

Connor rose to a seated position again. He could feel his sweaty, dappled bangs plastered to his forehead, his dress shirt disheveled and sweaty. Slowly, he rocked back onto Logan's girth until Logan began to thrust. And he could tell that Logan knew, knew the effort required of Connor to give this much of his body this hard and this fast and in rapid succession. And slowly Connor let go. Let Logan take control from the bottom. Let Logan grip his hips and grind his teeth and stare into his eyes as he drew closer and closer and closer.

Words as profane as everything they were doing bubbled up in him. As if Logan had become the locus of every debauched fantasy Connor had ever had, every slick and delightfully degrading act Connor had wanted visited on his body was now Logan's terrain, Logan's kingdom. Connor fell forward and brought his mouth to Logan's ear. "Own it," he whispered, "own it, 'cause it's yours. Own my ass, Logan."

Logan unleashed. Connor felt like he was suddenly riding a wave of muscle animated by a force pulsing from beyond this world. He straightened, straightened and accepted the final upward assault of Logan's desire, rocking back on it. Riding it, hands braced on Logan's sweaty, heaving chest. Delighting in the way Logan's eruption turned the expression on his face from something that could have been mistaken for rage into something suffused with wonder.

It was Logan who reached up and brought their mouths together. Some of the energy had gone out of his kiss, but not the need. Connor wilted, giving himself entirely to Logan's embrace.

Slowly, Logan rolled Connor onto his back, which allowed him to carefully withdraw from Connor's aching heat.

I love you.

Connor could feel the words inside of him, pressing against his lips. But it was too soon, too dangerous. Too childish to say them right in the flush of passion like this. But they circled in his head, pulsed inside his chest. *I love you. I love you, Logan.*

He couldn't. Not yet. Had to put some distance between himself and abandon before he gave voice to it. Only then could its truth stand apart from the moans and cries of release, only then could its significance and consequences be acknowledged for what they truly were. What they truly could be.

But when Logan started to pull away, probably to remove the condom, Connor stopped him. "Just wait. Just leave it and wait for a second."

"Of course," Logan whispered.

I love you, Logan, Connor thought, but what he said was, "Don't let me go. Don't let me go yet."

Logan answered by snuggling up against his back, spooning them into the covers, wrapping his arms around him. Holding him. And for a frightening moment, Connor feared Logan might not say anything in response. Surely he'd sensed the sudden flood of fear that had pulsed through Connor. Was he now scared too? It was always a risk with two men. There was always a little sandpit of shame waiting for two men after they had sex. And if they took the wrong step, suddenly it was drowning them in the voices of old bullies and old bigots. But Logan's embrace,

Connor was sure, could protect him from those voices, protect him from shame's quicksand. Still, Connor wanted him to say more, even as he fought against saying the words that were trying to force their way out of him.

"Never," Logan whispered into Connor's ear. "I'll never let you go."

And even if it was a platitude made easier to say by the afterglow of great sex, it was enough. For now. Enough for Connor to feel at rest in Logan's arms. Enough for him not to say the words he wanted to say. Yet. Enough to believe that maybe what Logan had said just might be true.

Logan was dreaming of lying on a beach with Connor in his arms. Somewhere distant, but as beautiful as Sapphire Cove. Someplace where they were together and content instead of trying to be together and content while also saving a hotel. It felt like Hawaii, but he'd never been, so he couldn't be sure. Wherever it was, there were palm trees greener than any Logan had seen in real life, and the ocean was as blue as Connor's mouthwash.

The ocean also sounded like it was trying to warn him something was on fire.

An electronic, insistent sound. It wasn't coming from his dreams, but the phone on his nightstand.

Recognizing the special ring he'd assigned Donnie, Logan groped for his earpiece and found it by its blinking blue light.

"Yep," he said.

"My boys are freakin', Murdoch." Donnie only called him by his last name when something was seriously wrong. Logan sat up fast, lighting flames in his injured shoulder.

"What's going on?" Logan asked.

"Some blogger outed them, and that crazy woman's Twitter is having a field day. She's using their *real* names, man. Brandon's mom just called him screaming from Ohio. She had no idea."

"Shit."

Next to him, Connor stirred.

"You better get down there and talk to them," Donnie said.

Connor turned on his bedside lamp, blinking sleep from his eyes.

"They're not getting fired." On his feet now, Logan stumbled toward his overnight bag and the pile of T-shirts within.

"Doesn't matter," Donnie said. "I'm doing what I can, but if you don't talk them down from the ledge, they're going to jet."

Logan checked the clock. Almost eleven p.m.

"When did this go live?" Logan asked, pulling clothes on.

"The blog post went up this evening, but she got a hold of it about two hours ago and now it's got five thousand retweets."

"Read me the tweet."

"*Porn star staff and a hotel full of kids. Is this what a new day at Sapphire Cove looks like?*" Donnie read. "Then she's got screen grabs of their O-faces right next to their real names. This woman's a friggin' rage machine. She's going after people who didn't even work there when her husband was blackmailed. *The Washington Post* doesn't even dox porn stars."

"What's going on?" Connor asked.

Phone to his chest, Logan gave him a brief synopsis.

"We need to go downstairs and talk to them before they quit," Logan said. "If they walk, we're down two men on the overnight shift, and I might not have anyone to cover the fire stairways to this floor."

"You're already dressed. You go."

"We should stay together."

"I won't leave the room, promise," Connor said.

"You *promise* this time?"

"Absolutely. Don't waste time on me. Go. I'll keep the doors locked."

Logan moved to Connor's side of the bed and knocked three times fast and then two times slow on the edge of the nightstand. "That'll be me and only me. Don't open the door for anyone else."

"Got it," Connor said.

Logan set his phone down on the nightstand, gave Connor a brief, hard kiss on the lips, mostly intended to distract his boss from the fact that he'd opened the lowest nightstand drawer and pulled out his M18 Sig Sauer and the waist holster that went with it.

"Woah," Connor said.

"I had Brandon run it over earlier. Don't worry. I've got a permit."

"Does the hotel?" Connor asked.

"Nope. I'm carrying this as an off duty private citizen, if anybody asks."

Once he was finished fastening the holster, he gave him another kiss on the lips, then headed for the door.

"Throw the deadbolt after me," Logan said.

Connor nodded.

Logan lifted the phone to his ear and was out in the hallway.

"Where are they?" Logan asked Donnie.

"Management offices," he answered.

Shit, so they've already left their posts.

Connor threw the deadbolt on the entry door, then slid into a T-shirt he'd tugged from his suitcase. He checked the lock on the door to the adjoining guest room. They'd kept it unoccupied in case they needed it for workspace, something damage control related they didn't feel safe discussing in the warren of management offices, but so far it had gone unused. The lock was firmly in place. The suite's sliding door was open a crack, letting in warm ocean breezes, but they were four stories up, and solid concrete walls separated all of the terraces.

No way was he going back to sleep. So he ducked into the bathroom. A little mouthwash would make sure he didn't subject Logan to a late-night version of morning breath when he got back.

He flicked the light switch and set his phone down on the counter, assuming the creak behind him was the bathroom door drifting shut. Then he realized, too late, it was the glass door to the shower stall. And it was opening. The combined stench of body odor and booze hit him in a wave. A hand reached around him and seized his phone, then sent it sliding away down the counter with a flick of the wrist.

Before Connor could scream, Rodney's other hand clamped down over his mouth.

20

"We need to talk, sport." Rodney's breath was hot in Connor's ear. His palm was greasing Connor's lips with sweat and something worse, something that tasted like black tar smelled.

He'd either been hiding outside for hours or sheltering in some filthy place with no AC. His black T-shirt and jeans didn't quite fit—which suggested they were either stolen or borrowed—and his face was dirt smudged, the grime standing out against a fierce fresh sunburn.

Now Connor had no choice but to meet the man's wild eyes through the mirror in front of him, which also forced him to take in the awful reality that he was both barely dressed and half his uncle's size. His mind raced to figure out how the hell Rodney had gotten in. Connor and Logan had both used the bathroom on several occasions earlier. There'd been no trace of him then.

He thought of the only open door to the room. The terrace. Four stories up.

And his hands tasted like tar.

The roof. He dropped down from the roof and came in through the terrace.

The thought of his uncle dangling off the edge of the building like a deranged Spiderman somehow made this moment more horrifying. If he was that committed to a confrontation, what was his end goal?

"No screaming, sport," Rodney said. "Blink twice if you're not going to scream."

Connor complied. His uncle lowered his hand.

"Are you armed?" Connor whispered.

"My guns are at home. I can't go home. What do you think?"

"Were you hiding on the roof?"

"Been here a while."

"When did you get in?"

"You guys were out cold."

In his mind's eye, he saw Rodney creeping past their bed while he and Logan slept. He had trouble drawing his next breath. "The hotel. How long have you been in the *hotel*?"

"A while. Helps if everyone's looking for some missing kid, I guess." He released Connor with a little shove but held his ground between Connor and the only exit. Connor felt his butt thump against the edge of the counter.

"What do you want, Rodney?"

"I'm going to clean this whole thing up, best I can."

"Okay. How?"

"I'm going to withdraw my not guilty plea."

"Okay," Connor said.

"That's all?" Rodney whined. "Okay. Just *okay*? Do you have any idea how hard this is for me?"

"I appreciate you sparing the hotel a trial, but did you have to break in to tell me that? Like, what about an email? Through your lawyer?"

"I didn't break in." Rodney sounded like a petulant child. "I didn't *break in*, okay? This is my fucking hotel. I built Sapphire Cove. I did everything your grandfather never wanted to do. I got up to my knees in the mud every day so he could cruise through this place like some dignitary. So your dad could huddle over the books and avoid his least favorite thing on earth, other people."

"Your record with other people is pretty wobbly right now too," Connor said.

"Oh, so you're going back to being a smart ass now, I see."

"And you're going back to calling me names like you did yesterday."

"Yeah, well, you made out all right. You got Murdoch wrapped around your finger, that's clear. Shoulda fired that guy last year. That's what Buddy wanted. Funny part is we'd just started putting pressure on him. We were even writing him up for the first time. He probably would have been out of here in another month."

"Why did you wait?" Connor asked.

Rodney shrugged, and his hooded eyes showed how drunk he was. "He had actual skills."

"Besides blackmail, you mean?"

"Whatever," Rodney said. "He gave you your little moment on the news and now I'm the villain. All that matters, right?"

"You showed up drunk with a camera crew," Connor said.

"And you had plenty to say about it. Like at the press conference."

"The press conference was about trying to get Sylvia Milton off our backs. And I was as polite as I could have been. I gave you a chance to leave and you called me a faggot and told me shit about my dad."

"Yeah, well, that's also why I'm here."

When Rodney turned to the door, Connor thought he might lead them into the bedroom. A stupid move, but one a drunk man might make, and a good development for Connor because it would bring him closer to a possible escape. Instead, Rodney pushed the bathroom door closed and leaned against it. When the lock clicked into place, Connor's heart resumed its race toward panic.

"I'm listening," Connor said.

"None of that shit was true."

"None of what shit?" Connor asked.

"Your dad, he didn't say those things. About you being gay. About wanting a daughter instead."

I will not cry in front of Rodney. Under no circumstances will I cry in front of my shitbag uncle.

"Why did you say them then?" Connor asked.

"I was pissed. About the press conference. I swear, where did you get your mouth? It's got to be your mom, 'cause your dad always took twenty minutes to answer a question. So busy looking at all the options. Figuring out what was safe."

"Is that why you hate me so much?" Connor asked. "Because my dad didn't answer your questions fast enough?"

Rodney licked his lips and cleared his throat, probably because they were dry as bones. "Do you know what it's like to feel different from everyone around you?" he finally asked.

"You're not serious, are you? Are you actually asking the only gay member of your family if he's ever felt different?"

Rodney waved his hands through the air. "You being gay never had a damn thing to do with a damn thing, is what I'm saying."

"Well, that's news. What was it then?"

"You were like them. You thought you were *good*. You were all about process and not results. You would take every step and show off while you were doing it. You were about things that sounded good but didn't make any damn money. I didn't give a shit if you sucked dick or zucchinis. I couldn't have you at the hotel. Watching over my every move, reporting back to them. I was using what I had to try to get some space."

"You didn't use what you had," Connor said quietly. "You used what I am."

Rodney's glare reminded Connor that, weapon or no weapon, his uncle was still twice his size.

"So were you so eager to keep me out because even five years ago you knew you'd eventually blackmail the guests here?"

"Oh, come on. They weren't angels. That Milton, before he got cancer, he used to talk to the staff here like they were lower than dirt. Then he has the nerve to turn one of our villas into a private cancer ward? You want to know how we found out? One of our housekeepers almost got stuck with a hypodermic needle so I called him myself to try to figure things out, figuring it might be a drug thing we should keep on the down low. He lied through his teeth about it and told me no general manager worth his salt should be bothering himself with a guest's trash, then he lectured me for twenty minutes on how I didn't measure up against the GMs at the supposedly much fancier places he stayed with his wife. What the fuck ever. But that's the hotel business. Trying not to drown in everyone's entitlement. Keeping a smile on your face twenty-four seven even though all you're seeing is the worst side of everybody."

"That sounds like what you chose to see," Connor said.

Rodney shrugged, then his eyes glazed over and suddenly he was searching Connor's face for something he seemed to desperately want but couldn't find. "What did he say, Connor?"

"Who?"

"Your dad. You said he left you a letter. About me. About stuff I did. In the past. What did it say?"

Connor had never seen his uncle so wide-eyed and afraid, as vulnerable as a young boy. But when he thought of his father's letter, its combination of sentiments seemed hopelessly tangled, and sharing any of that with Rodney made this hostage scene feel like even more of a violation.

"Step away from the door and I'll tell you," Connor said.

"Come on, Connor. Just tell me," Rodney said.

They both heard it at the same time. Three fast knocks, followed by two slower ones. On the suite's entry door, a few yards away but a galaxy of distance in this moment.

"This place will eat you alive, sport," Rodney said. "You don't have any idea what it's like to run a family business this size. There's no corporate office. No parent company to support you. The bank is *not* your fucking friend, and don't you ever forget it. If you screw up, they have a fiduciary responsibility to sell the place right out from under you."

The thought of stumbling into a firefight he wasn't prepared for made Connor's throat feel like sandpaper. "Rodney, tell me the truth. Do you have any kind of weapon on you?"

"Sell it, Connor. Every problem our family ever had came from this hotel. Your grandfather only knew how to promote it and make everyone feel like they were part of the family. Sell it. If you try to run it, mark my words, you'll have no one left in your life."

"Connor!" Logan's voice boomed.

As scared as he was for his own safety, no way could Connor let Logan burst into the room without warning if Rodney had lied about not having a gun or even a knife.

"Do you have a weapon, Rodney?" Connor asked.

More of Logan's special knocks, thunderously loud this time. Loud enough to wake Orange County.

"Connor! Open the door! Now!"

"He'll break it down if I don't answer," Connor said.

"We'll see. You're cute, but you're not that cute. And besides, word on the street is Murdoch's more of a hit it and quit it kind of guy."

Crash wasn't the right word for what they heard next. It was a solid, resonant collision, like a pair of two by fours being struck together, followed by a series of crackling sounds that sounded like a dragon was taking a bite out of the nearest wall.

Rodney jerked upright, stunned by the symphony of destruction.

"Sounds like he just hit it," Connor said.

The bathroom door flew inward from an incredible force, smashing into Rodney's face and sending him skittering backward into the counter. Suddenly Logan was filling the doorway in a shooter's stance, the Sig's barrel inches from Rodney's bleeding nose. The bathroom's marble walls turned it into an echo chamber of their shouts. Logan's sounded furious, Rodney's desperate. But Logan was shouting the same words over and over again.

"On your fucking knees!" Logan bellowed.

Rodney sputtered, word salad coming from his mouth.

"On your fucking knees!"

Rodney complied, hands going up in a fateful, familiar pose. But he was still sputtering, and the only word Connor kept hearing was relax. *Big mistake.*

"I'll relax when you're in jail, asshole. Connor?"

"Yes." Connor was surprised by the stammer in his voice.

"Are you okay?" Logan asked. "Did he hurt you?"

The protectiveness in Logan's voice, the surging concern, broke through the dam Connor had been using to hold his fear back. The reality of what he'd endured swept him from head to toe, and it felt like every bone in his body had started to shake. He'd been alone and trapped and half naked with his drunken, criminal uncle. And if Logan hadn't come back, there's no telling how it would have ended.

"I'm fine," he finally managed. "Nothing physical. I'm fine." But he didn't sound fine.

"All right, baby," Logan said. "I want you to just walk out of the bathroom behind me, okay? I'm going to stay right here with your uncle until the cops get here. Because newsflash. They're already on their fucking way."

Connor hated that he couldn't throw himself into Logan's arms. But the reason softened some of the fear. Thanks to Logan, his uncle might be leaving his life for the foreseeable future. But that meant he had to stay under the gun until he was in handcuffs.

The sight didn't please him as much as he thought it would, watching Rodney, his nose bandaged, escorted to a police car by two Orange County Sheriff's deputies as the few remaining reporters who'd stayed late trained their cameras on him.

A few yards away, close to the valet stand, Logan was in a huddle with the FBI agents who'd been by the day before.

Good timing had saved Connor, good timing and Logan's devotion and courage. Once Logan had convinced Scott and J.T. that Connor would never fire them over their porn pasts going public, they'd agreed to see out the rest of their shifts and discuss next steps the following day. Same with Brandon, who'd been off duty and resting at Logan's place when his mom called him sobbing over the revelations. He'd promised—

for now, at least—not to head back to San Diego.

"Hey," Connor said once Logan was approaching.

"Howdy."

"Your hero points are off the chart tonight, mister."

"Thanks. I try."

"How's your shoulder?" Connor asked.

"The pain in my leg from kicking in the door is a good distraction."

Connor winced on his behalf. "Oh, babe."

Logan smiled. "I got two."

"So what did the FBI have to say?" Connor asked.

"Rodney wasn't armed, and when they breathalyzed him he practically broke the machine. We'll review camera footage, see exactly how he got in and what he did before he broke into our room. Doesn't really matter. He's going to jail anyway."

"If he didn't have a weapon, what was his plan? Hide in our bathroom all night?"

"He says he wanted to talk to you."

"That couldn't have been his plan."

Logan gripped Connor's shoulders. It looked like he was searching Connor's face for injuries or scratches that might have escaped his notice the first time. "FBI says his old friends were all giving him the boot and telling him to turn himself in. And he clearly didn't have the means to get out of the country. He'd hit the end of the road."

"Rodney has friends?" Connor asked.

Logan laughed.

"Speaking of friends, you all wrapped with your FBI buddies?"

"Basically," Logan said.

"That doesn't sound final."

"They wanted to talk about the gun."

"Oh, yeah?" Connor asked.

"And I said I wanted to talk about the agents that were supposedly watching the hotel for Rodney. We agreed to call it a draw."

"Nice," Connor said.

"So what did he say to you in there?" Logan asked.

"It was his idea of an apology."

"So it was really shitty?"

"Basically, yeah," Connor said. "He also wanted me to tell him what my dad had said about him in that letter I told him about."

"Did you?"

"You showed up to save the day before I had to."

"Just doing my job, Mr. Harcourt." Logan winked like he did the night they met.

"He said something else. About you."

Logan's eyebrows went up.

"Were they writing you up before the raid?" Connor asked.

Logan nodded.

"Well, the plan was to drive you out. Buddy wanted you gone last year, but Rodney wouldn't do it."

"I figured."

"But that's not all he said, mister."

"Oh, yeah?"

"Yeah. He said he thought you wouldn't break down the door if I didn't answer because you were more of a hit it and quit it kind of guy."

Logan closed the distance between them. It was obvious he wanted to draw Connor into his arms but given the lookie-loos peering out from the lobby, he didn't want to risk another on-camera incident.

"Well, he's right. Because if he goes anywhere near you again, I'm going to hit him until he's quit. For good."

"That's so hot," Connor whispered.

"You like the whole bathroom thing?"

"I like how it ended."

"Good. Why don't I take you upstairs so I can give you the hug I've wanted to give you since I sent that bastard to his knees?"

"Sounds like a plan."

They couldn't stay the night in the penthouse suite. Not until it got a new door. Logan's rescue had left a man-sized splintered hole in it.

After they moved their things into the adjoining room, Connor spent several minutes showering off his uncle's stench, refusing to let the brown marble and honey-colored light and brass fixtures remind him of the time he'd spent prisoner in the bathroom next door.

He toweled himself, put on some fresh boxers and a T-shirt, and found Logan sitting at the compact desk in their new room tapping out text messages, probably to Gloria and the rest of the department heads, advising them of the incident before they saw it on the news. Then Connor called his mother. He managed to keep his voice from shaking for the first part of the conversation, but the more upset she got, the harder the fight became. First, she demanded he leave the hotel at once. Then she insisted on coming to the hotel herself. Finally, once he described

Logan's heroic actions in detail, she calmed down, and by the end of the call she was calling him her baby and her precious darling boy.

After he hung up, Connor sank to the foot of the bed. He thought all he needed to do was catch his breath. But Logan, apparently, could sense it coming, could feel the eruption before it blew. He took Connor into his arms right as days' worth of exhaustion and stress caught up to him, riding the freight train of fear and violation he'd felt while being held hostage.

But Logan's embrace reminded him of how it all ended, saved.

And for the second time that night, he fell asleep in Logan's arms.

21

"Connor Harcourt." Janice shoved the restaurant's drinks menu in her son's face. "I hereby sentence you to a cocktail."

When Connor's mother had requested Logan and Connor's presence at an off-site lunch to celebrate Rodney's second arrest, Logan had expected to end up in the draperied dining hall of some exclusive beach club. Instead, they were in a rowdy chain restaurant with bright yellow furnishings and walls of glass looking out on to the adjacent shopping mall's crowded parking lot. The place rivaled Sapphire Cove for hustle and bustle, but without its recent burst of gun play and frantic search for a missing child. With Rodney in jail, Logan was breathing more deeply than he had in days.

And not simply because he loved California Pizza Kitchen, even though a few hours earlier, he would have been willing to bet the Harcourts had never dined at one in their lives. Not true, apparently. Janice knew the menu by heart. The drink menu, at least.

"I can't drink," Connor said. "I'm working."

"I clocked you out," Logan said. "Go ahead. Knock one back."

"I didn't know the security director had that kind of authority," Connor said.

"He does. And I think everyone at Sapphire Cove would agree you've done more than enough on behalf of the hotel in the past forty-eight hours. Do you disagree, Mrs. Harcourt?"

"Not one bit," she said. "But call me Janice."

"See?" Logan said. "Your mother's spoken. You're done for the day."

"Okay, well then, so are you," Connor said. "I actually am your boss."

"Until it's shower time." Logan waggled his eyebrows.

"Don't traumatize my mother. She's been through enough."

"Oh, I already know you're a huge bottom," she said with a wave of her hand.

"Mother!"

"I've had gay friends all my life. There's nothing you can surprise me with. I mean, I was the one who told you about poppers, for Christ's sake."

When the server came to take their drink orders, Connor asked if they had any cyanide pills on the menu. The server, to her credit, told him they'd sold out that morning.

"I don't use poppers," Connor hissed once the server had left.

"And I know, Logan, guys like you send him into orbit," Janice continued, undeterred. "When he was in high school, he had this box of collages where he'd cut all the images together so it looked like Matt Damon from those Jason Bourne movies was making out with Mark Wahlberg from that movie where he played the sniper."

"*Shooter.* Please stop, Mom."

"Relax. I'm not going to tell him how I found out you were gay."

"He used to make you sit through his plans for fantasy weddings and stuff?" Logan said. "I heard about it. The night we met. Right?"

Janice Harcourt's eyebrows went up. "Oh, is *that* what he told you? Oh, no. It was so much—"

Connor's hands covered his ears. "What do I have to do to make this stop?"

"How about you give me that inheritance you won't touch?" Janice said.

Connor turned red. "Mom, really?"

"What inheritance?" Logan asked.

"His inheritance from his grandfather and his father. They're both sitting in the bank. I bet they're calling you all the time trying to get you to invest it. Must be driving them insane it's not earning them any fees. My endowment could use it if you ever decide to let go of it. God knows, you're not spending any of it."

So Connor had a massive inheritance collecting dust, and presumably interest, in the bank. Logan was tempted to ask how big it was, but that would imply Connor's value to him was based in dollar signs. Their work situation was already complicated enough. One thing was clear — the very topic had Connor glaring at the table, lips puckered, cheeks aflame.

"*I* will tell Logan the story later if you never so much as say the word *inheritance* in our presence again. I will also give you permission to go back to talking about me like I chase military men around in a white van with a cage in the back."

"Agreed. However, I'm allowed one last mention of the inheritance before our deal takes effect. And it's this. If you plow your inheritance back into the hotel to save it, I will disown you. There." She turned to Logan. "He's a big fan of the armed services, Mr. Murdoch. Why, I remember the first time he went out with a Marine in college, he came home and said he was going to get a Semper Fi tattoo on one of his butt cheeks to surprise the guy with during sex, and I told him that was great and that he could pay for college."

"Mom, is this how you're processing Rodney's break-in?" Connor asked.

"Maybe. Now I'm sure he's told you about our little talk yesterday, Logan."

"He did," Logan said.

"But there's another problem I see here. And it needs to be dealt with. Quickly."

"Maybe you could give us a beat to change the management structure at the hotel first?" Connor asked. "I started the ball rolling this morning."

"This isn't work related. The problem is you're running mostly on lust. And a lot of it, given how quickly you came back together these past few days. But it's allowed you to skip over some very basic steps. Now I don't doubt for a second that you're both remarkable young men. With you, Connor, I know this to be true because you have my DNA. And you, Logan. You certainly bear all the signs."

"Thank you, Janice," Logan said. "I appreciate that."

"But what's missing is some intimacy. And yes, your apparently legendary showers, which both of you have seen fit to mention in my presence, do entail some degree of intimacy. But not the full mile. And that's what I see in you two. Two men who want to go the full mile together."

"Well," Connor said, "those are interesting thoughts, Mom."

"Ah. And now the dismissal."

Connor turned to Logan. "What do you think, Logan? Are we low on intimacy?"

"I think your mom has a good point," Logan said.

"You've already won her over," Connor said. "You don't have to suck up."

"I'm not," Logan said. "In fact, she's giving me an idea."

"Oh, yeah?" Connor asked warily. "What sort of idea?"

"Tonight we're going to do something for the first time," Logan announced proudly.

"Okay. What?" Connor asked.

"We're going on a date." Logan thought a winning smile would settle it, but Connor was staring at him with a furrowed brow.

"Okay. Well, you skipped the part where you asked."

"Really? Okay. Can I take you out tonight, Connor?" Logan asked.

"Sure. Where?"

"No," Logan said.

"What do you mean, *no*?" Connor said.

"No, you don't get to ask. It's a first date. I surprise you by showing you a good time without a ton of cues. You get to see what I enjoy doing so you can see if you want a second date."

"Is that how it works?" Connor asked.

"It does with me. And you're getting intimate with me, remember?"

"Okay, but it ends with penis, right? Because I don't want to do that part of the date where we don't know if there's going to be sex."

"No, we don't have to do that part," Logan said.

"Well," Janice chimed in, "if you boys *really* wanted to get to know each other, you might want to consider a little pause on the—"

"Silence, Mother, or I shall overturn the table and vanquish you to the far kingdoms." With a raised finger, Connor had spoken those words in a rasping whisper.

Janice smiled. "It's bolted to the floor, Tolkien. But point taken. I'm glad you two are enjoying that part so much."

"What time should I be ready, Logan?" Connor asked.

Logan checked the time on his phone. "Meet me in the motor court at four o'clock. Dress casual."

"What kind of date will we have in the *motor court*?" Connor asked.

"We're going to *leave*, Connor. We're not having our first official date at Sapphire Cove. I have a full security staff for the first time in days.

Thirty percent of the evacuees went back to their homes today. We can take a night off."

"Oh," Connor said.

"Hear, hear," Janice said, raising her wine glass. "We could all use a break from Sapphire Cove right now."

Connor seemed to be struggling with the thought, as if the idea of leaving the hotel for an extended period of time was on par with eating dessert before your entrée came. "Okay. What do you mean by dress casual?" he finally asked.

"Exactly what I said."

"No, no, no. See, you want to have a first date? This is another first-date thing. Guys say, 'Wear whatever you want,' and then surprise, you're going clam digging. Or they say 'dress casual' and you end up at a restaurant where the women are in evening gowns and he's in a blazer."

"I'm starting to see why this has taken so long," Janice said.

"Comfortable shoes," Logan said.

"Comfortable shoes," Connor repeated.

Connor smiled. Logan felt his own smile hurting his cheeks.

"I'm nervous," Connor said.

"Why?"

"It's our first date," Connor answered, then he reached under the table and squeezed Logan's knee in a way that made shivers dance up his spine.

His shirt with Michelangelo's *The Creation of Adam* printed on it wouldn't meet Logan's definition of casual, Connor thought, even if it was, technically, a band-collar tee.

So Connor opted for a light blue polo, some basic Diesel jeans, and an old pair of Skechers he was sometimes able to walk around New York in without his feet feeling knifed the next day. He hadn't packed any tennis shoes. If the date involved a trip to the mall, maybe he'd grab some.

His dressed-down appearance was such a dramatic change from the blazers and dress shirts he'd worn since his arrival, the doormen and valets didn't recognize him when he stepped into the motor court. One of the doormen asked him if he needed assistance, then, upon realizing it was Connor, he surveyed him from head to toe. "Are you all right, Mr. Harcourt?" he asked as if he thought Connor had mistaken his Vicodin for aspirin and accidentally dressed casual in an opiate-induced fugue.

A few minutes later, a cherry red pick-up truck pulled into the motor court, sparkling from a fresh wash, with one of the most beautiful men Connor had ever seen behind the wheel.

Connor had just gripped the door handle when Logan dropped down from the driver's side, hurried around the nose of the truck, and opened Connor's door for him.

"Wow. So old fashioned," Connor said. "On a first date?"

"Yep. My father set a good example."

"Really?" Connor asked.

"Yeah. So basically I do exactly the opposite of everything he'd do."

Logan waited until Connor's arm was clear, then he closed the door, addressing Connor through the window he'd left open. "Like right now, he'd probably hand you a bag full of Burger King and ask you which parking lot you wanted to have sex in."

"Well, if that's how we got little Logan."

"Who you calling little?" Logan asked.

"Nobody. All right, stud. Let's go clam digging."

There was no sign of the media as they pulled away, but there were plenty of curious looks from the doormen. As they snaked down the hill, Connor was so busy enjoying the feeling of slipping free of the hotel that he jumped when he felt something rustle against his arm. His first thought was, *Uh oh. He brought a dog.*

He liked dogs, just not on first dates. Then he realized he'd mistaken petals for puppy tongue.

Logan was handing him flowers. And not just any flowers. Red roses. Connor threw one arm around his shoulders and gave him a big kiss on the cheek.

"You know, guys with dicks as big as yours don't really need to get their dates flowers," Connor said.

"Connor, can you please let there be, like, a little bit of romance here?"

"Sorry. I guess I'm nervous. It's been a long time since I've had a date with someone I'm actually crazy about. Love the butcher paper. That's so first date."

"Get a lot of flowers on your first dates, huh?" Logan asked.

"Only the ones where I charge for my time." Connor batted his eyelashes, leaned against the door, and tried for his best odalisque pose.

"Oh, really. So how much is this night going to run me?"

"That depends," Connor purred.

"On what?"

"What you want me to do?" Connor answered. "Foot stuff is extra."

"Uh huh. I think I'm learning something about you on this little first date of ours."

"Oh, yeah. What?" Connor asked.

"You got a thing for role play," Logan said.

"What makes you say that?"

"You're really leaning in to the escort-client thing right now."

"It makes me feel desirable." Connor batted his eyelashes. "And expensive."

"You're both. A man like me would be lucky to pay full price for you."

"Every time you say that the price goes down. Okay. What first-date things are we going to do? And if you say Color Me Mine, I'm jumping out of the car." To show he wasn't serious about the suicide threat, Connor took Logan's hand.

"No, we're going to do the single most important thing you can ever do on a first date," Logan said.

"A full panel STD test?" Connor asked.

"No, way more important."

"I'm out of guesses."

"We're going to get stuck in traffic." Logan beamed and slapped the top of the steering wheel with both hands.

"Wow. That's hot." If Connor's tone had been any dryer, it would be Palm Springs.

"Maybe not hot, necessarily. But it's essential to a first date."

"Okay," Connor said. Then, when Logan didn't say anything else, he added, "Why?"

"A traffic jam allows you to do the single most important thing you can do on a first date."

"Road head?"

"Be serious, Connor." But Logan was only half serious himself, clearly fighting laughter. Which was good. The only thing Connor hated more than traffic was snakes. He'd never been in a traffic jam with Logan, though. That might change things.

"Throw stuff at other cars?" Connor asked.

"No. *Talk*. Better than that, talk without having to look the other person in the eye. That's how you get some of the best accidental disclosures. You know, when the other guy slips and says something that tells you right off the bat it's not a match. And then you know not to waste money or time on dessert."

"Now who's bringing the romance? What if I let you return the roses? Will that clear up some money for our dinner fund? I kind of had my heart set on a brownie sundae."

"Just kidding. I always pay for dessert."

"Awesome. I'm getting ice cream *and* a traffic jam?" Connor clapped his hands together several times in a row. "I hope our next stop's a wedding chapel."

"Marriage? It's a first date."

"With traffic. The best kind."

Connor knew he was acting like a six-year-old in the throes of a sugar rush. But that's kind of how he felt. He was alone with Logan, far from the hotel, with no clear idea of where they were headed and no expectation that he plan it. Or rescue it from scandal and ruin. And the best part, his uncle was no longer a shadowy threat out in the world.

When Logan smiled and moved their linked hands to his lap, the sugar-high feeling got higher, and he could feel his cheeks hurting from his smile.

They were descending a long on-ramp that curved high above the freeway and would soon deposit them into the river of stalled cars that made up the northbound lanes of the 405 Freeway.

"Perfect," Connor cried. "Traffic!"

"See? Toldja."

"And just in time. Because I have questions."

"Do you?" Logan asked.

"Yeah, this is the conversation part, right?"

"Sure, but I'm not sure an interview format is what I had in mind," Logan said.

"Oh, I am. What was your worst date ever?"

"Really? We're going to talk about other men on our first date?" Logan asked.

"We're going to talk about men who didn't get to first base. I mean, I want your *worst* first date."

Logan made the kind of face you make when you forget to bring a gift to the birthday party.

"Oh, is that face your way of telling me you've slept with most of the guys you've had bad dates with?" Connor asked.

"Sometimes that's what made them so bad." Logan grimaced.

"Uh huh. So my uncle was right?" Connor said.

"About what?" Logan asked.

"You're a hit it and quit it kinda guy?"

"Used to be. And see, I warned you. Not a good topic for a first date."

Logan was right, and Connor suddenly felt a strange blend of animosity and desire at once—a charge from the fact that the guy next to him was so desirable that most of his first dates wanted to get sweaty with him, but this desire was sparked with fear, the fear that a guy as hot as Logan Murdoch couldn't be pinned down for longer than a few weeks because another offer would always come along.

"Hey, you keep up the pouting and I'm going to pull this truck over and give that cute little ass a spanking," Logan said.

"Bet you love yourself some Grindr," Connor said, even as he told himself not to say it.

"I take it you don't?"

"Tinder, Bumble, and you know, all the other ones, that are for actual dating. And not just sex."

"Sex. Okay. I guess that's fair."

"Because that's what you used it for," Connor cried like a detective unmasking the killer in the final act.

"Let's talk about something else. But first slide over here and let me put my arm around you the way I never did anybody I hooked up with on Grindr."

"Liar," Connor muttered, but he was already complying, scooting across the bench seat until he was resting comfortably against Logan's chest. His heart, which had started to race at the thought of Logan with other men, was slowing some.

"It's weird," he said before he could think twice.

"What's weird, my prince?" Logan asked.

"A guy I dated in New York for three months suddenly wanted to have a bunch of three-ways and I didn't bat an eyelash. I dumped him, but it wasn't like I was torn up about it. But the thought of you with other men makes me want to track down all those twinks and put their heads on pikes."

"Heads on pikes is definitely not a first-date thing. And if it makes you feel any better, the words *guy you dated in New York* made me want to crack the steering wheel in half."

"But that's not the weird part, though," Connor said.

"You think I can crack the steering wheel?" Logan asked.

"No. The weird part is the thought of you with other men also makes me hard. It's like my mind's torn. Thinking about you doing anything sexual turns me on, even if I want to pitch the other person into a jet engine when you're done with them. It's, like, jealousy with a hard-on. Does that make sense?"

"Yep."

"You're not just indulging me?" Connor asked.

"Nope. I had exactly the same thought about you the day after we first hooked up," Logan said.

"Really?"

"Yep. Jealous with a hard-on. Those are good words for it."

"It's a sign, you know," Connor said.

"Of what?"

Connor felt it was the night before again, and he was tangled in sweaty bedsheets, three short but powerful words knocking at the backsides of his clenched teeth, the aftereffects of the pounding Logan had delivered rendering him molten and speechless and full of dangerous thoughts.

"That I'm crazy attracted to you," Connor said.

"Oh. For me, it's something different."

"Uh oh. What?" Connor asked.

"If I tell you, we have to make a deal."

"A *deal?*"

"You can't say anything in response to what I'm going to say for twenty-four hours, and after I say it, you can't say anything at all for five minutes."

Connor sat up like a gun had gone off, but Logan held a gentle grip on his neck with one hand, eyes still on the road. Maybe to avoid the shock in Connor's expression, or maybe to avoid rear ending the van they were crawling behind.

"What kind of deal is that?" Connor's heart was racing, and the heat in the back of his neck under Logan's palm felt unpleasant all of a sudden.

He's going to say he doesn't believe in monogamy.

How many first dates of his had been torpedoed by this very topic? Too many to count.

By guys so opposed to it, or so incapable of it, they felt they had no choice but to come out stridently against it before the coffee cups had even hit the patio table. It wasn't always so bad. Unless they couched their disclosure in a bunch of pseudo-evolutionary arguments about how it wasn't the natural state of the species, and those who attempted it were fools. That's when Connor would get pissy. *Own your sexual expression, by all means, but don't shame me for having mine.*

But for the most part, those who were exclusively polyamorous felt the need to get their identity out from the first breath. The ensuing cup of coffee or meal was never very fun, but they'd done him a favor by being so direct, he knew.

And sometimes—rarely, but sometimes—Connor had entertained the idea that monogamy wasn't the ideal for him either. But then he'd take a step back and realize that when it came to himself, this was one of a series of compromises he was making to try to jam a guy who wasn't a fit into a place he didn't belong. Namely, Connor's heart. Three-ways after years of marriage was one thing. But a guy who declared on the first date that he could never see you as number one in the bedroom, not even for a little while? Connor could never make that work.

And if that was a group Logan was about to join, the devastation would be intense.

But wouldn't it make perfect sense? Logan was jaw-droppingly handsome, muscled, tall, and a power top. In the eyes of most of the gay community, that was gold stars across the board. A porn fantasy come to life. Maybe he had no plans to stop taking advantage of that fact as long as the getting was good.

His mother's admonishment was going to haunt them both for some time to come.

They'd been running too fast with only lust as fuel, and they hadn't stopped to learn some essential things about each other.

Like this one.

It's my fault, he thought. *It's my fault for bringing up the jealous with a hard-on thing.*

"I'm totally freaked out all of a sudden," Connor whispered.

"I can tell."

"Should I be?" Connor asked.

"I don't think so, no."

"Okay, so the deal is, I can't say anything in response to what you're about to say for twenty-four hours, and I can't say anything at all for five minutes afterward."

"Yep."

Logan's expression didn't bear the tense hallmarks of a guy who was about to make a potentially relationship-ruining disclosure. Instead, he seemed at peace.

"Fine," Connor said quickly, before he could second-guess himself. "I agree. Say what you want to say."

"Jealous with a hard-on doesn't just mean I'm crazy attracted to you. It means I'm in love with you, Connor Harcourt."

The wind he'd feared was about to get knocked out of him filled his lungs. His eyes misted, and when he couldn't breathe it was because he didn't want to let go of the air, not because he was starved for it. Because letting go of the breath would somehow make the time between when Logan had said those words—especially the one that started with *L*—and each new subsequent second pass faster than Connor wanted it to go.

"Nothing for five minutes," Logan reminded him, his eyes on the road, his voice cool. "Five minutes of not saying something back because you think you have to. Five minutes neither one of us tries to laugh it off. Five minutes of you doing nothing but feeling what I said right down to your bones. Because it's one of the truest damn things I've ever said in my life."

Connor wilted against him again, held to him.

Finally, he breathed. It was working as Logan said it would. The implication surging through his whole body. Again and again in waves. And with no pressure to say something in return, and then obsess over whether he'd said it with the right words or the right tone, or whether it was true at all and if he'd said it to even the playing field, Connor had no choice but to feel Logan's words.

To feel Logan's love.

Connor closed his eyes and held to Logan's strong body, imagining it was the only solid thing in the world. The only solid thing he needed.

"Two minutes." Logan let him know.

Connor moaned lightly like he'd taken a spoonful of Nutella.

It's possible. Everyone tells you it isn't, that two men can't do it, shouldn't do it, weren't made by God to do it. But now I know it's possible for two men to fall in love.

But he couldn't say so, of course. That was the deal.

Three hours through rush-hour traffic, through stop and go streets of Los Angeles at dusk, over the shadowed green Hollywood Hills on a snaking canyon road, then down into the twinkling expanse of the San

Fernando Valley.

Connor had no idea where they were headed within the City of Angels, but as long as he was headed there with Logan, he was more than fine.

As they'd neared the vast city, he'd thought they might be headed to one of the trendy restaurants along Melrose or Hollywood Boulevard, or maybe one of the gay bars along Santa Monica Boulevard he and Naser used to frequent in college. Places where casual meant a designer pair of jeans that cost as much as a tax refund check and every generation of gay reality TV star was represented among the clientele.

And he hadn't been looking forward to it.

West Hollywood bars could be fun, but not on a first date.

Not with a guy who looked like Logan, especially given the jealousy-teasing topics of their traffic jam interview. The compact gay city was a shark's tank full of pumped up, blow-dried, comprehensively moisturized actors and models, both aspiring and professional, basically most of the gay men in America who'd been told they could make a lot of money off their looks. Its night spots were great if you were on the prowl—not so great if you were trying to settle in to a rhythm with someone special.

But now they were on a side street off Ventura Boulevard, itself a river of strip malls and Starbucks stores, and when Connor saw the twin neon signs up ahead, a rainbow themed Budweiser sign and the outline of a cowboy hat below a giant sign that read SLICK'S, realization hit, and he cried out with unbridled joy.

Logan laughed and threw one arm around his shoulders, pulling him close and kissing him on the forehead. "Surprised you didn't figure it out before now."

But Connor was too busy trying not to cry.

Five years later, Logan had finally made good on the promise he'd made in the sea caves.

They were going line dancing.

Inside the old warehouse, the walls were a jumble of cowboy paraphernalia and neon that looked more suited to Dallas or Ft. Worth. To Connor's eye, most of the patrons looked like regular LA guys who needed a break from the West Hollywood meat markets, and for them the cowboy hats and boots weren't just a costume, but a respite from business casual lives spent in office towers or on studio lots.

Connor felt instantly relaxed. Until he saw there were as many eyes on Logan as there would have been over the hill in Boystown.

Jealous. Connor was jealous, plain and simple. And it wasn't Logan's fault. Hell, he'd tried to steer them off the topic of other men in general, and it was Connor who wouldn't let it go.

"Eat your potato skins," Logan said.

"You realize *potato skins* means this is going to be an all oral evening, right?" Connor held one halfway to his mouth, so Logan could change his mind about their appetizer choice.

"Yeah, I figured that backside of yours could use a break after the workout we've given it this week."

"One night off, maybe. I mean, let's not go crazy," Connor said.

"Doesn't rule out spanking, though."

"Are we doing it again?" Connor asked.

"Doing what again?"

"Using humor to distract from the...intimacy," Connor said.

"Maybe. I think your mom's word was *lust*."

"Sex talk," Connor said. "Right."

"Okay. How's this for talk?" Logan said. "I want to know how your mother found out you were gay."

"Or we could play dodgeball with traffic instead," Connor suggested.

"Oh, now you're telling me."

"Or we could do the spanking now. Do they have a back room?"

"It's not that kind of place. Story, Connor."

"Please don't make me," Connor whined.

"I told you mine the night we met, and it was pretty embarrassing."

"Mine's, like, six thousand times worse."

"How is that possible? My dad walked in on me jerking off."

"I can't believe I'm telling you this," Connor said.

"You're not. Not yet."

"Okay. Fine. So you know my mom used to be a schoolteacher?" Connor said.

"I think so, yeah."

"Okay. So because of that, she can't just have fun. There always has to be a learning element. Like some women would have girlfriends they get together and drink wine with. Some people would play cards or a board game. A knitting circle, you name it. Not Mom. She always needs to turn it into a club. For a while, it was book clubs, but focused on a particular topic. Like true crime or historical fiction. Then it was a cinema club where each member had to give a presentation about their favorite scene from one of their favorite movies.

"Then she started an art club. They'd get together once a month and one of the ladies would give a presentation on one of her favorite artists. Then they'd all get buzzed and watch a Nancy Myers movie and cry. Anyway, so the group meets one day and it's my mom's turn and she's going to give a presentation on Michelangelo. So she sets this easel up in the living room and puts this big coffee table book on it that's got color prints of Michelangelo's sculptures. And she's all ready to do her spiel and…"

"And?" Logan asked.

"Well, what she didn't know was that I'd developed a real fondness for Michelangelo at the time. Especially his work with the male form. So the coffee table book had spent a lot of time in my room."

"You were jerking it to Michelangelo in your room?" Logan asked.

"Yes, and apparently my aim was off because my mom put the book up on the easel and started leafing through it during her presentation, and when she got to the section on male statues all the pages were stuck together."

Logan exploded with laughter so hard he had to grab the edges of the table to keep from going off his stool.

"Was she able to play it off at least?" he asked once he could breathe.

"No. Oh my God. The room went nuts. Half the women had sons. They knew exactly why the pages wouldn't turn. They all started screaming. Some of them ran out. They couldn't take it."

"Did she call you?"

"*I was home!*"

Logan was seizing with laughter now, red faced and gasping. It was the first time Connor had seen the guy almost lose control before, and it was beautiful. They'd watched each other achieve all manner of ecstasy in bed, but this was the other side of Logan's pure and unfiltered joy. And given how ramrod straight the guy was most of the time, it was great to see him come close to falling apart.

"I was upstairs," Connor said. "I ran into the great room because I thought somebody had been murdered, and there's my mom holding up this sticky coffee table book and screaming at me."

"Did everyone leave?" Logan asked.

"Oh, no. Some thought it was great. They were refilling their wine glasses 'cause they wanted to see what happened next."

"What happened next?" Logan asked between gasps.

"I ran."

"Where?"

"The ocean, I think. Drowning seemed like a good way to go. Seriously. It was the most embarrassed I'd been in my entire life."

Then, suddenly, a slender, smooth arm snaked around Logan's shoulders, and a stunningly gorgeous man in a straw cowboy hat brought his pouty lips inches from Logan's cheek. The guy was model hot, six foot tall and perfectly proportioned, muscles swelling inside a chest-hugging white tank top. The kind of full-lipped, perfectly bronzed supermodel type you'd expect to see making out with a guy like Logan on some Instagram account that's all photos of the perfect couple in question on the balcony of their villa in Mykonos or on the deck of some yacht in the Caribbean.

"Well, hello there, Sergeant Stud," the guy cooed in Logan's ear. Then he sank his hand into Logan's crotch and started kneading what he found there as if he was intimately familiar with it. He didn't seem wasted, just drunk on the confidence that came from his impossibly good looks. "You know, it's not good manners to ghost a guy after you tell him to get a sling. Although, I have to say, I like it when you're rude. And hard."

Connor didn't see red, he saw fuchsia.

His breath had caught in his throat. His pulse was roaring in his ears.

This wasn't jealous with a hard-on. This was straight-up jealous, and the next few seconds, however they played out, suddenly felt fateful.

"I know how you can make it up to me, though. You can break your number one rule..." The cowboy leaned in, and that's when one of Logan's hands went up to block the guy's puckering lips. When Connor found the courage to look down, he saw Logan had seized the guy's wrist and was lifting it off his crotch.

"I'm actually with someone," Logan said.

For a moment, Connor thought the guy might readjust, maybe even apologize for his disrespect. Instead, he cast a disapproving eye in Connor's direction. "Oh, my. How'd you rustle up this little nugget, Sergeant? Did you clap your hands because you believe in fairies? Who are you, Light Brite? Should we call your fairy godmother so she can take you home and I can show Logan a real good time?"

Logan bent forward, intercepting the cowboy's hand before he could pinch Connor's cheek.

"His name is Connor," Logan said, "and as far as you're concerned, he's worth a lot more than twenty minutes on a Wednesday afternoon."

This comment seemed to hit the cowboy where he lived. Which was on Grindr, apparently.

"It was a Friday," the cowboy said, sounding wounded.

"It was lunchtime," Logan said. "It was once, and I don't even remember your name."

"Well, it's not like I remember yours either." The cowboy laughed and then looked to Connor as if he thought he might also be amused.

Connor wasn't.

"Good," Logan said. "Then apologize to my boyfriend for insulting him."

The cowboy snorted, as if he thought the request wasn't serious. When he saw Logan's expression, he realized it was. But all Connor could hear suddenly was *boyfriend, boyfriend, boyfriend, boyfriend*. He was Logan's *boyyyyyffrrriiieeend*.

"Yeah, no thanks," the cowboy said.

"Okay, then," Logan said, "run along. And maybe start looking for a personality people will put up with after you develop a normal adult metabolism."

And with that, the guy turned and left as if he'd been slapped. Apparently he was a cowboy unaccustomed to getting shot off his horse.

"Boyfriend, huh?" Connor asked.

"I know. Boyfriend usually comes first, love comes second. But with us everything's always been a little out of sequence, so why buck a trend?"

"And I'm still not allowed to say anything about the love part, so…"

"Yep. Twenty-four hours," Logan reminded him.

"Twenty-four hours from five seventeen p.m. this evening."

"Oh, wow," Logan said. "You checked the time."

"Absolutely."

"You must really be eager to respond, then."

"I am," Connor said.

"Well, I'll look forward to what you have to say," Logan said.

"You should," Connor said.

"So," Logan said, "how did I do? With…" He gestured to the space that had been occupied by their interloper.

"The cowboy whose name you can't remember? Pretty great, honestly."

"Yeah, I figured you wouldn't be beaming if I hadn't," Logan said.

"I mean, I could have done without the part where his hand was on your crotch."

"Me too."

"He's got a sling now, though. Apparently at your recommendation. So he got something out of the deal."

"I don't remember saying that. I don't remember much about him, to be frank."

"He gave me an idea, though." Connor put his elbows on the table and leaned forward.

"Oh, yeah?"

"Maybe we could do a role play thing later. You could treat me like one of your Grindr tricks."

Logan nodded, pursing his lips as if he was considering the idea. "You think that'd be hot, huh?"

"I won't know until we've done it."

"Yeah," Logan said. "We could do the part where we both undress in a hurry without looking each other in the eye because we don't really want to see who the other person is. Or we could do the thing where we start with the door unlocked and you face down on the bed, so I never have to look into your eyes at all." Logan, it seemed, placed a very high premium on looking into Connor's eyes, and this realization made the way they'd fucked the night before seem all the more special and intense. But Logan wasn't done. "Or we could do the cat thing. That was my favorite."

"The *cat* thing?"

"Yeah, that's where I ask you in chat if you have a cat and you say you don't, but when I show up I smell a litter box and try to do a search for it on the fly because I know if you lied I'll start to snot all over you during sex because I'm allergic."

"Wow. That does sound hot," Connor said.

"Right. Endless role play opportunities."

"Yeah, on second thought…"

Logan's stare was intense now. "Sometimes it scratched an itch. Mostly it filled the time. But it never led to someone like you or something like this. And that's why I deleted it off my phone three days ago."

"I like how proactive you are. Deleting apps off your phone. Answering questions I'm too afraid to ask."

But there was another question Connor wanted to ask about Logan's past. The thought of it, however, brought a painful memory of the handsome cowboy fondling Logan without regard for who he might have come to the bar with. *What was your rule?*

"Yeah, and there's something else…" Logan's voice trailed off, and it looked as if he was searching the table between them for his next words. "I'm sorry about what I said in the car."

"Which part?" Connor asked, face hot.

"Not *that* part. No, the part where I implied I slept with all my first dates. I've felt weird since I said it. That's something you say with your friends when you're trying to show off. It's not something you say to someone you feel about the way I feel about you."

"I'm not sure I saw it exactly that way, but I appreciate it, and I accept."

"Well, I saw it that way, and I promise not to do it again." Logan stood and extended his hand. "Since you accepted my apology, will you accept this dance?"

It was a slow song, a female vocalist, something bittersweet with lyrics about love. He didn't recognize the song or the singer. But that's because he didn't know much about country music. After tonight, that would change. He'd learn. If only to keep all the positive associations of this evening alive in his mind, his precious memories of their first real date.

And, it looked like, their first real dance.

"We'll have a lot more room than we did in the caves," Logan said.

Connor took Logan's hand, and suddenly they were on the dance floor, surrounded by other swaying couples. A true first now. A slow dance in public. With another man. This man.

His man.

When a voice in his head started to speak up again, he wasn't sure if it was fueled by doubt or if the question he had was a valid one.

"Logan?"

"Yes, baby," he said.

"The cowboy said you had a rule."

"With all my hookups, yeah."

"What was it?" Connor asked.

Slowly, Logan brought their lips together. The kiss was slow, tender, and long. Then, finally, he broke, but didn't pull away, their noses almost touching. "No kissing," he whispered.

If Logan hadn't been holding him in his arms, Connor might have wilted right there. Even so, he had to glance down to catch his breath, and that's when he saw them. Little diamond-shaped flecks in a skin of rugged brown. And some tell-tale stripes where Logan had pulled the hot glued sides apart.

"The boots!" Connor cried.

Eyes twinkling, Logan nodded. "I've been waiting for you to notice all night."

"How did you find them?"

"They were on the side of the road right where you threw them."

"You kept them all this time?" Connor asked.

"Yep."

"Logan, they're the—"

"The wrong size. I know. They're fucking killing me."

"They were only for display. You weren't supposed to actually wear them. I didn't even know what your size was."

"Yeah, I figured that when I put 'em on today. I wore long jeans to cover up that the tops stop at my ankles. And I brought another pair of shoes in my truck."

"But you were waiting for me to notice them," Connor said.

"Yep."

"Well, we should get you out of them so your feet don't kill you tomorrow."

"After this song," Logan said, pulling Connor close. "After this dance," he whispered.

The dance turned into another, then finally, a quick trip to Logan's truck where Connor slid his boots off and gently wedged his giant feet into a pair of comfortably fitting tennis shoes. Then they were back inside in time for the line dancing class. Connor found himself a natural, maybe because his weight was low to the ground and most of the moves were in the hips, and because Logan snuck up behind him every now and then and put his hands on his hips as if to steady him, but Connor figured it was just an excuse to draw them close. And he didn't mind at all.

Then, once they were sweaty and tired, it was time to hit the road, time to curl up against Logan's body as they took to the traffic-free night highway with the windows down and the warm night air blowing over them both. And the luxury of being silent and unhurried and on their way to a place that had started to feel like home for them both.

Instead of the shower, they took to the bathtub this time, where the attention they paid each other's bodies felt less like a rush toward orgasm and more like languid extensions of their kisses. Deep, hungry kisses of the kind that Logan had reserved for someone special, someone like him.

All the next morning, Connor pretended to focus on work, on emails and the gathering of proposals from outside security companies, checked in on the security team to see if they'd found any footage of Rodney's movements after his break-in. They hadn't yet, but the review was ongoing. But mostly, Connor was watching the clock. The effort didn't distract him. It gave a larger structure to his day, an end point that made him feel focused and directed.

And when the hour finally came, he found Logan out on the pool deck, supervising a joint training session between the lifeguards and the security staff. It sounded like the lifeguards were teaching the security agents how to recognize the signs of a swimmer in distress. Since Logan wasn't the one doing the talking, Connor felt comfortable pulling him away by one arm.

"Everything okay?" Logan said.

"Yeah, one thing." Connor leaned in and brought his lips to Logan's ear. "It's been twenty-four hours," he whispered. "And I love you too."

He gave him a quick kiss on the cheek. When he withdrew, he saw Logan beaming, a twinkle in his eyes, fighting a desire, it seemed, to pull him in for a lip-lock right there.

"Back to work, Mr. Murdoch," Connor said.

Logan grunted and nodded, but it looked like he was saving up a burst of passion to unleash on Connor later that night when they were finally alone.

22

Logan's newest hire was twice the size of Logan, a giant Pacific Islander named Keoni Hale. As Connor squeezed himself into the new camera monitoring room after both men, he felt like a pebble crushed between two boulders. Logan and Keoni had worked together years before at a rowdy music venue where, to hear Keoni tell it, they'd subdued more than a few dozen brawls with minimal broken bones.

The old monitoring room had worked fine, but they'd decided to convert it into office storage for the same reason airlines took certain flight numbers off the schedule after one of the planes flying them crashed.

For someone who looked like he could plow through a brick wall without missing a step, Keoni was surprisingly soft spoken. But he was still bleary-eyed from watching hours of surveillance footage, so maybe the guy was simply tired. And after all that work, he'd only found a few glimpses of Rodney on the new security cameras.

"So it's like Rodney said," Keoni explained. "He came on the property while everybody was looking for that little boy."

Logan raised a hand. "Okay. Hold up. Sort of. He jumped a fence east of the villas then went up the east staircase of the main building while we were all huddling in the lobby coming up with a plan, so J.T. wasn't monitoring the feeds. Otherwise he would have seen him. As soon as we split into search teams, J.T. came back here, but he was so busy paging through all the live angles looking for Benji he didn't go back into the archive. *That's* why we missed Rodney."

"All right," Connor said. "Well, the system's only a few days old, so maybe we could all use some more training sessions."

"Copy that." Logan's nod told Connor he'd phrased the directive diplomatically enough not to raise his boyfriend's hackles. But the message was clear—J.T. had goofed up.

"He never came down off the roof again?" Connor asked.

"We can't find a trace of him on any of the other cameras," Keoni said. "Believe me. I've watched them all. He had to have stayed up there until he broke into your room."

"Which suggests," Logan said, "he really did come back because he wanted to talk to you."

"It's still weird he went straight to the roof and stayed there until the hotel went to sleep." Connor leaned closer to the freeze frame they'd been studying, hoping some telling detail would reveal itself once his nose was inches from the screen.

"Well, he didn't just stay there," Logan said. "He passed out drunk. He had a flask on him."

"Also, there's another thing," Keoni said. "I can't prove it, 'cause he had a cap on, but I think there might be a moment where he notices the new cameras."

"Which means," Logan said, "he realized he didn't know how to evade them. They're all in different places now, so if he had a map in his head of how he was going to sneak around for hours before he caught up with you someplace private, that was out the window. Also, he might have thought the whole system was still in smithereens after the raid. We moved hell and high water to get new cameras put in. Nothing moved that fast when he was GM."

"And he didn't have anywhere else to go, right?" Connor asked. "Didn't the FBI say his friends were all telling him to turn himself in?"

"Yep, and he obviously didn't have the means to leave the country either," Logan said.

"Good lesson there," Keoni said. "Gonna run a blackmail ring? Pack a go-bag."

"I know this might be hard to believe," Logan said, "but Rodney might have actually been feeling remorse about what he said to you. People change when they hit the end of the road. My dad did."

Maybe, but Rodney's apology hadn't been unconditional. There was something he'd wanted in return—for Connor to tell him what his dad had said about Rodney in his don't-open-till-I'm-gone letter. The thought of sharing something so personal and intimate with his uncle after everything the man had done made Connor's stomach lurch. Thank God Logan had broken down the door before Rodney could add a new level of menace to his demand.

"There's no comparing your dad to Rodney," Connor said.

"Today," Logan said. "*I* wouldn't have wanted to hang with my dad when he was on the streets. He still doesn't even like talking about some of the stuff he had to do out there."

There was a buzz in Connor's pocket, one of the urgent alerts he'd assigned to his department heads.

"Jonas," Connor said when he saw the screen.

"A 911 from *Jonas?*" Logan asked. "First event's not for three weeks."

"I better go talk to him," Connor said.

The special events office was by itself right next to the conference center. It shared a small hallway with a storage closet and an employee bathroom most of the staff seemed to have forgotten about. Jonas was standing outside the hallway's *STAFF ONLY* door, phone in hand, expression graver than any he'd worn in Connor's presence before.

"We have a problem," he said.

"Ditto," said another voice from behind Connor.

Gloria was next to him suddenly.

"Yikes," Connor said. "Well, the timing suggests they might be related. Jonas, you go first because you got to me first."

"I have an email from the Lighthouse Foundation's executive director," Jonas said.

"Nicole Richter? What does it say?"

"She wants to take a fresh look at some of the terms of their contract."

"A *fresh* look?" Connor asked. "What does that mean?"

"I have no idea," Jonas said. "But I wanted to check in with you before I talked to her. I know we said we'd let them walk without a cancellation fee. But renegotiating a few weeks out? Their contract's ten pages, and it predates my working here."

"All right, then," Connor said. "You and I will set up a call with them ASAP. In the meantime, I need a copy of the contract. Gloria, you're up."

"Sylvia Milton announced a press conference," Gloria said. "It's on the Stop Sapphire Cove Twitter feed."

"*Her* Twitter feed, you mean. And what is the subject, pray tell?" Connor asked.

"New revelations about the security staff at Sapphire Cove."

"What new revelations?" Connor asked. "Is there something in the news I didn't see?"

"We've been checking, and the last major item was Benji's rescue."

"Well, and also the professional history of some of our security team," Jonas said.

"Twitter was dragging her ass for using their real names, and nobody in the mainstream press was covering it," Connor said. "What else could she possibly be using against us now?"

"I guess we're about to find out," Gloria said.

Jonas's office was a time capsule. The puddling pink draperies framing the view of the Draco palms outside brought back painful memories of how the hotel had looked in Connor's youth, transporting him back to a more innocent time before the renovation, before his flight to New York. Connor would have preferred less memory-filled surroundings as he strapped himself in for Sylvia Milton's latest attack.

Jonas had turned his laptop screen around and was standing behind Gloria and Connor as they all watched.

Sylvia Milton stood behind a microphone-clustered podium on the steps of her lawyer's modern office building in downtown Phoenix. "This is what we know to be true about this alleged *new day* at Sapphire Cove. We know that all the members of the security team who worked there while my husband was being blackmailed have not, in fact, been arrested. Logan Murdoch, who worked for years alongside many of the conspirators who destroyed my husband's final days, is not only still employed, he's being lavishly rewarded with a very special kind of attention by the new general manager, as we all saw. A general manager, I might add, who claimed to have no connection at all to the previous regime that ran a criminal enterprise. And yet there he was, in a lip-lock with his security director in broad daylight. With children a few feet away."

Connor winced at this homophobic dog whistle. Gloria reached out and gripped his arm.

"So I ask you," Sylvia continued, "when Connor Harcourt says it's a *new day* at Sapphire Cove, when he assures his guests they will not be subjected to blackmail and a host of other criminal invasions, is he telling us the truth? Or is he telling us what he *wants* to be the truth because his sexuality has blinded him? This seems clear. Logan Murdoch has very special skills when it comes to avoiding the consequences of actions which happened right over his shoulder, and those skills include casting a seductive spell over his new employer."

"Blinded by my *sexuality*?" Connor asked. "Is that actually how she phrased it?"

"Yes." Jonas, usually placid as a pond, sounded like he wanted to rip his laptop in two.

"All that being said," Sylvia continued, "I do believe in second chances. And yes, I've seen the good work Sapphire Cove is doing with victims of the Palm Fire. And I'm aware the hotel employs many decent, hardworking people who had nothing to do with the Harcourt family's crimes. But it is entirely unclear if Logan Murdoch is one of those people, and given the compromising positions they've placed themselves in, Connor Harcourt is the last one who can make that determination for us. So if he truly wants to declare it a new day at Sapphire Cove, he should begin it without Mr. Murdoch. Thank you for your time."

And with that, Sylvia Milton left the podium, ignoring questions the reporters shouted at her.

"The Harcourt *family's* crimes?" Connor asked. "Is she implying I was in on the blackmail?"

"I'm not sure there's an end to what she was implying," Gloria answered.

For what felt like an eternity, none of them said a word.

"Get Lighthouse on the phone," Connor said. "Right now."

"Maybe we should handle one thing at a time," Gloria offered.

"Bet your bottom dollar they're the same," Connor said.

As Jonas picked up his desk phone and dialed, Connor tugged his cell from his pocket and texted Logan.

Did u see?

Yeah. Bad.

Come to Jonas's office?

Jonas was talking to an assistant on the other end of the line when Logan's response came through.

In a few.

Love you. We will beat this.

"Hi, Nicole. It's Jonas Jacobs. How are you? I've got Connor Harcourt and Gloria Alvarez here. I'm going to put you on speaker. Is that okay?"

Jonas didn't wait for a response from the other end.

"Hi, Nicole. It's Connor Harcourt."

"Good morning." The woman's usual frost had an extra fringe of icicles.

"So I understand you want to renegotiate the terms of your contract?" Connor asked.

"I'm not sure that's how I'd phrase it. And I thought we had an understanding certain terms were fluid based on a changing situation."

"One of those terms, yes," Connor said. "The cancellation fee. Are you electing to cancel?"

"No, as I said. We simply want to revisit a few things."

"How many things?" Connor said.

"One," Nicole answered.

"And it's not the cancellation fee?" he asked.

"No."

Connor's stomach went cold. "Okay. What is it?"

"Logan Murdoch needs to go."

Connor had felt it coming, but Gloria looked shocked, and Jonas sank into the ornate Louis XIV desk chair in the corner, hand clasped over his mouth.

"So your understanding is that you have a line item in your contract that permits you to make permanent personnel decisions at this hotel?" Connor asked.

"We have a duty to keep our conference attendees safe."

"And you're afraid they're in danger from a man who saves toddlers from drowning," Connor said.

"We're concerned management has shown a lack of judgment when it comes to the current security director."

Took the words right out of Sylvia Milton's mouth, and barely a minute after her press conference. What a coincidence, Connor thought.

"A lack of judgment. That's a pretty big accusation, Nicole. Could you possibly be more specific?"

"Our board is upset, Connor. Don't make this worse than it is."

"How big is it?" Connor said.

"Our board?"

"No. The donation Sylvia Milton gave you to take this position."

You could have heard a pin drop. For a second or two, Connor thought the woman might have hung up.

"I'm not sure I appreciate the in—"

"Fine. How about this, Nicole? Why don't you take the afternoon to see how the world reacts to the fact that Sylvia Milton attacked a ten-year veteran of the Marine Corps who saved a child's life this week? And that she did it using terms she'd never use to describe a straight couple in a million years. Why don't you kick back, see how all that unfolds on social media, and then you can decide whether your *literacy* organization should be dragged into the middle of this woman's media war?"

Gloria and Jonas were both statue still during the silence that followed.

"Nicole?" Connor asked.

"Let's touch base this evening," she said. "When everything's calmed down some."

"Sounds good."

"My assistant will reach out to Jonas and set a time." She hung up without a goodbye.

Connor rose to his feet, head spinning, shaking with anger. He moved to the office's floor-to-ceiling window and stared out at its view while only seeing red.

"May I ask what happens if Lighthouse walks?" Jonas asked.

"We can operate out of cash reserves for several months. But if we don't raise occupancy, and if their cancellation inspires others, a sale is inevitable."

"Christ," Gloria whispered.

No one said anything for a while.

"Did I screw up?" Connor finally asked.

As the silence wore on, he figured they might be too horrified to answer, but when he turned, he saw they were both staring at their phones.

"Oh, God," Connor moaned, "what now?"

"Check your email." Gloria had tears in her eyes when she looked up at him.

The newest message in his inbox was from Logan. He opened it, saw the other addresses it had gone to. All of the department heads, and Lois at the bank.

The words in the subject line smashed into Connor like a sledgehammer: **Letter of resignation**.

Connor was prepared for a fight, a fierce battle of words, or a heated discussion that might push the two of them close to the brink for the first time since they'd declared their love for each other. But he was not prepared for Logan to already be out of uniform, not fifteen minutes after submitting his three-sentence resignation letter. Logan was also calmly removing his blazers and khakis from the penthouse suite's closet, folding them neatly and tucking them inside his now bulging duffel bag. The finality of this scene tossed kindling on the fires of Connor's panic.

"What the hell are you doing?" Connor cried.

"What needs to be done." He avoided eye contact as he continued to pack. "Make Keoni interim security director. He's a solid dude, and he won't hesitate to call me if he has questions."

"You sent a letter of resignation to the bank without talking to me first?" Connor asked.

"I'm making it easier, okay?"

"For Sylvia Milton, maybe."

He hurled the blazer in his hands to the duffel bag at his feet. "For *you*, Connor. For you." Regretting his flash of anger, it seemed, Logan looked to the floor. "What was the 911 from Jonas about?" he asked.

"Logan, we just need to sit down with everyone and figure—"

"The first event's in three weeks. You haven't had an urgent text from your special events director since you started here. Why did you get one five minutes before that press conference?"

Connor couldn't bring himself to say it.

"They're saying the same thing, aren't they?" Logan asked.

Connor blinked back tears. All the answer Logan needed.

"And what do you want me to do, Connor? You want me to stick around and be the reason everyone loses their job? After I just redeemed myself in their eyes for a bunch of crimes I had nothing to do with. I mean, how much longer is this going to go on?"

"I wasn't lying when I said we could beat this."

"You weren't lying when you said you *thought* we could beat this, and I respect that, Connor, I do. But she won't stop until she has someone's head. And she's decided it's mine, so I've got no choice. And neither do you."

"She won't stop if you leave. What happened to her husband was wrong and terrible, but it's turned her into a bully. And bullies *never* stop. She'll find something else, and she'll start hitting at that. And she'll hit twice as hard if we hand her a victory now. I don't understand this, Logan. Where's the guy who broke down this door the other night?"

"That guy is right here, and he knows damn well that sometimes you use a weapon and sometimes you make a sacrifice. And sacrifices are not something you know much about, Connor Harcourt."

"Wait! Seriously?"

"Oh, I forgot. You ran off to New York to kill time before your giant inheritance showed up."

Connor felt like he'd been slapped. "I would not call being alienated from my family during the last years I could have had with my father and grandfather *killing time*."

"I'm sorry. I…"

"Are you?" Connor asked.

"It's not what I meant."

"What did you mean, Logan?"

"I'm just saying, you could have stayed and fought, but you didn't."

"Oh, okay. So which is it? You think I should have made a sacrifice by staying here five years ago and being abused by my uncle on the daily? Or you think I should understand why you're running away now because you think I ran then? I mean, since you're making all my decisions for me, why not tell me what to think too?"

"I'm not running. This is not *running*."

"Your bag is already packed. You're quitting with a three-line resignation letter you wrote in ten minutes. What is this if not running?"

"I'm sorry if I don't have the confidence that comes from having a giant pile of money sitting in the bank because I'm too proud to spend it."

"I don't, Logan!"

Connor's cry forced Logan back a step, but he couldn't tell if it was his tone or the information he'd just shared that did it.

"I don't have a giant pile of money sitting in the bank. The reason I never want to talk about it is because it's not there. I donated it all to charity the minute it came in. Anonymously. I didn't want a life built by people who didn't want me around. And I didn't ever want to be looked at or talked to again like that night when you accused me of having no idea how reality works. I didn't want to be that kind of person. So I gave it all away."

"You don't really expect me to believe you gave away a giant inheritance because I wouldn't go on a joyride in a Rolls-Royce with you."

"Here's what I believe. One, you're being a real dick right now. Two, you're an amazing and beautiful man, and in many ways you are more courageous than anyone I've ever met. But not when it comes to this."

"Comes to what?" Logan said.

"Not when it comes to what other people think of you. You have gone through life looking and sounding like what most gay men either want to marry or be, and if there's one thing you don't know about, it's what it's like to be in the other room while they come up with new and more sophisticated ways to call you a faggot. So if you want to come at me about family and sacrifice, ask yourself how things would have been with you and Big Chip Murdoch if you'd popped out of the womb talking and walking like me, Staff Sergeant Murdoch."

"Don't bring my dad into this," Logan said.

"I'm just saying, the next time you lecture me on privilege, you might want to factor in yours. I don't have the option of just not telling people I'm queer. They know the second I walk into the room and open my mouth. So I know a hell of a lot about sacrifices, thank you very much. I sacrificed the last years I could have had with my father and grandfather rather than compromise who I was. And I'm sorry, but I'm tired of you bringing up my financial background every time you're afraid."

Logan's jaw was rigid in a way that said he was clenching his teeth. His nostrils were flaring, and he was glaring at the dining table as if it had given him the finger. For a second, Connor was afraid he might storm out the door. When he didn't, Connor took a step toward him.

"But I also know what it feels like to be slandered," Connor said. "And that's what you were today, and I know how badly that hurts. But if you could have waited at least two seconds and *talked* to me before you sent that—"

Tears glistened in Logan's eyes. "Before the *world*, Connor. Not just my dad and grandfather in a living room. The *world*. Everyone I ever served with is going to see her calling me some white trash man whore who slept my way into this job after blackmailing people. It's not about your money. It's about *hers*. I can't go out and buy a new reputation. I have to work with the one I've spent years building, and she destroyed it in ten minutes. And she can do that once a week if she wants, with her fancy lawyers and her press conferences and the twenty-four hours a day she can spend on Twitter while the rest of us are trying to do our goddamn jobs."

"She did it because she's desperate, and she's losing the war she started. She did it because you saved a child's life and that was all anyone was talking about. This is another strike. She's only destroying something if you leave, Logan. We can fix this. *Together.*"

"Not if it takes this place over a cliff first."

"You don't trust me to do better than that?" Connor asked.

"It's not about trust."

"It is, though. It is. I'm five foot four. I'm barely a hundred thirty pounds. I'm never going to be able to break down a door for you. But this? Negotiating with powerful people who think they should run the world. This is what I've done for years. This is what I'm good at, and if you won't let me do it for you, you aren't letting me fight for you. And I know I might be some little fem twink, but every now and then I'm going to want to save you too. And I can't do that if you walk away from us."

"Us?" Logan looked so stunned, Connor wasn't quite sure what had happened. "You think I'm walking away from *us*?"

"I meant we're doing this together. We're supposed to be partners in this."

"Or we can't be partners at all?" Logan asked.

"I didn't say that!"

"What did you say? Because you're acting like if I don't stay here then we don't stay together."

"I'm just afraid, okay? We came together when we started working together, and I'm worried that if we lose that—"

"Then we lose each other? You're afraid that if you don't have a job to offer me, I'll leave you? I'm sorry, Connor, but how is that any different from what Sylvia Milton said on TV? I mean, is that who you think I am? Someone who would walk away if you didn't have Sapphire Cove to give me?"

"That's not what this is about. You resigned without talking to me."

"From the *hotel.* Not from you. But you're acting like they're the same, and I don't even know what to think about that. You sound just like her."

Logan went for his bag, stuffed the spill of clothes inside the zipper and yanked it shut, then hefted it up off the floor in one arm powered by anger.

"Please, Logan. Please don't leave."

Hand on the knob, Logan stopped and turned, but Connor saw only hurt and anger in his eyes. "Five years ago I walked through the front doors of this place with as much fear hanging over my head as I had riding through a combat zone. And five *minutes* with you and I wanted to chuck it all and walk back out those doors with you in my arms, and by God, I would have done it if it wouldn't have sent my dad's life down the tubes. Sapphire Cove has never been the reason I want you, Connor Harcourt, but somehow it always turns into the reason I can't have you."

The door slammed.

And by the third time Connor called his name, it was clear that Logan wasn't coming back.

His ears weren't ringing like they had after he was struck by an IED, but he felt just as deafened, and he could barely follow what the two men on the other side of his dad's office were saying. A different and more painful song was playing in Logan's ears—the sound of Connor calling out to him as he'd walked off down the carpeted corridor, each time with more fear in his voice. He could still feel the anger that seized his limbs, drowning out the call of his heart, driving him forward. Forward and away. Away from that terrible moment in which the man he loved saw him exactly as Sylvia Milton had described him.

Given how intently his dad was studying him now, Logan could tell he was doing a lousy job of hiding his hurt. How could he hide something he felt in every inch of his body?

"She spent that whole press conference dancing along the line of defamation," Logan's attorney was saying. Benjamin Bullfinch had been his dad's buddy for years and always dressed like one corner of a boxing ring, but he knew his stuff. "Point is, I'd have no trouble pointing out where her feet landed on the wrong side, if you know what I mean."

It hadn't been Logan's idea to meet with his lawyer. Instead, he'd wanted to get down to business with his dad about starting work at Chip's Kicks. But when he arrived at the Irvine location, his vision wobbly, his jaw aching from grinding his teeth, the lawyer had been waiting for him in his dad's office, dressed better than he'd been the day he met Logan.

"But she's got money to burn, right?" Chip said.

"Maybe," Bullfinch said, "or maybe that's only how it looks on TV. You find out those kind of things in a lawsuit."

"I'm not sure I'm ready to jump feet first into a lawsuit right now," Logan said.

"Maybe not a suit," Bullfinch said. "Maybe just a really good cease and desist letter to shut her up. You can always go for an apology and a retraction without suing somebody."

"Hold up here a second, son," Chip said. "You're saying you and Connor both thought it would be best if you resigned. I mean, how does that prove the lady's wrong? It makes you look guilty."

"Conferences were threatening to cancel," Logan said. "We had no choice."

We. Yeah, right.

"Look," Bullfinch said. "I know a lot's happened today, but let me bottom line this shit. This woman's sloppy. You don't go on TV and imply someone's a blackmailer because you don't like who they're sleeping with. It might be easy to shut her down if we strike while the iron's hot."

"My primary concern right now is the hotel," Logan said.

"Where you don't work anymore," Chip said.

"Ben, I appreciate you coming over." Logan got to his feet and extended his hand to the attorney. "I really do, but I'm not ready to talk about all this today. I kinda want to get started with my new work situation."

Because if I go home, I'll get so drunk I might drown in my sofa cushions.

"That's my son." Chip dropped his feet from the edge of the desk to the floor. "Never a day off."

Logan shook Bullfinch's hand, then steered him to the door. Then he and Chip were alone with Logan's lies hanging over their heads like a smoke cloud.

If Logan didn't strike first and hard, Chip would own the conversation. He turned to his dad and clapped his hands together. "So I was thinking virtual workouts. Maybe a live streaming thing to add to the YouTube channel. We could roll it out over the next year, beef up your camera equipment capabilities. Maybe hire some new tech guys and—"

"Wait, what are virtual workouts?"

"We can have the trainers do kickboxing classes online. Live stream it. Maybe even charge for it. Like a members' only thing. Then it archives and we can share it to other social media platforms and—"

"I don't do other social media platforms. I can't figure any of them out, and they all make me feel senile. The channel's fine. And I don't put the trainers on the channel unless we're doing session videos, and those are only focused on one exercise. A class is going to last maybe thirty, forty-five minutes. My metrics crash if I do a video longer than fifteen."

"Well, maybe it's time to look into some new ways of doing things, new stuff."

"Why?" His dad sounded suspicious.

"To expand," Logan said.

"With your tech savvy? All you know how to do on a computer is download porn."

"I was sixteen," Logan said.

"Oh, and after that you just quit?"

"Can we focus, please?"

"Is that what we're doing? Focusing?" Chip's tone was so pregnant with implications it was about to deliver on the office floor. "I don't need to expand. My business is fine. Why would I expand?"

"To make more money. Isn't that the point of a business?"

"The channel makes money when I say crazy shit. The people who care about the kickboxing? That's like fifteen percent of my audience. Have you even watched my channel?"

"I've been kinda busy, Dad."

"I meant, like, ever."

My God. What have I done?

"Well, what were you thinking I'd do, Pop?" Logan asked.

"Towel hampers are pretty full out there. You know where the washer is."

Logan glared at him.

"Or you could stay in here and we could talk about how it *really* went with you and Connor this morning." Chip grinned like the Joker.

Logan nodded and stepped from the office, taking care not to shut the door too hard behind him, even though he'd made it pretty damn clear he'd rather swim in dirty laundry than tell his dad how things had actually gone down.

"Come back later, please," Connor barked after the second knock. He'd meant it to sound professional, but the frog in his throat had other plans.

"Yeah, I don't think so, Blondie. Open the door."

Naser, shit.

Technically, Connor had stayed at work, even if he'd spent every break between frantic phone calls curled into a fetal position under the covers, the same thought blazing through his head as he sobbed.

After Gloria called to tell him Nicole Richter's assistant had scheduled a call with Connor for that evening, his assistant general manager also made several attempts to lay eyes on Connor. In each instance, he'd put her off. He'd told the staff calls were coming in so fast and furious on his cell he didn't have time to leave the suite. That was, of course, bullshit. The truth was, after his initial sobs had abated enough for him to catch his breath, he'd pulled off his work clothes and hurled them into a rumpled ball in the corner. Since then, he'd spent the day in pajamas and Wheat Thin crumbs, with crying jags in between frantic business calls. None of the possible scenarios if Lighthouse canceled could be described as remotely good. Harris Mitchell felt Sylvia Milton had gone so far over the line Connor and his mother had no choice but to file a defamation suit. It all came down to four words—the Harcourt family's crimes. Right now, Connor had about as much stomach for that as he'd had for the black tar smell on his uncle's hands the night of his assault.

He opened the door a crack, and Naser gave him a once-over, from his bedhead to his bare feet, which he'd done such a terrible job of slathering with lotion they looked like they were shedding melting wax. Naser raised one eyebrow.

"I'm working out of my suite today," Connor mumbled.

"Really? 'Cause it looks like you're attending a hoedown with the Keebler elves."

"Never. I hate those queens. They're too into meth."

Naser smiled. "Well, you still have your sense of humor. That's good."

"Who called you?" Connor asked.

"Gloria. She said her next call was going to be your mother."

"Shit. Come in so we can barricade the door before she gets here. Mom canary-yellowed me the other day, and I'm still recovering."

Closing the door gently behind him, Naser examined the suite as if he expected to find corpses littering the floor. "All right, well, nothing's broken, so that's good," he said. "But you placed nine room service orders for Wheat Thins, which the staff interpreted as a cry for help."

Connor picked up the nearest open box and held it out for Naser. "Help yourself."

Connor flounced down onto the love seat at the foot of the bed. With a sweep of the hand, he gestured for Naser to sit anywhere he liked.

"Gloria's worried," Naser said. "*I'm* worried."

"You didn't have to leave work for this," Connor said.

"Connor, it's five thirty. I've been off work for half an hour."

"What?" Connor sat up, checked the view beyond the windows, and saw the early-evening light that presaged dusk. "Christ, I've got a call with the Lighthouse Foundation in thirty minutes. I hope they're nicer when they're teaching people how to read."

Naser sat down on the love seat next to him. "What happened?"

"So did he make some big dramatic exit?" Connor asked.

"No. Gloria said they didn't even realize he was gone until they checked the lot for his truck."

"That's good, I guess."

"Maybe."

"I didn't accept his resignation. And I accused him of giving up without a fight. And of not letting me fight for him."

"And what did he say?" Naser asked.

"He said I was making it sound like him working here and our relationship were the same thing."

"Did you?" Naser asked.

"It's how it came out. Kind of."

"Kind of?" Naser asked.

"It's exactly how it came out." Connor struggled for his next words. "I said he was walking away from us. I want to think I didn't mean it, but I'm worried it was like a Freudian slip. Only the kind that, you know, destroys a relationship."

"Why would it destroy your relationship?"

"Because he said if I believe he only sees me as a job opportunity, that's no different than what Sylvia Milton accused him of this morning."

Naser grunted softly.

"I know that grunt."

"Do you?" Naser asked.

"Yeah, that's the *I have something to tell you but I'm not sure if you can take it* grunt."

"Sometimes our insecurities can sound like insults outside of our heads."

"Deep. I assume the insecurities you're referring to are mine."

"So do you want advice?" Naser asked.

"Yes."

"Do you want best friend advice or ass-kicking therapist advice?"

"Are those really the only two options?" Connor asked.

Naser crossed his legs and sucked in a deep breath. "Logan was right. You're afraid that if he doesn't work here anymore, he won't want to be your boyfriend."

"Great. So I can't have a relationship unless I'm sexually harassing someone at work?"

"I didn't say that."

"What are you saying?"

"I'm saying that you're still the same guy who brought a Rolls-Royce on your first date with him because you thought you wouldn't get a second date without it. And you did it to distract from the fact that you have the voice of a kid from a Pixar film and the only thing you've ever topped is a bicycle."

"You're one to talk, queen."

"I speak from experience, gurl. There's gay shame, then there's bottom shame, and then there's femme shame. And if we've got all three, and we don't watch it, they'll work together to destroy our happiness. You didn't get bullied much in high school, did you?"

"Some. I turned in an English class assignment on bright red laser printer paper once, and Pierre Boston asked if it was perfume scented and the other kids laughed."

"Devastating. I spent most of sophomore and junior year getting stuffed in lockers by this stupidly hot football asshole who I was also jerking off to every night before bed. My point is, that's how I got treated for how I talked and how I walked. And it sounds like you had an easier ride. Maybe because they knew who your family was or they were impressed by the hotel. I don't know. And I'm not saying I wish you'd gone through what I did. But on some level, you have, and you know. You know that the flash and the glam and the money can protect you from the shitty things people think about us for not talking and acting like Logan Murdoch. I know you know because I've seen you use it."

"How?" Connor said.

"Oh, honey. Don't make me litigate it. It's just…if we were out to dinner with somebody's straight friends, you'd always pick up the check. In New York, if some big butch queen was hanging out with us, you'd start name dropping celebrity clients to try to impress him. It's just a thing. We all wrestle with it. I try to be the best little boy in the world who manages my family's finances, and sometimes I go too far. And God knows, I don't love you any less over it. But when it comes to a guy like Logan, your way of wrestling with it, it worries me."

"How?" Connor asked.

"Even if you're being generous, if you act like the hotel and everything that comes with it are the greatest things you have to offer the people in your life, all you're going to do is remind a guy like Logan of all the choices you've always had that he never did."

Naser gave Connor several minutes to digest these hard truths. That was good because he needed them. He also needed Wheat Thins, but he didn't feel like getting up to get some. Also, he was still nauseated from the last box, so maybe *need* wasn't the right word in this instance.

"There was something else Rodney said that night that I overheard him." Connor wilted into the sofa cushions.

"What?" Naser snuggled in next to him.

"He was describing Logan, and he said, he's gay, but it's fine, because he keeps it reined in."

"Asshole," Naser whispered.

"But in my head, I thought that meant…" Connor's tears seized his voice, and the next thing he knew Naser was gripping one of his hands and resting his head against his shoulder. "I thought that meant my dad and my grandfather would have wanted me around if I was more like Logan. If I talked like him, if I sounded like him. I thought it meant I was the wrong kind of gay for my own family. And that was somehow worse than thinking they didn't like gays at all."

Naser sat up as if a gun had gone off, but his grip on Connor's hand tightened, and suddenly they were nose to nose. "You are *not* the wrong kind of gay, and Logan is not the right kind of gay. There's no such thing. And you don't know what your father or your grandfather thought because they didn't speak up. And that's on them. But now you know they did want you around. It's why you're here, Connor. And if Logan was only interested in you because of this place, he would have thrown you up against the wall five years ago and plowed you three ways from Sunday because that's when he really needed a job."

"I've never thought about it like that. But I guess I didn't really know how I was thinking about it. And then today it slipped out. And he was so hurt. It was like I was as bad as she was."

"Sylvia Milton, you mean?"

"Yeah."

"Have you talked to him since he left?" Naser asked.

"No. I was begging him not to leave. And he did. So I feel like if I call him it's bullying."

"All right, well, let him cool off for a bit. It's been so intense since you got here, and I'm sure you guys are both exhausted."

"Oh, God. What time is it?" Connor asked.

"Time for your call," Naser said.

"Could you stay?" Connor asked.

"Of course. On one condition."

"What?"

"No more Wheat Thins, and we get a real meal up in here."

Connor got to his feet, and so did Naser. "Deal."

Naser's hug was strong and firm.

"You want me to step out on the balcony while you scream at these people?" Naser asked.

"No. Stay close. That way I won't scream."

Naser nodded. Connor fetched his phone off the nightstand.

A few seconds later, Nicole Richter answered her direct line.

"Hi, Nicole. It's Connor Harcourt."

"Good evening," she said with her usual lack of charm. "I'm sorry to say our position hasn't changed."

"Okay then. How much time do I have?" Connor asked.

"Time?"

"To consider this request."

"In all fairness, it's not really a request," Nicole said.

"How much time do I have to consider your ultimatum, Nicole?"

"Forty-eight hours," she answered.

"Seventy-two."

There was a stilted silence from the other end.

"I'll have to run that by my board," Nicole finally said.

"Let me know."

Connor was about to hang up when Nicole said his name, softly and without her usual bite.

"I'm here," he said.

"Just…I… You're a very perceptive person. That's all."

She hung up, probably because she was afraid of slipping and revealing other details of their internal negotiations.

"Well?" Naser asked.

"I was right. Sylvia Milton made them a donation they couldn't refuse."

"Shit," Naser whispered.

For a while, neither of them said anything. Finally, Connor set his phone down on the nightstand. The bathroom door was half open, and its honey-colored lamps sent a triangle of light across the nightstand's glass-topped surface. He'd struggled to set foot inside the bathroom that day. The stress of his fight with Logan had made him even more vulnerable to traumatic flashbacks of Rodney's subtle but menacing assault.

But suddenly, those memories were striking very different nerves.

"I have an idea," Connor finally said.

"Don't save a job he doesn't want, Blondie. That's not going to be the best thing for you two in the long run."

"It's not about the job," Connor said. "It's about him."

The judge was so furious with Rodney for violating the conditions of his bail she'd ordered him into Orange County Central Men's Jail. While he'd looked pathetic the night he'd broken into Sapphire Cove, after several nights in the company of accused murderers, Connor's uncle now looked broken. His yellow jumpsuit was so rumpled it looked like he'd been spending most of his time in his cell curled into the fetal position. No longer shining with product, his hair was a dry mat atop his head, his eyes both haunted and vulnerable. Expectant. They were also clear. *Sober.*

Connor wasn't sure if that would aid his agenda or not.

Connor probably didn't look much better. He'd tossed and turned most of the night, distracting himself from how badly he missed Logan's weight in the bed next to him, with thoughts of all the ways his plan could go wrong.

A new lawyer was sitting next to Rodney at the meeting room's metal table, a crisp and professional-looking woman with a Jackie-O bob, a strand of thick pearls, and an expression that said nothing much fazed her. She nodded as Connor took a seat across from them. Because Rodney couldn't shake hands, thanks to the cuffs that secured them to the table in front of him, none of them did.

"I don't suppose we can do this alone," Connor asked.

"No, I don't think so," the lawyer said. "And just to confirm, we're here to discuss the events of your encounter at the hotel this week and not the other charges. Does that continue to be our understanding?"

Connor nodded. The lawyer nodded, and then Connor looked to his uncle. "How are you?"

"Shitty," Rodney answered. "You?"

"Dealing with Sylvia Milton," Connor said.

"Yeah, well, maybe when we announce my plea, she'll back off a bit."

"So you didn't change your mind?" Connor asked.

"Why would I change my mind?" Rodney asked.

"Change of heart. Change of blood-alcohol level. That sort of thing."

"Yeah, well, I meant it." He studied his handcuffs.

"I had them review all the security camera footage from that day," Connor said.

"Why? I mean, you had me arrested so…"

"You got yourself arrested, Rodney. And for a lot more than breaking into Sapphire Cove."

"Still, you know I was on the property. Why'd you need to review the footage? What, you thought I was there to steal something?"

"And again," the lawyer said, "we're here to discuss the contents of your conversation at Sapphire Cove this week and not anything—"

"It was not a *conversation*. Your client prevented me from calling for help and barricaded me in the bathroom while I was half naked. It was an assault, and you should be grateful I'm not bringing charges. May we continue, please?"

"Carefully," she said.

Connor returned his attention to his uncle. "I had trouble believing you came onto the property just to talk to me. That's why I reviewed the footage."

"And now?" Rodney asked.

"I think you're more capable of feeling guilt than I wanted to believe. A man changes when he hits the end of the road. That's what Logan said to me the other day. About you. Is it true?"

"It was the look on your face," Rodney whispered.

"When?"

"In the lobby. When I said that stuff about your dad. The look on your face was…" Rodney swallowed and studied the metal table between them. "I always saw you as just some kid. Maybe that made it easier to push you around. You know, like, you'd eventually grow up and get over anything I did, and so why was it a big deal?"

"A dazzling approach to child rearing." Connor's fake smile hurt his cheeks.

"But when I saw the look on your face that day... I knew if I didn't say something I'd be seeing it every night. In jail."

Connor hadn't been prepared for this answer, and apparently that was clear from his expression, but his uncle was studying him closely.

"You believe me, sport?" Rodney asked.

Connor couldn't fight his wince. "Why do you call me that? It always sounds like an insult."

"You don't know the story?"

Connor shook his head.

Rodney smirked, and Connor prepared for a story more insulting than the nickname.

"You were about five years old and we were in the backyard of Dad's old place in Dana Point, and I was trying to teach you how to throw a football and you weren't getting it. I was giving you a hard time and Dad came out and said, 'Knock it off, Rodney. That kid's already a genius. He's not going to need sports like you.' That's how it always was, Connor. You came along and they let you be whoever you wanted to be, but me, I had to stay in this narrow lane to keep their respect."

"The luxury resort you had control over for decades would be the *narrow lane* you're referring to here?" Connor said.

Rodney nodded.

"You're making it sound like you never wanted the job," Connor said.

"It was the only way they'd see me. It was the only way I could exist for them. Without it, I was a fuckup. Your dad was the brains. Your grandpa was the heart, and I was just everything they didn't want to be lumped into one thing. Person. Whatever."

"But you stayed on after they died."

"Yeah." Rodney's grin was a leer. "And my love for the place is really shining through now, isn't it?"

Connor wasn't there to question Rodney's version of the past, no matter how self-serving he thought it was. He wasn't even there for Rodney.

Or himself.

He reached inside his blazer pocket and removed a folded piece of paper he hadn't touched since the day after he landed at John Wayne Airport. He placed it on the table but kept his hand atop it so it wouldn't drift open. His palm felt hot. It twisted his gut, bringing this last gift from his father, this private message his mother had guarded and protected for years, within his uncle's reach. The alternative, he knew, would feel much worse.

"But that's not the only reason you came back to the hotel the other night, is it?" Connor asked.

"What is that?" the lawyer asked, gesturing to the letter.

Rodney's wide eyes suggested he knew exactly what it was.

"You wanted me to tell you what my dad said in the letter he left for me. Isn't that right?"

"Don't play with me, sport," Rodney whispered.

"I'm not playing, but I am dealing."

"What do you want?"

"I will let you read this entire letter, including everything he wrote about you in it. On one condition."

"I'm listening," Rodney said.

"This morning I spoke to a producer at CNN who wants to do a live interview with you tomorrow evening here at the—"

The lawyer sat up as if a gun had gone off. "That is *absolutely* out of the—"

"Let him finish," Rodney barked.

Once it was clear the lawyer wasn't going to interrupt again, Connor continued. "And during this interview, you will explain in detail everything you said to me the other night. About Logan. You will tell them that not only did Logan Murdoch have nothing to do with your little blackmail scheme, but that Buddy Haskins wanted you to fire him last year and you refused because he was so competent and skilled. You'll also include the detail that the day of the raid you were planning to have him written up over bogus charges as part of what would be a larger pressure campaign to drive him out because you knew good and well that you could never make a man as good as him, as loyal as him and as honest as him, a part of your crimes. You will say that clearly and without reservation and you will say it to the world. Is that clear?"

For a long while, no one spoke, and the most haggard breaths seemed to be coming from Rodney's attorney. She finally broke the silence. "It is my duty as your legal representation to strongly advise you against doing any press or media prior to your sentencing."

"Maybe some honesty now will play well with the judge when that time comes," Connor said.

"I'll do it," Rodney said. "Just read it to me."

"*After* you do it," Connor said. "Deal?"

The lawyer sighed.

Rodney glared at him for what felt like an eternity.

"Deal," he finally said.

Evacuees were departing, returning to homes spared by the fire. Moments of healing for them, but the quiet they left behind exposed the wounds the hotel had suffered and made Logan's absence echo. As the sun sank toward the ocean, Connor dreaded another night alone in his palatial bed, had even considered changing rooms. But what would it matter? Penthouse suite or closet, it would be another night spent tossing and turning, obsessively checking his phone as he searched for any attempt by Logan to break the silence he'd plunged them into after walking away.

Watching sunset from the very spot at the balustrade where they'd first talked probably wouldn't help pass the night, but as soon as work had died down, he'd felt a magnetic pull.

Now, he was hit by a blast of Chanel No. 5. Suddenly his mother was next to him, chest up as if she was carrying every single call he hadn't returned atop it.

"Am I to understand that you actually met with Rodney today?" she asked.

"I did."

"And you didn't think this was worth discussing with me?"

"I had a bolt of inspiration," Connor said, "so I went with it."

"I want you to step down," she said.

"You're not serious," Connor said.

"I am."

"It'll force a sale."

"Good."

"Everyone will be out of a job. You want that on my head?"

"No, I want it on *Rodney's* head. Where it belongs."

Her giant sunglasses were heavily tinted, but he was confident her eyes blazed with anger behind them. She quickly returned her attention to the sunset, as if embarrassed by how abruptly she'd snapped.

"It's not a given a new owner will let everyone go," she said.

"Mom, this place is consumed with scandal. They'll clean house in a week and change the name."

"Then I'll pull from the endowment and—"

"Your endowment is bringing drinking water to villages fighting famine. I'm not going to have you spend it on a beach resort."

"Well, I'm not going to have you lose your first love over a *beach resort* either. For Christ's sake, Connor, you've placed the future of you and Logan in the hands of that monster, after everything he's done."

"I haven't. That's not what this is about."

"What is it about then?" she asked.

"I don't know if I can get Logan back. I've never seen someone look at me the way he looked at me yesterday. I've never hurt someone that much. I don't know if you come back from that. I don't have the experience."

"You can," she whispered. "You *can* come back from that. I *do* have the experience."

"The point is, it's not why I did it. If I have to say goodbye, I want this to be my goodbye and not what happened yesterday."

His mother placed one hand atop his clasped ones.

"Oh, honey," she whispered. "There's no telling what Rodney will do. I mean, it's a national interview and it's live. He could say anything. And now he sees how much you love Logan. He could try to use it against you."

"I have to do something. There's only one voice right now that will speak louder than Sylvia Milton's and it's his."

"Maybe it's your voice Logan needs."

"This is my voice."

His mother tightened her grip on his hands. "This is all my fault," she whispered.

"How?"

"I should have explained everything to you on the phone and given you an out when you were still in New York. The private plane thing, I imagine it was a lot of pressure."

"Kinda, yeah."

"But the truth is, I wanted you to come back. I thought it would be justice, you taking the reins after the way you were treated. But not if you lose Logan over it."

The word *lose* struck him like a blast of cold air in the face. He had to change the subject or the tears he'd been holding back since last night would return.

"Rodney says the only way he could earn respect from our family was if he worked here."

"Oh, my ass hurts," his mother growled. "Did he really say that?"

"I'm afraid so."

"Your father and grandfather could not have lost more sleep trying to figure out how to make that man feel loved. I mean, half of the reason your grandfather always stuck around here even after he retired is because he knew he had to make the staff happy to make up for all of Rodney's weaknesses. Honestly, I think that's why the benefits are so good here. They moved heaven and earth for your uncle, to give him a place in this world as he left wreckage everywhere he went. And this is how he repaid them. So forgive me, my son, if I'm concerned about how he might repay you tomorrow night."

It was a chilling prospect, but not an irrational one.

And he'd thought of it himself multiple times.

But the reward, if Rodney came through, outweighed all the negatives.

"Nas is coming for dinner. Care to join us?"

"Well, it just so happens I'll be around," she said.

"Oh yeah?"

"Yes. I'm staying at the hotel now that you've had a bunch of rooms open up. That way, it'll be impossible for you to ignore my calls."

She pulled him close and kissed him on the cheek.

"I wasn't ignoring them," Connor said. "I was preparing for them."

"Likely story."

23

Logan couldn't decide which thing was worse, his father's yelling or the high-pitched squealing coming from the giant device Logan couldn't figure out how to turn off.

"Are you out of your goddamn mind, son?"

Two days after he'd resigned and both nights since he'd managed about three hours of shut-eye tops. Maybe because he was staying late at the gym and crashing on his dad's office sofa to avoid going home, reaching for Connor in his fitful dreams and palming scratchy office carpet instead. He'd filled the largely sleepless hours by reviewing all of his dad's files, without his dad's permission. And that morning, courtesy of gas station coffee, he'd driven hell for leather to Los Angeles and returned with the contraption that had turned Chip's Kicks Irvine into a nightmare of squeals, beeps, and Klaxon bursts.

A few grizzled-looking customers stepped through the gym's glass doors and saw the new metal detector blocking their path. One of them stopped and threw out his arms. "You running flights to Puerto Vallarta out of this place now, Chip?"

"Go around the thing, guys." But as soon as he said it, Chip realized that would require them to move the giant trash cans Logan had set up on either side of it. So he did, giving Logan looks that said he wanted to tear his head from his neck.

Finally, Logan found the manual override switch and killed the screaming. "It's got a reserve battery, apparently. That's why it didn't go off when I unplugged it."

"Why did you buy a metal detector without talking to me?" Chip growled.

"For the last time, I didn't buy it. It's on loan from a buddy of mine who owns the company. You have security issues, Pop."

"Says who?"

"Your insurance files. I found payouts for two fights."

"When did you go through my files? Jesus! They weren't *fights*. They were sparring matches that spilled off the ring and the guys got hurt and threatened to sue, so insurance settled because it was barely anything. Nobody's ever drawn a weapon here. This isn't some dive bar."

"Well, once we figure out the settings, I'm sure we can make it work," Logan said.

"A metal detector in a boxing gym is never going to work. Eighty percent of our members have metal plates in their heads. This thing's going to scream all day like a robot getting murdered. And there's no lobby, so everyone on the floor's going to hear it. Does that sound like *making it work* to you?"

"I said I'll figure it out."

"Take it back and get your money back."

"For the last *freaking* time, old man," Logan growled. "I didn't buy it. It's *on loan*."

Chip recoiled from Logan's teeth-clenched rage. But he didn't look scared. He looked satisfied, as if a suspicion of his had been confirmed.

"In my office," Chip said, "now."

Feeling ten years old again, Logan followed his dad across the floor, past clients working with trainers and others pumping iron on the weight machines.

Once Chip had slammed the office door behind them, he pointed to the leather sofa. "Sit."

"Look, the problem is we need to have a planning meeting about—"

"*Sit down!*" Chip roared.

Logan flounced down onto the leather sofa. The hard shell he'd held to himself for almost seventy-two hours now was cracking. Maybe because of his dad's anger, or maybe from hitting the sofa like a disciplined child. He braced himself for a lecture on getting out of line and what would be asked of him—and not asked of him—if he stayed on as an employee of Chip's Kicks. "Tell me what's really going on," his father said instead.

"You know the story," Logan growled.

"You've been sleeping here. Why?"

Logan's exhale turned into a low, throaty growl. "The off-shift guys are staying at my place, and I don't want to answer questions."

"You don't want them telling Connor where you are or what you're doing."

"Maybe," Logan said.

"All right, then tell me what's really going on with you two."

"I don't want to talk about it."

"Yeah, I'm clear on that. But the shit you're doing to avoid talking about it is going to make me bury you off the Ortega Highway, so fess up, son. I'm not asking you to be tough. I'm asking you to be honest. Did he fire you?"

"No."

"Did you quit?"

Logan nodded.

"And?" Chip asked.

"I didn't talk to him before I did it."

Once again his dad looked like a suspicion of his had been confirmed. This time he didn't seem satisfied, though. He looked afraid. He sat down behind his desk. "And he didn't want you to, I take it."

"I was trying to make things easier for him, but he said I wasn't letting him fight for me. And the way he said it, it was like he thought our relationship and the job were the same. Like he thought I would eventually walk away if he didn't have the hotel to offer me. And how was that any different from what that woman said about me on TV? If I wanted to use my body for money, I would have made porn with Donnie years ago."

Chip gulped. "That was a consideration?"

"For a minute. But the money's behind the camera, not in front."

"Oh. Okay."

"I'm just saying. You see my point, right?" Logan asked.

"I'm your dad. I see *you*."

"Aw, what does that mean, old man?"

"Son, I gotta say some shit. It's been knocking around in me for a while, but I'm saying it now because I think it's going to help. And God knows, if there's one thing I haven't done enough for you, it's help—"

"Dad, that's not true. You—"

Chip spread his arms like he was declaring a baseball player safe. "No, you need to stop. You need to stop with this story about how I was a great dad. 'Cause I wasn't. And you don't need to keep spinning it to keep me in your life. I got a lot to make up for, and I'm here until I've made up for all of it, at least. So I'll be in your life until I kick the bucket."

"What are you talking about?" Logan asked.

"I'm talking about how your mother's death gutted me for ten years, and if you hadn't put dinner on the table for us most of that time, it wouldn't have made it there. And if you hadn't been you, you hadn't been this amazing, unstoppable kid who did stuff and made it work, I would have driven you to Fallbrook way sooner and left you with your aunts to make sure you didn't die of exposure.

"I was not a great dad, son. I wasn't even a good dad. I used to say I wasn't cracked up to be a single parent. Then that therapist you sent me to busted my ass. She said I hadn't been cracked up to be any kind of parent at all. Because what examples did I have? The mom who OD'd? The dad who grieved with a fuckin' belt? I never planned for anything, and I always went with my gut, and the results were fucking shitty, to be frank.

"But *you* were great. So I didn't have to be. And that was a miracle. For both of us. That was your mother working in my life. But if there was one thing neither one of us could teach you—her 'cause she was gone, and me 'cause I was fuckin' Chip Murdoch and nobody could tell me anything—it was how to be taken care of. It was how to trust that someone else would do for you. Because nobody ever did that for you except for your aunts. And they were part time. You give me a lot of credit for not kicking you out when I found you beating your meat to man-on-man stuff, but that's a pretty low bar these days. And you were worth more than that. You still are. And that guy who loves you, that sweet guy, he's trying to take care of you. And you're not letting him. And right now, that's the biggest problem you got."

Logan was stunned.

There was truth in his words. Lots of it. There'd been so many things Logan had to teach himself, do himself, worry about all on his own. His dad was never a falling-down drunk or physically abusive. Sure, he'd shout and rave and sometimes lose his patience on a dime. But for most of Logan's early life, it felt like a part of Chip Murdoch was missing. Gone with the ghost of Logan's mom, never to return, leaving Logan to prove he was worthwhile enough to make that part of his dad come back, if only for dinner.

Or at least that's what Logan thought. And then came Chip's accident and his therapy and a new pair of glasses through which the man came to view the world and start a business that changed his life. Both of their lives, Logan realized, because he'd removed the burden of his future from his son's plate.

"So Connor thinks the job will hold you guys together and he's wrong," Chip said. "I mean, would that be such a bad thing if you weren't already thinking he was better than you just because he was born rich?"

"I don't think he's better than me. I think he's different than me and maybe this whole thing, this whole situation, made that clear."

"Made what clear?"

"That it's a problem for *me*."

"His money?"

"I said this thing about his inheritance. I didn't even realize how much anger I had over it. But he was so hurt, and I'm not sure I can take it back."

"Why'd you say it?" Chip asked.

"I don't know. Because he was mad. Because he didn't want me to quit. And he was lecturing me."

"Yeah, I know you, son. You're one of those guys who thinks anything you don't want to hear is a lecture."

"Wonder where I got that from?"

Chip shrugged. "I'm not saying Connor didn't have a part in this whole thing. But you did plenty of work to turn Connor and Sylvia Milton into the same person in your mind. That woman's the one who's made this mess, not Connor. Don't take this all out on him."

Logan wasn't sure if he was convinced by his dad's words or just running out of steam.

"Rodney Harcourt's the one who made this mess," Logan whispered.

His dad shrugged, conceding the point.

Neither one of them spoke, but his dad didn't seem in any rush to leave or break the silence. And that meant something, something subtle and profound, that after everything they'd been through over the years, his dad was willing to sit with him in thoughtful silence while Logan tried to see through the hurt, the anger, the confusion.

"I don't know if I can take back some of the things I said."

"We can't take anything back," Chip said. "We can only do better today. That's what I've been trying to do with you for years. You and

Sapphire Cove might be done. And honestly, maybe that's for the best. The place is way too pink, and those chandeliers look like something growing on a dead person's foot. But my point is, you and Connor have a shot. But you gotta trust that he might be the first person to really do right by you. And since you look at him the way I used to look at your mom, you should really fuckin' try."

"What happened to my hard-ass dad?"

"Here he is." Chip stood up, crossed to the office door, and opened it. "You put that goddamn metal detector in your truck and you drive it back to your friend in LA or so help me God, you and I are going to be a *Dateline* episode before today's through."

"Copy that."

Logan stood, nodded, and headed for the door. But before he stepped through it, his dad grabbed his shoulder and squeezed. "Today, kid," he said softly. "It's about what we do today."

Logan looked back and saw feeling swimming in his old man's eyes the way it had that evening he'd had to leave him on the sofa during his first shift at Sapphire Cove. Logan squeezed back, then left the office, enjoying the comfort of following an order.

Leaving Irvine, he was sure he wanted a future with Connor. And the drive north to his pal Johnny's warehouse in Burbank gave him time to meditate over his dad's advice. But as soon as he offloaded the metal detector and headed south again through soupy traffic, his calm departed, and a future with Connor once more seemed pocked with landmines.

Could they go back to where they'd been before Logan walked out? Or had the path forked toward the edge of a cliff, and if they started up again, a plummet would be inevitable?

Or could they start back at square one? Start fresh, free of Sapphire Cove?

Would Connor allow it?

He'd asked Connor point blank if he saw the job and the relationship as the same and Connor had deflected and turned things back on Logan, and so Logan had left.

You left.

The words ricocheted through his mind as he drove, the windows down, the wind blowing across the spot where Connor had been curled against him a few days before.

Now he was making the same drive home without him, an awful foretelling of things to come. Connorless nights, Connorless mornings.

It's easy to storm out of a fight, harder to turn your back on the promise of a bright future.

You left.

He hadn't given Connor more than a minute to sort through the volcano of anger that had erupted that morning for them both. Driven to the surface by Sylvia Milton's latest strike.

But the question remained, what would they be without Sapphire Cove? What *could* they be?

Connor seemed so frightened by the prospect, he didn't want Logan to leave its ranks.

And maybe it frightened Logan too.

Maybe that's what his dad had been hinting at. And maybe that's why Logan had reached for Sylvia Milton's accusations like a life raft, flipping them into accusations against Connor.

Because the truth was something worse. The fear that had really plagued him as he'd typed those three lines of text, hit *send* on the resignation letter, marched back to the penthouse suite, and started packing his bags was altogether different and entirely his own.

If I can't stay here without getting everyone fired, how will I be his hero?

He'd tipped his hand during their fight, let something slip that had stuck with him in the hours since. He'd called himself white trash, attached it to the insult of man whore, which did seem borne of Sylvia Milton's insinuations, but the woman hadn't attacked his background or his economic status. He'd added that one to the kettle himself. And set it to boil.

He wanted Connor, wanted him always. He wouldn't be sleepless and half crazed if he didn't. And he'd sure as hell take Connor without Sapphire Cove in the mix.

But would Connor take a version of Logan Murdoch who didn't come in a tailored blazer bearing the bright gold logo of his family's legacy? Dinner parties with Chip Murdoch were one thing, but would he take a Logan who worked part time at a gym while he tried to put together a new future for himself in law enforcement or firefighting or something that wouldn't have him standing beside Connor as he greeted celebrities and politicians and corporate titans?

Was he guilty of the very things he'd accused Connor of? Of not being able to love him, cherish him, value him unless they were both wrapped in the glittering elegance of a luxury beach resort?

By the time he rolled back into the parking lot at Chip's Kicks, he was exhausted. He'd done what he always did in matters of the heart: litigated it a hundred different ways to try to find a way to avoid spilling his truth.

You're the one who left, so you're the only one who can go back. Not to the hotel, not to the past. To Connor.

How many times had he checked his cell phone over the past two days, hoping for some bleep, some emoji, anything to break the silence? But what right did he have to expect one? The silence was his. He'd brought the ax down.

Twice.

What if five years ago he'd started a conversation instead of making a decision? What if he'd told Connor his family situation, told him why he was so afraid, told him what the risks were and given them a chance to try at something anyway?

On another day, when he wasn't in this much pain, he wouldn't have indulged what ifs, but if you ignored a what if for too long it could turn into a not again.

He pulled his phone out now. Stared at the screen and saw a text from his dad.

How far are you?

Just parked, he wrote back.

Then he was staring at his phone again.

Probably exactly like Connor had stared at his right before he wrote that text that made Logan float up out of his body right there in that tiny trailer he'd been sharing with his dad five years ago.

And hadn't Logan been a few seconds away from writing a swoony text in response? Hadn't he been thinking of all the passionate things he'd say back as soon as he'd snuck into his bedroom to get some privacy? And then his hands froze up and the text had died.

It hadn't just died. He'd killed it. Fear had killed it, killed it like it drove him from the hotel the other day even as Connor called out to him, more and more pain abrading his voice with each cry.

Logan opened the notes feature, figuring he needed to draft the thing first to make sure fear didn't guide his pen.

Their path had forked, but maybe not toward a cliff. Maybe toward something new that Logan couldn't yet see through the mist. A future for him and Connor that didn't include Sapphire Cove.

He'd typed only a few words when there was a harsh knock against the window next to him. He jumped and looked up to see his dad on the other side of the glass. "Come inside, son. There's something you're going to want to see."

Logan obeyed.

His dad's office played host to a knot of people, all focused on the television, which was tuned to CNN. Danny, the Irvine manager, along with Jed and Petey. Bullfinch was there, too, which could only mean one thing, and it wasn't good. This was about Sylvia Milton or Sapphire Cove. Probably both. Or it would be in another second or two, since the report on screen was news from the other side of the world.

Then an anchor who looked like an action movie star filled the screen, live from some studio in New York. His dad turned up the volume.

"And now we turn to an ongoing scandal out of Orange County, California, where a posh resort is alleged to have played host to a criminal conspiracy that made headlines last week, a conspiracy to blackmail several of the guests, allegedly masterminded by the hotel's former general manager, Rodney Harcourt. With Harcourt now in jail for violating the terms of his bail, the result has been an escalating media war between the hotel's current management and the widow of one of the scheme's alleged victims. In a fiery and controversial press conference earlier this week, Sylvia Milton waged a series of accusations asserting the hotel had not done enough to purge itself of those who might have participated in the crimes against her husband."

The report cut to an audio clip of Sylvia smearing him. Logan shut his eyes, wincing. Jed and Petey both booed and thumbs-downed the television.

"But are those allegations true?" the anchor continued. "And if the FBI has seen no reason to arrest security director Logan Murdoch, was the attack on him earlier this week warranted? Here tonight in a live, exclusive interview to shed light on this very question is the alleged orchestrator of the conspiracy himself, former Sapphire Cove general manager, Rodney Harcourt."

When Rodney, in a yellow prison jumpsuit, filled the other half of the screen, Jed and Petey both cursed under their breath. Benjamin Bullfinch sat up so straight it was like a gun had gone off. But the sight of Logan's dad sitting quietly slowed Logan's pulse a bit. Someone had let him know this was coming, and if he was this relaxed, maybe there was a chance it was good.

Logan turned his focus to the screen and did his best to inhale.

"Mr. Harcourt, I appreciate you joining us this evening," the anchor said.

Rodney nodded and cleared his throat, but it looked like he couldn't manage a polite response in return. Connor sat forward on the sofa and clasped his hands over his mouth. Rodney's nerves could be the result of doing live television for the first time and not a hesitancy about what was to come. Only the next few minutes would tell. Connor would be lucky not to suffer a stroke before then.

Connor had tried to watch alone, but his mother wouldn't have it, and now Naser, Gloria, and Jonas were all present, clustered into the penthouse suite's seating area, watching the screen with laser focus. Jonas had gotten up from the sofa so many times as the minutes counted down toward the interview Janice had finally suggested he pace. Which he'd done, right up until the interview started.

"Now while we want to discuss the accusations Sylvia Milton made this week, we also need to start with your situation currently. You've been sentenced to confinement at Orange County Men's Jail for violating the terms of your bail, and it's likely you will be there until your trial. This is your first interview since you were arrested at the hotel earlier this week. Mr. Harcourt, are you guilty of what you have been charged with?"

Rodney stared into the camera, jaw working.

Connor learned for the first time what it truly meant to feel like your heart was in your throat.

"As to the matter of several charges that have been brought against me by the FBI, I will be changing my plea to guilty."

Connor's mother let out a breath it sounded like she'd been holding in for days, reached blindly for one of Connor's hands, and gripped it as they continued to watch.

"Can you tell us which charges those are?" the anchor asked.

"I cannot comment on the individual charges at this time."

"Can you comment on the blackmail? That's obviously the most serious one."

"I will be pleading guilty to the blackmail charges."

Jonas slapped the back of the sofa he was standing behind. Gloria's hands shot to her face.

"This is obviously a shocking turn of events," the news anchor continued, "for those who have watched this case. Earlier this week, you were caught on camera in what's being described as an attempted assault on your nephew, who has taken over your position at the resort. You violated the terms of your bail. I have to ask what many people are thinking in this moment. What triggered the change of heart?"

Rodney stared straight into the camera. "Memories." A silence fell, the kind that usually means trouble on live television. Maybe the anchor was as surprised as the rest of them. But then Rodney broke it. "I...uh...I've had a lot of time to reflect. In jail. About my actions. I've had time to consider what role my use of alcohol and other substances might have played in what I...what I've done. And while I don't seek to absolve myself of blame, it should go without saying that I have not been living my best life, and my actions have hurt others in ways I couldn't have predicted."

"You couldn't foresee that a blackmail scheme would hurt people?" the anchor asked.

Naser clapped, but Connor was nervous. He needed Rodney to clear Logan's name. A spat with the interviewer over Rodney's plea might leave no time for that.

"I am ashamed to admit that I rationalized inexcusable actions by targeting victims who I thought could afford to...pay what we were asking."

"Lawyer scripted that one, I bet," Connor's mother muttered.

"I need him to get to the part I scripted," Connor whispered.

"And those victims who could afford to pay, as you put it, included Walter Milton, the CEO of a financial services company based out of Phoenix, Arizona, who was secretly receiving cancer treatments in one of Sapphire Cove's villas," the anchor said. "Are you confirming that Mr. Milton was a victim, Mr. Harcourt?"

"I am."

The anchor seemed genuinely shocked. He had to swallow before continuing.

"Very well then. Let us turn now to the allegations made by Milton's widow earlier this week."

"I can't believe this," Bullfinch muttered for the third time. "His lawyer must be shitting bricks."

Logan had taken a seat on the edge of his father's desk, but in Logan's vision, the rest of the office seemed to have melted away.

"Only one member of the resort's security department was not arrested during the FBI's raid on the hotel, and that's Logan Murdoch," the anchor said, "who earlier this week was the subject of a press conference held by Sylvia Milton. Many are interpreting her remarks as implying that Murdoch was a part of the blackmail scheme and that the hotel's current general manager has overlooked that fact due to a romantic relationship that's developed between the two men. Now I'd like to read for you, and our viewers, a statement we received this evening from Pacific Crest Bank, which manages the family trust that owns Sapphire Cove."

The screen went to a title card showing the text of the statement as the anchor read it aloud. "We here at Pacific Crest Bank can assure you that the management of Sapphire Cove is in full cooperation with the FBI's investigation into the alleged blackmail scheme carried out by the previous general manager and former members of the hotel's security department. We can also state without qualification that after an exhausting initial investigation, the FBI has not made us aware of even the barest suspicion that Logan Murdoch might have been involved in these crimes. In the eyes of his coworkers and the bank, he is a model employee, a decorated veteran of the United States Marine Corps, and a cherished asset to Sapphire Cove."

"Hot damn," Chip said next to him.

Logan's vision blurred before he realized he was blinking back tears. When he succeeded, he saw Rodney on screen once more.

"Now the FBI did decline to comment on this, saying they don't make statements about ongoing investigations," the anchor said. "It's unclear if that will change now that you've admitted guilt to many, if not all, of the charges, Mr. Harcourt. But now, I must ask you, point blank, the question so many of us want an answer to after this week. Was Logan Murdoch involved in your crimes?"

Logan stood up. His heart was racing like it had when he'd first stumbled out of the bus at the Recruit Training Depot and the shouts and orders had started and he thought, *My God, what have I done?* It was racing like it had his first night at Sapphire Cove as he'd hesitated coming out to Buddy Haskins, racing like it had right before he'd kissed Connor Harcourt for the first time.

"No," Rodney said.

Chip let out a war whoop. Jed slapped his thighs, and Bullfinch wilted back into the sofa.

"There is absolutely no truth to that whatsoever," Rodney continued. "In fact, there was a plan to fire Logan the previous year because we doubted we'd be able to involve him, and it just so happens that the day of the raid, we had him written up for the first time over nothing."

"You say you knew you couldn't involve him. Did you want him to quit because you feared he would detect the scheme?"

"Correct," Rodney said.

"So I have to ask, why didn't you fire him a year ago?"

"He was very good at his job," Rodney said.

"Good at security, you mean?" the anchor asked.

"Yes," Rodney said.

"Not so good at blackmail?" the anchor asked, one plucked eyebrow raised.

"I wouldn't know because he never did any with me."

Logan felt his dad's hand on his shoulder, gripping him like he had that night in Fallbrook when he'd told him he would always be his boy. Even though he was embarrassed by the tears in his eyes, he turned to face his old man anyway.

"Connor called you?" Logan asked. "He told you this was going to happen?"

"Yep." Chip squeezed his shoulder. "Looks like he fought for you anyway, son."

"Yeah," Logan croaked. "Yeah, he did."

Then Chip gave him a light slap on the back, and Logan knew exactly what it meant.

Knew exactly what he must do.

He was out the door and behind the wheel of his truck several minutes later, heading west under a darkening sky still threaded with pinks and oranges and deep blues, just like it had looked that night five years ago as he'd headed to his first shift. West toward the coast. West toward a new and frightening but exciting future. West toward Sapphire Cove.

West toward Connor.

Scott and J.T. saw his truck as it pulled into the motor court and ran out to meet it, both breathless with excitement.

"Logan! Did you see it?" Scott asked.

"I saw. I saw it. Where's the valet?"

"I'll park your damn truck, just go," J.T. shouted.

"Where is he? Where's Connor?"

"Penthouse suite," Scott said. "They were all watching. *Go!*"

Logan ran through the lobby, then couldn't bring himself to wait for the elevator, so he ran up the fire stairs, down the long, carpeted hallway he'd walked so many times, hallways he thought he might never see again, and then there it was, the recently replaced door to the penthouse suite, beyond which fantasies had come true and all dreams had seemed possible.

Before he was within reach of the knob, there was Connor, big blue eyes bright and full of tears. Tears of relief, Logan hoped. Had they given him a heads-up that Logan was on his way?

"You fought for me," Logan said. "Even though I left, you fought for me anyway."

"Damn right I did. I wanted it to be our first fight, Logan Murdoch. Not our last."

He didn't remember closing the last few feet of distance, but suddenly he was taking Connor in his arms and he was bathing in his smell, his warmth. His protection.

24

They'd greeted him like he was a war hero, and the whole time Connor wouldn't let go of his hand, even as Janice threw her arms around him and then Naser pulled him into a hearty half hug. Logan gripped Connor's hand right back, marveling at how the seemingly casual connection could feel so anchoring. Then came polite, formal partings Logan didn't really hear, and suddenly he and Connor were alone, the taffeta curtains billowing in the warm ocean breezes, and all of it feeling so dreamlike and perfect Logan wondered if he'd hit his head and would wake up on the floor of his dad's office in another minute or two.

The dream didn't end. Instead, he took Connor into his arms, and for a while they held each other as if they'd both jumped out of the path of a speeding truck at the last possible second and were now tangled together on the curb, trying to breathe again as gratitude swept them from head to toe.

"What did you do, my prince?" Logan finally whispered. "What did you do to get him to say all those things?"

"I know a guy on the inside. He made my point for me."

"Seriously?"

Connor laughed. "No, Logan. Not seriously."

Logan stiffened and drew back so he could look into Connor's eyes. "The letter. You read him your dad's letter."

"Not yet," Connor said. "But now that he gave the interview, I kind of have to."

"You can't."

"I can and I will because I want to for *you*."

Logan pressed his lips to his forehead, knowing he wanted to go lower but hesitating for some reason. Thinking that a kiss might be something he'd have to earn back.

"Are you hungry?" Connor asked.

"Yeah. I haven't eaten in two days. Haven't slept much either."

"Me neither."

But he couldn't let Connor go, couldn't stop caressing his cheeks and planting his forehead with tender kisses.

"I shouldn't have walked out," Logan whispered.

"You were attacked on national television. I should have been easier on you. I shouldn't have gone after you like that for resigning. I was asking you to take your time and work with me, but I came at you like a freight train because I was so afraid I'd lose you. And you're right. I mean, you're half right."

"About what?"

"I was afraid that if I didn't have Sapphire Cove, I wouldn't be good enough for you. Not because I think you're some manipulative operator. But because I worry that I'm…that I'm…"

Logan smoothed Connor's bangs from his forehead. "That you're what?"

"Well, Naser says I have a voice like a child from a Pixar film and the only thing I've ever topped is a bicycle."

"Are either of those bad things? Pixar's great. So are bottoms."

Connor laughed through his tears. "You know what I mean."

"I don't, actually. I just know it's a very accurate description of a guy I'm in love with."

"The night I overheard my uncle with my dad and my grandpa," Connor said, "Rodney was describing you and he said 'he's gay but it's okay because he keeps it reined in.' And in my head, for years, I took that to mean that if I had been more like you, my family would have wanted me around. It's weird sometimes to be in love with someone who's a better version of me."

"I am not a better version of you, Connor Harcourt. Who put that bullshit thought in your head?"

"I want to say Rodney, but I think it's me."

"Well, what can I do to get it out?" Logan asked.

"Coming back was a nice start."

"Yeah, and maybe not leaving so quickly will be a better start next time."

Connor nodded, smiling through his tears. "That would really work for me, to be frank. The not leaving so quickly part."

Logan pulled him close, letting Connor dry his tears on his T-shirt.

"Logan, I don't care if you never work another day here in your life. I mean, as the general manager I'd be devastated to lose the best department head ever and a man who helped pull this place back from the brink. But as the guy who loves you, I'd take you any way I could get you." Logan pulled him in closer.

Neither of them spoke for a while, but Logan felt like he could stand here forever, rooted in place, holding Connor up in his arms, savoring his weight and heat.

"I never should have sent that letter," Logan finally said. "Job or no job, I can see why that scared you, to have the man you love just...*act* like that without including you, talking to you. If you'd done the same to me, I might have freaked out too. And I have to admit, part of the reason Sylvia Milton got to me is because I think I should have been able to tell what was going on here, and I blame myself for missing it."

"I don't," Connor said.

"I know, but I do, and I have to own that and move past it and not take it out on you."

"That'll be easier to do when I'm not pelting you with my insecurities," Connor said.

"I do understand what you meant, Connor. I do. I haven't experienced it, but I'm aware of it, and I'll try to be more understanding."

"Which part? I have *a lot* of insecurities."

"You're right. I've been one of those guys who can go through life, and if I don't out myself, sometimes nobody notices and nobody asks, and I can keep my mouth shut and skate. And it means I get treated differently, and there're things about what you've gone through that I don't understand."

Connor nodded and gently rubbed Logan's chest, but Logan could sense him struggling with something else.

"What?" Logan whispered. "Say it, my prince. Say it all. God help us, I don't ever want to go through seventy-two hours like that again."

Connor took a deep, fortifying breath. "Do you really think I should have stayed five years ago? Do you really think I ran?"

"No," Logan said. "I ran. You don't have to fly five hours to run. You can run by staying put. You can run by withdrawing. By turning down a chance to get hurt, by refusing to let someone fight for you. I ran five years ago, and I ran three days ago because I wouldn't give you the chance to be bigger than my fear. My dad says I have to learn how to be taken care of because he didn't do the best job. Maybe he's right. But there's one thing I know for sure. You're the only man I'd ever want to teach me how."

And just like that, it seemed, he'd earned the right to a kiss, a true one, a long one, a lingering and grateful one that coursed with gratitude, connection, and relief.

"I have to ask you something," Connor finally whispered.

"Ask away." Logan smoothed Connor's bangs back from his forehead.

"Knowing that I will take you any way I can get you, do you still want me to accept your resignation?" Connor asked.

"What are the conferences saying?" Logan asked.

"I have to let the Lighthouse Foundation know of our decision soon. And it looks like Sylvia Milton is giving them a donation to get them to hold the line."

"And if they cancel?"

"It's not good any way you slice it. A sale might be likely. Especially if it inspires other conferences to pull out. But the interview might change things. There's no telling how they'll feel tomorrow."

"I don't think they'll want Sylvia Milton's money any less, and I'm not sure heaven and earth could get that woman to change her mind about all this."

"I wish I could disagree, but I can't," Connor said.

"I love this place," Logan said. "I really do, always have. But I love you more, and I can't turn you into the reason everyone might lose their job in a few months. I can't be the reason either. We wouldn't just be making a decision for us. We'd be making a decision for everyone who works here. I can't live with that, and neither can you."

Suddenly, Connor was looking over Logan's shoulder. Worried he'd angered him, Logan reached up and caressed the side of Connor's cheek with one bent, crooked finger. But Connor was thinking, deeply. Planning.

"What if we don't make the decision?" Connor asked.

Connor thought they might have trouble wrangling at least a handful of Sapphire Cove's employees. But the crowd that greeted them in the Seahorse Ballroom the next morning was expansive, and Lois Penry assured him it included everyone currently employed by the hotel.

The cushioned conference chairs were arranged in close, even rows, spanning the length of the hotel's smaller ballroom. Behind them, a wall of glass offered a view south down a coast painted with morning sun. Through it, a few lingering wildfire evacuees paused during their morning strolls to gaze curiously inside, wondering what urgent matter called for assembling the hotel's staff in such an organized way.

Lois Penry and Harris Mitchell stood off to one side, watching the gathering crowd with blank expressions. And then there was Logan, standing by himself, a few feet from where Connor was getting ready to speak into the wireless microphone they'd handed him. The sight of Logan back inside his typical uniform of blue blazer and khakis made Connor wobbly inside.

Behind Connor were two rolling white boards. When it was time, Lois Penry would turn them so the room could see the large-print bullet points taped to the other side.

The room needed no time to settle. There'd been no conversations or whispers as everyone filed in. They could feel the seriousness in the air, and their eyes were glued to Connor from the minute they sank into their chairs.

He took a breath, raised the microphone, and began to speak.

"I want to thank all of you for gathering on such short notice. Especially those of you who came in on your day off. Although, for most of us, days off feel like a thing of the past." There was some gracious laughter, all of it telling him the attendees were as nervous as he was. "As some of you may already know, the Lighthouse Foundation is scheduled to host their annual conference with us in three weeks. What you may not know is that three days ago they contacted us and made a specific request. If this request is not met, they will very likely cancel their conference altogether. If that were to happen, there's a good chance that in the next few months Sapphire Cove will have to seriously engage an outside buyer. In other words, we'd have to sell the hotel." A few gasps went up from the crowd. "And given the actions of my uncle and Buddy Haskins and others, there's a high likelihood a new buyer wouldn't agree to retain most of the current staff, most of you."

Connor took the quietest deep breath he could and continued. "The request the Lighthouse Foundation has made is that Sapphire Cove would be required to terminate Logan Murdoch's employment immediately."

More gasps this time, and a low murmur of angry conversation. Connor waited for them to settle.

"The reasoning expressed is that he's the only remaining member of a security department that was once supervised by Buddy Haskins and my uncle. And for those of you who haven't heard, Buddy Haskins entered a guilty plea this morning. Now as you're probably all aware by now, Logan Murdoch and I have entered into a relationship, and as a result of this relationship we feel strongly that neither one of us is objective enough to make a decision of this magnitude on behalf of all of you. And so we're going to put this matter to a vote. A vote by you, a vote by secret ballot. And while I would have preferred to give everyone more time to consider their decision in this matter, given the time frame placed on us by the Lighthouse Foundation, this vote will need to be conducted within the next few hours."

Connor signaled to Lois. She stepped forward and turned both rolling boards so that they faced the audience. Most of those seated sat forward a little to better read the large, bright print spelling out the consequences of a vote to accept Lighthouse's condition on one, and a vote to reject on the other.

"The matter on which you'll cast your vote is whether to accept or reject this condition placed on Sapphire Cove by the Lighthouse Foundation. On the boards behind me, you'll see a clear outline of the consequences of both votes. These bullet points were not prepared by me or by Logan Murdoch, nor were they subject to our approval. They've been prepared by the manager of the trust that currently owns this hotel, using detailed financial projections, and in the most objective and comprehensive manner possible so as to give you a clear, unbiased portrait of how a certain vote will impact the hotel and your employment here. We also have handouts for each of you to review before you cast your ballot."

Connor had only been able to bring himself to look at the other sides of the boards once before his stomach clenched up. The phrase *possible cascade of cancellations into the next calendar year* was as far as he got on the REJECT board. But right now, all he could see was the sea of faces before him. Some were sad. Others looked shocked. A few were openly angry.

"As I said, your ballot will be secret," Connor continued. "There will be no repercussions from me or anyone who answers to me as a result of this vote. Everyone's vote counts the same, whether you've been here three years or three weeks. All of you, everyone sitting in this room, had the opportunity to abandon this place during its worst moment, and all of you chose to stay and fight it out."

The next point was the hardest for him to say. Logan had insisted on it. Connor hadn't fought. But still, it was a bitter pill, and he hadn't swallowed it all the way yet. "Given the magnitude of the decision, a simple majority will not suffice. The winning choice will require a three-fourths vote.

"Now I need to say something before I turn the microphone over to Logan," Connor said. "My grandfather founded this place on a single principle—that if he treated the employees well, they would treat the guests well, and he would have a successful business because of it. For the most part, this place has done its best to stay true to that spirit. To his spirit. But there's no doubt my uncle's crimes will tarnish that legacy for some time to come, and it will take years of work to overcome it. And so it's my job to stay true to it now. Sapphire Cove isn't a building. It isn't a piece of property. It isn't a bunch of rooms. It's certainly not the general manager, and it isn't even the guests. It's you. You deserve the right to decide its future. Not me, not the bank. Not a room full of lawyers or board members. But all of you."

Connor nodded at Logan. He approached and took the microphone. They both avoided each other's eyes, knowing they'd probably tear up if they didn't.

Maybe it was the power of the microphone, or maybe it was the power that always seemed to live in Logan's voice, but he barely had to speak up for his voice to fill the vast ballroom. "Thank you for coming together on such short notice. I want to say, I'll understand whatever decision you make. But make it based on your future, your families, your savings. Make it knowing I'll have nothing but respect in my heart for each and every one of us who fought through this time together. Like Connor said, in these past few weeks alone, you've all given this place more than it deserves. I don't know. Maybe that's up for debate, I guess. But what isn't up for debate is that each one of you have earned the right to cast this vote and decide what comes next. For you and for this place."

When Logan handed the microphone back to Connor, there were expressions of shock over Logan's brevity.

"Wait!" a voice said. It was Gloria's. She'd risen to her feet, and the tissue she'd been holding to her face was damp with tears. "*Wait.* I have something to say. And as someone who's been here longer than probably everyone, I think I've earned the right to say it."

"Of course." Connor gestured for her to come forward and take the mic.

Once she had it, she gulped a few breaths before her tears stopped. "I've been here forty-five years. I started at the front desk while I was in night school. I've worked in almost every department. Except lifeguarding, because you all know I hate the ocean. It's where sharks live, and don't tell me otherwise." A ripple of tension-easing laughter swept the room. But Gloria's eyes were on Logan. "And I can say, without a doubt, I have never in all of my time here seen an employee like Logan Murdoch. And so I understand, Logan, why you're not pleading your case right now, given the stakes for us all. But *I* will plead your case. I will remind everyone that in the long history of this place, you are the only employee who has ever saved a child's life on the grounds of this resort. That on the night the FBI showed up and we thought the death threat calls would never stop, you sat with our operators until two a.m. just to make them feel safer. And you'd spent all day chasing reporters out who'd tried to sneak in. You are a fine man. A man who fought for this country and fought for this hotel.

"I don't know what happens to me if this place sells. But I know I'm not broke, and I can get other jobs. And telling me the only way I can hold on to this one is if we fire one of the best people who's worked here because of something other people, bad people, did... Well, I'm sorry. We've done a lot for this place, but that's a bridge too far for me. I'll be voting to reject."

There was a vigorous burst of applause, but not enough to suggest Logan was saved. Most people still looked shocked and overwhelmed by the revelations.

Gloria took Logan's face in her hands, stood on her tiptoes, and gave him a firm kiss on the forehead. Because Connor knew it was only seconds before he and Logan would lose their bid to stay dry-eyed, he took the microphone from Gloria and cleared his throat once, then twice. "And now I've asked Lois Penry from Pacific Crest Bank to come forward and explain some more about how the voting process will work."

Connor gave Gloria a quick hug, feeling Lois gently tug the microphone out of his hand where he held it against Logan's back. Then the next thing he knew, he and Logan were in the hallway outside. His mother was there, throwing her arms around him.

"I'm so proud of you," she whispered in his ear. "And your father would be too."

He kissed her on the cheek. She turned to Logan and threw her arms around him. He returned her embrace, bowing his head over her shoulder and pursing his lips in a way that said he might be in danger of unleashing the tears Connor had already set loose. Knowing briefly, Connor hoped, what it felt like to have a mom. She told them she was going to head outside to the pool deck if they needed her. Then the two of them were alone in the large, empty corridor, listening to the sound of Lois Penry's more official-sounding voice echoing through the ballroom next to them as she explained how the voting would take place in three of the nearby conference rooms, how the groups of voters would be organized by the first letter in their last names.

"So," Logan said as he took one of Connor's hands, "I heard there are sea caves here. You want to show me?"

But they didn't make it to the sea caves.

The sea caves had given rise to their fair share of passions. They were also a place of secrecy and shadows. And now, with everything out in the open, Connor steered them to one of the beach loungers instead, where a bright blue umbrella flapped in the ocean breeze.

For a while, they lay in each other's arms. The sea was roiled that day and the surf sounds were steady. Connor's ear rested on Logan's broad chest.

"What are you going to do, Logan, if they vote to accept?"

"Well, if my dad and I come close to killing each other again, which is a distinct possibility, I've got a buddy down in San Diego putting together a private security firm. He said he'd want to take me on. But honestly, even if they vote to reject, I might have to do the same. Not sure a new buyer's going to be any more excited about me than Sylvia Milton is."

"We'll see," Connor whispered.

At the very least, engaging with new buyers would present new unknowns, new risks, but also new opportunities to preserve what was valuable about Sapphire Cove. Before yesterday, those unknowns had seemed unacceptable. But now, with a single conference client trying to force an unreasonable demand on the hotel, they seemed worth exploring.

"San Diego," Connor said. "That's a commute."

"He said the jobs would be all over Southern California." Logan tightened his embrace around Connor. "I'd stay right here."

"Good." Connor straightened and turned. "I want to show you something." He reached inside the pocket of his blazer and pulled out a small brown envelope. "Open your hand."

Logan complied, and out spilled the big bronze room key Connor's father had sealed away as a special gift years before.

"Oh my God," Logan said. "Is this an original room key?"

"Yep. It was in a letter from my dad. And now…"

"Are you going to cry again?" Logan asked.

"Probably."

"That's okay, baby. But try to get more than three words out so I can know why you're crying."

"Like it's any mystery why I'd be crying today. What I wanted to say is that this key is yours now. Because no matter what happens, no matter how the vote turns out, as far as I'm concerned, a part of this place will always be yours."

"Well, you should hold on to it then," he said.

"Why?"

Logan reached into the pocket of his blazer, just as Connor had done, and pulled out an envelope that was about the size of Connor's. But the key he shook out into Connor's palm was a lot smaller. A lot less impressive. But, Connor realized, its implications were far more momentous.

"As it happens," Logan said, "I went and got you a key too. It isn't quite as groovy, but there are a lot of privileges that come with it."

"Like what?" Connor asked.

"Like going to bed with me every night. Fighting over whether we're going to watch my History Channel stuff or your design shows. And you'll be able to hold on to the original room key, 'cause we'll share it like we share everything else."

"Because I'll live with you," Connor said.

"If you get tired of the penthouse suite, of course," Logan said.

"I don't know, the penthouse suite's pretty nice."

"It is, but I don't charge fifteen dollars for a bottle of water."

"Is that what we charge for bottled water?" Connor barked.

Logan nodded gravely.

"Okay. That's going to change."

"Maybe wait 'til the hotel's in the black again. But speaking of changes, chances are you're not going to be seeing much of me during the day anymore. So what do you say, Mr. Harcourt? Will you accept this key even if I don't have the schematics for your four-story shoe closet ready yet?"

"That's so unfair. I barely brought any shoes."

"Yeah, 'cause they're all still at your place in New York, I bet, and you're going to have to get them, right?"

"Maybe," Connor said with a sheepish smile.

"That's what I thought. But don't worry. I'm more than prepared."

Connor smiled and took the gold key from Logan's hand. "I'd get rid of every pair of shoes I have for the chance to spend every night with you."

Their kiss was perfect.

For about fifteen seconds. Then Connor felt Logan stiffen, and not in a way that said sexy times were afoot. Something had distracted him.

Connor drew back and took Logan's face in his hands. "What?" he asked.

"I probably shouldn't ask this, but it's been bothering me, and I can't let go of it."

"Okay."

"How much was it, Connor?" Logan asked.

"How much was what?" Connor asked, even though he knew exactly what Logan meant.

"Your inheritance."

Connor swallowed, looked out at the sea, saw no escape there, so he looked back at Logan. "I'll tell you. On one condition. Well, two actually."

"Okay," Logan said.

"You can't respond to what I'm about to say for twenty-four hours, and you can't say anything at all for at least five minutes."

Logan's laugh was long. "I guess I deserve that."

"Maybe a little. So do you agree?"

"I do," Logan said.

Connor leaned forward and whispered the combined total figure into Logan's ear, then recoiled. Logan's nostrils flared. The veins in the sides of his neck bulged. The sounds that came from his throat were strangled and high pitched, as if eight hundred different responses were trying to fight their way out of him at once, and he was stuffing down every single one with all the muscles in his body.

"See?" Connor said. "Now you know how it feels."

Logan managed to suck in a long, deep breath that sounded vaguely like Lamaze.

"Kiss me, big boy," Connor said. "It'll make the time go by faster."

Logan did. After a while, he began to yield. But it was a long while. It was a lot of money.

As their umbrella shielded them from the noonday sun, the exhaustion of the last two days overtook them, and suddenly they were dozing in each other's arms, kissed by the warm winds. And in the moment right before he nodded off, it felt to Connor like they were surrendering to whatever might come next. Letting their guard down beneath the big open sky and unstoppable power of the sea and whatever fate was assembling itself in the conference rooms above.

Then he was pulled from vague dreams filled with ocean sounds by a louder and more insistent sound, the sound of sneakered feet punching sand nearby. Logan had also stirred. Scott was running toward them across the sand, breathless with excitement or alarm, Connor couldn't tell.

"I've been instructed to ask you both to come upstairs," he said.

"By who?" Connor asked. "I'm your boss."

"By the bank," Scott answered, gasping.

"What happened?" Connor asked. "Did they count the ballots?"

"Just come up, okay? I've got one job here and it's to get you guys off this beach. I'm going to do it right."

Scott turned and ran for the wooden stairs.

Connor and Logan exchanged a look. "Hoo boy," Logan whispered. "Here goes."

Connor took Logan's hand forcefully, then they followed the instructions of their breathless security agent. Connor held Logan's hand as they ascended, a reminder to the man he loved that he'd stand by him no matter what came next.

When they arrived at the top of the stairs, they both froze at the sight before them, of the entire staff assembled on the steps of the Dolphin Ballroom. He spotted Naser in the front row. As Connor had asked, he'd shown up after the vote and not before so he could be there to help them deal with the consequences.

And apparently one of those consequences would be a gathering of the entire hotel's staff set to rival an appearance of the Mormon Tabernacle Choir. Logan's hand tightened around Connor's.

Connor was so stricken by the scene he was startled when Lois Penry stepped forward from several feet away.

"Mr. Murdoch," she said, crisply, professionally. "It's my responsibility to inform you as the trustee for the Sapphire Cove Trust that the ballots have been counted and the vote certified. The decision was unanimous. The staff of Sapphire Cove has voted to reject the Lighthouse Foundation's request, and as a result of this vote, your employment here will not be terminated."

"Well, damn," Logan said under his breath in a trembling voice. "Well, how about that." And Connor could see his eyes were glistening. He was pretty sure that in a different circumstance, Logan would have run like hell to the nearest bathroom to hide the emotions welling in him. But he couldn't bring himself to leave the scene. And Connor wouldn't have let him run away if he had tried.

Was it suicide for the Sapphire Cove they all knew and loved? Maybe. But when given the choice, the staff had made their vote and decided Logan Murdoch shouldn't be swept aside.

When Logan turned to Connor, he was chewing his bottom lip harder. But it was a losing battle. The tears had already come.

"Kiss him!" Naser cried.

Could they really do it? Right out in the open, in the bright afternoon sun, before the eyes of the entire hotel? On the spot where they'd first met, before secrecy and shame, lies and abuse had conspired to separate them for half a decade? Logan took Connor into his arms, and the cheers got louder.

"You saved me," Logan whispered, "again."

"All I did was give them the chance not to throw away a hero," he said.

Logan pulled back and took Connor's face in his hands. "You're my hero now, Connor Harcourt."

Then Logan planted one on him that rivaled the first kiss they'd ever shared, and the staff's cheers swam in a fresh sea of applause.

25

First came the weddings.

All three of them same sex couples. The two male couples both said the same thing. After skyrocketing real estate prices and an old tween reality show had unseated Laguna Beach's long-held status as a bohemian arts colony years before, they'd never considered Orange County to be a welcoming destination for a gay union. Sylvia Milton's attack on Connor and Logan had changed that, and they'd since broken off conversations with possible venues in Palm Springs and San Diego.

As for the female couple, during their site visit, one of the brides-to-be took Connor aside to tell him how Sylvia's tone and phrasing during her press conference had reminded her of the time she'd lost her temper with the senior partners at her first firm after they asked her not to bring her girlfriend to the Christmas party. It might upset the other lawyers, they'd said. "Of course, they didn't care how upset *I* was," she'd said. "In fact, they actually told me I was the one who should calm down. It wasn't exactly *blinded by my sexuality*, but it was damn close."

But those were precisely the words that had rocketed across social media, inspiring their own hashtag among those eager to call out Sylvia Milton for what they saw as her not-so-subtle attempts to paint queer relationships as marked by a feverish level of lust that obscured sound, professional judgment. Relationships she'd depicted as a danger to any child who might witness their displays of affection. #NotBlinded had even trended briefly in the United States, and someone had sent the hotel a package of T-shirts printed with the phrase in rainbow letters.

Despite the shows of support, in the end, Connor thought it was a close call. Amongst the rarely predictable twists and turns of social media wars, Sylvia's throttling was the result of a few poorly chosen words. If she'd stuck to the question of whether or not a workplace relationship during a time of scandal was the right choice for the hotel, she might have been able to lob a weakening strike without bribing the Lighthouse Foundation in the process. Having Logan report to an outside management company could have played defense for a round or two. Or maybe not. At any rate, the feud would have continued.

Had Sylvia Milton simply been sloppy with her language and become a victim of a PC mob as a result? That's what some of her vastly outnumbered right-wing defenders thought. Or was she actually a bigot?

Connor was sure of only one thing. Considering her word choice along with her performance that day, she'd seemed all too eager to mobilize bigotry on her behalf.

And she was paying the price for it.

When word of the vote hit the news, the Lighthouse Foundation, which had followed through with its threat to cancel, had been widely accused of participating in a baseless smear campaign against a veteran of the Marine Corps who'd saved a child's life, and because Sylvia Milton's money remained too good for them to pass up, they'd been forced to weather the storm. If it hadn't been for the weddings and the social media pushback, the patent attorneys might have canceled too. Instead, they made Connor wait on pins and needles for forty-eight hours before they notified him they were hanging in. Then the Equality Defense Fund, a political action organization that dispatched some of the nation's best lawyers to argue on behalf of LGBT rights in the courts, moved their annual conference to Sapphire Cove from a giant LA convention hotel that was unlikely to miss the business. And suddenly, the hotel could breathe again.

Brought to the brink by Rodney and his coconspirators, then brought back to it by Sylvia Milton, Sapphire Cove had survived two brushes with death. And now its staff—Connor and Logan included—walked its halls with a new skip in their step and an energy that bordered on giddy.

More importantly, the Stop Sapphire Cove Twitter feed had gone dormant.

Harris Mitchell still believed a defamation suit was required. Nothing else, in his view, would put the Sylvia Milton matter to bed once and for all. But Connor dreaded the thought of another lawsuit. Wanted a life for him, for Logan, for the staff at Sapphire Cove that was temporarily free of scandal, lawyers, and tweets that sent everyone running in all directions.

Two weeks after the vote that had saved Logan's job, Connor was explaining these very thoughts to Logan as they stood together in the lobby, amidst a trickle of incoming guests. When Logan's face suddenly fell at the sight of something over Connor's shoulder, Connor turned, half expecting a Bengal tiger to nose its way through the entry doors.

He was close.

At first, he didn't recognize the approaching woman. Her sunglasses were enormous, and she'd changed her hair since the press conference. Once a platinum cascade, it was now slicked back in a confining-looking updo held in place by a bright silver, jeweled barrette. Her black pantsuit had a subtle sheen. When the fabric shifted as she walked, the sheen seemed to pulse. She was taller than Connor expected, around six feet even, but that made sense given she'd worked as a model. But that wasn't the detail that struck him most.

Sylvia Milton was alone.

No assistant, no lawyer, no bodyguard, and no reporters.

His feet feeling like smoke, Connor approached her. "Good afternoon, Mrs. Milton."

A handshake seemed too pushy given their history, so he turned his nod into a subtle bow. She removed her sunglasses and sized him up with cold eyes. She was a hard woman. An injured woman. A *grieving* woman, he reminded himself. And, whether he wanted to admit it in this moment or not, nothing could change the fact that she and her husband had been wronged.

"Mr. Harcourt," she said. "Mr. Murdoch."

"Ma'am," Logan said with a nod of the head.

"Congratulations on weathering your recent troubles." It was an admission of defeat, Connor knew, and it cast this unexpected meeting in a suddenly strange light. "I thought perhaps we could have a drink, Mr. Harcourt."

"Sure, if Mr. Murdoch joins us."

Her pursed lips told Connor she didn't like this idea one bit, but she didn't feel like she was in a position to negotiate. *Tough shit.* If she was going to stage a surprise attack, she'd have to do it in the presence of the man she'd smeared.

"Of course," she whispered.

"And perhaps we could do it someplace off site," Connor said.

"I promise I'm not here to make a scene."

"I was thinking mostly of your comfort," Connor said. "You choose the place, and we'd be happy to meet you there."

"I did. We're here. Let's sit, shall we?"

The hostess for Camilla's regarded them with eyes gone saucer wide. Connor and Logan sitting down to a casual lunch with the hotel's public adversary. It was a reaction that spread silently, and not so subtly, throughout the surrounding staff as Connor led the three of them to a table by the window. He instructed the server to get Sylvia whatever she wanted, and Sylvia ordered a glass of the most expensive Chardonnay on the wine list.

Then a tense and uncomfortable silence settled. Sylvia studied their surroundings with a suspicious squint.

"He never brought me here," she finally said. "This was his special place, I guess. Which is surprising. No offense, but it's a level down from where we'd usually stay when we traveled together. The Ritzes and the Mandarin Orientals."

If letting Sylvia cast insults against Sapphire Cove was the price he'd have to pay for a meeting that would end this once and for all, Connor was willing to do it.

"I'd expected to hear from your attorneys by now," Sylvia said.

"I understand the civil suit is proceeding accordingly," Connor said.

"Not that. You know I don't mean that. I'm referring to our…exchanges."

"On Twitter, you mean."

Her eyes flashed to his. She'd never publicly connected herself to the Stop Sapphire Cove account. Would she do so now? Instead, she looked up at the server who'd brought her wine, studied the glass for a beat as if she was checking for the powdery threads of poison, then took a careful sip.

"It seems I was an old woman playing a young person's game," she finally said, swirling her glass. "My choice of words was intemperate. And it sent the wrong impression."

"Some of your best friends are gay, right?" Connor asked.

For a second, he regretted the remark, but she seemed slightly amused by his sarcasm. Then she shifted her attention to Logan. "I meant to say that you are so devastatingly handsome, Mr. Murdoch, that your good looks would be capable of driving anyone to distraction, whatever their sexual identity."

"Gee," Logan said, "thanks."

"The point is, I didn't make my point, and that's on me."

"Your point was that Logan was a criminal and I didn't have the good judgment to see it," Connor said. "And with all due respect, neither was true."

Sylvia sipped her wine.

"Should I get us lunch menus?" Connor asked.

"In all honesty, how much respect do you think I'm due, Mr. Harcourt?" she asked.

"You haven't heard from our lawyer. That should answer your question."

"It does. But only in part."

"A few years ago I lost my grandfather, then shortly after that, my father. Sometimes the grief hurt so badly I couldn't speak. I can't imagine how bad that pain must be when it's your husband. After your press conference, Logan and I spent three nights apart, and our future together was…not exactly sure. They were some of the worst days of my life."

"Ah, so you pity me, then." Sylvia sipped her wine bitterly.

"I sympathize. It's not exactly the same thing. And I'm no stranger to my uncle's abuse. And neither was your husband."

She looked studious and wary now, and not quite so rigid.

"And apparently you played a pivotal role in getting him to publicly admit his guilt," she finally said. "That was not lost on me."

Connor nodded but figured it was best not to take too much credit for anything until he had a better sense of where this unexpected meeting was headed.

"I'll take the Twitter account down as soon as I leave here," she said, "provided we both agree to never speak about this publicly again. If I'm called upon to make any statements about the civil suit, I'll be sure to direct them at your uncle and his henchmen and not either of you or the hotel."

"And in exchange?" Connor asked.

"We bury the hatchet. You won't make any public statements about me either. And, of course, there'll be no further legal action in this matter."

Sylvia Milton was a shrewd negotiator. What she wanted was something she hadn't said aloud. She wanted to avoid making a public apology to the hotel. To Connor and Logan. And for a second, he wanted to protest. But he reminded himself of how badly she'd been throttled, and of the not so simple fact that her husband had actually been blackmailed inside of these very walls.

"Is that all?" Connor asked.

"No." She took another slow sip of wine. When she looked at him again, there was something unguarded in her eyes. "I want to see it. Six E, right? I'm told that was his villa of choice."

Connor looked to Logan for confirmation of this, and he nodded.

Did she really want to visit the scene of her husband's blackmail as if there were a headstone there? Or was she after something else?

He had to find out. After checking with registration to make sure it was vacant, the three of them started for the villa. There were only nine in all, terraced in three rows on the south coast-facing hillside. Each had a side door that opened onto a walkway that traveled downhill between each row. They were newer than the main building. Imitation adobe with red tile accents, but the same brightly colored furnishings that matched the renovated lobby's color scheme, the same plush carpeting and taffeta drapes as the main rooms. Each one had a cathedral ceiling and a tiny backyard with a plunge pool. Six E had gone unoccupied since the scandal broke. As they entered, Connor pulled the drapes and opened the balcony door so ocean air could drive out the vaguely musty smell.

When he turned, he saw Sylvia Milton standing in place, turning slowly to take in her surroundings. The bright blue chaise lounge in the corner had captured her attention. It was positioned so its occupant could take in the sparkling ocean view. Her eyes filled. Was she imagining her husband sitting in it, attached to the IV drip of whatever punishing treatment had been intended to drive his cancer into submission?

As Logan took up a position next to him, as they both watched Sylvia's silent tears, Connor did the math in his head. She had never been here before. Her husband had kept this place a secret from her. And that meant there was another secret he might have kept from her as well.

The silence between them stretched to what felt like a breaking point. "Mrs. Milton, may I ask you a question?"

It seemed to take effort, but she roused herself, nodded, and dug a tissue from her purse.

"We were told your husband was keeping his diagnosis secret from his company," Connor said.

"That's correct," she whispered.

"Did he also keep it a secret from you?"

When he looked into her eyes, he saw the pain there, saw it in the sudden sag in the corners of her mouth, the fresh sheen of tears in her radiant eyes. The single sharp exhale she took through her nose, as if she'd planned to take several but couldn't manage the next few.

"First, he had me travel all over. Told me he'd be closing some big deals and would be less around than usual. Then *he* started to travel. Or, at least, that's what he told me. But he was coming here. When he couldn't hide it anymore, he told me it was an infection he'd picked up on one of his trips. By the time the doctors told me what it really was, he was slipping away. It was terminal, and there was very little hope. Apparently he didn't want me to know. And then came the letter."

Connor was tempted to tell her he had his own experience with letters left by the departed, but this was her moment.

She walked to the chaise lounge and ran her fingers gently along the head. "I used to think it was a good thing that he always saw me as that young party girl he practically picked up off the runway and turned into his wife. I never stopped being young in his eyes. Who doesn't want to be young forever? But the flip side was he never saw me as very competent either. It might be why he never tried to trade me out for a younger model. And it feels cruel now, but I always thought the fact that he was old would be my best hope in that regard. Because eventually I would get to care for him and show him there was more to me than my…beautiful smile. But he didn't let me. In the end, he said he wanted to spare me the pain. But what he really did was spare me the chance to be his wife."

After a while, she returned to the center of the room and gave it one last survey, her expression turning flinty again.

"So," she said, "do we have a deal?"

Connor turned to the man next to him. "Logan?"

Logan looked surprised to be consulted, then pleased.

"Of course," he said.

She turned to Logan and extended her hand. "With my apologies, Mr. Murdoch."

Logan accepted her handshake. "Thank you, ma'am."

"Would you like us to show you out?" Connor asked.

"No, I'm fine, thank you."

Sylvia went for the door, but as soon as her hand closed on the knob, she turned to them. "Do you love each other?" she asked.

"More than words can say," Connor said.

"What he said," Logan added. "And then some."

She nodded. "Good. But it won't be enough just to feel it. You'll also have to receive it. Trust me. Sometimes that's the hardest part."

And then her footfalls were clacking up the walkway back toward the main building, and Logan took Connor's hand in his. A few minutes later, they left the villa, left its ghosts and grief, and stepped out into the sun. Downhill a few steps was a paved walking path that sat right below the lowest row of villas, skirting the top of the cliffs. It was one of the hotel's little secrets, and right now they had it all to themselves. Drained by Sylvia Milton's unexpected display of emotion, Connor wilted into Logan, letting himself be supported by his powerful embrace.

"It meant the world to me that you asked me before you accepted her offer," Logan said.

"She made more of a target out of you than she did of me."

"We were both targets."

"True. So did you mean it?" Connor asked.

"What, the more than words can say thing?" Logan asked.

"That was my part. You said the *and then some* part."

"Yeah, 'cause it was true."

"Good. Just checking. I mean, now that you know I can bake I figured it's a lock, but maybe you don't appreciate muffins."

Logan tightened his embrace. "They were *really* good muffins."

"Muffins are only the beginning. The banana bread's going to make you mine forever."

"What if I don't like bananas?" Logan asked.

"You will when you have my banana bread." Connor smiled up at him and waggled his eyebrows.

"I do love your determination."

"And my baking."

"And your powers of perception," Logan said.

"How so?"

"How could you tell her husband didn't tell her he was sick?" Logan asked.

"It was the way she looked at the room. There was this longing in her expression. I'd expected her to be angry, you know. But instead it was like she was staring at doors that had been closed in her face."

Logan crooked his finger under Connor's chin and lifted it until their eyes met. "She's right. Sometimes it's harder to receive the love than it is to give it. But after a while, maybe it becomes second nature. So what do you say? Let's do it every day, so it becomes a habit."

"Sounds like a plan," Connor whispered, then graced him with a quick and tender kiss.

Then it was time to get back to work. Together.

Six Months Later

26

"Logan, let me help, please," Connor said for the fourth time.

"Not a chance, my prince."

Donnie was in the kitchen, warming up the dish he'd brought, and the other guests would be there any minute. But Logan had already spent twenty minutes trying to screw a hook for the string lanterns into the back wall of their new home. He didn't seem to be making progress, and Connor was getting nervous. "Tonight's my show, remember? That's the deal."

"Well," Connor said, batting his eyelashes, "maybe I just want an excuse to rub up against you on that ladder."

Logan unleashed several more fires of the automatic drill. "You'll have plenty of time to get all up on this later. But *I'm* doing this one. We agreed."

As good as Logan looked in his Levi jeans and hunter green polo, Connor was more interested in getting handsy with the preparations than with his boyfriend. Throughout their grassy backyard, Connor saw a litany of design choices in desperate need of improvement.

Logan had already put the place settings on the folding table even though it would be an hour before they ate, an hour in which they would be dusted with whatever their sycamore tree felt like shaking loose in the warm, canyon breezes. Now he was spending way too much time setting up the string lanterns that would soon—Connor hoped—stretch across the entire backyard, hopefully providing more illumination for their dinner than the candles on the folding table. Candles that had no covers or wind shields.

"I'm just saying," Connor continued, "if you did the lanterns in an X over the backyard instead of two parallel strands then maybe—"

"*I'm* doing this one." Logan emphasized his point with several fires of his drill in rapid succession. "Have some faith, all right? Does the downstairs bathroom have all the new tile you picked out or not?"

"It does," Connor conceded.

Their new house was a fixer upper, and in the few weeks since they'd moved in, Logan had proved his mettle as a skillful contractor. The speed with which he'd redone the floor in the downstairs bathroom was a definite point in his favor. But he'd also cleared and finished a space in the kitchen for a refrigerator twice the size of the one the previous owners had used. And he'd replaced all the metal air conditioning vent covers with wooden ones that didn't rattle. The fact that they matched the surrounding walls was an added plus.

They'd planned to buy a place closer to Sapphire Cove. But a little way south, in Mission Viejo, they'd found the perfect combo of the big backyard Logan had always craved and a manageable mortgage that wouldn't require Connor to ask for help from his mom. Added perks? A peaceful eastern view of the surrounding hills, plenty of closet space off the master, and a deep enough kitchen counter for Logan to take Connor missionary atop it, something they'd done almost every day since they moved in. While the commute was twenty minutes on a good day, neither one of them minded. After all they'd given the hotel these past months, they could both use a bit of distance between their work and home lives.

"Don't bother fighting him, dude." Donnie emerged through the sliding door with a Heineken in each fist. "He's serious about this one. I went with him to pick up the folding table, and he shook it like he was trying to get gold out of it just to make sure it wouldn't collapse. I'm like, what are we having for dinner? A giraffe?"

Connor took the beer out of Donnie's left hand and saw Donnie give him a startled look.

"What?" Connor asked.

"The beer was for Logan," Donnie said.

"Oh, sorry. Didn't mean to cut in line."

"No, it's fine. I can get him another one. I kinda thought you weren't a beer person. I was going to make you a vodka soda."

"I can drink beer." Although, now that he thought about it...

"It's not supposed to be, like, an endurance thing," Donnie said.

To prove a point, Connor brought the bottle to his mouth, slugged, and winced. "Oh, God. It tastes like jet fuel. Why is this a thing at all?"

"Some guys in the Middle Ages thought it up, I think," Donnie said.

"Hand over the Heineken," Logan demanded.

Connor passed the bottle up to him as he shook his head and shivered like a wet dog.

"I'll get you a suitable cocktail," Donnie said. "Is Naser coming?"

"Who wants to know?" Naser asked, stepping through the open back door with a covered casserole dish in both hands.

Donnie blushed and looked to his feet. "Just wondering if I should brush up on my math."

"It was actually a logic problem you couldn't solve, not a math problem. And you really need to let it go."

"It's a stupid problem," Donnie grumbled. "There's no such thing as *half* a hen so *half* a hen can't lay *any* eggs."

"It was three months ago, Donnie," Naser said.

"Or was it three *half* months ago?" Donnie grumbled.

"Whatever," Naser said. "I need refrigerator space."

"Second shelf is all yours," Connor said.

"Oh, also, your mom's driving in circles around the neighborhood because she probably can't find the place," Naser said as he stepped back inside.

"She's been here three times already," Connor said. "She's driving in circles because she doesn't want to get off the phone with her friend Lisa, who's going through a dramatic divorce."

"*Where the gays at?*" a booming male voice called from inside the house.

"Dad!" Logan barked, then fired the drill a few more times and let out a triumphant war whoop when the hook didn't come loose under his jiggling hand.

Chip Murdoch stepped through the sliding door past Naser, but not before clapping the guy on the back so hard he stumbled and rolled his eyes. Now that he went almost everywhere with his girlfriend of five months, Donna Langdon, he'd stopped wearing the Chip's Kicks branded gear he'd worn to every outing except for the dinner party where he met Connor. Neither one of them looked ready to dance at the Rainbow Room, but their jeans looked ironed, and Donna had clearly made Chip wear one of the few T-shirts he owned that didn't have an offensive saying written on it.

"How's everybody doing?" Chip boomed. "Is Nas helping you guys cheat on your taxes too?"

"We are not *cheating* on your taxes," Naser shouted from the kitchen. "We're filing them on time so you don't have to pay a penalty. I know it's a big change for you, but it's not against the law. Quite the opposite, in fact."

"Are you paying in *half* hens or whole hens?" Donnie grumbled.

"I heard that, Donnie!" Naser called.

Once he finished securing one end of the lantern strand to the hook he'd screwed into place, Logan descended the ladder and started unspooling the rest of the strand across the grass.

"Honestly," Chip said, "given the taxes we pay in this state, we should have a monorail that goes to the front door of everybody's house."

"No politics, Chip." Donna said. "It's a housewarming, not a barn burning."

"Well, if I want to burn through my own money, I should be able to burn through it on something stupid. Like buying my son a drill he can figure out how to use."

"Dad, seriously?" Logan barked. "Donnie, go get some of that red wine and turkey casserole we got for the old man. He could use a nap before dinner."

"Oh, don't worry about him," Connor said. "Now that he's got Donna, he tires out after a few minutes and goes quiet."

"Yeah, well I gotta save up energy for this one." Chip grinned. "She keeps me burning the midnight oil, if you know what I mean."

Donna whacked Chip across the back of the head so hard it was a good thing he didn't wear dentures. But that only made Chip's grin widen, suggesting this kind of roughhousing was exactly what kept them up so late.

Connor's mother emerged from the back door like a hurricane of bright couture, sunglasses still on, phone still in hand. Connor couldn't tell if her hair was windblown or if she'd styled it that way on purpose. "Boys, I'm so sorry I'm late."

"You're not late." Connor threw his arms around her.

"It's my friend Lisa, her divorce…it's just endless. It's just an endless, unfolding disaster of successive disasters."

And if I don't stop this now, we will be talking about it all night.

"Oh, I know," Connor said. "It's just awful when affluent women get millions of dollars in a divorce settlement from a husband they've been with for six months."

"Mind your tongue, young man. She actually sort of liked this one. When you find a tech billionaire that's willing to learn foot massage for you, you hold on to him. Until he sleeps with your cousin. Anyway."

"Yeah, well, I've got a former Marine who does stuff to my body that none of you want to hear about," Connor said.

In the end, there weren't so many twigs in the dinner plates that they couldn't shake them out with minimal effort, and the potluck-style buffet had something for everyone's liking. And the string lanterns, even in parallel strands, sent a lovely glow across the grassy but still unfinished backyard. Even if the candles blew out after three minutes. Connor was willing to take the wins along with the losses. Sometimes the things about a guy that allowed him to wreck your ass to your satisfaction also meant he'd wreck your dinner party before the guests showed up.

At the end of the meal, Logan rose from his folding chair and lifted a glass of wine. "A toast," he said, "or I should say, a series of toasts."

"Oh, boy," Connor muttered.

"First, to the chaplains at Mendota Federal Prison, who I hear are doing a bang-up job handling Rodney Harcourt's super convenient conversion to Christianity, which they'll have to tolerate for three years at least since a term of his plea deal was no parole."

There were whoops and hollers around the table.

"God bless 'em all," Connor said, and they all raised their glasses and drank.

"And second, to Sapphire Cove's insurance company for reaching reasonable settlements with most of Rodney's victims. Although I'm told the other negotiations are proceeding in a positive direction."

"And we are barred from disclosing the content of those negotiations at this time," Connor interjected quickly. "But we should still toast them nonetheless."

Everyone drank.

"No offense here," Chip said, "but don't we rattle off who the toasts are for and then drink once? I mean, if we keep this up, I'm going to have to whiz before we get to the part where we thank Jesus."

"Since when are you remotely concerned for Jesus?" Donna grumbled.

"Hey!" Chip wailed.

"Facts are facts, Dad. Now pipe down. All right, so I thought long and hard about what I was going to get Connor for a housewarming present, what with it being our first house and all. And then an idea came to me. I know all of you know the story of how we met five years ago. But what you might not know is the night after we met—"

"After you *made out* in the sea caves, you mean," Naser barked.

"Yeah, that, exactly. So that night Connor sent me a text asking how I was doing and I *might* have sent him a thumbs-up in response."

"*Might* have?" Connor cried. "That's exactly what you did."

"Yeah, and it was kind of lame, and whatever. But my point is that the next morning Connor sent me a longer text and it was… Well, it was really great."

There was a nervous shake in Logan's voice Connor wasn't used to hearing there. Logan was usually good in front of a crowd. Maybe it was the intimacy of the setting, how well he'd come to know everyone present, but Connor was suddenly curious about where this was headed.

"And anyway, we all know how it went after that, so that's my toast. Who wants pie?"

There were groans and moans as Logan pretended to sit down. When Donnie's napkin slapped him in the chest, Logan grabbed it and stood up again. Then he reached into his pocket, and Connor's heart stopped. Until he pulled out his cell phone.

"So, my prince, for your housewarming present, I thought I'd take us back to the moment when I got your text, and instead of asking you to meet for coffee so I could shoot the whole thing down, I'd write what I really wanted to write you in that moment. I'd write what was in my heart. With a little something extra added in at the end. But I'll explain when I get to that part. You'll see. Anyway. Here goes." Logan cleared his throat and took one of Connor's hands in his as he began to read.

"Hey," he said, which got a laugh from the whole table. "So that was maybe one of the most amazing texts I've ever gotten. And I'm kinda scared to write back because I want whatever I say to make you feel the way you made me feel. With words alone. Because the way you made me feel is like everything I felt last night when I saw you the first time, when I heard you laugh, when I heard your beautiful, sweet, seductive voice, when I looked into your blue eyes and against my better judgment gave them a nickname on the spot. All of that made me feel like something I'd always been told about wasn't just a myth, wasn't just a song I heard on the radio when I was a kid. You made the room stop when I first saw you,

Connor Harcourt, and I think that means we should pay a lot of attention to each other. Starting now. So how about dinner tonight and maybe a long drive after? And then we see what happens. No plans, no judgments, no fears. Just us and the future."

Blinking back tears, Connor looked to the rest of the table, and that's when he saw most of them were tearing up too. They were also looking directly at him, watching him closely. Expecting something.

"And here's the part I added recently," Logan said.

Logan put the phone down on the table. When he sank to one knee and revealed the ring box in his other hand, Connor's breath left him in a single, excited huff. It was like Logan had described that long-ago night. Time stopped, and everything that wasn't Logan—everything that wasn't *them*—seemed to fade away. Then Logan opened the ring box in his hand to reveal a brilliant sapphire embedded in a silver band.

"Connor Harcourt," Logan said, "since you told me you'd take me any way you could have me, I want you every way I can get you. Will you marry me, Baby Blues?"

First he nodded it, then he managed to croak it out once, twice through his tears, then he felt the delicious tug of the ring sliding onto his finger, then it felt like he was airborne. Because he was. Logan had picked him up in his arms as everyone around the table cheered, as his mother dabbed furiously at her tears with a paper napkin, as Chip Murdoch turned his head away from the table and coughed to hide his own, as Donnie roared like he was at a football game, and Naser whistled and clapped.

"Now you see why I wanted to plan this party?" Logan asked.

The guests stayed late, and for most of the night, Connor felt like part of Logan's clothes, that's how fast and tenderly they held to each other. Then when the guests departed, leaving behind the pleasant memory of their laughter, Logan guided him upstairs and into their bed.

There were less acrobatics now, less frenzy. Their bodies joining with the stealth familiarity provides. The tests they'd agreed to had been taken—the medical ones and the emotional ones—and now, as Connor reclined, blissfully exposed, drawing his legs back in hungry submission, their union was defined by skin on skin, heat meeting heat, trust meeting trust. It had become his favorite position, lying on his back as he gave himself entirely, letting Logan claim him while he watched the passage of every emotion, strain, and eruption pulse across his handsome face. At the moment of Logan's release, Connor embraced him tightly as he bellowed and shook and emptied, absorbing all of it with no barrier between them. Holding tight to the rock and roar of him, the strength and passion, the union of commitment and desire.

And then there was the silent, blissful aftermath of letting their heaving breaths fall into a matching rhythm, of lying in a sweaty tangle before the shower called them both.

A shower big enough for two—Connor had insisted on it.

And when they returned to the sheets together, cleaned and exhausted and sated, Connor thought for what must have been the hundredth time that we find what we most need while answering calls we at first resist.

Saving Sapphire Cove had saved a part of him. Saving Logan had saved the rest.

Theirs had once been a secret passion concealed within the shadows of a cave. When morning came, it was promises kept within the walls of a new home bathed in light.

THE END

Keep reading for a sneak peek at C. Travis Rice's next steamy and emotional installment in the Sapphire Cove series...

Sapphire Spring
Sapphire Cove, Book 2
Coming September 6, 2022

Under his new pen name, C. Travis Rice, *New York Times* bestselling author Christopher Rice offers tales of passion, intrigue, and steamy romance between men. The second novel, SAPPHIRE SPRING, once again transports you to a beautiful luxury resort on the sparkling Southern California coast where strong-willed heroes release the shame that blocks their hearts' desires.

Naser Kazemi has never met a problem a good spending plan couldn't fix. But working as the chief accountant for his best friend's resort isn't turning out to be the dream job he'd hoped for. It doesn't help that his fashion designer sister is planning an event that just might bring Sapphire Cove crashing down all around them. When the wild party unexpectedly reunites him with Mason Worther, the gorgeous former jock who made his high school experience a living hell, things go from bad to seductive.

The former golden boy's adult life is a mess, and he knows it's time to reform his hard partying ways. But for Mason, cleaning up his act means cleaning up his prior misdeeds. And he plans to start with Naser, by submitting to whatever the man demands of him to make things right. The offer ignites an all-consuming passion both men have denied for years. But can they confront their painful past without losing each other in the process?

Excerpt:

Naser's first thought when he saw his sister's best friend dragging Mason Worther toward him across Sapphire Cove's pool deck was that he was imaginings things. That the stress of dealing with his sister's event had triggered a hallucination of his former high school bully.

Naser's next thought was, *Why is he still so goddamn hot?*

Ten years after graduation, Mason Worther looked like a *True Blood* era Alexander Skarsgård, his navy blue designer suit tailored to a lean and muscular body he'd never stopped working on.

And yeah, chances were he'd stayed a cornsilk blond thanks to a good colorist, but he'd grown into his height, and his blue eyes blazed in the light of the surrounding tiki torches. That neck Naser had fantasized about gripping with both hands as Mason drove into him with rageful abandon was even thicker and more muscular now. And he gazed at Naser with the same wide-eyed openness he'd used on him back in school. Eye contact as bait, Naser was sure—designed to draw him in so Mason and his football friends could treat him like a rag doll deserving of ridicule.

Before Fareena could get a word out, Mason Worther cried, "Nas!" in a big, booming voice that turned heads.

Like they were old friends.

Suddenly Naser was wrapped in the same powerful arms that had worked day after day to blend desire and menace into a combination that still haunted him, still warped the edges of his fantasies in ways he tried to flatten with both hands.

"How you doing, buddy?" Mason boomed.

Naser couldn't think of what to say, so he didn't say anything at all. He went rigid instead. Mason wobbled a little bit, but he didn't pull away. Maybe he thought that would only make this more awkward.

"Well," Fareena said, "you two know each other, it seems."

"Damn right. Laguna Mesa Panthers. Leave 'em on the field in pieces, right, Nas?"

One arm wrapped around Naser's shoulders, Mason pulled back and raised his other fist. Mason Worther, the guy who'd torn his backpack off him more times than he could count, was expecting Naser to greet him with a fist bump. He did. Weakly.

"Or in lockers," Naser said.

Mason cackled.

Fareena looked at Mason, then at Naser, as if they'd both grown additional heads. "You played sports in high school, Nas?"

"Is dread a sport?"

Mason went to ruffle Naser's hair and encountered a solid plate of hair product that would have had him wiping his hand with a napkin if he'd been more sober. "Aw, come on. We loved Nas. I mean, look at those eyes. How could you not love those eyes?" The *s* on the end of eyes lasted longer than it should have. The guy was plastered. Which explained the hug. Maybe.

Fareena seemed to be realizing it too. "What happened to one beer?"

"Drank it like I told you, sweetness."

Fareena pointed a manicured nail at him. "*This* is not one beer."

Mason shrugged, as if to say, *Women, amIrite?*

Naser glared back at him, but what he was thinking was, *Did Mason Worther just compliment my eyes? Also, Fareena's right. This is not just one beer.*

"All right, all right," Mason slurred. "It's true. We did kinda give Naser some shit in high school. I mean, just a liitttllle"—Mason raised his thumb and forefinger as if he were indicating the world's tiniest penis— "Just a little shit, right?"

"Actually, more like a whoooollle"—Naser spread his hands as if indicating a giant loaf of still-baking bread, which forced Mason to drop his arm from Naser's shoulders and take an unsteady step backward—"lot of shit. Like a whole, whole football field of shit." He kept spreading his hands until his arms were thrown open wide. "I mean just year after year after *year* of shit."

Fareena gripped one of Mason's shoulders to keep him from stumbling into the swimming pool behind him. "Before this exchange drowns me in class, may I ask how we're defining *shit* here?"

Mason sputtered, waved a hand through the air in front of him. "Oh, you know. Just guy stuff. Right? Just guys being guys. And stupid. You know, stupid guys. Right, Nas?"

Maybe if he hadn't looked to Naser for confirmation, for unearned split-second forgiveness, Naser could have held his tongue and let it slide. But Mason Worther was as smug and arrogant and good looking as he'd been back then. And Naser wasn't a scared teenager anymore.

"Yeah, *guy stuff*. Like when you broke the lock on my PE locker and stole all the towels out of the locker room so I had to walk across campus naked to get help."

Which he hadn't done, but no doubt, that had been their intention.

The guilt in Mason's glassy-eyed stare satisfied Naser like a glass of water after a long run. The truth was, Naser had always partly blamed himself for that particular incident. After all, he was the one who chose to wait until all the other boys had showered and left before showering himself—easier to avoid the humiliation of an unwanted boner that way. And he hadn't walked naked across campus for help. Instead, he'd cowered in the shadows until a janitor showed up, and when he got busted for missing three classes in a row, he'd lied and told the teachers he was throwing up in the bathroom. But Fareena knew none of this, so her face remained icy and blank as she studied her date for the evening. Naser figured it was the same expression she gave insanely rich clients when they complained that the forty-million-dollar beach house she'd just shown them didn't come with more than one helipad.

"Today we'd call that sexual harassment, Mr. Worther," she finally said.

Mason's mouth opened as if he were going to defend himself, but the sound that came out was like a creaking door in a haunted house. He looked so pathetic Naser considered holding his tongue. Then the pain of those years came surging back, and Naser let his tongue fly.

"But that wasn't my favorite round of *guy stuff*. Not by a mile. No, that distinction went to when you and your buddies used an anonymous email account to write a letter to the assistant baseball coach where you pretended to be me and professed my sexually explicit love for him. Even though I was a minor and not out of the closet yet. That was an amazing piece of guy stuff that resulted in so many *amazing* conversations with my mom. And the school."

Mason's mouth snapped shut. His labored breaths caused his chest to rise and fall. His crew had never been held responsible for that little stunt, but this stunned reaction was all the confirmation Naser needed.

Fareena's professional mask cracked down the middle. "Oh my God, Mason."

The guy swallowed, squinted as if Naser and Fareena were flickering in and out of existence before his glassy eyes. Then he cleared his throat. It seemed like an attempt to gather himself, but the sound was so stuttering and weak it only made clear how wasted Mason Worther was.

"What can I say? I'm a piece of shit?" He shrugged as if the fact was so obvious it didn't bear repeating. Then he gazed into Naser's eyes, and Naser saw something there that shocked him—pain. Pure pain. Suddenly there was pressure on the back of Naser's neck. Mason, he realized, was gripping it in one powerful hand. His first urge was to tell the guy to get off him and back up. But the grip, while forceful, didn't feel hostile. It felt hungry. Desperate. Maybe the need in Mason Worther's eyes was just a selfish desire for forgiveness. Gooseflesh swept down Naser's spine, bouncing off nerves all over his body. "And like all pieces of shit, I should be flushed—"

Mason was underwater before he could finish the sentence. He'd turned and walked right into the pool.

The splash wasn't big enough to draw much attention.

In an instant, Naser and Fareena were slack jawed, watching the man they'd just been talking to swim toward the pool's opposite end, ducking under floating candles as he went. He'd only break the surface for a second or two, like he thought he was invisible when submerged.

Jonas, who'd been conferring with security near the entrance to the restaurant, raced toward the edge of the pool Mason was headed for, carrying towels the security team had just swiped from the cabanas. They swaddled Mason as they led him inside, then Jonas looked back, met Naser's stare, and opened his arm in a clear gesture of, *What just happened with this guy?*

A few minutes later, once he'd managed to extract himself from the party, Naser hurried into the lobby. A janitor was scrambling to mop up the wet trail Mason had left across the marble floor. He told Naser they'd taken the swimmer to the events office, which bothered Naser deeply. He and Jonas occupied a private little corner of Sapphire Cove, and Mason's presence there felt like a violation. That said, escorting him to the management offices would have meant letting him drip over a long expanse of carpet, so Naser couldn't fault Jonas for the call.

The group he was looking for had gathered inside the employees-only corridor. Minus one. Mason Worther. The two security guys hovering outside Naser's closed office door were a study in contrasts. Keoni was a giant Pacific Islander who carried himself like an NFL player, and J.T. was a pasty white boy with a twangy Southern accent and the calculated musculature of someone whose last job involved having sex on camera.

"Do you know this guy?" Jonas whispered, tugging Naser into his office.

"We went to high school together." He tried to keep it from sounding like the loaded statement it was and succeeded.

"Think you can get him to sign this?" Jonas handed him a clipboard holding some papers.

"Where is he?" Naser asked.

"Your office."

"Dripping all over everything? Thanks, Jonas!"

Jonas recoiled. "He finished toweling off in the bathroom and then we gave him some hotel merch to change into. He's not wet, I promise."

"Sorry, I didn't mean to…"

"No, I'm sorry. I thought you guys were friends. Don't worry about it. I'll have him sign the release myself."

"No, it's fine."

"Is it?"

Before Jonas could ask twice, Naser was knocking on his own door, Keoni and J.T. parting on either side of him like the Red Sea.

Mason told him to come in.

Naser obeyed, pulling the door shut behind him, realizing, too late, he was suddenly alone with a spectacularly shirtless Mason Worther, who was looking at him with one eye as he pulled a pair of hotel-branded sweatpants up over his very bare ass. Of course he'd ditched his underwear. They were soaked, and Sapphire Cove didn't sell any. He'd run his hands through his thick, wet hair, and now he looked less like a party accident and more like a fashion model preparing for a beachside photo shoot.

"You told me—" Naser turned, grabbed the knob. "I'll come back."

"It's fine. Come in, Nas."

Mason turned to face him, the sweatpants leaving little to the imagination.

Discover More Christopher Rice

Dance of Desire
By Christopher Rice

When Amber Watson walks in on her husband in the throes of extramarital passion with one of his employees, her comfortable, passion-free life is shattered in an instant. Worse, the fate of the successful country music bar that bears her family's name suddenly hangs in the balance. Her soon-to-be ex-husband is one of the bar's official owners; his mistress one of its employees. Will her divorce destroy her late father's legacy?

Not if Amber's adopted brother Caleb has anything to do with it. The wandering cowboy has picked the perfect time for a homecoming. Better yet, he's determined to use his brains and his fists to put Amber's ex in his place and keep the family business intact. But Caleb's long absence has done nothing to dim the forbidden desire between him and the woman the State of Texas considers to be his sister.

Years ago, when they were just teenagers, Caleb and Amber shared a passionate first kiss beside a moonlit lake. But that same night, tragedy claimed the life of Caleb's parents, and the handsome young man went from being a family friend to Amber's adopted brother. Has enough time passed for the two of them to throw off the roles Amber's father picked for them all those years ago? Will their desire for each other save the family business or put it in greater danger?

DANCE OF DESIRE is the first contemporary romance from award-winning *New York Times* bestselling author Christopher Rice, told with the author's trademark humor and heart. It also introduces readers to a quirky and beautiful town in the Texas Hill Country called Chapel Springs.

READER ADVISORY. DANCE OF DESIRE contains fantasies of dubious consent, acted on by consenting adults. Readers with sensitivities to those issues should be advised.

Desire & Ice
by Christopher Rice

Danny Patterson isn't a teenager anymore. He's the newest and youngest sheriff's deputy in Surrender, Montana. A chance encounter with his former schoolteacher on the eve of the biggest snowstorm to hit Surrender in years shows him that some schoolboy crushes never fade. Sometimes they mature into grown-up desire.

It's been years since Eliza Brightwell set foot in Surrender. So why is she back now? And why does she seem like she's running from something? To solve this mystery, Danny disobeys a direct order from Sheriff Cooper MacKenzie and sets out into a fierce blizzard, where his courage and his desire might be the only things capable of saving Eliza from a dark force out of her own past.

The Flame
By Christopher Rice

IT ONLY TAKES A MOMENT...

Cassidy Burke has the best of both worlds, a driven and successful husband and a wild, impulsive best friend. But after a decadent Mardi Gras party, Cassidy finds both men pulling away from her. Did the three of them awaken secret desires during a split-second of alcohol-fueled passion? Or is Mardi Gras a time when rules are meant to be broken without consequence?

Only one thing is for certain—the chill that's descended over her marriage, and her most important friendship, will soon turn into a deep freeze if she doesn't do something. And soon.

LIGHT THIS FLAME AT THE SCENE OF YOUR GREATEST PASSION AND ALL YOUR DESIRES WILL BE YOURS.

The invitation stares out at her from the window of a French Quarter boutique. The store's owner claims to have no knowledge of the strange candle. But Cassidy can't resist its intoxicating scent or the challenge written across its label in elegant cursive. With the strike of a match and one tiny flame, she will call forth a supernatural being with the ultimate power—the power to unchain the heart, the power to remove the fear that stands between a person and their truest desires.

The Surrender Gate
A Desire Exchange Novel
By Christopher Rice

Emily Blaine's life is about to change. Arthur Benoit, the kindly multimillionaire who has acted as her surrogate father for years, has just told her he's leaving her his entire estate, and he only has a few months to live. Soon Emily will go from being a restaurant manager with a useless English degree to the one of the richest and most powerful women in New Orleans. There's just one price. Arthur has written a letter to his estranged son Ryan he hopes will mend the rift between them, and he wants Emily to deliver the letter before it's too late. But finding Ryan won't be easy. He's been missing for years. He was recently linked to a mysterious organization called The Desire Exchange. But is The Desire Exchange just an urban legend? Or are the rumors true? Is it truly a secret club where the wealthy can live out their most private sexual fantasies?

It's a task Emily can't undertake alone. But there's only one man qualified to help her, her gorgeous and confident best friend, Jonathan Claiborne. She's suspected Jonathan of working as a high-priced escort for months now, and she's willing to bet that while giving pleasure to some of the most powerful men in New Orleans, Jonathan has uncovered some possible leads to The Desire Exchange—and to Ryan Benoit. But Emily's attempt to uncover Jonathan's secret life lands the two of them in hot water. Literally. In order to escape the clutches of one of Jonathan's most powerful and dangerous clients, they're forced to act on long buried desires—for each other.

When Emily's mission turns into an undercover operation, Jonathan insists on going with her. He also insists they continue to explore their impossible, reckless passion for each other. Enter Marcus Dylan, the hard-charging ex-Navy SEAL Arthur has hired to keep Emily safe. But

Marcus has been hired for another reason. He, too, has a burning passion for Emily, a passion that might keep Emily from being distracted and confused by a best friend who claims he might be able to go straight just for her. But Marcus is as rough and controlling as Jonathan is sensual and reckless. As Emily searches for a place where the rich turn their fantasies into reality, she will be forced to decide which one of her own long-ignored fantasies should become her reality. But as Emily, Jonathan, and Marcus draw closer to The Desire Exchange itself, they find their destination isn't just shrouded in mystery, but in magic as well.

Kiss The Flame
A Desire Exchange Novella
By Christopher Rice

Are some risks worth taking?

Laney Foley is the first woman from her hardworking family to attend college. That's why she can't act on her powerful attraction to one of the gorgeous teaching assistants in her Introduction to Art History course. Getting involved with a man who has control over her final grade is just too risky. But ever since he first laid eyes on her, Michael Brouchard seems to think about little else but the two of them together. And it's become harder for Laney to ignore his intelligence and his charm.

During a walk through the French Quarter, an intoxicating scent that reminds Laney of her not-so-secret admirer draws her into an elegant scented candle shop. The shop's charming and mysterious owner seems to have stepped out of another time, and he offers Laney a gift that could break down the walls of her fear in a way that can only be described as magic. But will she accept it?

Light this flame at the scene of your greatest passion and all your desires will be yours...

Lilliane Williams is a radiant, a supernatural being with the power to make your deepest sexual fantasy take shape around you with just a gentle press of her lips to yours. But her gifts came at a price. Decades ago, she set foot inside what she thought was an ordinary scented candle shop in the French Quarter. When she resisted the magical gift offered to her inside, Lilliane was endowed with eternal youth and startling supernatural powers, but the ability to experience and receive romantic love was removed from her forever. When Lilliane meets a young woman who seems poised to make the same mistake she did years before, she becomes determined to stop her, but that will mean revealing her truth to a stranger. Will Lilliane's story provide Laney with the courage she needs to open her heart to the kind of true love only magic can reveal?

About Christopher Rice writing as C. Travis Rice

C. Travis Rice is the pen name New York Times bestselling novelist Christopher Rice devotes to steamy tales of passion, intrigue, and romance between men. He has published multiple bestselling books in multiple genres and been the recipient of a Lambda Literary Award. With his mother, Anne Rice, he is an executive producer on the AMC Studios adaptations of her novels The Vampire Chronicles and The Lives of the Mayfair Witches. Together with his best friend and producing partner, New York Times bestselling novelist, Eric Shaw Quinn, he runs the production company Dinner Partners. Among other projects, they produce the podcast and video network, TDPS, which you can find at www.TheDinnerPartyShow.com. Learn more about C. Travis Rice and Christopher Rice at www.christopherricebooks.com.

Sign up for the Blue Box Press/1001 Dark Nights Newsletter
and be entered to win a Tiffany Lock necklace.

There's a contest every quarter!

Go to www.TheBlueBoxPress.com to subscribe.

As a bonus, all subscribers can download
FIVE FREE exclusive books!

Discover 1001 Dark Nights Collection Nine

DRAGON UNBOUND by Donna Grant
A Dragon Kings Novella

NOTHING BUT INK by Carrie Ann Ryan
A Montgomery Ink: Fort Collins Novella

THE MASTERMIND by Dylan Allen
A Rivers Wilde Novella

JUST ONE WISH by Carly Phillips
A Kingston Family Novella

BEHIND CLOSED DOORS by Skye Warren
A Rochester Novella

GOSSAMER IN THE DARKNESS by Kristen Ashley
A Fantasyland Novella

DELIGHTED by Lexi Blake
A Masters and Mercenaries Novella

THE GRAVESIDE BAR AND GRILL by Darynda Jones
A Charley Davidson Novella

THE ANTI-FAN AND THE IDOL by Rachel Van Dyken
A My Summer In Seoul Novella

A VAMPIRE'S KISS by Rebecca Zanetti
A Dark Protectors/Rebels Novella

CHARMED BY YOU by J. Kenner
A Stark Security Novella

THE CLOSE-UP by Kennedy Ryan
A Hollywood Renaissance Novella

HIDE AND SEEK by Laura Kaye
A Blasphemy Novella

DESCEND TO DARKNESS by Heather Graham
A Krewe of Hunters Novella

BOND OF PASSION by Larissa Ione
A Demonica Novella

JUST WHAT I NEEDED by Kylie Scott
A Stage Dive Novella

THE SCRAMBLE by Kristen Proby
A Single in Seattle Novella

Also from Blue Box Press

THE BAIT by C.W. Gortner and M.J. Rose

THE FASHION ORPHANS by Randy Susan Meyers and M.J. Rose

TAKING THE LEAP by Kristen Ashley
A River Rain Novel

SAPPHIRE SUNSET by Christopher Rice writing as C. Travis Rice
A Sapphire Cove Novel

THE WAR OF TWO QUEENS by Jennifer L. Armentrout
A Blood and Ash Novel

THE MURDERS AT FLEAT HOUSE by Lucinda Riley

THE HEIST by C.W. Gortner and M.J. Rose

SAPPHIRE SPRING by Christopher Rice writing as C. Travis Rice
A Sapphire Cove Novel

On Behalf of Blue Box Press,
Liz Berry, M.J. Rose, and Jillian Stein would like to thank ~

Steve Berry
Doug Scofield
Benjamin Stein
Kim Guidroz
Social Butterfly PR
Ashley Wells
Kasi Alexander
Asha Hossain
Chris Graham
Jessica Johns
Dylan Stockton
Dina Williams
Kate Boggs
Richard Blake
and Simon Lipskar

CPSIA information can be obtained
at www.ICGtesting.com
Printed in the USA
LVHW041923120322
713152LV00004B/39